HAMLET, REVENGE!

Michael Innes is the pseudonym of J. I. M. Stewart, who was a Student of Christ Church, Oxford, from 1949 until his retirement in 1973. He was born in 1906 and was educated at Edinburgh Academy and Oriel College, Oxford. He was lecturer in English at the University of Leeds from 1930 to 1935, Jury Professor of English at the University of Adelaide, South Australia, from 1935 to 1945, and lecturer in Queen's University, Belfast, between 1946 and 1948.

He has published many novels – including the quintet *A Staircase in Surrey* (*The Gaudy, Young Pattullo, A Memorial Service, The Madonna of the Astrolabe* and *Full Term*) – several volumes of short stories, as well as books of criticism and essays, under his own name. His *Eight Modern Writers* appeared in 1963 as the final volume of *The Oxford History of English Literature*, and he is also the author of *Rudyard Kipling* (1966) and *Joseph Conrad* (1968). His other books include *Andrew and Tobias* (1981), *The Bridge at Arta and Other Stories* (1981), *A Villa in France* (1982), *My Aunt Christine and Other Stories* (1983), *An Open Prison* (1984), *The Naylors* (1985) and *Parlour 4 and Other Stories* (1986).

Under the pseudonym of Michael Innes he has written broadcast scripts and many crime novels including *Appleby's End* (1945), *The Bloody Wood* (1966), *An Awkward Lie* (1971), *The Open House* (1972), *Appleby's Answer* (1973), *Appleby's Other Story* (1974), *The Appleby File* (1975), *The Gay Phoenix* (1976), *Honeybath's Haven* (1977), *The Ampersand Papers* (1978), *Going It Alone* (1980), *Lord Mullion's Secret* (1981), *Sheiks and Adders* (1982), *Appleby and Honeybath* (1983), *Carson's Conspiracy* (1984) and *Appleby and the Ospreys* (1986). Several of these are published in Penguin together with two omnibus editions, *The Michael Innes Omnibus* containing *Death at the President's Lodging, Hamlet, Revenge!* and *The Daffodil Affair* and *The Second Michael Innes Omnibus* containing *The Journeying Boy, Operation Pax* and *The Man from the Sea*.

MICHAEL INNES

HAMLET, REVENGE!

A Story in Four Parts

PENGUIN BOOKS

PENGUIN BOOKS

Published by the Penguin Group
Penguin Books Ltd, 27 Wrights Lane, London W8 5TZ, England
Penguin Books USA Inc., 375 Hudson Street, New York, New York 10014, USA
Penguin Books Australia Ltd, Ringwood, Victoria, Australia
Penguin Books Canada Ltd, 10 Alcorn Avenue, Toronto, Ontario, Canada M4V 3B2
Penguin Books (NZ) Ltd, 182–190 Wairau Road, Auckland 10, New Zealand

Penguin Books Ltd, Registered Offices: Harmondsworth, Middlesex, England

First published in Great Britain by Gollancz 1937
First published in the USA by
Dodd, Mead & Company, Inc., 1937
Published in Penguin Books 1961
9 10 8

Printed in England by Clays Ltd, St Ives plc
Set in Linotype Pilgrim

CONTENTS

1

PROLOGUE

The actors are come hither my Lord. . . .
We'll hear a play tomorrow.

WHEN you spend a summer holiday in the Horton country you must not fail to make the ascent of Horton Hill. It is an easy climb and there is a wonderful view. The hill is at once a citadel and an outpost, dominating to the north the subtle rhythms of English downland into which it merges, and to the south a lowland country bounded in the distance by a silver ribbon of sea. The little market-town of King's Horton, five miles away, is concealed in a fold of the downs; concealed too, save for a wisp of blue-grey smoke, is the near-by hamlet of Scamnum Ducis. And almost directly below, beyond a mellow pomp of lawn and garden and deer-park, stands all the arrogantly declared yet finally discreet magnificence of Scamnum Court. Perhaps it is not the very stateliest of the stately homes of England. But it is a big place: two counties away it has a sort of little brother in Blenheim Palace.

And yet from the vantage-point of Horton Hill Scamnum looks strangely like a toy. The austere regularity of its façades, the improbable green of its surrounding turf, the perfection of its formal gardens bounded by the famous cliff-like hedges imitated from Schönbrunn – these things give some touch at once of fantasy and of restraint to what might easily have been a heavy and extravagant gesture after all. Here, Scamnum seems to say, is indeed the pride of great riches, but here, too, is the chastening severity of a classically-minded age. Mr Addison, had he lived a few years longer, would have approved the rising pile; Mr Pope, though he went away to scoff in twenty annihilating couplets, came secretly to admire; and Dr Johnson, when he took tea with the third duke, put on his finest waistcoat. For what is this ordered immensity, this dry regularity of pilaster and parterre, but an assertion in material terms of a prime moral truth of the eighteenth century: that the grandeur of life consists in wealth subdued by decorum?

Here, shortly, is the story of Scamnum and its owners.

Thirty years before the birth of Shakespeare, Roger Crippen, living hard by the sign of the Falcon in Cheapside, had been one of Thomas Cromwell's crew. A sharp man, uncommonly gifted in detecting a dubious ledger – or in concocting one when need drove – he had risen as the religious houses fell. His sons inherited his abilities; his grandsons grew up hard and sober in the tradition of finance. When Elizabeth ascended the throne Crippens already controlled houses in Paris and Amsterdam; when James travelled south Crippens stood as a power in the kingdom he had inherited.

The Civil Wars came and the family declared for the King. At Horton Manor thousands of pounds' worth of plate was melted down; and Humphrey Crippen, the third Baron Horton, was with Rupert when he broke the Roundhead horse at Naseby. But bankers must not be enthusiastic: Crippens too controlled tens of thousands of pounds that were flowing from Holland across the narrow seas to the city and the Parliament men – and during all the monetary embarrassments of the Protectorate they lost no penny. Meanwhile – themselves in ostentatious exile – they patiently financed the exiled court and at the Restoration the family of Crispin came home to a dukedom. Since the first grant of a gentleman's arms to Roger Crippen there had passed just a hundred and thirty years.

Crispin remained a banker's name. And on banking, in the fullness of time, Scamnum Court was raised. Far more fed the Horton magnificence than the broad acres of pasture land to the north, the estate added to estate of rich arable to the south. 'You can't', the present Duke would ambiguously remark, 'keep a yacht on land' – and the yacht, the great town house in Piccadilly, the Kincrae estate in Morayshire, the villa at Rapallo, Scamnum itself with its monstrous establishment ('Run Scamnum with a gaggle of housemaids? Come, come!' the Duke had exclaimed when he shut it down during the war) – these were but slight charges on the resources controlled by the descendants of Roger. For Crispin is behind the volcanic productivity of the Ruhr; Crispin drives railways through South America; in Australia one can ride across the Crispin sheep-station for days. If a picture is sold in Paris or a pelt in Siberia Crispin takes his toll; if you buy a bus or a theatre ticket in London, Crispin – somehow, somewhere – gets his share.

And here, from the windy brow of Horton Hill, the wayfarer

can look down on the crown of it all, his reflections dictated by his own philosophical or political or imaginative bias. There lies Scamnum, a treasure-house unguarded save by the marble gods and goddesses that stand patiently along its broad terraces, or crouch, narcissus-like, beside its ornamental waters – Scamnum unguarded and unspoiled, a symbol of order, security, and the rule of law over this sleeping country-side. The great wing to the east is the picture-gallery: there hang the famous Horton Titian; Vermeer's *Aquarium*, for which the last Duke paid a fortune in New York; the thundery little Rembrandt landscape which the present Duchess's father, during his Dublin days, had got for ten shillings in a shabby bookshop by the Liffey – and for which, ten years later, he sent a flabbergasted bookseller a thousand pounds. And that answering wing to the west is the Orangery. Sometimes, of a summer night, they will hold a dance or a ball there – the long line of lofty windows flung open upon the dark. And a curious labourer and his lass, seeing the procession of cars sweep into the park, will climb the hill and stretch themselves in the clover to gaze down upon a world as remote as that other world of Vermeer's picture – tiny figures, jewelled and magical, floating about the terraces in a medium of their own. Now and then, as the wind veers, wisps of music will float up the hill. It is strange music sometimes, and then the spell is unbroken, the magic unflawed. But sometimes it is a lilt familiar from gramophone or wireless – and man and girl are suddenly self-conscious and uneasy. And Scamnum in general has long understood the necessity of keeping its own hypnotic other-world inviolate. Many a Duke of Horton has unbent at a farmers' dinner, many a Duchess has gone laughing and chattering round Scamnum Ducis. But all have known that essentially they must contrive to be seen as from a long way off, that they have their tenure in remaining – remote, jewelled, and magical – a focus for the fantasy-life of thousands. We are all Duke or Duchess of Horton – this is the paradox – as long as the music remains sufficiently strange.

From Horton summit it is possible to see something of Scamnum's great main court and of its one architectural eccentricity. For here some nineteenth-century duke, a belated follower of the romantic revival, has grotesquely pitched a sizable monument of academic Gothic in the form of a raftered hall. As it stands it is something of a disreputable secret: the hill-top apart, you are aware of it only from certain inner windows of the house, and aware of it probably but to regret the famous fountain which it has obliterated. In the family it is known sometimes as Peter's Folly, and more regularly – with that sub-dued irony which Crispins have assimilated with the aristo-cratic tradition – as the Banqueting Hall. It is a trifle damp, a trifle musty, and there is painful stained-glass. No use has ever been found for it. Or rather none had been found until the Duchess had her idea, the idea which was unexpectedly to draw the attention of all England upon Scamnum and to bring streams of chars-à-bancs with eager sightseers to the foot of Horton Hill.

Even now, strange events are preparing. But this flawless afternoon in June knows nothing of them yet: from the dove-cot beyond the home orchard floats the drowsiest of all English sounds: the jackdaws wheel to the same lazy tempo above the elm walk; a bell in the distant stables chimes four; Scamnum slumbers. On the hill no tourist, field-glass in hand, disturbs the gently nibbling sheep or speculates on such activity as Scam-num reveals. There is no one to identify as the Duke the little knicker-bockered figure who has paused to speak to a gardener by the lily-pond; no one to recognize in the immaculately breeched and booted youth sauntering up from the stables Noel Yvon Meryon Gylby, a scion of the house; no one to guess that the tall figure strolling down the drive is his old tutor Giles Gott, the eminent Elizabethan scholar, or that the beautiful girl, looking thoughtfully after him from the terrace, is the Lady Elizabeth Crispin. Nobody knows that the restless man with the black box is not a photographer from the *Queen* but an Ameri-can philologist. And nobody knows that the Rolls Royce ap-proaching the south lodge contains the Lord High Chancellor of England, come down to play a prank with his old friend Anne Dillon, the present Duchess of Horton.

Scamnum, doubtless, is in the minds of many people at this moment. In Liverpool, serious young men are studying its ground-plan; in Berlin, a famous *Kunsthistoriker* is lecturing on its pictures; its 'life', brightly written up for an evening paper, is selling in the streets of Bradford and Morley and Leeds. Scamnum is always 'Interest' : presently it is to be 'News'.

The Rolls Royce swings under the odd little bridge joining the twin lodges and purrs up the drive.

*

'And her Grace', said Macdonald magnanimously, 'can hae as muckle o' roses for the Banqueting Ha' as she cares to demaun'.'

'Good,' said the Duke, concealing the consciousness of a victory unexpectedly won. 'And now, let me see' – he consulted a scribbled envelope – 'ah yes, sweet-peas. Enough sweet-peas to fill all the Ming bowls in the big drawing-room.'

'The *big* drawing-room!' Macdonald was aghast.

'The big drawing-room, Macdonald. Big party this, you know. Quite an event.'

'I'll see tae't,' said Macdonald dourly.

'And, um, just one other thing. Dinner is in the long gallery –'

'The *lang* gallery!'

'Come, come, Macdonald – a big dinner you know. Quite out of the ordinary. About a hundred and twenty people.'

Macdonald reflected. 'I'm thinking, wi' great respect, it'll be mair like the saloon o' a liner than a nobleman's daenner in ony guid contemporary taste I've heard tell o'.'

Macdonald was one of the curiosities of Scamnum. 'Have you met our pragmatical Scot?' the Duchess would ask gaily – and the favoured visitor would be taken out and cautiously insinuated into the head-gardener's presence and conversation. Nevertheless, the Duke felt, Macdonald could be *very* trying.

'Be that as it may,' said the Duke, unconsciously supporting himself on what had been the pivotal phrase of his celebrated speech in the House of Lords in 1908 – 'be that as it may, Macdonald, the fact is – carnations.'

'May it please your Grace,' said Macdonald ominously, 'I had a thocht it might be the carnations.'

'Carnations. The long gallery is to have a single long table, and they've raked up thirty silver vases from the strong-room –'

'*Thirty*,' said Macdonald, as if scoring heavily.

'To be filled with the red carnations –'

'Horton,' said Macdonald firmly, 'it canna be!'

When Macdonald resorted to this feudal and awful address – eminently proper, no doubt, in his own country – affairs were known to be critical. And the Duke had been expecting this crisis all afternoon.

'It canna be,' continued Macdonald with a heavy reasonableness. 'Ye maun consider that if ye hae a hunnert and twenty folk tae daenner in your lang gallery, I'm like tae hae a hunnert and twenty folk walking my green-hooses thereaufter. And ye maun consider that the demaun's already excessive: a' but a' the public apartments and forty bedrooms – let alone what the upper servants get frae my laddies when my back's turned! And it's my opeenion,' continued Macdonald, suddenly advancing from reasonableness to an extreme position, 'that flu'ers hae no place in the hoose at a'. Unner the sky and unner glause, wi' their ain guid roots below them, is the richt place for flu'ers.'

'Come, come, my dear Macdonald –'

'I'm no saying there's no a way oot o' the difficulty. Maybe your Grace is no acquaintet wi' Mistress Hunter's *Wild Flu'ers o' Shakespeare?*'

'I don't know –'

'No more ye need. It's no a work o' ony scholarly pretension. But it's in the library and it might persuade her Grace –'

'Come, come, Macdonald!'

'– that Shakespeare's wild flu'ers doon that lang table would be mair appropriate than my guid carnations. Do you see to that, your Grace, and I'll set the lassies at the sooth lodge to get a' that's wanted fraw the woods. .... In thirty sil'er bowls too' – added Macdonald enthusiastically – 'it'll be a real pretty sight!'

The evasiveness of the Duke's response revealed him as judiciously giving ground. ' 'Pon my soul, Macdonald, I didn't know you were a student of Shakespeare.'

'Shakespeare, your Grace, was well instructed in the theory o' gardening, and it becomes a guid gardener to be well instructed in Shakespeare. In this play that's forrard the noo, there's eleven images from gardening alone.'

'Eleven – dear me!'

'Aye, eleven. Weeds twa, violet, rose, canker twa, thorns, inoculate old stock, shake fruit frae tree, palm-tree, and *cut off in bloom* – the thing ya shouldna dae. It's a' in Professor Spurgeon's new book.'

'Ah yes,' said the Duke incautiously, 'Spurgeon – clever fellow.'

'She's a very talented leddy,' said Macdonald.

Powerful, precise, world-wide, the Crispin machine ground on. And did Macdonald, bringing this interview to a triumphant close, ponder in his metaphysical Scottish brain some deeper irony – conscious, amid all this familiar ducal ineffectiveness, of the lurking dominance of that steel-hard Crispin eye?

Macdonald trudged down the drive to the south lodge.

*

The Rolls stopped in its tracks. Lord Auldearn stood up behind his impassive chauffeur and made a dramatic gesture as Giles Gott advanced.

'Barkloughly Castle call they this at hand?'

Gott shook hands – with the bow one gives to a slight acquaintance who keeps the King's conscience in his pocket. Then he laughed.

'There stands the castle, by yon tuft of trees.'

'Mann'd with three hundred men, as I have heard?'

'Presently to be manned with about three hundred guests, as far as I can gather. In the Duchess's hands the thing grows.'

'Get in,' said the Lord Chancellor with unconscious authority. And as the Rolls glided forward he sighed. 'I was afraid it would turn into that sort of thing. Anne must always pick the out-size canvas. A mistake her father never made.'

'Didn't she run old Dillon?'

'I think she did – as a clever woman can run a genius. She kept him to the portraits, picked the right moment for capitulating to the Academy, and so on.' Lord Auldearn paused. 'I know my part, I think. What's yours?'

'I'm producing. And I've built a sort of Elizabethan stage.'

'Good Lord! Where?'

'In the Banqueting Hall.'

'Mouldy, gouty hole. So it's all very serious – striking experiment in the staging of Shakespeare – crowds of your professional brethren watching, eh?'

'There is a bevy of them coming down on the night. And an American about the place already, I believe. The Duchess is never wholly serious – but she's working tremendously hard.'

'Anne always did. Worked underground for weeks to contrive a minute's perfect effect – a minute's perfect absurdity, it might be. That's how she got here. What's she doing – the dresses?'

'Not a bit of it. She's been reading up the texts. Got out the Horton Second Quarto and borrowed somebody's First Folio. I'm terrified she'll start scribbling enthusiastically in the margins. And she's been studying the acting tradition as well. She's impressed by the accounts of Garrick, particularly his business when he first sees the Ghost. She's almost ready to coach Melville Clay in it.'

'Coach Clay!' Lord Auldearn chuckled. 'Do him good. Make a noisy success of a part in London and New York – and then be coached in it by a woman for private theatricals. What's he doing it for?'

The question, abruptly pitched, seemed to make Gott reflect. 'Glamour of Scamnum,' he suggested at length.

'Humph!' said the Lord Chancellor – and a moment later added: 'And Elizabeth – how does she like it? Rather a thrill playing opposite Clay?'

'No doubt,' said Gott.

For a moment there was silence as the car sped up the drive. Macdonald, stumping past, touched his hat respectfully.

'And Teddy?' Lord Auldearn continued his inquisition. 'What does Teddy think of the size the thing's apparently grown to?'

Gott looked dubious. 'I can't quite make out what the Duke thinks – on that or anything. I'm a distant Dillon, you know, and the Duchess strikes me as essentially readable. But the Duke puzzles me. I shouldn't like to have to put him in a novel – or not in the foreground. He's a nice conventional effect while in the middle-distance, but disturbing on scrutiny.'

Lord Auldearn paid these remarks the tribute of some moments' silence. Then he pitched another question: 'Do you write novels?'

Confound you, thought Gott, for the smartest lawyer in England – and replied with polite finality: 'Psuedonymously.'

But the Lord Chancellor, vaguely curious, was not to be put off. 'Under what name?' he said.

Gott told him.

'Bless my soul – mystery stories! Well, I suppose it goes along with your ferreting sort of work – just as it might with mine. And what are you writing now? Going to make a story out of the Scamnum theatricals?'

'Hardly a mystery story, I should think,' replied Gott. Lord Auldearn, he reflected, was not impertinent – merely old and easy. But Gott was shy of any mention of this hobby of his. And it was perhaps with some obscure motive of diversion that his hand at this moment went out to a crumpled ball of paper which he had discerned in a corner of the car.

'What's that?' asked Lord Auldearn.

Gott smoothed out the paper – to stare unbelievingly at three lines of typescript on an otherwise blank quarto page. 'More Shakespeare,' he said, 'like our greetings a few minutes ago. But this isn't *Richard II*; it's *Macbeth*.'

Lord Auldearn was again vaguely curious. 'Read it out,' he said. And Gott read:

> *'The raven himself is hoarser*
> *That croaks the fatal entrance of Duncan*
> *Under my battlements.'*

The Rolls had stopped – Scamnum towering above it. 'Curious,' said Lord Auldearn.

*

It was half-past seven. Noel Gylby sat on the west terrace, dividing his attention between a cocktail, *Handley Cross*, and his former tutor, who had sat down with a brief 'Hullo, Noel,' to stare absently and a shade disapprovingly at the beginnings of a garish sunset.

'There's going to be a decent party at Kincrae for the Twelfth,' said Mr Gylby presently. 'Last August Aunt Anne took the bit between her teeth and the moors were like an O.T.C. field-day. But Uncle Teddy's put his foot down this time.'

'Has he,' said Gott.

'He's asking you,' said Noel, turning *Handley Cross* sideways to look at an illustration. 'Going?'

Gott shook his head. 'I think I may be in Heidelberg,' he said austerely.

'Humph.' Noel had been an impressed observer of the Lord Chancellor's mannerisms during tea. And after a silence he added 'I'm getting a new 12-bore.'

In the technical language of his generation Noel was an 'aesthete'. His normal conversation was much of his contemporaries the youngest poets. He ran a magazine for them and wrote editorials sagely discussing André Breton and Marianne Moore; it was rumoured that he had been to a tea-party with Mr Ezra Pound. But in the atmosphere of Scamnum some atavistic process asserted itself; he took on the colour of the place – or what a lively imagination prompted him to feel the colour should be. He read Surtees and Beckford; he made notes on Colonel Farquharson on the Horse. He discoursed on stable-management with the head groom; he spent hours confabulating with the one-eyed man in the gun-room.

'A half-choke, I think,' said Noel – and the subject failing to excite he added after a moment: 'Why didn't you take a cocktail?'

'Habit,' replied Gott. 'The old gentlemen at St Anthony's don't drink cocktails before dinner, and I've got the habit.' He smiled ironically at his former pupil. 'I'm at the age when habit gets its hold, Noel.'

Noel looked at him seriously. 'I suppose you *are* getting on,' he said. 'What are you?'

'Thirty-four.'

'I say!' exclaimed Noel. 'You'll soon be forty.'

'Quite soon,' responded Gott coldly.

'You know,' said Noel, 'I think you should –'

He was interrupted by the appearance of a dinner-jacketed figure at the end of the terrace. 'Here's your pal Bunney. I'll leave the savants together. Little chat about Shakespeare's semicolons may do you good.'

'My pal *who*?'

'Bunney. Dr Bunney of Oswego, U.S.A. Dying to meet a real live Fellow of the British Academy. I suppose' – Noel added innocently – 'it's something to make that even at thirty-four? Well, cheery-bye, papa Gott.' And Mr Gylby strolled off.

Gott eyed the advancing figure of Dr Bunney with suspicion. The man was carrying a largish black box which he set down on a table as he advanced to shake hands.

'Dr Gott? Pleased to meet you. My name's Bunney – Bunney of Oswego. We are fellow-workers in a great field. *Floreat scientia.*'

'How do you do. Quite so,' said Gott – and assumed that charming, charmed, and tentatively understanding expression which is the Englishman's defence on such occasions. 'You have come down for the play?'

'For the phonology of the play,' corrected Dr Bunney. He turned and flicked a switch on the black box. 'Say "bunchy cushiony bush",' said Dr Bunney placidly.

'I beg your pardon?'

'No. "Bunchy cushiony bush".'

'Oh! Bunchy cushiony bush.'

'And now. "The unimaginable touch of time".'

'The unimaginable touch of time,' said Gott, with the suppressed indignation of a good Wordsworthian forced to blaspheme.

'Thank you.' Bunney turned and flicked another switch. Instantly the black box broke into speech. *"Say bunchy cushiony bush I beg your pardon no bunchy cushiony bush oh bunchy cushiony bush and now the unimaginable touch of time the unimaginable touch of time thank you,'* said the black box grotesquely.

Bunney beamed. 'The Bunney high-fidelity dictaphone. Later, of course' – he added explanatorily – 'it is all graphed.'

'Graphed – of course.'

'Graphed and analysed. Dr Gott, my thanks for one more instance of that friendly cooperation without which learning cannot increase. *Hee paideia kai tees sophias kai tees aretees meeteer.* There are drinks?'

'Sherry and cocktails are in the library.' And as Dr Bunney disappeared Gott chanted a little Greek of his own.

'Brek-ek-ek-ex! Ko-ax! Ko-ax!' said Gott. *'Brek-ek-ek-ex! Ko-ax!'*

'Giles, have you laid an egg – or what?' The Lady Elizabeth

Crispin had emerged on the terrace, bearing a luridly-tinged cherry speared on a cocktail-stick.

'I was only telling a rabbit what the frogs thought of him,' said Gott obscurely – and began laboriously an unhappy academic explanation. 'Aristophanes –'

'Aristophanes! Isn't Shakespeare quite enough at present?'

'I think he is. Shakespeare and Bunney between them.'

'It was Bunney, was it? Has he black-boxed you?'

'Yes. Bunchy cushiony Bunney. How did he get here?'

'Mother picked him up at a party. He black-boxed her and she was thrilled. He's going to black-box the whole play and lecture on the vowels and consonants and phoneems and things when he gets home. Only mother hopes he's really something sinister.'

'Sinister?'

'The Spy in Black or something. Black-boxing secrets of state. Have my cherry, Giles.'

Gott munched the cherry. The Lady Elizabeth perched on the broad stone balustrade. 'Another hideous sunset,' she said.

'Isn't it!' exclaimed Gott, electrified at this agreement. But Elizabeth had returned to the subject of the American.

'I suppose Bunney's quoted Greek and Latin and the Advancement of Learning at you?'

'Yes.'

'And you've been eyeing him with the polite wonder of the St Anthony's man?'

'Yes – I mean, certainly not.'

'Dear Giles, this must be an awful bore for you – beaning Shakespeare to make a barbarian holiday. You're very nice about it all.'

'It's not beaning. Everybody's being remarkably serious. And I want to see Melville Clay on something like an Elizabethan stage. And I particularly want to see you.'

Elizabeth wriggled gracefully into a position in which she could inspect her golden slippers. 'I wish about three hundred other people weren't going to. How morbidly Edwardian-Clever Mother is! Don't you think?'

'Age cannot wither her,' said Gott.

'Yes, I know. She's marvellous. But who but an Edwardian-Clever would think of celebrating a daughter's twenty-first by dressing her in white satin to be talked bawdy to by a matinée-idol and drowned and buried to make a big county and brainy Do?'

This breathless speech had evidently been simmering. Gott looked surprised. 'You don't really object, do you, Elizabeth?'

Elizabeth swung off the balustrade. 'Not a bit. I think I love it. Clay's beautiful.'

'And extraordinarily nice.'

'Yes,' said Elizabeth. 'And – Giles – I do hope I'll speak it all so that you approve!'

'Ironical wench.' Gott was out of his chair. 'Round the lily-pond before dinner, Elizabeth!' And they ran down the broad steps together.

Returning, they met Noel waving a letter.

'I say – Giles, Elizabeth! The Black Hand!'

Elizabeth stared. 'Do you mean the black box, child?'

'Not a bit of it. The Black Hand. Something in Uncle Gott's own lurid line. Preparing to strike – and all that.'

Gott understood. 'You've had a scrap of typescript?'

Noel withdrew a quarto sheet of paper from the envelope and handed it to Elizabeth. All three stared at it.

> *And in their ears tell them my dreadful name,*
> *Revenge, which makes the foul offender quake.*

'From *Titus Andronicus*,' said Gott.

'Rubbishing sort of joke,' said Noel.

*

Far away, St James's Park was closing. The melancholy call, as of the archangel crying banishment from Eden, floated faintly through the open window. The Parliamentary Private Secretary, glancing obliquely out across the parade, could catch a glimpse of his old berth. He and Sir James were well past that stile together ... but this was a nervous elevation. His fingers drummed on the window-sill.

'Here in a few minutes now,' said the Permanent Secretary unemotionally.

'In a Bag?'

'Hilfers is bringing it back ... Croydon.'

'Oh.' The Parliamentary Secretary was frankly raw, frankly impressed. There was silence, broken at last by footsteps in the long corridor. An elderly resident clerk came in.

'Captain Hilfers here, sir.'

'We'll go over to the deciphering,' said the Permanent Secretary briskly to the Parliamentary Secretary. He picked up a telephone. 'And have the great men over from their dinner.'

At this the Parliamentary Secretary grew suddenly cheerful. 'Of course they must come over straight away,' he agreed importantly.

*

The Prime Minister summed up the deliberations of an hour.

'Get Auldearn,' said the Prime Minister.

'Auldearn's at Scamnum,' said the Parliamentary Secretary.

'Get What's-his-name,' said the Prime Minister.

'Get Captain Hilfers,' elucidated the Permanent Secretary into a telephone.

*

The near-midsummer dusk is deepening on Horton Hill. The sheep are shadowy on its slopes; to the north the softly-rolling downland is sharpening into silhouette; and below, Scamnum is grown mysterious. Its hundred points of light are a great city from the air. Or its vague pale bulk is the sprawl of all Europe as viewed from an unearthly height at the opening of *The Dynasts*. And here, as there, are spirits. The spirits sinister and ironic look down on Scamnum Court these nights.

2

THERE had been a time when Anne Dillon's large canvases were notorious. Lionel Dillon, moving dubiously amid the gay, indistinguished, and overflowing companies which his daughter gathered in their rambling Hampstead house, had been inclined to charge her with a merely quantitative mind. Dillon himself was austerely qualitative in those days. He would stand grim and baffled before a single canvas for a year on end, and count every moment not so spent lost – fit only for drink and violence, to be followed by confession, Mass, and renewed concentration afterwards. He was of the time before the nineties. 'One should do nothing to make oneself conspicuous,' was the motto of his quiet spells; and he painted in a dress indistinguishable from that of his father, the Dublin solicitor.

Anne, taking charge of the widower in her later teens, had had to change all that. It was in itself, she knew, not a good picture to present to the declining century; and it was otherwise dangerous. Brandy once a month was the fatal Cleopatra of that generation; she ruled it out and established instead more intimate and respectable relations with claret. 'Dillon,' she would say – for she exploited all the minutiae of the cult of genius – 'Dillon was born a glass too low'; and the daily glass, working out in practice at three-quarters of a bottle, was provided. There was nothing merely quantitative about the claret; it was the best one could readily buy in London, and it came into the cellars regularly twice a year even if the rent or Anne's dressmaker had to wait. And it worked. The awkward thought disappeared from the canvas to be replaced by the fluent handwriting that was acclaimed miraculous in London, in Glasgow, in Paris. And although Lionel Dillon knew the early studies as the things for which men would one day bid high he did not protest. It was not altogether Anne's doing : he had felt the twitch of his tether, knew both the level at which he had shot his bolt and the level at which he had a future. And the orthodoxy that had come upon him like a revelation in Toledo was still heterodox enough in England – heterodox enough for the picture Anne was composing.

The period of the big parties had been the critical time. Making scores of undistinguished Bohemian people interesting to each other, imbuing them with poise, confidence, and urbanity for a night, had been stiff labour; and even on unauthentic champagne-cup and mixed biscuits it had come expensive. But again it worked. A mere law of averages mingled in those promiscuous gatherings certain of the emerging Great. Selection came later.

Perhaps the turning-point had been the famous Academy Banquet. It might have gone like a damp squib, been written a tasteless fiasco : the paper probabilities were strongly that way.

But Anne had brought it off. There had been hard work behind the perfection with which the dozen chosen young men had impersonated the venerable President of an august English institution – twelve snowy beards, twelve courtly stoops. And Anne kept her head. She vetoed out of hand the exuberant suggestion that the real President should be lured unawares to the party; she firmly locked up in a lavatory a young actress who came brilliantly disguised as the President's undistinguished wife. Dillon and his bosom friend Max Cope, each in his own bravura manner, dashed off for the occasion a couple of travesties of the most discussed 'pictures of the year'. And a powerful London dealer, catching with the prescience of his kind a something in the air, bought these broad jokes on the spot at prices far exceeding what was being asked for the originals at Burlington House. The whole affair was kept beautifully dark – something half London had in confidence – and it marked alike the height and end of the Hampstead period. The play-acting period, Dillon called it.

The nineties had been quiet. There was Wilde's too-beautiful white dining-room; later there was Whistler, and Lionel Dillon's emergence, under that dazzling stimulus, as a dinner-table wit. The big portrait-commissions came in; the assault on the fashionable world was accomplished classically, as an assault by the fashionable world. There followed frequentation of the great London houses : Dillon, grown not unlike Lord Tennyson and in a resplendent Order secured at the expense of two goodish pictures sent to Central Europe, moving blandly through parties at which there was always royalty at the other end of the room. Finally there came the *concordat* with the Academy and, about the same time, Anne's engagement to the Marquis of Kincrae, the Duke of Horton's heir.

All this is not to say that Anne Dillon was a careerist. Always she had been a creature fundamentally detached; a priestess, a famous wit had laid it down, of the Comic Spirit, dynamic with hidden mockeries. Her choice, she would say, had been most horridly limited; and squirarchy, any professional caste, any continental nobility would have bundled her out at once; only a great Whig house would have accepted her. And if she had grown into Scamnum with the years she yet kept something of her fallen days about her. Alone in the little Gibbons-style drawing-room, she would stand by the piano measuring herself against the girl who stood by the piano in Whistler's portrait on the wall. The identical poise was there; for what time had softened and subdued in the flesh that delicate and sombre artistry had softened and subdued on canvas long ago.

And still for the Duchess life must be delicately odd always, with phases of bolder comedy interspersed. It was the Dillon brandy-drinking coming out perhaps, this periodic indulgence in a larger scale. And the present frolic was an instance, a prank elaborated to a point at which even the Scamnum world would blink. Just such a big affair she would have organized in Hampstead times, her father now ridiculing and now joining in. But Lionel Dillon was dead these ten years, and of his set nobody remained but Lord Auldearn – Lord Auldearn and Max Cope, a crazy old man with a snowy beard and a courtly stoop, come down to bear this part by painting perhaps his last picture for the Academy: 'The Tragedy of Hamlet played at Scamnum Court'.

•

The play was only three days off. Members of the house-party had been arriving intermittently throughout the afternoon and the Duchess was still busy with introductions in the last minutes before dinner.

'Diana, this is Charles Piper, who is going to excite you tremendously. Charles, Proust put a cousin of Miss Sandys's in *Sodome et Gomorrhe* – or was it refused to put him in? Diana will tell you all about it. Diana, find out about Mr Piper's new book for me. Look at poor Dr Bunney!' Bunney, having apparently decided with a struggle that the black box would be an impropriety at this ceremonial hour, was standing before the fireplace without a motive in life. 'Dr. Bunney, come and have introduced to you Timothy Tucker – the strikingly handsome man in the corner. He published Piper's book you know. Mr Tucker, let me introduce you to Dr Bunney: he too is passionately interested in phonetics.' The Duchess gave a commanding nod at the ugly publisher, who instantly entered on a subject about which he knew nothing at all; such gmynastics were demanded as a matter of course at Scamnum parties. 'And what', asked Tucker gravely, 'do you think of this younger German school?' The question was ninety-nine per cent safe. Bunney was enchanted. Conversation went smoothly and efficiently on.

Melville Clay, the veritable handsome man in the room, was introduced formally and without comment to Lord Auldearn. Gott stood by a window receiving squeaky but racy reminiscences of Beardsley from Max Cope. Gervase Crispin, the Duke's elderly cousin, was coping with a strange American lady and her disconcertingly identical twin daughters Elizabeth had been sent to insinuate to the little black man – another of her mother's recent finds – the extent to which he might properly discuss politics with the Lord Chancellor. Noel was conversing with Gervase's Russian friend, Anna Merkalova, in the polished French proper to a future member of the Diplomatic – and casting most undiplomatically venomous glances at Mr Piper, earnestly discoursing with Miss Sandys, meanwhile. The Duke, cruising amiably round, estimated the probable length of the dinner-table. He detested a meal at which his wife was not within hail and general talk possible. It was a small party, praise God, so far; but there would be another bevy by the late train And meanwhile the widow with the twin fillies, he supposed, was his pigeon. He hurried round to the Duchess to refresh his memory on this lady's name. Mrs Terborg. And just in time.

The minute hand of the Dutch bracket-clock dropped to the horizontal of eight-fifteen. Bagot, Scamnum's venerable butler, appeared through a vista of opening doors. The Duke carried off Mrs Terborg without more ado. Noel, releasing himself from Anna Merkalova an improper moment before that lady was handed over to Bunney, made across the room. He was too late Mr Piper and Miss Sandys, in unbroken talk, had been waved forward by their hostess. Timothy Tucker and Melville Clay had a Terborg twin apiece. Elizabeth held on to the black man, having to superintend – as Noel, gloomily returning, explained to Gott – the special oriental nosebag, Gott and Noel, with Gervase Crispin and Max Cope, went forward together as momentarily superfluous bachelor familiars of the house. The

Duchess followed with Lord Auldearn. 'Mixed biscuits, Ian,' she said, 'and champagne with an "h" in the Reims!'

The Lord Chancellor chuckled. 'And a barrel of apples in the studio for those in the know.' To the Duchess of Horton, Lord Auldearn admitted what a rocky manner still hid from the world : that he was a man mellowed and appeased by success, slipping into that final mood – reminiscent, yet remote, tolerant yet comprehensively critical – in which one who has made his mark in the world prepares to take leave of it. And because there existed between him and Anne Dillon a long-standing and delicately handled sentimental relationship he would speak his thoughts to her as to no one else. 'Not much more apple-picking for me now,' he said, giving the apples a characteristic twist into some remote literary allusion. 'And not much more Shakespeare either. Just a year, I think, with Horace and Chaucer – and then a hunt through Hades for a few affable and familiar ghosts.'

'We don't think of you as a ghost here, Ian. We've cast you, you see, as a very lively, wise old man.'

Lord Auldearn shook his head. 'A slippered pantaloon and a figure of fun. And Polonius is a ghost before the play's ended.'

The Duchess pressed his arm. 'So are we all,' she replied; 'except young Charles Piper, who must live to write a great many more conscientious novels.' Piper was to be Horatio.

'Did you know Gott writes novels?'

'Yes. But he's ashamed of them because they're *not* conscientious. He thinks they're time stolen from all this business of old texts. I've been looking at that sort of thing for the play and it seems to me rather immoral labour. I have a feeling that such good wits should be in the Cabinet.'

'My dear Anne, how seriously you've come to regard the burden of rule! What of seducing me from affairs of state for a week? But they do call in Gott's sort, you know – for an emergency. It's an odd thing, but there's nobody like your professional seeker-out of truth for inventing a four-square, coherent system of lies. When propaganda is needed the don is the master of it.'

'Touching lies,' said the Duchess, 'have you heard Gervase's explanations of his Russian friend there?' And she turned to arrange her table.

Gott, unconscious of his potential role as a well of deceit in times of national emergency, was looking round the gathering with a producer's eye. More and more he was realizing that the Tragedy of Hamlet played at Scamnum Court had assumed alarming proportions. It had begun as a family frolic. And now, although it would not be publicly reported, the dramatic critics were coming down as if to an important festival. Professors were coming to shake learned respectable bald heads over a fellow-scholar's conception of an Elizabethan stage. Aged royalty was coming to be politely bewildered. Most alarming of all, 'everybody' was coming – for the purpose, no doubt, of being where 'everybody' was. And even if it was a select and serious everybody – a known set before whom a Lord Chancellor might mime without misgiving – it was still a crowd, and its reactions were unpredictable.

The company that was to present *Hamlet* had one initial advantage. It was thorough. Its members possessed that tradition of thoroughness that goes along with Scamnum traditions of leisure and responsibility. The habit that would prevent the airy Noel from touching a cricket bat or a tennis racket without making a resolute onslaught on county form, the habit that would send Elizabeth forward from Somerville next year miraculously perfected in sundry dreary Old and Middle English texts, the habit that brought Gervase Crispin to his feet in the House of Commons to discuss battalions of figures with his eye innocently fixed on the roof – this would make *Hamlet* as good as efficiency could make it. But Gott was dubious all the same. Acting is such a difficult business that only one thing will make it pass – economic necessity. Act-or-out-you-go is the only really effective producer.

'Don't you think acting is the most unnatural thing in the world?' It was the voice of one of the indistinguishable Misses Terborg – Miss Terborg One – on Gott's right.

'I was just thinking so' – Gott noted to himself the absence of that sense of miraculous coincidence that had accompanied Elizabeth's observation on sunsets earlier in the evening. 'But some people would say that we most of us act uninterruptedly.'

28

'Ah, but that's different, isn't it? We are always impersonating our own idealized image of ourselves – our *persona*, is it called? – in order to shine in our own eyes or in other people's. Or we're shamming something quite false in order to get something that our real self wants. But this business of becoming someone else and taking on his image and *persona* and desires – pure falsification, in fact – surely that is unnatural?'

Gott on the one side and Melville Clay on the other regarded Miss Terborg One with some curiosity. Gott with his tutor's instinct was placing this young lady's mind provisionally among the good Two-ones; Clay was attracted by discussion of the theory of acting. He broke in eagerly :

'It is the most unnatural thing in the world. Which is why it's still thought rather disreputable – and why it's so absorbingly interesting. One never *becomes* someone else. There's no someone else to become; it's only a bad and confusing metaphor. They talk about how the great actor lives his part and so on; but isn't that just woolly thinking too? Acting's *acting* – every exquisite moment when one's on form. And that's why it's difficult for amateurs; because it's all technique.'

'Well,' said Gott, '*Hamlet* is fortunately an almost indestructible play. And with the thing chiefly on your shoulders we'll scrape home with it.'

'Oh, more than that! This show's already been a revelation to me of how rapidly clever people can acquire a specific skill. Lady Elizabeth's good. And the Duke's marvellous. They've both found the vital truth. If acting is a hundred per cent technique, technique is about seventy-five per cent timing.' And Clay turned to enlarge on timing to the Duchess on his right.

Yes, in the rehearsals so far held, Elizabeth had been good – and the Duke marvellous. It was difficult to get the master of Scamnum on the stage; at the appointed hour he would be engaged in instructing his bailiff, being instructed by his agent, or playing austere croquet with the vicar's wife on the farther cedar lawn. His attitude to the whole affair was one of vague dubiety. But, once planted on Gott's great platform stage in the Banqueting Hall, his part fell upon him like a mantle. Whether or not it were a matter of technique, Shakespeare's cunning usurper Claudius stood completely realized amid his court.

'Anne,' the Duke was saying down the table, 'about those flowers for the Long Gallery on Monday. What about having Shakespeare's wild-flowers? I was looking at a book about them in the library, and at this time of year we could get almost the whole lot.'

'Daisies pied,' interposed Bunney firmly, 'and violets blue, and lady-smocks all silver-white.' He smiled round the table as one who has contributed neatly to the general elegance of the proceedings. Everyone looked kindly on Bunney except the Terborgs, who looked cold. Nowhere more than in the United States, Gott reflected, are there chasms.

'Let's go out and gather them,' said Diana Sandys.

'They would have to be gathered on Monday,' objected the Duchess, 'when we should be much too busy. But it's a nice idea.'

The Duke considered. 'We might persuade Macdonald to send some of his lads into the woods for them – or perhaps the children from the lodges. I'll speak to him.' And, nodding over the possibility, he proceeded to give Mrs Terborg particulars on Shakespeare's interest in gardening. Mrs Terborg, taking up the subject of flowers, made efficient conversation out of gloxinias, antirrhinums, chionodoxas, kolkwitzias – matters more familiar probably to Macdonald than to his employer. Charles Piper, some way down the table, attended with the undisguised concentration of a man who always makes notes before going to bed. Some lady in some future fiction would talk efficiently of gloxinias, antirrhinums, chionodoxas, kolkwitzias.

'Who', asked Miss Terborg One, 'is the young man listening so attentively to my mother?'

'Charles Piper, the novelist,' replied Gott. 'He has just published a very successful book called *The Bestial Floor*.'

Miss Terborg One could almost be discerned flipping over some voluminous card-index in her mind. 'Of course: "The uncontrollable mystery on the bestial floor." I suppose it's about Christ?'

'No. It's about the childhood of Dostoyevsky.'

'Dostoyevsky', said Miss Terborg One firmly, 'was very interested in Christ.' Across the chasm, thought Gott, threads of connexion can always be traced. 'Do *you* write novels?' asked Miss Terborg One.

Unconsciously, the Duchess came to the rescue. 'And I decided we must have firemen. Giles, were there firemen in the Elizabethan theatre?'

'There were fires,' replied Gott cautiously.

'Well, I've arranged for three men from King's Horton – and I've said they must bring helmets. There will be one at each door beside the footmen.'

'Anne,' came Max Cope's piping voice from up the table, 'have you arranged for a detective too? Don't you think a detective –'

'A detective, Max!'

'I mean, there will be a lot of jewellery and so on, won't there? And a mixed crowd. And you've already got some pretty queer –'

'Fish, sir?' murmured Bagot, deserting his wines and breaking silence with inspired indecorum. Everybody at Scamnum knew that an eye had to be kept on old Mr Cope. His wits were gone: there was nothing left in him but a mere, sheer painting. He was promptly taken charge of by Mrs Terborg on the one hand and Gervase Crispin on the other for the rest of the meal.

Lord Auldearn was conversing with the black man – with that remorseful deference which the English raj accords the Oriental visitor to the heart of Empire. Timothy Tucker was entertaining Elizabeth with fantastic anecdotes of a fellow-publisher.

'... But Spandrel's best stroke was with the Muchmoss. You've heard of her? She was a nice old party living in Devon and she sent him, years ago, a manuscript called *Westcountry Families I Have Known*. Spandrel has a nose and he smelt not family chat but novels in her. And sure enough he turned her into a solid market success. She was a nice old party with a good brain tucked away, and soon the Muchmoss Westcountry was esteemed. So after a few years Spandrel decided to build up a school. He found several other parties, not quite so old, and most luckily the Muchmoss – kind old soul – thought no end of them all. So you see, the Muchmoss sold them and they in turn were healthy for the Muchmoss. Well, that was all right – until the Muchmoss died. She died, unhappily, a bit too soon – before the Muchmoss atelier could do all its own heave and shove. Spandrel was stumped for a bit, but one day he had a revelation. He was walking in the Park, he says, when it came to him quite suddenly: the knowledge that the Muchmoss was *still* enjoying the Muchmoss school no end – in heaven. So he arranged a séance –'

Noel, it occurred to Gott, was making surprisingly heavy going with Miss Terborg Two. He had plainly reached that desperate stage at which one drops this disconnected observation after that into a horrid well of silence. But at this moment one of these observations had a startling effect. Miss Terborg Two gave a loud scream.

The literary activities of the Muchmoss ghost, Lord Auldearn's polite questions on *yogis* and *gooroos* died, with other miscellaneous topics, round the table. Everybody looked askance at Noel – particularly Gervase, who jumped to the conclusion that he had retailed to an innocent virgin an anecdote which Gervase himself had published to the billiard room earlier in the day.

Noel was apologizing profusely and confusedly both to the lady and to the table at large. 'I'm most frightfully sorry; never thought of it as actually startling; just the story –'

'Story!' said Gervase grimly.

'Just the story of the Black Hand, you know.'

Miss Terborg Two made an agitated gesture upon her boyish bosom. 'Stupid of me. Duchess, I'm so sorry – but secret societies and things have made me scared ever since a kid. . . . The Black Hand!'

The Duke looked with mild severity on his youthful kinsman. 'What's this foolery, Noel?'

'Nothing at all, sir. Rubbishing joke. . . . Elizabeth's seen it . . . sort of threatening message. Thought it might amuse. Most terribly sorry to have distressed Miss Bertog – I mean Miss Terborg –'

This was most sadly remote from the suave success with which Noel must one day dine about the embassies of Europe. Elizabeth took on the burden of further explanations. 'A type-written slip that came to Noel by post. It's just a scrap from Shakespeare; something about revenge.'

In the buzz of speculation that followed Gott glanced at Lord Auldearn. But the Lord Chancellor said nothing. That a similar joke had been played on himself he did not propose, apparently, to announce. Here, even in dealing with a pointless prank, was the statesman's impulse to keep mum. But another statesman reacted differently. Gervase Crispin took Elizabeth up sharply: 'Revenge! That's odd. I had the same sort of thing myself the other day.'

Mild curiosity ran round the table.

'Yes. I had a telegram at the House before coming down here, Just two words.'

This time Lord Auldearn spoke: 'Two words?'

'*Hamlet, revenge!*'

*

'Curious about those messages,' said the Duke when the men were alone. 'Who would play a trick like that?' He looked lazily and amiably round his guests; the very anti-type, thought Gott, of King Claudius of Denmark. 'Funny thing.'

'A *bad* thing!' said the black man suddenly and emphatically. It was his first utterance to the company at large, and everybody started. 'It is *very* wicked to send a curse!'

'I don't know about its being a curse,' said Timothy Tucker easily. 'I think it's just what we call a practical joke; and rather a feeble one at that. It's curious that a person educated enough to know his Shakespeare should do such a futile thing.'

'Odd the people who do know their Shakespeare,' the Duke remarked. 'I discovered this afternoon, for instance, that Macdonald, my head-gardener, knows his inside-out.'

'Macdonald!' said Lord Auldearn sharply. 'Mr Gott, was it not Macdonald that we passed coming up the drive?'

Gott nodded absently. 'There's a little more than mere knowledge of Shakespeare involved,' he said.

At this Max Cope, who had all the appearance of dozing comfortably in his chair, suddenly burst into high-pitched speech. 'In fact, it's "Puzzle find the oyster-wife" – eh?' And looking cunningly round the table, he ended in the embarrassing giggle of great age. As far as Gott could judge, everyone except Lord Auldearn was bewildered by this. But no one seemed inclined to interrogate the venerable painter. Max slumbered again.

'Cope means', Gott explained, 'that Crispin's message, "Hamlet, revenge", is not – as you may remember – actually from Shakespeare's play. It was probably a line in an earlier play, now lost, and is first quoted as a joke in Lodge's *Wits Miserie* in 1596: there is a reference there to a ghost that cried miserably in the theatre, like an oyster-wife, "Hamlet, revenge." It doesn't follow that our joker has any special erudition, but he does seems to have browsed about in an antiquarian way.'

As Gott concluded this explanation he looked speculatively at Melville Clay. Clay, it occurred to him, should not have been bewildered by the oyster-wife; during the past few days he had been displaying a pretty thorough knowledge of the round-abouts of the Elizabethan drama. But Clay dissipated this speculation now. 'Of course!' he said eagerly. 'I'd quite forgotten. And there are other references too. It was quite a familiar quip.'

Gott nodded. 'Yes. But it doesn't really help us to the identity of the joker. What about where the messages came from?'

'Mine,' said Noel, 'was posted in the West End this morning.' There was a pause in which all eyes were turned on Gervase Crispin. But Gervase kept silence until directly challenged by the Duke. Even then he spoke with a shade of reluctance.

'My telegram,' he said quietly, 'was sent off from Scamnum Ducis.'

At this it was suddenly clear to everybody that speculation about the messages, pushed forward idly enough, had reached some point of obscure uncomfortableness. Everybody except Piper, who saw nothing in the conversation that would write up, was interested; even Max Cope could be discovered on scrutiny to have one eye open still. But equally, everybody knew that the subject must be dropped. The Duke rose, and taking Cope's arm, led the way to the drawing-room.

Fresh arrivals were expected and the party was keeping together to welcome them. The Duchess contrived to establish one large circle and start a general discussion of the play. For a time it ran on practical lines: dresses, make-up, the next day's rehearsals. Then it took a historical turn and the talk narrowed to those with special knowledge: Gott, the slightly uncomfortable specialist; Lord Auldearn, with rather more than a smattering of everything; Melville Clay, genuinely learned in the histories of all Hamlets that had ever been; and the Duchess, fresh from intensive reading. Garrick's trick chair that overturned automatically on his starting up in the closet scene, the performance on board the *Dragon* at Sierra Leone in 1607, Mrs Siddons and other female Hamlets, the tradition that Shakespeare's own best performance was as the ghost: the talk ran easily on. Mrs Terborg gave a formidably perceptive account of Walter Hampden's celebrated Hamlet in New York in 1918. Elizabeth remembered how Pepys had once spent an afternoon getting 'To be, or not to be' by heart. And this gave the Duchess her chance. She immediately turned Clay to presenting Mr Pepys delivering the soliloquy to Mrs Pepys. Anything that Anne Dillon had once been used to impose on obscure young men at Hampstead she would never hesitate to impose on the great and the famous at Scamnum.

There can be nothing more trying to an actor than being required to extemporize before a drawing-room – even a drawing-room of quick and sympathetic spirits. But Clay showed no trace of annoyance; the difficulty of the odd task had wholly possessed and absorbed him in a moment. He stood with knitted brows for perhaps twenty seconds, and then – suddenly – Pepys was in the room. And Gott, with no great opinion of the wits of actors, had the feeling that this two minutes' *tour de force* – for it lasted no longer – was one of the most remarkable things he had ever seen. Anyone might know his Pepys and his Hamlet, but instantly to produce the sheer and subtle imaginative truth that was Clay's picture of Pepys *as* Hamlet was a miniature but authentic intellectual triumph. Looking round the room amid the ripple of delighted exclamations, Gott saw Lord Auldearn's eyes narrowed upon Clay as upon something suddenly revealed as formidable; saw that Charles Piper's mind was racing as a writer's mind will race when something extraordinary has occurred. And the thing had even got across to old Max Cope; the painter was cackling with delight. Only the intelligent Hindoo was looking intelligently bewildered. No doubt he had – following the weird system of education imposed upon his country – been examined both in Shakespeare's *Hamlet* and Pepys's *Diaries*. But this sudden telescoping was beyond him.

For the Duchess all this led up to something else. She now turned to a subject she had already frequently debated with Clay: Garrick's Hamlet, and particularly his first encounter with the Ghost.

> '*On the stage he was natural, simple, affecting;*
> '*Twas only that, when he was off, he was acting,*'

quoted the Duchess.

'Yes, but this wasn't natural. It's clear he took it too slowly; theatrically, you would put it. The *St James's Chronicle* said so; even Lichtenberg said so – and Lichtenberg was an enthusiast.'

Here, thought Gott, was a man who could talk his own shop in a mixed company, without a trace of self-consciousness. And everybody was interested.

'And Garrick overstressed mere physical terror. That was Johnson's opinion, Fielding's opinion.'

'One sees you see it,' the Duchess let fall.

And Clay was obviously seeing it. He was on his feet still, his brow again knitted, his eye upon David Garrick on the stage of Drury Lane nearly two hundred years ago. 'The cloak and the big hat,' he said softly, 'it was all built up from them.'

In an instant Noel was out of the room, to return with an enveloping opera cloak and a soft black hat – a hat with a monstrously exaggerated brim such as undergraduate devotees of the Muses delight to wear. 'The hat's not what it was,' he explained cheerfully; 'it and I have been pitched into the St Anthony's fountain together before now. But it may serve.'

Clay took the cloak at once and threw it round himself; then he jammed the hat apparently at random on his head. Gott felt sub-acute discomfort in himself; divined it in others. They were confronted by something grotesquely incongruous: a man in exquisite evening dress, set off by the black and scarlet of a twentieth-century dandy's cloak, with a parody of a Montparnasse hat perched on his head – and now proposing to convert this elegant drawing-room, with its Whistlers, Dillons, and Copes, its Ming and 'Tang, into the battlements of Elsinore. But

Clay, with a glance round at the lighting, had stepped to a door and flicked at the switches to get the effect he wanted: one area of subdued light in a farther corner of the darkened room. 'Horatio,' he called gaily, 'remember your lines!' And he took up his position in the little circle of dim illumination.

And then quietly, without any attempt at dramatic illusion, and as a teacher might enunciate Shakespeare from behind a lectern, Clay spoke Hamlet's lines as they follow on the noise of revelry borne up to the battlements:

> *'The king doth wake tonight and takes his rouse,*
> *Keeps wassail and the swagg'ring upspring reels:*
> *And as he drains his draughts of Rhenish down,*
> *The kettle-drum and trumpet thus bray out*
> *The triumph of his pledge. ....'*

And, obediently, from the midst of the little audience came the voice of Piper as Horatio:

> *'Is it a custom?'*

Clay looked across and smiled – still Melville Clay reciting quietly in the Scamnum little drawing-room:

> *'Ay marry is't,*
> *But to my mind, though I am native here*
> *And to the manner born, it is a custom*
> *More honoured in the breach than the observance.'*

And as the speech proceeded Clay imperceptibly, like a cinematograph trick – faded out and Hamlet – David Garrick's Hamlet – grew into being. Shakespeare in the eighteenth century – here was another scholar-actor's subtlety indefinably but lucidly conveyed. Gott, watching fascinated, heard beside him Bunney's gasp of astonishment as the very vowels and consonants came over with the shading of 1750. The knotty, difficult speech, that throws the hearer's mind into a half-darkness of its own, proceeded – accompanied by an increase of mere physical blackness. A turn of the shoulder began to hide the lower part of the face; an inclination of the head brought the hat over the eyes. For a moment there was a mouth, a nose only; then blackness save for two eloquently moving hands. The voice searched on:

> '... these men,
> Carrying I say the stamp of one defect,
> Being nature's livery, or fortune's star ...'

One hand disappeared; then the other: the speech ended in darkness answering darkness, the voice dying away in the impenetrable obscurity of the final lines:

> '... the dram of evil
> Doth all the noble substance of a doubt,
> To his own scandal.'

The cloak had fallen annihilatingly round the immobile figure. There was a long moment's silence in which Gott had time for the fleeting reflection that Miss Terborg Two might well make this juncture occasion for another scream. Then Piper's voice:

> 'Look, my lord, it comes!'

No one missed the actual presence of the Ghost in the minute that followed. With the rapidity of an athlete Clay had whirled round upon himself and stiffened as instantly into a convention of retarded motion at once wholly theatrical and wholly terrifying. The hat had slipped to the ground, the cloak fallen back. Legs straddled, left arm flung wide and high, right arm bent with the hand hanging down and the fingers wide apart, the whole trembling figure of the man answered to the fixed, glaring terror on the face. Second after second of absolute silence crawled by. Then, on the hiss of an outgoing breath, came speech:

> 'Angels and ministers of grace defend us!'

With what seemed shattering rapidity there followed Melville Clay's own musical laugh. The lights snapped on. The actor was patting Noel's hat into shape with ironical precision. He had not turned a hair. 'Garrick,' he said, 'was more effective, of course; but that was the idea.'

Gott looked round the room. Lord Auldearn had disappeared. Nearly everybody seemed to be under the influence of a species of stage shock: the evocation, and more the abrupt dissipation of a piece of supreme theatre, had left the audience somewhat in the air. It was the Duke who lowered the tension. 'You know,

if I were the Ghost I think I'd be the more scared of the two!'
The Scamnum drawing-room recovered its momentarily shattered identity; congratulation, comment, animated discussion flowed on.

Nevertheless, Gott felt a hint of constraint in the air. Elizabeth was looking, in some remote way, troubled; the Duchess was working particularly hard; the Duke had retreated a little further into the light-comedy part he seemed to cultivate. And there was a perceptible feeling of relief when the purr of cars on the drive announced the distraction of arrivals by the evening train.

*

Ten-thirty at night is not a wholly polite hour at which to arrive for a long week-end: explanations, previously offered no doubt by letter, were reiterated now. Lord and Lady Traherne had been giving one of their colonial parties: never such oceans of colonials as this year! Sir Richard Nave had been lecturing to the Society for Improving Sex on 'The Psychological Basis of Matrilinear Communities'. Professor Malloch had been conducting viva-voce examinations in his native Aberdeen. The Marryats had felt that a week away from London so early would be an *experience*, but things turned up so that only five days were *possible*. Tommy Potts explained that in Whitehall now one was worked like a nigger; one might as well be in the second grade. Pamela Hogg had been stepping into the midday train when she had had the most frightful news about Armageddon – intelligence obscure and even alarming until one realized that the matter concerned a horse. Mrs Platt-Hunter-Platt had been demonstrating at the Albert Hall against something ill-defined but outrageous. An undevotional-looking banker was loud in laments at having missed the midday service: Paris-Croydon, it turned out to be – and the sequel of a novel and apparently remarkably hazardous route by land and water. A sparkling lady in full evening-dress declared herself as having come straight from her old governess's funeral. A podgy M.P., unconscious of a faint residual smear of lipstick on his bald head, murmured obscurely of committees.

Sandwiches, whisky, hot soupy stuffs as if after a dance; some three dozen people, almost crowding the little drawing-room, laughing, chattering, exclaiming, eddying: was it, Gott wondered, what Elizabeth had called it – a barbarian holiday? Or was it really a polite society, with sufficient of a common code – tastes, attitudes, assumptions, intentions – to go through with this elaborate affair in front of it pleasedly and confidently? Did the Lord Chancellor of England and Pamela Hogg belong to a structure still sufficiently solid, sufficiently homogeneous for the one to play Polonius before the other? Or had the Duchess fabricated the idea of such a society out of the novels of her girlhood – and was the whole thing going to be an uneasy sham? What did Lord Auldearn think of this growing gathering? But Lord Auldearn was still invisible.

Gott disengaged himself from Mrs Platt-Hunter-Platt, who wanted him to sign some sort of manifesto or petition to the government of Brazil; dodged Professor Malloch, advancing with technical Shakespeare-scholarship in his eye; dodged Sir Richard Nave, discoursing blandly of the twilight of the Christ mythus, and slipped out upon the terrace. An uncertain moonlight was haunting the gardens, glittering on a sheet of water far below, adding folds and shadows to the silhouette of Horton Hill beyond. The babble of voices floated out through the windows; Gott strolled down broad steps to find silence on the farther terrace below. He stopped where the long flow of balustrade was broken by a massive, dimly-outlined marble – a Farnese Hercules perhaps – and let his eye travel along the line of the downs. He was worried about this play.

Yes, decidedly there was some uncomfortableness in the air; an uncomfortableness which must not grow if disaster was to be avoided. And it had its origin, he now felt, in the trivial foolishness of the mysterious messages. To begin with, the whole *Hamlet* plan was a little out – a whim imposed on this Scamnum world rather than something growing naturally from it. He himself had been to Scamnum often enough, but always before he had shed here his professional role of scholar and antiquary. Talking and contriving Elizabethan theatre in the Duchess's drawing-room was disturbing; it induced a self-consciousness such as a Fellow of the Royal Society would feel if asked down to demonstrate the peculiarities of atom and electron. Centuries ago that sort of thing would have marched: when Fulke Greville and Giordano Bruno disputed on the Copernican theory in the drawing-rooms of Elizabethan London; when the noble family of Bridgewater moved through the stately dance and rhetoric of Milton's *Comus* at Ludlow Castle. But now show was shop; and theatricals were theatricals – and the basic attitude of a scurrying contemporary society to them was that expressed by Sir Thomas Bertram when he put a stop to such nonsense in *Mansfield Park.*

Leisure had gone. Of these people gathered here the abler were absorbed in the increasingly desperate business of governing England, of balancing Europe. And the others were not so much leisured as laboriously idle : fussing over Armageddon or demonstrating against brothers in Brazil. All in all, the Tragedy of Hamlet played at Scamnum Court, however seriously taken up by the persons chiefly committed, had to come to birth in a precariously viable air. True, the Duchess had carried out a sort of air-conditioning process with some subtlety. Tucker, Piper, the American ladies so ingeniously materialized from Henry James : these blended with Scamnum – or with the aspect of Scamnum the Duchess was concerned to emphasize – well enough. And here Gott arrived at the view that it was not after all so much a matter of the people as of the place. In its comparatively brief two hundred years of existence this enormous mansion had contrived to become heavy with tradition; and it was not a tradition – despite its Whig pretension of accepting whatever interested or amused – that squared readily with eccentricity. Just as the whole physical pile frowned down upon Peter Crispin's Gothic hall, so the spirit of the place frowned rather upon the play that was to be performed there. Hence the effect upon the house-party of the scraps of typescript : they gave just that hint of a lurking, unfriendly presence which was needed to start this other feeling of a lurking incongruity in the whole affair – the incongruity which had been felt again when Melville Clay performed his dazzling tricks in the drawing-room.

Gott's hand, groping for a cigarette-case in the pocket of his dinner-jacket, closed upon a proof of the printed programme that would be distributed on Monday night. 'The play produced by Giles Gott, M.A., F.B.A., Hanmer Reader in Elizabethan Bibliography, Fellow of St Anthony's College.' Everyone else had been shorn of distinction; Claudius was 'Edward Crispin' and as Polonius the Lord Chancellor of England was plain 'Ian Stewart' as he had been in Hampstead long ago. But with her producer the Duchess – with a sound eye for effect, no doubt – had piled it all on. And Gott recalled the slightly satirical eye of Professor Malloch in the drawing-room. He was up to the neck in it and it must go through.

His mind turning to ponder over detail, he climbed back to the upper terrace at the eastern end of the main building. Here there is a colonnade, lit at night by a vista of subdued lights in the entablature. Under the lights was the Lord Chancellor. And Gott suddenly saw that his own speculations and doubts of a moment before were something of infinitesimal significance in the world.

Lord Auldearn was pacing absorbedly up and down, with a strange, forward-lurching gait that suggested more than the beginnings of physical decay. Indeed, he seemed very old; older by ten years than when he sat gaily talking to his hostess at dinner. In his hand was what appeared to be an official document. On his face sat an utter gravity, the utter gravity of a great savant or a great statesman in some crisis of thought or action. Gott watched him for a long moment; then turned round and retreated as he had come.

3

LOOKING back on the days immediately preceding the play Gott was to see them – and that despite the practical bustle with which they were filled – as an orgy of talk. Serious, pseudo-serious, and idle, relevant to *Hamlet* and irrelevant, general and *tête à tête*, sustained and fragmentary; there was talk in every category. Most of it was talk that would naturally fade from the mind in a day. But soon circumstances were to compel Gott to dredge up every accessible scrap of it from oblivion, to sift and search it as he had never perhaps sifted and searched before.

Saturday morning saw an encounter with Charles Piper in

their common bathroom. 'I can usually', said Piper over the turning of taps, 'get five to eight hundred words out of a hot bath.'

'Often', replied Gott, unwarily stepping into the position of a fellow-author, 'I get a new start from brandy and muffins.'

'Really ... and *muffins*? I never heard of that.' Piper eyed Gott as one might eye a suddenly perceived object of minor but authentic interest in the Victoria and Albert Museum. 'And what', he asked with sober interest, 'brought you to detective-stories?'

'Moral compulsion. The effort to give a few hours' amusement as a sort of discount on many hours' boredom.'

Piper dropped this response after a moment's consideration into some mental pigeon-hole – was it *Evasion* or *Unsuccessful Humour* or *Academic Psychology*? – and proceeded to further interrogation. 'Would you say', he asked solemnly, 'that fiction proper and narrative melodrama are absolutely distinct kinds?'

'I doubt if there is necessarily an absolute line. Dickens wrote a mix-up of novel and melodrama – and very successfully.' Gott paused to turn on the shower. 'Of course fiction commonly uses a finer brush all through. It avoids labels except where they are functionally necessary: Hot, Cold. Melodrama runs on big splashy labels: Bath Mat. None of your aristocratic restraint.' And Gott pointed to the unembellished cork surface at his feet.

Piper, again with a pause for the docketing procedure, turned from question to statement. 'I think myself that they come from different parts of the mind. Fiction belongs to what's called the Imagination. Melodrama belongs to the Fancy; it's a bubbling up of the suppressed primitive, a subconscious on holiday, *fantasy*.'

'I think that's a novel notion,' said Gott, looking at Piper with an innocent and admiring eye. But Piper, delaying only to record *Irony* in his invisible notebook, pursued his thought.

'I see the difference in my own waking and dream life. My waking life is given to imaginative writing – writing in which the chief concern is values. But my dreams, like melodrama, are very little concerned with values. The whole interest is on a tooth and claw level. Attack and escape, hunting, trapping, out-witting. A consciousness all the time of physical action, of material masses, and dispositions as elements in a duel. And, of course, the constant sense of obscurity or mystery that haunts dreams. If I wrote melodrama it would be out of dreams.'

'And what of Shakespeare's drama of primitive intrigue, *Hamlet*? Is that an example of the melodramatic and the imaginative working together?'

Piper meditated. 'Perhaps', he said, 'it's a failure on that account. The melodramatic material taken over by Shakespeare may not have been susceptible —'

But this was a theme on which Gott conducted some dozen laborious discussions with some dozen more or less laborious undergraduates every year. During some part of Piper's following remarks, in consequence, he was guilty — like the Great Lexicographer in similar circumstances — of abstracting his mind and thinking of Tom Thumb.

'. . . And I should find it irresistible,' said Piper.

Gott nodded comprehendingly. 'Irresistible.' But Piper was not deceived. He made his invisible note, *Donnish exclusiveness; inattentive to outside opinion*, and patiently began again.

'I probably suppress the melodramatic in myself: I don't read it, for one thing. But it's there waiting to bubble up. And as it doesn't get into my writing it would like, I think, to get into my life. If a sort of Ruritania came my way — cloak and sword adventure — I should jump at it. And, as I say, in real life I should find your sort of business — neatly disposing of a corpse and so on — irresistible.' Piper adjusted the large horn-rimmed glasses through which he normally contemplated the world. 'As irresistible', he added conscientiously, 'as a lovely and willing woman.' He threw open the bathroom window. 'Do you do deep breathing? I always do.'

*

It was possible, said the Duke as he hovered indecisively between the kidneys and the bones, that his mother might come over from Horton Ladies' for the play. Diana Sandys, sitting beside Anna Merkalova, observed that the dowager Duchess was a *very* strict old lady. Piper made his note, *All girls cats by twenty*; Noel looked reproachfully at Diana; Elizabeth looked speculatively at Gott. Bunney, surrounded by an irreproachable

44

American breakfast, was interested. 'How old?' he asked the Duke.

'Eh? Oh – ninety-four.'

Bunney's eyes widened. 'Vigorous?'

'Uncommon.'

'Not – deaf, by any chance?'

Mrs Terborg was looking sternly at her countryman over her coffee. The Duke replied that his mother was certainly not deaf, but added that she now lived in almost unbroken retirement. Bunney nodded inexplicably. 'Most important!' he said. 'Do you think she would cooperate? Ninety-four and living out of the world; you see how important that is?' He looked almost pleadingly at the Duke. 'Your mother is probably substantially uncontaminated.'

'Uncontaminated!'

'Uncontaminated.' Bunney made brief calculations. 'I think,' he said – his eye fixed meditatively on Timothy Tucker – 'she will almost certainly say *hijjus*. And *indjin*,' he added – looking at Mr Bose. Suddenly a gleam came into Bunney's eye. 'She may even say *gould*! It would be a big thing to find a *gould*.' He turned to Gott as to a fellow sage. 'You remember Odger maintains *gould* to have died with the late Lady Lucy Lumpkin in 1883?'

The Scamnum running breakfast was now at its busiest. Some twenty people were scattered round the big tables; three or four more were foraging among the hot plates. But Bunney had now attracted the attention of the whole company. And he expanded under notice. 'Your butler is an interesting man,' he told the Duke, 'a most interesting man. He was born, you know, in Berkshire, and so were his parents. But almost certainly the family came from Kent. There are certain slack vowels. . . .' And just as interest in Bunney was dissipating itself he succeeded in recalling it abruptly. 'Bagot was good enough to cooperate last night. I asked him to repeat the Lord's Prayer.'

The Duke looked blankly at his guest. 'Asked Bagot to repeat the Lord's Prayer! Really, Dr Bunney, you must meet my head-gardener, Macdonald. You would interest each other.'

'The Lord's Prayer,' affirmed Bunney, beaming round. 'It affords a number of interesting collocations of speech-elements.

45

Bagot was good enough to cooperate, and here it is.' And stooping down to his feet, Bunney produced the black box and flicked a switch. The table fell silent in somewhat shocked expectation. Then the black box spoke, in a high falsetto.

'I will *not* cry Hamlet, revenge,' said the black box.

There was a startled pause and then a dry voice spoke from down the table. 'An unfamiliar version, my dear sir.' This was Sir Richard Nave.

'Kentish or Berkshire, Dr Bunney?' This was Professor Malloch : both these had arrived since the mysterious messages had been in prominence.

Bunney was staring at his machine much as Balaam may have stared at his ass. Noel took it upon himself to enlighten the new arrivals. 'If Miss Terborg will steel herself, I'll explain. It's the Black Hand. He was operating yesterday and here he is again. Only he seems to have changed his mind; quite turned over a new leaf, in fact. He will *not* cry "Hamlet, revenge." '

'Why should he change his mind, I wonder?' It was the competent Mrs Terborg who took up the theme. The previous evening, no doubt, she had realized as Gott had done that the Black Hand was generally disturbing; now she saw the advantages of giving the subject an airing on a whimsical plane. 'I think Black Hands ought to pursue a more consistent policy if they want to impress. Not that Dr Bunney doesn't seem impressed.'

'It's a comfort to think', Miss Terborg One carried on briskly, 'that even if we don't discover the identity of the Black Hand Dr Bunney will be able to identify his grandfather's and grandmother's home-town.'

'I think it's creepy,' said Miss Terborg Two.

*

Gott, Noel, Nave, and Malloch made their way to the Banqueting Hall together. It was rather awkward, Noel felt, about Malloch. *Crucible*, Noel's publication, did not usually much concern itself with the merely learned of the world; it contented itself with occasional shadowing of all such under the generic figures of a certain Professor Wubb and his assistants Dr Jim-jim and Mr Jo-jo. But it had taken notice of Professor Malloch; in fact it had reviewed his Hamlet study, *The Show of Violence*. And Malloch had written a dry little reply. Confronted now by Malloch as a guest at Scamnum, Noel was disposed to see this reply as having been, in a way, a compliment. At the time, it had seemed an incitement: Professor Malloch and Professor Wubb had in consequence been ludicrously interwoven in certain editorial paragraphs of *Crucible*. Noel had just read these over in bed and although they still seemed funny – Noel's editorials were usually considerably gayer than the productions of his contributors – they had struck him as distressingly childish as well. And here was Malloch in the flesh; dry, courteous, incredibly learned, and apparently a constant and critical reader of *Crucible* from cover to cover. It was really very awkward.

'And the story', Malloch was saying, 'of the hydrocephalic children at the funeral of the girl who used to torture the cats – I wonder if the writer took medical advice?'

'I suppose he is a little unbalanced,' said Noel uncomfortably.

'Ah, yes. But I mean advice on the likelihood of the story. Nave, do you read Mr Gylby's journal? There was a story about hydrocephalic children....' And Malloch proceeded to enlist the physician in the task of demolishing the pathological basis of *Crucible*'s last masterpiece. Yes, he was incredibly learned; he seemed to know more about it all than Nave himself. That was always their way, Noel thought. Accumulate enormous stores of information – always the right factual brick ready to throw at you. Meanwhile, anxious Crispin courtesy was the rule. Respectfully, he drew attention to a magnificent Fantin-Latour on the wall. Whereupon, Malloch made certain knowledgeable observations on Fantin-Latour.

Gott had taken up another semi-medical theme with Nave. 'Have you noticed the American twins? It's impossible to tell them apart – until they begin talking. Vanessa is distinctly intelligent and Stella is almost witless. That's unusual, is it not?'

Nave nodded. 'Distinctly so. They're clearly identical twins' – he searched for the technical word – 'uniovular. That means that they have an identical hereditary equipment. If their intelligence is markedly unequal it's an extraordinary interesting thing psychologically. because the difference must be an accident of nurture or environment. I must have a talk with them.'

47

The psychologist was plainly interested. But Gott had a problem of his own. 'They are physically identical to the naked eye – but would they be that microscopically, so to speak? What about finger-prints, for instance?'

Nave, who was probably unaware of Gott's hobby, looked vaguely surprised. 'I'm really not sure. But I should think ...'

Malloch, walking behind with Noel, interposed: 'Galton investigated the finger-prints of uniovular twins. He found that, although remarkably similar, they were never indistinguishable.'

Gott abandoned an interesting possibility. Noel, pacing beside the invincible Malloch, could almost be heard to groan. At the door of the hall he positively embraced the hovering figure of Mrs Platt-Hunter-Platt.

And now one of Gott's nervous moments had arrived: his stage was to undergo its first expert scrutiny.

'Ah,' said Malloch, 'the Fortune.'

'Yes. The hall being rectangular, I thought it best to take something like the Fortune as a model.'

Malloch looked dubious. 'I should have been inclined to take the Swan. However unreliable De Witt's drawing may be ...'

And the two authorities drifted away in a courteous battle of technicalities.

Meanwhile Mrs Platt-Hunter-Platt's voice rose in a squeal of protest. 'But there's no curtain!'

Noel grinned. 'Oh yes there is – a little one there at the back.' And the amusements of delivering himself in his old tutor's best lecture-room manner suddenly striking him, he continued gravely: 'It is necessary to remember that the Elizabethan theatrical companies originally presented their plays in the yards of London inns –'

'In public-houses?' exclaimed Mrs Platt-Hunter-Platt. 'A most disorderly arrangement!'

'So the puritan faction thought. They produced manifestos and protests about it which you would probably find technically interesting. Well, as I say, the players simply put up a platform in the yard of an inn and acted on that. The expensive part of the audience sat looking down from the galleries or rooms of the inn –'

'Or sat on the platform itself,' interposed Nave, who had abandoned the scholars.

'Or sat on the platform on three-legged stools beside the actors,' agreed Noel, 'the nasty one spitting tobacco and crying "filthy, filthy!"'

'Disgusting,' said Mrs Platt-Hunter-Platt.

'And the common people simply stood on the ground round the platform; they were called the groundlings.'

'Why?' asked Mrs Platt-Hunter-Platt blankly.

'I think because they stood on the ground. They were also occasionally called the understanders –'

'Understanders?'

'Perhaps a joke. Well, the platform was surrounded on three sides by the audience, and the fourth no doubt abutted on certain rooms that the actors used for dressing-rooms, entrances, and exits, and so forth. When they began to build theatres of their own what they built was still uncommonly like a platform in an inn-yard. Here it is.' And Noel led the way forward and assisted Mrs Platt-Hunter-Platt to mount the low platform which projected from the middle of the hall. 'This platform is the front stage, where most of the action of a play takes place. It ought to be under the open sky, just as an inn-yard was. And, as you see, we shall try to get a similar effect on Monday by lighting it from directly above with arc-lamps. The audience, sitting round the hall, will be more or less in shadow. Gott felt a bit dubious about a modern audience feeling comfortable in a full light.'

'The effect', remarked Nave, 'should be rather like a boxing-ring in a stadium.'

'Boxing!' said Mrs Platt-Hunter-Platt, in tones that conveyed whole manifestos against Degrading Spectacles.

Noel nodded. 'Yes. Only here the platform or arena isn't actually islanded in the audience. On one side it runs back to what is the really interesting part of the theatre. You remember I said that in the inn-yard one side of the platform abutted on certain rooms and so forth? Well, the players used a bit of the galleries in that quarter as well. They liked to be able to act on two levels. So they used the first gallery at the back of the stage for "aloft" and that sort of thing. The upper stage, it's called.

Enter Lord Scales upon the Tower, walking: then enter two or three citizens below.'

'Lord Scales?' said Mrs Platt-Hunter-Platt, looking dubiously round the hall for one of Scamnum's plentiful peers.

'In *The Second Part of King Henry VI*. And they used another gallery above that, maybe, just for blowing trumpets and so forth. But what is chiefly interesting is what happened *below* the upper stage, on the level of the front stage or platform proper. That's where a curtain comes in. They simply hung a curtain from the gallery and the result was something very like a modern stage on a smallish scale right at the back of the platform. It was just a deep recess, with its own entrances, and across which they could draw and undraw a curtain. It's called the rear stage. And just as the upper stage was used for "aloft" – Juliet's balcony, city walls and that sort of thing – so the rear stage was "within" : Prospero's cave in *The Tempest*, Desdemona's bedroom in *Othello* –'

'Or the Queen's bedroom in *Hamlet*!' said Mrs Platt-Hunter-Platt with sudden enormous intelligence.

'Wrong, as a matter of fact.' It was Gervase Crispin who had strolled up and who spoke. 'The Queen's bedroom will be played on the front stage because the rear stage is needed for Polonius hiding behind the arras. Hamlet stabs through the curtain, pulls it back – and finds the corpse.'

'I think', said Mrs Platt-Hunter-Platt, 'that Shakespeare is sometimes rather dreadful.'

Gervase laughed gruffly. 'Not so dreadful as some of the others. Tell Mrs Platt-Hunter-Platt about the Jew's trap-door, Noel.'

'There's a trap-door between the upper stage and the rear stage. We know it should be there from Marlowe's *Jew of Malta*. The Jew sets a sort of man-trap in his "gallery" – the upper stage, that is. He arranges a concealed hole in the floor, with a nice boiling cauldron underneath. Then he falls through it himself, the curtain of the rear stage is withdrawn – and there he is nicely cooking in his own pot.'

Piper had joined the group. 'But there's no trap-door here, is there?' he asked. 'It's not necessary in *Hamlet*?'

'*Hamlet* only needs a trap in the front stage. But Gott had the upper stage one built in, all the same. It's there', Noel added as Malloch and Gott approached once more, 'to satisfy nice antiquarian sensibilities.'

Timothy Tucker strolled up. 'You know, this is very suggestive.' He waved his hand around and addressed Gott. 'It gives me an idea. You remember Spandrel's idea when he published *Death Laughs at Locksmiths*? It was a story that all turned on skeleton keys. So Spandrel bought up about three thousand yards of copper wire and enclosed a foot with every copy. And soon everyone was trying to make their own skeleton keys to pick their own locks –'

'Encouraging criminality,' said Mrs Platt-Hunter-Platt severely.

'Not at all,' said Sir Richard Nave with equal severity; 'on the contrary, a healthy resolving of suppressed criminal tendencies in fantasy.'

'Skeleton keys are apparently all nonsense anyway,' said Tucker easily. 'But what strikes me is this. Here's a perfect material setting for a mystery: upper stage, rear stage, trapdoors, and what not. Why not write it up, Gott, and we could issue it with a cut-out model of the whole thing – Banqueting Hall, Elizabethan stage, corpse, and all? Toy-shops have the kind of thing: "Fold along the dotted line," you know. I dare say we could run to coloured cardboard and a bright scrap of curtain. Everybody would set up his own model and study the mystery from that.'

The publisher wandered away. 'Dear me,' said Malloch, 'Mr Tucker seems to think you greatly interested in sensational fiction.'

Noel, having suffered so much on account of *Crucible*, was ruthless. 'Mr Gott,' he explained courteously, 'is the pseudonymous author of the well-known romances, *Murder among the Stalactites*, *Death at the Zoo*, *Poison Paddock*, and *The Case of the Temperamental Dentist*.'

Malloch turned to Gott with no appearance of surprise. 'This is most interesting. But in *Death at the Zoo*, now: I readily believe that the creature could be trained to fire the fatal shot. But the training of it by means of the series of sugar revolvers to swallow the real revolver? I asked Morthenthaler – you know his *Intelligence in the Higher Mammalia?* – and he seemed to think. . . .'

It was Gott's turn to groan. To have an expert scrutiny of his stage remorselessly followed up by an equally expert scrutiny of his fantastic hobbyhorse was a stiff beginning to the day's exertions. But just as Malloch was showing dangerous signs of proceeding from the natural history of *Death at the Zoo* to the toxicology of *Poison Paddock*, a diversion appeared in the form of the Duchess carrying a telegram.

'Giles,' she said briskly, 'Tony Fletcher, the First Grave-digger, has mumps. I've sent for Macdonald and if you approve I'll ask him. Everybody would be delighted, I think; and with luck I can persuade him.'

Gott considered. 'I don't know that Macdonald is just the cut of a Shakespearean clown. I rather suspect him of being something much more like Prospero. But the Doric would be pleasant – and a real feast for Bunney's box. Try him by all means. Here he is.'

'Macdonald,' said the Duchess, 'I wonder if you would play the Sexton?'

Macdonald reflected, 'Your Grace will be meaning the First Clown?'

'Yes. The Grave-digger.'

'I could dae't,' said Macdonald, with conviction but without enthusiasm.

'And will?'

'Weel, ma'am, I dinna ken that I can rightly spare the time. Wi' twa ignorant new laddies aye speiring aboot matter o' elementary skill, and wi' the green-hooses like to be half-pillaged o' blooms. . . .'

'But we're really relying on you, Macdonald. There's nobody else who can possible get it up.'

There was a remote gleam of interest in Macdonald's eye. 'I'm no Kempt or Tarlton, your Grace, and I rather misdoot the songs. But there's no question but it's an interesting pairt. And wi' a verra richt-thochted reference to the gardening craft – though ill-confoonded wi' ditching and grave-making. And I'd hae to consult wi' Mr Goot here on the queer reference to Yaughan. . . .'

'Why, Macdonald,' exclaimed Gott, 'you know the part already.'

'I hae a common reader's knowledge o' the text,' replied Macdonald with dignity. 'And though the time's short, your Grace, I'll no say ye no. I'll awa' to study it noo, and hae a guid pairt o' the lines by the afternoon.' And Macdonald composedly withdrew.

'Macdonald', said Noel, 'knows the Elizabethan clowns and the *cruces Shakespearianae*; a village Gott, in fact; a mute, inglorious Malloch; a pedant guiltless of his pupils' blood.'

'Mr Gylby', explained Bunney to Lord Auldearn, 'is paraphrasing Gray's celebrated *Elegy*.'

4

By tea-time on Sunday Gott found his anxieties about the play lightened. His mind was now concentrated on this definite point and that; his more comprehensive doubts had dwindled. He felt that the tragedy of Hamlet was winning. That first lurking sense of uneasiness; the embarrassed feeling that the house-party was making itself a motley to the view; the apprehension lest some emanation of personification of Scamnum, like a ghostly Sir Thomas Bertram, might abruptly appear and bring all to a huddled and ignominious close – these things were gone. Instead, some thirty people had agreed to put an antic disposition on – and were enjoying it. The Duchess had worked hard; Mrs Terborg had talked amateur theatricals through the centuries: Elizabeth Kenilworth, Voltaire's Ferney, Mme de Staël's Coppet, Doddington under Foote, the Russian Imperial Court – she had talked, in fact, all she knew, which was a lot. The Black Hand, moreover, had gone out of business; or those favoured by its communications chose to be silent. And Macdonald's last-moment accession to the company – calculated stroke of a clever hostess that it was – was an immense success. Behind stage during rehearsals, the head-gardener held a sort of court. And he repeated the Shorter Catechism and 'The Cotter's Saturday Night' for the benefit of Bunney and – as he later discovered with some indignation – the black box.

The practical business of those final days, with all the actors assembled, was, of course, that of fitting everything together. The principal characters were already well-drilled and the main tones of the production, Gott felt, were satisfactorily established. Melville Clay, with infinite tact, had perfected what was in effect a first-rate amateur Hamlet: quiet, with a minimum of business and movement, relying chiefly on the formal beauty of the verse and prose. In that virtuoso display of his in the little drawing-room he had glided imperceptibly in sixteen lines of blank verse from an enunciation merely academic to the full compass of a great actor in the grand tradition. On the stage in the Banqueting Hall it was as if he had found, somewhere in that progress, just the right point at which to halt for the purpose on hand. With this nursing of the company by an acute theatrical intelligence, with the ready acquiescence of the others in Clay's simplified dramatic formula, with the absence of disturbing professional association which the novel staging would ensure, the play was likely to go well. All the principal players had amateur experience: the Duke had done that sort of thing – in Greek as far as he could remember – at school; the Duchess had played Portia to the satisfaction of Mr Gladstone; Piper had been in the O.U.D.S. – and so on. Nevertheless, to get a large amateur cast to run smoothly through a long play, far more rehearsal than that available would be necessary. There were bound to be hitches; Gott and Clay between them were busy foreseeing and eliminating what they could.

Much was to depend on the rapidity and continuity of action which the reconstructed Elizabethan stage made possible. The play was to begin at nine o'clock; there was to be one interval only, taken at the end of the second act; it was to be over just before midnight. There was no scenery to change, and few properties to manipulate. Now on one and now on another of the three stage spaces – front stage, rear stage, upper stage – the action would run smoothly forward. As the first scene, 'The Battlements of Elsinore', ended on the upper stage, Claudius and his court would enter in procession for Scene Two, 'The Council Chamber in the Castle', on the front stage. And as soon as the last characters in this scene had made their exit the curtain of the rear stage would be drawn back, revealing Laertes and

Ophelia in Scene Three, 'A Room in the House of Polonius'. The curtain would no sooner be drawn again on this than Hamlet and his companions would appear 'aloft' for the meeting with the Ghost in Scene Four. In this way the play was assured something of the impetus it enjoyed three hundred years ago. An audience accustomed to the constant dropping of a curtain over a proscenium-arch and to a succession of elaborate stage sets might be disconcerted for a time, but they would be seeing *Hamlet* played in the manner in which Shakespeare himself had played in it.

No expense – as Bunney commented – had been spared. The hall had been divided in golden section by a tapestried partition in the centre of which, and fronting the larger area, had been inset rear stage and upper stage, with a sort of dwarf turret crowning all, and with the front stage projecting far up the hall to the tiers of seats arranged for the audience. In the part of the hall behind the partition, there had been adequate room for all behind-stage necessities, including a green-room and a number of dressing cubicles. The hall was thus a self-contained unit, a complete playhouse in itself. Once the play began, no scurrying about between hall and the main buildings of Scamnum would be necessary.

Just before the Saturday afternoon rehearsal, Gott was busy with a final review of properties. It was surprising, he was finding, how little paraphernalia – costumes apart – were either necessary or desirable when producing in the old way. A property too much and the non-representational character of the stage would be marred, with an uncomfortable result as of a fragmentarily set-up scene. Moreover, it was necessary to keep the front stage as bare as possible. The Elizabethan producer had cared almost nothing for continuous visual illusion; he would thrust a mossy bank – or even a lady in bed – out upon the front stage in the middle of a scene without a tremor. But a modern audience must not be unnecessarily disconcerted, and there must be as little shifting of properties on the open front stage as possible. Gott had finally reduced the front-stage properties to two thrones, with two benches added for the play-scene, and a table added to that again in the last scene of all – furniture which servants could whisk on and off unobtrusively enough. To all intents and purposes the front stage was to be simply a bare platform throughout.

The rear stage was different; behind its curtain one could move on and off anything one liked. Here, therefore, there would be more properties: different tapestries in different scenes, and various pieces of Scamnum's most exquisite Jacobean furniture. Gott was contemplating the rear stage as set for the King's prayer scene when the Duchess entered.

'Giles, we can take that ungainly monster' – and she pointed to a bulky *prie-dieu* which took up a good deal of the scene – 'back to its home. I've got the most perfect faldstool – and a much better crucifix too.' As she spoke two footmen came in bearing a crate. 'I remembered the faldstool at Hutton Beechings, and I rang up Lucy Hutton and she's sent it and the crucifix as well.'

'It's not a crucifix,' said Gott when they had unpacked. 'It's a plain iron cross, which is perhaps better. And the faldstool is exquisite. They'll do both for the King in the prayer scene and for Hamlet to point to at "Get thee to a nunnery". By the way, has Yorick's skull come? I've decided I don't want any bones; only the skull.'

'Old Dr Biddle is coming over to dinner and bringing it with him.' Dr Biddle was the local practitioner, and he had promised to provide whatever remains of Yorick were required. 'And, incidentally, he's very keen to walk on. Do you think he could?'

Gott nodded. 'Certainly he can. . . . There are plenty of spare costumes and he'll make a most convincing attendant lord or venerable counsellor. I thought of putting Mr Bose on' – Mr Bose was the black man – 'but I am afraid he would look a little *outré*; something strayed in from a *cinquecento* Adoration of the Magi. As it is, he's a capital prompter; knows the text backwards and has terrific concentration. I don't think his mind will stray for a split second throughout. See where he comes.'

'He would make a capital Ghost,' said the Duchess, and seeing that the approaching Hindu had heard something of this remark, added: 'Mr Bose, you should be the Ghost. Your movement is not earthly.'

Mr Bose smiled – and his smile was something on which Charles Piper might have sat up all night elaborating paragraphs. It had at once the subtlety of Mona Lisa and the spontaneous gaiety of a Murillo beggar-boy; it was remote and utterly intimate, limpid and fathomless – the paragraph would have to be stuffed with such contradictions. And above all it was a sort of disembodied smile, just as the motion to which the Duchess had referred was a sort of disembodied motion. In his fictions Gott sometimes permitted himself a mysterious Oriental who was credited – on what he had described to Piper as the Bath Mat principle – with moving like a cat. Mr Bose moved not in the least like a cat, but strictly like a spirit, an *esprit* who had been caught by a spell and constrained to talk a giggling, difficult English, to charm and puzzle and alarm. Mr Bose giggled delightedly now.

'I do not go tramp, tramp about your place, Duchess? It is because I do not eat too much, I think!' Mr Bose radiated his quintessence of gaiety. He could give to mere facetiousness, Gott reflected, a something that made the finest Western irony *gauche*. And when he took a plunge into seriousness, talking with alarming suddenness and simplicity of the soul, he made one feel – as Noel put it – a great pink lout. Yet Mr Bose was a Bath Mat Oriental as well; he was ingratiating and he was wily, undoubtedly wily. And if one were surrounded by millions of Mr Boses most certainly one would feel that only the wiliness counted.

'But in winter', Mr Bose was proceeding more seriously, 'perhaps I shall eat an egg. I have my father's permission for an egg – if constitutionally necessary.' Mr Bose looked dubiously into the future; the possibility plainly troubled him. He stood on one leg, his habit when feeling unhappy.

'I was saying', Gott remarked, 'that you are better than the best professional prompter. You know every line of the play.'

Mr Bose forgot the threatening diet and giggled again with delight. 'In my country our education is *very* largely memory – *very* largely. A Brahmin of the old school would not teach from books; much is thought too sacred to be written in any book. It is part of our training to learn by heart many thousands of lines of sacred texts. And so memory is developed. *Very* quickly I know an English text by heart; but to know what it means – *that* is more difficult. So I found, studying for the B.A. degree at

University of Calcutta. Now I understand nearly everything – even Chaucer and much of Mr James Juice.' Mr Bose sparkled to the Duchess in modest pride.

But Gott was apprehensive lest Mr Bose, despite his efficiency as a prompter, might be feeling out of it. 'I'm sorry', he said when the Duchess had moved away, 'that you're not in the play. But you wouldn't fit the colour-scheme, would you? I wonder if the Grand Mogul or somebody had an ambassador at the court of Elsinore?' Mr Bose, Gott knew, delighted in banter of this sort. And now Mr Bose laughed.

'One day at the Duchess's place I will play Othello the dusky Moor! And meantime I learn much – very much. If the Queen, though, had a little black boy ... but that was later, was it not? And on this old sort of stage you cannot disguise people – eh? Black cannot be made white, nor old young, nor plain lovely?'

'No; that is one of the points that have emerged. Very little make-up is possible on a platform stage. And that makes it important that people should be like their parts to begin with.'

'Mr Clay', said Mr Bose, 'is very like the Melancholy Dane.'

'Yes; but I doubt if Gervase Crispin is at all like Osric. And Bunney, whom we've had to call in, is an unconvincing Gentleman of the Guard. And the Vicar, unfortunately, is peculiarly unlike a Doctor of Divinity – though he is one. And think of Lord Auldearn: was Polonius that sort of disconcerting mingling of Shakespeare and Caliban?'

This was neat enough: the Lord Chancellor, with his dome-like forehead, heavy jaw, and characteristic lurch, suggested just this combination. But Mr Bose was rather shocked. 'Lord Auldearn', he said emphatically, 'is a very good man, a learned and enlightened prince! He is a little infirm because of his great years. In my country we consider great years very holy.'

Convicted, thought Gott, of a barbarian lapse and gently reproved. But Mr Bose, with politeness, continued the theme just as if he had not been shocked. 'Lady Elizabeth, I think, does not look her part. She is too beautiful, is she not?'

This was percipience. Could one, after fifty years in India, say anything as understanding as that of an Indian drama? It went straight to a point round which Gott had been fumbling for days. Ophelia, so hopelessly under the weather throughout the play, should be forlornly pretty; never more than that. And Elizabeth's looks would not knit themselves to the part; they spoke too clearly of a spirit with which poor Ophelia could not be credited. What was Elizabeth's beauty? It was not something that could be dissociated from uncommon qualities of mind; but it was not, again, the highest and always tragic sort of beauty – heavy, fateful, perversely crossed by melancholy or intellect. It was not Rosamund, Cordelia, Desdemona, the Duchess of Malfi. In fact, there was no real place for Elizabeth in the Elizabethan age; she represented something of later birth – an invention of Fielding's, or Meredith's. And this astounding revelation of deficiency in the Elizabethan drama, so casually indicated by Mr Bose, was perhaps the chief intellectual shock which Giles Gott experienced during these by no means uneventful Scamnum days. Now he looked at his watch. 'Time to begin,' he said briskly.

*

Hamlet has thirty speaking parts, two or three of which are nearly always omitted. With bold doubling, one can give the play with nineteen speaking players. In addition, one needs a few supers: a Dumb-show King and Queen, two servants, and if possible an extra Player, Lord, and Lady. There is no crowd, but in Act Four, Scene Five, everybody not actually on the stage must be prepared to stand off and shout to represent 'Danes'.

These were the Scamnum arrangements. It would have been easy to avoid doubling; there was no lack of minor amateur talent available for the smaller parts. But partly because the original plan had been for an entertainment *by* Scamnum, and more particularly because Gott was concerned to avoid that common source of amateur disaster, an over-crowded greenroom, the cast had been kept down. It would finally stand in the programme like this:

CLAUDIUS, *King of Denmark*	Edward Crispin
HAMLET, *Prince of Denmark, son to the late, and nephew to the present King*	Melville Clay
POLONIUS, *Principal Secretary of State*	Ian Stewart

HORATIO, *friend to Hamlet*	Charles Piper
LAERTES, *son to Polonius*	Noel Gylby
ROSENCRANTZ | *formerly fellow-students*	Thomas Potts
GUILDENSTERN | *with Hamlet*	Timothy Tucker
OSRIC, *a fantastic fop*	Gervase Crispin
A Gentleman	Rupert Traherne
A Doctor of Divinity	Samuel Crump
MARCELLUS |	Richard Nave
BARNARDO | *Gentlemen of the Guard*	Edward Bunney
FRANCISCO |	Peter Marryat
First Grave-digger	Murdo Macdonald
Second Grave-digger	Gervase Crispin
FORTINBRAS, *Prince of Norway*	Andrew Malloch
A Norwegian Captain	Peter Marryat
English Ambassador	Richard Nave
Messenger	Vanessa Terborg
Sailor	Timothy Tucker
GERTRUDE, *Queen of Denmark, mother to Hamlet*	Anne Crispin
OPHELIA, *daughter to Polonius*	Elizabeth Crispin
Players	Andrew Malloch, Gervase Crispin, Anna Merkalova, Diana Sandys
Dumb-show King	Giles Gott
Dumb-show Queen	Stella Terborg
A Lord	Henry Biddle
A Lady	Lucy Terborg
Attendants	
The GHOST *of Hamlet's father*	Noel Gylby

This represented, Gott believed, a body manageable within the space available. Just thirty people all told would have business behind the scenes: the nineteen speaking players, the seven supers (including Gott himself as the Dumb-show King and two footmen dressed in Tudor liveries as 'attendants'), Mr Bose as prompter, the Duke's man and two professional dressers, male and female, brought down from London. A vexed question at the moment was whether there should be a thirty-first in the person of Max Cope. Cope was working on two sketches: one from the minstrel gallery at the back of the audience's part of the hall; the other from a corner of the upper stage, where he would be tolerably unnoticeable and get an interesting angle on the front stage. He was undecided still as to which he would work at on the night. Gott wished him safely away in the minstrel gallery, but as it would doubtless be by Cope's picture that the Tragedy of Hamlet played at Scamnum Court would go down to posterity he could hardly insist.

The cast, as the cast in any amateur theatricals must always be, was odd in one or two prominent places and shaky in several minor ones. Lord Traherne, as a Gentleman, unfortunately lost the character the moment he stepped on the boards, and became instead an awkward, though gentlemanlike, schoolboy. Peter Marryat, one of the untried late arrivals with two small parts, appeared dangerously half-witted. He was absent-minded enough, Clay declared, to begin his Norwegian Captain's speech while making his brief appearance as Francisco in the first scene – and obstinate enough, Gott added, to carry firmly on with it to the end. Stella Terborg was fairly safe in a silent part; but as her business was that of being poisoned in the dumb-show by someone uncommonly like a Black Hand she might very conceivably break through the convention with a scream. The more formidable Vanessa as a boy messenger, and Diana Sandys as a boy player who should speak the prologue in the play scene, both had parts less considerable than their competence deserved. Gervase Crispin had rather too much; it was doubtful if his foppery as Osric and his clownery as the second Grave-digger would be as distinct as was desirable. And Noel was rather an unfledged Ghost. The part had been marked originally for Dr Crump, the Vicar of Scamnum Ducis; but when Dr Crump found it involving an acrobatic disappearance down a trap, followed by a longish crawl beneath a three-foot stage, he had retreated to the more familiar business of officiating at Ophelia's burial. Noel, however, was shaping well. Being the orthodox Crispin six feet, and a master of the precocious bass, favoured on public-school parade-grounds, he had the essential qualifications. All in all, Gott reiterated to himself, things should go well.

And this first dress-rehearsal on Saturday afternoon began

excellently. Peter Marryat gave it a good start, by some terrific effort speaking Francisco's eight dispersed lines correctly and in the right place. Bunney, although he insisted on delivering himself according to his own theory of Elizabethan pronounciation, was a surprisingly military Barnardo. Sir Richard Nave, in life a most drily unpoetical person – as who must not be, the Duchess said, that wants to improve sex? – brought out the lyrical strain in Marcellus well enough. Noel's Ghost, coached by Clay, stalked and turned on the upper stage as if on fifty yards of frosty battlement.

The first scene, however, tells one little of how the play will run. It is a tremendous start and the interest it instantly commands has to be caught up and sustained in the succeeding council scheme. Once that is got compellingly under way the play is launched. And now it was going as Gott wanted it to go. The right atmosphere was being generated.

Gott's *Hamlet* was not the *Hamlet* in which Clay was accustomed to play on the professional stage. It belonged to what Malloch dubiously called 'the new historical school'. It was a *Hamlet* in which, through all the intellectual and poetical elaboration of the piece, a steady emphasis was given to the basic situation of wary conflict between usurper and rightful heir. The sense of desperate issues, of wits matched against wits in a life-and-death struggle, was to be perpetually present. The battle of mighty opposites – one side the crafty king and his equally crafty minister Polonius; on the other the single figure of the more formidably because more intellectually cunning prince – this was to be the heart of the Scamnum *Hamlet*. Whereas Clay's usual *Hamlet* sprang in considerable part from the ruminative minds of Goethe and Coleridge, Gott's sprang not a little from the minds of Shakespeare's full-blooded predecessors.

Into this newer reading of the play, Clay – though it had meant much work – had thrown himself with enthusiasm. And now in the second scene the result was beginning to unfold itself. Here in Claudius and Hamlet were two men who must fight to the death; here was the opening of a duel that would be instantly clear to any Renaissance audience. And as the action proceeded it came to Gott that he was watching not merely a careful and competent amateur *Hamlet* but a *Hamlet* which

62

was – as far as its embodiment of this main conflict went – positively remarkable. Clay was a great actor, a fact Gott had barely realized before this Scamnum venture, though he knew him to be brilliant and successful enough. And – what was something more remarkable – the Duke of Horton was a great actor as well. He had been startling on his few and scrappy appearances at rehearsal earlier; he was astounding now. And the play as a result was catching the drift that Gott designed. The meditative Hamlet was revealed as only a facet of the total man; the Queen and Ophelia were pushed back; the play showed itself as turning predominantly from first to last on Statecraft. And it was the statesmen who were important; on the one side the dispossessed Hamlet; on the other Claudius and Polonius.

Gott watched the play unfold with the discriminating delight with which one studies an infinitely complicated thing that one has studied long. Mysterious power of dramatic illusion! Here was Melville Clay fronting the Duke of Horton and Lord Auldearn on a bogus Elizabethan stage in this bogus Gothic hall – and impossible not to believe that the fate of a kingdom lay at issue between them.

> *'The play's the thing*
> *Wherein I'll catch the conscience of the King!'*

Hamlet's voice rang out in triumphant anticipation of his plot. The first part of the dress-rehearsal was over.

*

Nave came up in the interval, watch in hand. 'How quickly it moves!'

'As quick as the talkies,' said Clay.

Gott nodded. 'The talkies help. They bring the ear up with the eye again. And you notice how the speeding-up is carried over from the play? Everybody's brisker. Look at the Duke – bustling about like a works manager.'

'I should be inclined to put it', said Nave, 'that there is rather a species of rebound. They have all been acting, and now they fall back more than they commonly allow themselves on what they would call their real selves. The carry-over from the excitement of the play brings out what used to be called the ruling passion – or what your Elizabethans called the predominant humour.'

Nave's science was young and pushing, and the man was always ready to preach, even in a bustling pause for rehearsal. Now, as Clay hurried away, he continued to talk to Gott. 'Look at young Gylby. He's after that girl Sandys. He's twenty-two, I suppose, and she's probably the first girl he's ever become extensively aware of – such, Mr Gott, are our extraordinary educational conventions! And the result? A high degree of infatuation, a high degree of bewilderment, and a painful lack of technical knowledge as to how to proceed. But masquerading as a projection of sixteenth-century superstition has loosened him up. He's come back to his dominating purpose with a bound, and is achieving a markedly enhanced degree of sexual efficacy.'

Gott was somewhat too old-fashioned a person to relish the psychologists's terminology. But he had to admit the justice of the observation. Noel was taking Diana Sandys very seriously. And at the moment, clad still in the Ghost's gleaming armour and with his helmet on his arm, he was going about his business with all the directness of a knight in some distinctly pre-Tennysonian Arthuriad.

'Do you know anything of the girl?' asked Nave.

'Miss Sandys? She's a school acquaintance of Elizabeth's, and rather older. And, come to think of it, she too is a psychologist.' He looked with just sufficient whimsicality at Nave to make the coming thrust pass inoffensively. 'Or rather an applied psychologist, working on the mass subconscious in the interest of soaps and stockings and patent foods. Copy-writing, I believe it's called.'

Nave nodded coolly. 'Well, advertising is one of the more harmless perversions of science, after all. And whatever she is, she's as hard as nails.' The tone indicated that, for Sir Richard Nave, to be hard as nails was one of the major maidenly virtues. And now abruptly he changed the subject. 'By the way, what exactly are the relations between the Player King and Player Queen?'

Gott, perhaps because he was obscurely disturbed, failed for an instant to grasp the question. And Nave, misinterpreting the hesitation, added: 'I ask as an old friend of the family.'

'Gervase Crispin and Mme Merkalova? I am not in their confidence.'

But Nave would not admit Gott's system of reticences. 'In other words, you share the general impression that she's his mistress? But that's just what's curious. I don't see quite the mechanisms one would expect. A Russian woman in such a situation, and moving in this sort of society, would insist on certain conventions – a little extra distance and formality between them – which would make the matter conveniently plain to the instructed, and leave the uninstructed equally conveniently ignorant.'

'Dear me,' said Gott, honestly feeling that he knew less of polished ungodliness than a romancer ought, 'you instruct *me*, Sir Richard.'

'Instead of which they are – well, not exactly as close as innocent lovers, but as thick as thieves.'

Gott laughed. 'If Gervase Crispin wanted to make the biggest haul in England, he'd have to crack his own safe. I hardly suppose the lady can be his accomplice in crime.'

•

The later hours of Saturday afternoon saw the arrival of another bevy of guests. Tea on the cedar-lawn, with the players moving about in their costumes still, had the appearance and proportions of a charity pageant. Gott had the impression that Lord Auldearn, viewing the swelling throng, was none too delighted. And presently he had what seemed confirmation. Auldearn, who had been talking earnestly to the Duke, swung round and approached him.

'Mr Gott, I have to go away. In anything you do tomorrow somebody must read my part. I shall be back on Monday morning – God willing.' And with this abrupt speech Lord Auldearn disappeared into the house. Twenty minutes later he stepped into his car and was whirled down the drive. The Duchess, Gott thought, was not undisturbed; there was something like an extra dash of resolution in the ready gaiety with which she was going round. And the unwonted briskness which he had noticed in the Duke after rehearsal was gone. The master of Scamnum was vaguer than ever.

Noel had lured his Diana away to croquet; she was pinning up the Ghost's closet-scene dress – a sort of dressing-gown – to prevent its getting in his way. Pamela Hogg, the Armageddon woman, was fascinating Tommy Potts with equine lore. Mrs Terborg sailed about, knowing most people; discovering with others common friends in Paris, Vienna, Rome; skilfully circulating Vanessa among judiciously selected intellectuals, skilfully circulating Stella among less warily chosen Propertied Oafs. And by all these things Gott was obscurely troubled.

Dinner that night was an expansive affair. Bagot, unable to cope with introducing the first course, was of the technical opinion that it was a banquet. His master, contemplating a wife diminished into the middle distance, was just discernibly of the opinion that it was a bore. Max Cope, observing Gott's eye on the Duke, transferred his own gaze significantly to the panelling over the fireplace. Gott saw the point. There hung Kneller's portrait of the first Duke: an oldish man, competently painted, competently turned out as a Restoration type – and with over the keen features the same veil of indifference that now distinguished the eighth Duke at the head of his table. Gott looked round for this queer habit of the will in the other members of the family. Gervase had nothing of it. Noel, a Crispin in some collateral line, was going to have it one day. And Elizabeth? Elizabeth was a Crispin rather than a Dillon, but it was not there nevertheless. A hereditary characteristic, perhaps, latent in the female. And for the remainder of the meal Gott contemplated a very simple fact. He was not, and never had been, disturbed about the Tragedy of Hamlet played at Scamnum Court. It was not in his nature to be disturbed by such an affair, and any anxieties he felt were transferred anxieties. Fuss over x while preparing to plunge at y.

Curious how the keyed mind would cling to inessentials, to the merely practical consequences, all the corollaries on less bewildering planes. A Fellow of St Anthony's, for instance, could not marry a Duke's daughter and get away with it – be as he had been. Either, Gott knew, he would have to quit, or inevitably on old Empson's retirement he would be President. Elizabeth, now at college because she had an eccentric mother, would be planted in the President's Lodging, entertaining dons' wives, undergraduates, itinerant Bunneys.

Irrelevant anxieties – and wandering later through the moon-lit gardens with Elizabeth he continued to start them in his mind. Twenty-one and thirty-four. Thirty-one and forty-four, forty-one and fifty-four, seventy-one and eighty-four. . . . And – more formidable still – it had once been six and nineteen. Elizabeth had been a familiar creature then; now, walking beside him where he could remember balancing her on her first fat pony, she was remote as the stars and secret as the farther hemisphere of the moon.

They were pacing silently down one of Scamnum's famous avenues, the high, impenetrable hedges stretching interminably as in a dream; the pedestalled statues, a whole Olympus of marble deities dimly marshalled in extended file on either side, ghostly against the dark, cañon-like cypress-walls. At the end of the vista, etched in moonlight, stood one of Peter Crispin's minor eccentricities, a picturesque cow-house. A cow-house is not a common amenity in a formal garden, but Peter Crispin had liked to have his curiosities within an easy walk. When there were visitors at Scamnum he had been accustomed to give orders that cows be installed; and his friends, taking their first stroll, would exclaim in dutiful delight when the animals were discovered commodiously lodged in what had outwardly all the appearance of a ruined priory. And now the cow-house was picturesque still, but a cow-house no longer: they kept chemical manures there. Just beyond it, concealed by a high wall, ran the main road to King's Horton.

Elizabeth had paused for a moment by an untenanted pedestal. 'The Pandemian Venus,' she said. 'My grandmother had it removed because she thought it was particularly indelicate. Like Dr Folliott, Giles, in *Crotchet Castle*.' The light irony was Crispin; Giles, after all, *might* have been Elizabeth's tutor.

Six more statues to the cow-house. And there were those horrid words of Nave's: 'Twenty-two . . . a high degree of infatuation, a high degree of bewilderment, and a painful lack of knowledge as to how to proceed. . . .' Noel, twenty-two; Gott, thirty-four. Thirty-four and twenty-one, eighty-four and seventy-one. . . .

Three statues to the cow-house. 'Auldearn went off suddenly,' said Gott, baulking badly.

'He heard of something important.' It was an absent but possibly ominous reply.

Two statues ... one statue ... round the cow-house.

'Elizabeth –' began Gott.

Elizabeth laid a hand on his arm. 'Look!'

The figure of a man had appeared from behind the bogus priory. There was a low whistle, some small object flew over the boundary wall in the moonlight, there was an answering whistle and the figure had vanished. A moment later there came the smooth crescendo and diminuendo of a high-powered car.

'Some servants' intrigue,' said Gott.

'With a Daimler waiting?' There had come into Elizabeth's voice – astoundingly – a far-away echo of the Duke's lazy indifference. 'No; it's something we've had occasionally at Scamnum·ever since my enterprising mother hit on making daddy an Elder Statesman.' She gave a little puckered smile. 'A species of excitement your austere art sniffs at, Giles. *Spies.*'

*

And in the early hours of Monday morning the Black Hand put up its most effective show. Suddenly and hideously in the darkness the whole great fabric of Scamnum re-echoed to the uproar of a tremendous bell. It reverberated through the corridors and flooded a hundred lofty rooms, first in peal after solemn peal and then in a wild gallop, grotesquely loud. And as the startled household hurried out of bedrooms and along corridors, and while the Duke, a surprisingly commanding figure at the head of the main staircase, was shouting that there was no danger of fire, the bell abruptly ceased – to be replaced a moment later by a thunderous but oddly familiar human voice :

> *'Ere the bat hath flown*
> *His cloister'd flight, ere, to Black Hecate's summons*
> *The shard-borne beetle with his drowsy hums*
> *Hath rung night's yawning peal, there shall be done*
> *A deed of dreadful note. . . .'*

Echoing bewilderingly from every direction, the speech could yet be distinguished as coming from somewhere below. It was Gott who, with a sudden gesture of enlightenment, ran downstairs. The voice grew in menace:

> *'Come, seeling night,*
> *Scarf up the tender eye of pitiful day,*
> *And with thy bloody and invisible hand*
> *Cancel and tear to pieces that great bond*
> *Which keeps me pale! Light thickens ...'*

Silence. Gott remounted the stairs. 'The radio-gramophone,' he said. 'Turn a knob and get as much volume as you like. And it changes its own records. First record, a carillon chime – the horror of the ringing bell. Second record, Mr Clay recording from *Macbeth*. Another petty jest.'

Clay, beautiful in a brocaded dressing-gown, nodded easily. 'I thought the voice had a homely ring,' he said. 'I made that record a long time ago, and I think it was a mistake. What was that most apposite quotation?'

Vanessa Terborg turned from calming Stella, her master-passion for showing herself always on the spot roused at once. ' "The clangour of the angels' trumpets and the horror of the ringing bell." Well, I don't think anybody's scared.' Her eye went back firmly to her sister.

Gott doubted the assurance – of others besides the timid Stella. He was scared himself. The mind that could contrive so violent an effect was a mind that thought in terms of violence.

5

(3, 4) *The Queen's closet hung with arras, represented by the rear-stage curtain*

The QUEEN *and* POLONIUS

POLONIUS: A' will come straight. Look you lay home to him,
Tell him his pranks have been too broad to bear with.
And that your grace hath screened and stood between
Much heat and him. I'll silence me even here.
Pray you be round with him.

HAMLET (*without*): Mother, mother, mother!
QUEEN: I'll war'nt you,
   Fear me not. Withdraw, I hear him coming.
      [POLONIUS *hides behind the curtain of the rear-stage.*
      HAMLET *enters.*]
HAMLET: Now, mother, what's the matter?
QUEEN: Hamlet, thou hast thy father much offended.
HAMLET: Mother, you have my father much offended.
QUEEN: Come, come, you answer with an idle tongue.
HAMLET: Go, go, you question with a wicked tongue.
QUEEN: Why, how now, Hamlet?
HAMLET: What's the matter now?
QUEEN: Have you forgot me?
HAMLET: No, by the rood not so,
   You are the queen, your husband's brother's wife,
   And would it were not so, you are my mother.
QUEEN: Nay then, I'll set those to you that can speak.
   [*Going.*]
HAMLET (*seizes her arm*): Come, come, and sit you down, you
      shall not budge,
   You go not till I set you up a glass
   Where you may see the inmost part of you.
QUEEN: What wilt thou do? thou wilt not murder me?
   Help, help, ho!
POLONIUS (*behind the curtain*): What, ho! help, help, help!
HAMLET (*draws*): How now! a rat? dead, for a ducat, dead.
   [*He makes a pass through the curtain.*]
POLONIUS (*falls*): O, I am slain!
QUEEN: O me, what hast thou done?
HAMLET: Nay, I know not,
   Is it the king?
      [*He lifts up the curtain and discovers* POLONIUS, *dead.*]
QUEEN: O, what a rash and bloody deed is this! ...

Aged royalty, perhaps with royalty's instinct for keeping
clear of anything a trifle odd, had decided not to come after all.
So decorations had been put away; young ladies, hearing the
news when half-way to the drawing-room, had scurried back to
their rooms to change into more intriguing frocks; Bagot had

had a busy half-hour putting away the plate which Scamnum produces only for members of a Reigning House. And now in the hall the Dowager Duchess was sitting in the front row in solitary state, on her right hand the two empty chairs that had been destined for the 'real' Duchess and the 'real' Duchess's lady. The Dowager was formidable enough in herself and Gott received with relief Noel's report that the old lady seemed disposed to take out most of the play in sleep. It was a quite unexpurgated *Hamlet*.

Peter Marryat had caused some anxiety. After dinner he had declared that he felt all muddled, and piteously inquired of Noel as to which *was* the one that came first: Francisco or the Norwegian Captain? And Noel having recklessly decided that the answer might be found in a good stiff brandy, the first scene had at moments conveyed the impression that the sentries of Elsinore were a trifle too familiar with the regimental canteen. But as Claudius's court was well known to be in a condition of festivity and swagg'ring upstart reels, this might have passed as the stroke of a venturesome producer; indeed, Gott could see in Malloch's eye the prospect of its being humorously so represented in many Common-rooms hereafter. But there had been no major mishaps. The first part of the play had run rapidly and well and ended in a thunder of applause.

And now the audience, who in the interval had been wandering all over the stage and hall, to the accompaniment of that quite deafening chatter which is the hall-mark of large and polite parties, had been shepherded back to their seats; Bunney had set his black box going on the floor beside the Dowager; the players had returned to the green-room and Tommy Potts, who had turned out to be skilful in such things, heralded Act Three, Scene One with a flourish on a trumpet. A second flourish and the rear-stage curtain was drawn back on 'The lobby of the audience chamber'. The King and Queen, with Polonius, Rosencrantz, and Guildenstern, came on in a little confabulating, plotting knot; and behind them came Ophelia. The second half of the play was launched.

3.1 bristles with technical difficulties; Gott, standing off-stage in his costume as Dumb-show King, was following it intently. Rosencrantz and Guildenstern had come off – heads together, plotting still. And the King's voice continued, tense and secret yet carrying clearly through the hall :

> *'Sweet Gertrude, leave us too,*
> *For we have closely sent for Hamlet hither,*
> *That he, as 'twere by accident, may here*
> *Affront Ophelia:*
> *Her father and myself, lawful espials,*
> *Will so bestow ourselves, that seeing unseen,*
> *We may of their encounter frankly judge ...'*

The Queen came off; Ophelia was set with her book at the faldstool; the King spoke the ticklish guilty aside that prepares for his remorse in the prayer-scene; he and Polonius concealed themselves. Hamlet came on; walked far up the front stage.

> *'To be, or not to be ...'*

To the actor, this is the most formidable speech in drama, formidable because it has established itself at the heart of English poetry, and every word is a legend. Now it came, grave and level, from Melville Clay :

> *'For who would bear the whips and scorns of time,*
> *Th' oppressor's wrong, the proud man's contumely,*
> *The pangs of disprized love, the law's delay,*
> *The insolence of office ...'*

Slowly Hamlet was rounding the great stage, the rhythm of his movement answering the rhythm of the speech. Now he was approaching Ophelia :

> *'Thus conscience does make cowards of us all,*
> *And thus the native hue of resolution*
> *Is sicklied o'er with the pale cast of thought,*
> *And enterprise of great pitch and moment*
> *With this regard their currents turn awry,*
> *And lose the name of action ...'*

He had seen Ophelia; there followed, Gott thought, the most beautiful lines in the play :

> *'Soft you now,*
> *The fair Ophelia – Nymph, in thy orisons*
> *Be all my sins remembered.'*

And now the moment had come which was to tax the utmost limit of Clay's technique. Without direct word spoken, it had to come to the audience that Hamlet had recognized of a sudden that Ophelia's presence was part of a plot. From that moment he would be speaking to her – savagely – with the skin of his mind; all his faculties concentrated on his lurking enemies. This sudden understanding – because it is prepared for only by a fragment of business buried six hundred lines before – is extraordinarily difficult to convey. The point can be made broadly by the King or Polonius accidentally giving their presence away; but there is no warrant for that. It can be – and often is – ignored; but then Hamlet's brutality becomes revolting. If the thing is to be perfectly effective Hamlet must *recollect*.

Clay recollected. He froze.

> *'Are you honest ... are you fair?'*

The words came as if from one in trance. And each succeeding speech, while tremendous in itself, was yet queerly automatic. The surface of the mind ran on, to finish in threadbare railing: women and their painting! For all the forces of the man were now concentrated elsewhere. Here was a Hamlet for whom only one fact was any longer real: the presence of his enemies hidden somewhere here about him; plotting, preparing their final trap. Here, in fact, was the Hamlet of the historical school come rather terrifyingly to life.

He was gone. If Gott had been given to conventional gestures he would have mopped his brow. And now Ophelia's voice – Elizabeth's voice – was moving clearly and tragically through her final soliloquy :

> *'O, what a noble mind is here o'erthrown!*
> *The courtier's, soldier's, scholar's, eye, tongue, sword,*
> *Th' expectancy and rose of the fair state,*
> *The glass of fashion, and the mould of form ...'*

The King and Polonius were out of hiding again, heads together, Polonius eager to be hiding once more:

> 'My lord, do as you please,
> But if you hold it fit, after the play,
> Let his queen-mother all alone entreat him
> To show his grief; let her be round with him;
> And I'll be placed (so please you) in the ear
> Of all their conference. If she find him not,
> To England send him; or confine him where
> Your wisdom best shall think.'

Polonius, his plan to hide in the Queen's closet settled, withdrew. The King turned full to the audience and raised a dramatic hand in keeping with the rhetorical menace of his concluding couplet:

> 'It shall be so.
> Madness in great ones must not unwatched go!'

He stepped within the rear stage and the curtain closed.

*

3. 2.

3. 3.

3. 4. ... Again the rear-stage curtain had closed on the King, this time as he knelt at his vain prayers by the faldstool. At once the Queen and Polonius took the front stage for the closet-scene.

Mr Bose, crouched in his place to the side of the rear stage, was following the speech of the invisible players, syllable by syllable. Polonius's injunction to 'lay home'; Hamlet's call for admittance; the rustle of the rear-stage curtain as Polonius slipped through from the front stage to 'silence himself'. ...

The altercation between Hamlet and the Queen grew. The Queen's cry rang out:

'Help, help, ho!'

From the rear stage came the echoing voice of Polonius:

'Help, help!'

Mr Bose, his eye fixed on his text, stirred in his seat. A pistol-shot rang through the hall.

2

DEVELOPMENT

Good now, sit down, and tell me, he that knows,
Why this same strict and most observant watch?.
What might be toward, that this sweaty haste
Doth make the night joint-labourer with the day:
Who is't that can inform me?

MR JOHN APPLEBY of Scotland Yard was at the theatre. Being the new sort of policeman he was at the ballet, waiting for *Les Présages* to follow *La Boutique Fantasque*. Being paid the old sort of wage, and having the most modest of private fortunes, he was sitting in what his provincial childhood had known as the Family Circle. But being unmarried he was unaccompanied by a family, and being serious and shy, he was without the distraction of a female friend. As a consequence, he was able to devote the interval to reflections on ballet as Pure Muscular Style. Appleby contrived to read the latest books on such things. He was just meditating the awkward case of Japanese tumblers – they were certainly not ballet, but might they not be Pure Muscular Style too? – when the lights were lowered and Tschaikowsky's music, heavy with observations on the Mysterious Universe, filled the theatre.

The constant patrons, who treat the stalls so impressively after the manner of a drawing-room, were strolling and edging back to their places. The woman next to Appleby shut her chocolate-box and stowed it under the seat. Portentously, the curtain rose on Masson's sub-Dantesque stage: hit or miss, Appleby thought, whether you were excited or felt that here was a nice design cruelly run in the wash.

The puce ladies, vaguely Spanish from the neck down; the green and brown gentlemen, ever so slightly ashamed of themselves (one ashamedly and philistinely suspected) from the neck up; Action, in pleasing pleats and extracting miraculous grace from impossible angularities ... they were all at it again, thought Appleby – who was half-way to being a hardened amateur. And certainly it was exciting; Pure Muscular Style – in stately capital letters – scarcely put the matter excitingly enough. The trouble was that these galvanic figures were obscurely up to something, insinuating something, endeavouring – the fatal image would come – like the deaf and dumb to utter through a laborious periphrasis of gesture. And now, against the backcloth, the gentlemen were leaping from wings to wings in three unbelievable hops; now they were charging across the same path in couples, the ladies held out in front of them, head-high, like battering-rams. And all, evidently, with the largest cosmic intent ... articulative, like the music, of the Nature of Things. But the oftener you came, thought Appleby, the less satisfactorily did it build up, the more did you get your pleasure from the fragmentary movements – the exquisite precision, for instance, of the *pas de deux* which the programme called Passion. Yet what delighted him most in *Les Présages* was something essentially dramatic, the entrance of Fate. It was a pity that Fate was got up like a queasy Ethiopian in off-black; it was a pity that he had to make that merely pantomime exit backwards on his heels. But his entrance perfectly blended the dramatic and the choreographic.

Appleby remembered his uncle George, who used to recite at parties a poem beginning 'A chieftain to the Highlands bound' – and at 'bound' *bound* into the middle of the room. ... Fate did not come on like that. On the great stage the common traffic of life was proceeding with an even, untroubled rhythm – and then Fate was *there*, his entrance unnoticed, his menace waiting to strike home.

It was nearly over. The gentlemen had appeared in a new and yet more cosmic kit; they were machines, they were infantry crossing broken ground under fire. The evil in Man, as the programme had it, had aroused the angry passion of war – and the puce ladies, also metamorphosed, were themselves subjected by the martial glamour. If only as mere miming, this was impressive; the symbolism pierced to the contemporary nerve. And now the finale: dubious victory; the Hero leaping to a tableau on somebody's shoulders, stretching out arms – perhaps to the Future, but unescapably as if to an invisible trapeze, so that one thought of tumblers again and half expected the *corps de ballet* to clap hands and make admiring Japanese noises.

The woman in the next seat groped for her chocolate-box.

Appleby emerged from the theatre and walked luxuriously through the London night, discoursing with himself on his own character as a modified philistine. He worked hard as a police-man, he often made his work his play, it was pleasant to have given three hours to something that could have no possible bearing on shop – the monotonous pursuit of burglars in Earl's

Court and injudicious philanthropists in the City. Coming down the Duke of York's Steps, his eye rested on the Admiralty and travelled along the jumbled line of government buildings. One had Palmerston to thank that the Treasury – or was it the Foreign Office? – was not a monument of Ruskinian Gothic. High up, just beyond Downing Street, there shone a solitary light. Were his more orthodoxly gifted contemporaries who had made their way here similarly immersed in a dull routine? What were they doing up there now?

Appleby had one of the humblest flats in one of the largest blocks in Westminster; his three rooms, he suspected, had originally been intended as a bathroom, a kitchenette, and a shoe-cupboard for some more magnificent tenant. But the situation gave him St James's Park as a detour to and from work; his living-room window commanded Mr Epstein's admirable Night while ignoring his less admirable Day; and sitting up in bed he could distinguish the upper half of the flag-staff on Buckingham Palace. Approaching the entrance of this building now, Appleby quickened his pace. A car was standing outside, a car which meant business. A moment later he became aware of a second car, and whistled. And when he saw a third car – a car which every policeman must know – he ran.

The night-porter, usually inaccessible to any under six-room tenants, came scurrying out of his cubby-hole to say something Appleby didn't stop to hear. The lift-boy, hitherto familiar and conversible, looked at him on this occasion with awe. He ran along the corridor and burst rather breathlessly into his room.

It was an overwhelming spectacle. The Chief Commissioner was pacing up and down the available eight feet of floor. Appleby's immediate superior in the c.i.d., Superintendent Billups, stood, plainly bewildered and slightly affronted, in a corner. In the only easy chair sat the Prime Minister, holding a large gun-metal watch some three inches from his nose.

'Good evening, gentlemen,' said Appleby. The words represented, he felt, one of the major efforts of his career.

The Prime Minister exploded. 'Is this the man? Haddon, if you have a plain Number One man don't let him clear out of sight again. Theatres have names, you know, and theatre-seats numbers. Ask your doctor.'

While prime ministers speak to commissioners thus, detective-inspectors look modestly down their nose; Appleby attempted this. But now the Prime Minister tucked away his watch and sat back as if he had simply dropped in for a chat. 'And *where* have you been, Mr – um – Appleby?' he asked amiably.

'*Les Présages*, sir.'

The Prime Minister shook his head. 'The ballet's gone modern since my day. When Degas was painting, now ... but the point is the Lord Chancellor's been shot. At Scamnum Court, playing at *Hamlet* apparently – a strange play, Mr Appleby, a strange atmosphere about it. Shot thirty-five minutes ago by goodness knows whom. But whatever it's about the business has no political significance. You understand me?'

'No political significance,' said Appleby.

The Prime Minister rose. 'But, you know, I like *Les Sylphides*. And now, Mr Appleby, come along and don't stand there talking. I'll tell you about it in the car.'

Appleby opened the door, and felt the blood tingling in his finger-tips as he did so – perhaps it was with the increased physical consciousness that follows ballet. '*Les Sylphides*, sir?' he murmured demurely.

'Yes. Damn it – no! Auldearn.' The Prime Minister turned conciliatingly to the Commissioner. 'Excellent plan coming on here, Haddon; got our man at once. Advise keeping that lead on him another time, though.' His eye strayed to Superintendent Billups. 'You'll see that Mr Dollups works a machine or net or what not in town here if it's necessary? I suppose he'll get his instructions direct from Mr Appleby at Scamnum.' The Prime Minister was innocently oblivious of the hierarchies of the police. And having during the proceedings sacrificed some forty seconds to the conscientious whimsicalities that endeared him to the electorate, he now pushed Appleby into the lift and cried 'Down!' so fiercely that the already overwrought lift-boy lost his head and shot them straight to the top floor. It was, Appleby thought, an excellent prelude to adventure.

And so was the fire-engine. Billups would not have thought to requisition a fire-engine; the Prime Minister had. Its bell, he explained, gained more respect than did a police siren – and in addition the sound was somewhat less disagreeable. So the fire-engine tore through the rapidly thinning night-traffic towards Vauxhall Bridge, the Prime Minister's car followed, and the police car – it was the great yellow Bentley that always gave Appleby a schoolboy's thrill – brought up the rear.

Appleby looked cautiously at the silent figure of the Prime Minister humped in his corner; he was not quite sure that he was not part of a dream. Only fifteen minutes before he had been skirting the Horse Guards', murmuring against routine and looking as from an immense distance at an enigmatical light in the Foreign Office that had symbolized the very vortex of Empire. Now, far out on either side of him, Earl's Court with its burglars and the City with its twisters, were hurtling into the thither darkness at forty miles an hour – a sweeping turn at the Oval and the pace was working up to fifty on the Clapham Road. It was a gorgeous and fantastic procession, and Appleby thought comfortably of the fourth car going off in another direction, with a grim Commissioner giving Billups a gloomy lift to bed. He stole another glance at the great man beside him. Yes, it was true. This was the Prime Minister and ahead of them lay one of the famous houses of England. *Death at Scamnum Court* – what a title for Giles Gott!

The Prime Minister had out his ostentatiously rural watch again; when the road narrowed in New Wimbledon and the pace dropped he swore. It was his only utterance until, a mile down the Kingston by-pass, the fire-engine swung right for Putney and disappeared. Then, as the cars opened out, he talked.

'Lord Auldearn motored down to Scamnum on Friday afternoon. He meant to stay five or six days and join in this *Hamlet* business ... you don't know the Duchess?'

Mr Appleby confessed to not knowing the Duchess.

'Remarkable woman – and fond of that sort of thing. Daughter of Lionel Dillon – fellow who could make prosperous counter-jumpers look like saints in El Greco. Well, Auldearn went down on Friday and that same evening' – the Prime Minister hesitated – 'something important came in. We sent it straight down to him.'

'To the Lord Chancellor.' The matter-of-fact amplification was as near to a fishing question as Appleby thought it discreet to go. The Prime Minister took up the implication easily; he pursed his lips, evidently feeling his way.

'Auldearn's death', he said carefully, 'is a terrific blow – not merely personally to many of us, but nationally. He had more political wisdom and experience than anyone. And a wonderful brain. And he had a curious career – for a lawyer. He was Foreign Secretary, you remember, at a very ticklish time.'

'Of course,' said Appleby. There was a long silence. Some unidentifiable South London common was slipping past, at once banal and mysterious under the garish London sky. Far to the east a train whistled – the profoundly disturbing whistle of a train in the night.

'On Saturday afternoon,' the Prime Minister continued quietly, 'Auldearn decided he must come back to town. On Sunday there were various ... discussions. But he made it a point of honour to return to Scamnum for the play today. You will readily guess that he made no sacrifice of public duty to do so. Only ... he took with him for study another document. Mr Appleby, I wish to God he had not done so.'

The Prime Minister, so shortly before practising his pertinacious eccentricity of speech and manner, had become direct and grim. 'At eleven-five tonight they brought a telephone into my dressing-room – an urgent call. It was the Duke of Horton. He told me that Auldearn had been shot dead on the stage, apparently in circumstances which afford no light on his assailant. That is very extraordinary, but I suppose it may be so. Horton either knew or guessed that public issues might be involved. He said he was holding everybody tight and he begged me to act at once. He particularly asked for somebody who would not be scared by a high and mighty mob; he was referring, no doubt, to the sort of house-party he has down there. When I got hold of Haddon he named you.' There was a pause. 'Much may depend on you.'

Appleby said nothing. He would not have liked to swear that at the moment, at least, he was wholly unscared. But when the Prime Minister suddenly thrust forward a cigar-case his hand was perfectly steady under the other's gaze. It was a sort of ritual of confidence. Efficiently, Appleby supplied matches.

The Prime Minister drew a rug round himself and spoke

again. 'There is no reason to suppose that this horrid affair is other than an act of random madness or of private vengeance. All public men are a mark for such things. And for that reason cannot afford to go straight to the Intelligence. Who is known and marked there one can never know, and the knowledge that they had been sent down might be undesirable. And so we send' – the Prime Minister smiled wanly – 'a straight policeman.'

Appleby asked his first question. 'Was he guarded?'

'He would never hear of it. I am sure they would never let me get away with such an attitude, but Auldearn carried it.' The Prime Minister eyed his own detective sitting beside his chauffeur and sighed. 'He was a powerful man.'

The cars swerved through Esher. 'Please Providence, Mr Appleby, this document is now safe and undisturbed in Auldearn's despatch-case. But should it be involved you will be able to carry on for a time without being at a disadvantage with the specialists. If they have a line on anything at Scamnum at present the information will be waiting for us at Guildford, where I shall leave you. Have you struck the fringes of that sort of thing – espionage?'

'Yes, sir,' said Appleby briefly.

'So much the better. It's a crazy and surprising business; a complicated game that every country plays at – with a big bill and, just occasionally, a successful piece of mischief to show. What is to be remembered, I think, is that it is crazy – continually offending against probability, like bad fiction. You never know who's in on it, particularly – I'm told – among the women. To put it absurdly, Mr Appleby, don't trust anybody, not even the Archbishop of Canterbury should he be there. Trust nothing but your own nose.'

Appleby pondered these skilfully imparted instructions for a few moments before venturing on a question. 'Can I have more information on the nature and importance of the document, sir?'

The Prime Minister answered readily. 'The document concerns the organization of large industrial interests on an international basis, in the event of a certain international situation. The general drift towards the matter such a document embodies cannot, you will realize, well be secret; nothing big can be secret. But the details may be. And this document might be useful in two ways: the detailed information might be useful to one powerful interest or another; and accurate possession of the details, as circumstantial evidence of something already known in general terms, might be useful to an unfriendly government. And that is why I am gravely concerned: the document at this moment would be a lever, a lever where a lever is being looked for. Or call it a switch, Mr Appleby; a switch that might release a spark.'

Again there was silence. The Prime Minister contemplated the glowing end of his cigar. And Appleby had before him in the darkness – and with a new impressiveness – Masson's angry stage and Massine's loam-coloured personifications of conflict, beating out their obscure warfare to that mounting chaotic music. 'War?' said Appleby, carried to generalities despite himself, 'the springs of war are surely not in spy-work and filched papers?'

His companion regarded him with a new interest. But his voice was harsh and rapid as he answered. 'War! No, no – that is something no bigger than a man's hand. It must remain so.' He tapped the window at his side. 'Do you know this part of the country? Out there somewhere, a couple of miles short of the river, there's a little place called Mud Town. War means Mud Town for Europe, Mr Appleby. And do you know what's ahead of us – just north of Bisley, suitably enough? Donkey Town. War means that too. Certainly its springs are not in filched papers! Its springs are in the profound destructiveness deep in each of us, the same madness that has killed Auldearn – yes, however calculated that killing may turn out to have been. But these things, documents, plans' – he returned obstinately to his former figure – 'can be levers; damnable engines.'

He let the dead ash fall from his cigar. 'Well, Mr Appleby, so much you must certainly know, if you are to face the unexpected. And you must know how to identify the document. It is endorsed *Ministry of Agriculture and Fisheries: proposed Pike and Perch Joint Scheme*.' He smiled on the astonished Appleby as he revealed this Cabinet secret.

'Auldearn's last joke,' he said. 'And not without salt.'

*

Just beyond the environs of Guildford the car drew to a halt. And almost instantly a dim figure appeared at the window and opened the door. The Prime Minister, followed by Appleby, got out.

'Captain Hilfers?'

'Yes, sir; beaten you by five minutes. There's no report whatever. I've had the Scotland Yard people up since I left you, and our own people as well. There has been trouble at Scamnum twice in the last five years. Once when you yourself were there an undesirable guest was discovered and quietly turned out; and once a servant was found to be taking money from a well-known agent. But just now – we have knowledge of nothing.'

'You're an experienced man; just how much does that mean?'

'Little enough, sir. But if there's been shooting I think the thing incredible. And on the other hand I've found myself sparring with the incredible before now.'

The Prime Minister nodded impatiently in the darkness. 'Yes, yes. No government, no bureau would venture such a thing. But no doubt there are amateurs ... irregulars.' He laughed shortly. 'Well, we have our own irregular. Hilfers, you know Inspector Appleby? Mr Appleby, come along.'

To the north the sky still held the ruddy smear of London; to the south were stars and a low-riding moon. They trudged in silence to the police-car. Huddled in the back were the Yard's best searchers, man and woman – evidence that the Prime Minister left little unthought of. Appleby, wasting no time, sprang into the front. The Prime Minister shut the door, tossed in his cigar-case. 'You may have time for another. And you'll find there the telephone-number I'll be at the end of for the next twelve hours. . . . Did you see Woizikowsky?'

'In *Les Présages*, sir? Yes, as Fate.'

'Fate? ... Well, good luck.' The Prime Minister turned on his heel and with Captain Hilfers – that mysterious Mercury – melted into the darkness.

'Let her go, Thomas,' said Appleby. The Bentley rocketed south.

*

Just at twelve-forty, with some eight miles to go, they met the first car – a large limousine dimly lit within, and with a footman beside the chauffeur. 'Nobs,' said Thomas as they flashed past with dipped headlights.

'The Brazilian Minister,' Appleby responded absently; he had spotted the flag. A moment later Thomas had to swerve violently to avoid a sports car cutting a vicious corner in the darkness. It held a hatless youth in tails, one hand on the wheel, one resigned to a lady submerged in white fur. And close on its tracks followed an enormous scarlet sedan.

'Earl of Luppitt,' said Thomas, well-informed on the equipage of one of England's sporting peers. 'Party on somewhere hereabouts.'

'Thomas, what's down this way?'

Thomas considered. 'Nothing much except Scamnum, sir.'

Another car flashed past and then another. Away to the right, along some ridge of downland, a succession of gliding, swerving lights sped westwards towards Hampshire. 'Push along,' said Appleby quietly.

Thomas pushed along, only to draw up abruptly on the crown of a little bridge, the Bentley's bonnet almost touching the running-board of a dapper coupé, awkwardly stalled in the middle of the road. Its sole occupant was a man, an opera-cloak on his shoulders, the immortal invention of M. Gibus on his head, and a look of uncommon anxiety discernible on his face. He was thrusting angrily at his self-starter.

'Hullo, Happy!' The gentleman in the opera-hat jumped at the voice from the darkness. 'Thomas, this is Mr Happy Hutton; as part of your education – mark him well.' Appleby leaned across the Bentley and swivelled the spot-light. Mr Happy Hutton's anxiety was clearly revealed as changed to abject terror; his engine spluttered into life, his clutch engaged, he lifted his opera-hat nervously, and bounced on into the night.

Appleby chuckled. 'Happy's always polite, even when scared stiff. Useful information, Thomas, but not our quarry. Push along.'

This time Thomas pushed along unimpeded. The remaining miles melted away. The Bentley pulsed up the south drive of Scamnum Court.

TAKE a revolver down to the far end of the garden for a little target-practice and your neighbours (unless they be timorous folk) will merely complain of your 'potting away.' Let fly at someone you dislike in the street and the resulting disturbance will be supposed by nine bystanders out of ten to come from a motor-bicycle. But fire a revolver in a raftered hall and you will produce the equivalent of a thunder-clap.

The unknown – presently to be revealed as death – had irrupted upon the Scamnum theatricals with an effect of astounding violence; and it was because of this, perhaps, that the audience felt everything that followed as pitched incongruously low. The shot brought several people to their feet; brought cries from others. But the audience was quickly still again – waiting and watching. They saw Melville Clay hesitate in front of the curtain towards which he had been advancing with his rapier – hesitate with the actor's instinct to gain time when something has gone wrong. Then he took a swift step forward and vanished through the curtain. An agitated voice called out 'My Lord!' and a moment later the Duchess rose and slipped quietly off stage.

A minute went by and then the Duke of Horton, King Claudius's wig limp in his hand, appeared from the rear stage and said: 'There has been a serious misadventure: please all stay where you are.' A murmur – acquiescence, support, concern – answered him as he disappeared. A few people began to whisper, as if in church; most were silent; but all heads turned sharply when Giles Gott, still in his costume as Dumb-show King, walked rapidly down the hall, spoke to the fireman at the farther door, and returned silently behind the scenes once more. Five minutes later the Duke appeared again. With an ominous slowness he traversed the whole depth of the front stage and it was seen that he intended to speak to his mother. He dropped down from the stage, and taking her hand, spoke earnestly a couple of sentences. Then he climbed back to the stage and faced the audience. The hall was very silent.

'I have bad news. The pistol-shot you all heard was aimed at

Lord Auldearn. He is dead.' The Duke paused to let the ripple of horror produced by the spare announcement subside. Then he added: 'For the moment, nobody must leave the hall. And it will be best that none of you should come upon the stage or behind the scenes. I ask you to stay where you are until the police arrive.'

Again there was a docile murmur, this time not a little awed. A guest of consequence – a stray ambassador who had turned up at the last moment – called out: 'We will do just what you direct.' And at this the Duke nodded and retreated again.

By this time the crowd in the hall was conscious that it was behaving well in difficult circumstances; that it was helping to handle an appalling situation efficiently. The lighting had not been changed and for the rows of people sitting in shadow there was perhaps something hypnoidal in the empty stage with its sharply focused arc-lamps; everybody continued to sit still as the minutes went by. It was as if that peculiar merging of consciousness which comes upon an audience watching drama had been furthered rather than broken up by the advent of veritable catastrophe: the audience for a long half-hour behaved as a single impassive spectator. Only a judicious murmur of conversation was kept up here and there to minimize the strain.

There was little to observe. The Duke came back to speak for a few minutes to his mother; he was followed by Gervase and then by Dr Biddle, who had succeeded in walking on as an attendant lord and who now brought the Dowager a drink in his everyday capacity as medical attendant to the family. After he had retired old Max Cope made a slightly disconcerting appearance on the upper stage, surveying the hall placidly, palette in hand, as if nothing whatever had happened. Presently he was joined by Melville Clay – clad in a sombre dressing-gown, as if he kept a stock about him for all emergencies – and led off. A minute later Clay emerged below, crossed the front stage and dropped down beside the Dowager. He sat down and talked quietly, the soothing murmur of his musical voice audible in snatches to the people near by. Then he went away again, returned with Max in tow, set the old man safely down beside the old lady, and disappeared once more. Twice a telephone buzzer could just be heard behind the stage; the murmur of voices there occasionally rose into a half-distinguishable phrase. Then at eleven thirty-five the door at the rear of the hall opened and a police sergeant and three constables entered, ushered by Bagot.

One constable stopped by the door, the others walked rapidly down the hall, eyes front. They disappeared behind the scenes.

And that was all. *That* – several people remarked next day, with the changed attitude that the chasm of sleep will bring – was all that the audience got from the violent death of a Lord Chancellor. That and an extra cup of coffee, for at eleven forty-five footmen wheeled in quantities of this decorous refreshment. For fifteen minutes cups were handed and accepted; sandwiches were handed and either declined as frivolous or consumed as a species of funeral baked meat according to the temperament of the individual. At three minutes past midnight the Duke appeared for the last time. He was brief and quiet as before, but in his voice some subtle change – it might have been relief – was distinguishable.

'It is not necessary that you should stay longer. Will those of you who are stopping with us go back to the house? There will be no need for you to stay up longer than you want to. For the others the cars are coming round now. It will be best that we on this side remain in the hall a little longer.' Again the Duke descended to speak to his mother; he secured two ladies to look after her and then steered Max Cope behind the scenes. The guests filed out. It was the end of the Tragedy of Hamlet played at Scamnum Court

When the last tail-coat had vanished and the doors were shut once more the players began to percolate by ones and twos into the main body of the hall – foraging. One of the big coffee urns was empty, but the other was full; they fell to. They ate the sandwiches without delicacy; theirs had been the chief shock and they were beyond fancied proprieties. The two footmen in their Tudor liveries, together with the Duke's man, handed salvers with something like imperturbability. The two dressers from London sat in a corner and sipped and nibbled, scared and a little indignant. The police sergeant had gone off with one constable – for the orthodox purpose, it was said, of interviewing the servants – and a second was invisible on the rear stage, guarding the body. Macdonald waited on the Duchess, still considerably more like Prospero than a first Gravedigger. Most of the players had felt it seemly to discard as much of their theatrical appearance as possible, but all had not been equally successful. The women had removed the slight make-up from their faces and thrown on cloaks. Gervase had abandoned Osric's grotesque cap but not his fantastical doublet. Noel had cast Laertes's cloak over the Ghost's nightgown. Dr Crump had hastily taken off his vestments but forgotten his tonsure. Dr Biddle's white hose were stained with blood. All in all, it was discernibly the ruins of King Claudius's Court at Elsinore, disrupted by a mine more deadly than any Hamlet had devised, that stood or wandered about Peter Crispin's folly. A queer sight ... and the courtyard clock was tolling one when the door opened and a young man strode rapidly in, swept up the scene at a glance and said: 'The Duke of Horton, please. I am from Scotland Yard.'

The tone was unaggressive, but it represented all that firm control of a situation which the Duke himself had been sustaining these two hours. And now from the Duke something seemed to fall away.

'Then surely we can get this cleared up.' The Duke looked irresolutely round his guests. 'Well – come, come.'

The Duchess sighed. And everybody had the irrational feeling that after an evening's madness the normal had reasserted itself.

*

But presently the Duke, emerging from the rear stage with Appleby and conducting him to the deserted green-room, thought it desirable to concentrate once more.

'Lord Auldearn was shot during the progress of the play and where you have just seen his body, in the curtained recess, that is, what they call the rear stage. He was playing Polonius and there comes a point' – the Duke looked speculatively at Appleby: the higher constabulary might be expected to know a little Shakespeare – 'you will remember there comes a point at which Polonius hides behind a curtain in the Queen's closet. He calls for help when he supposes Hamlet to be attacking the Queen, and then Hamlet stabs through the curtain, draws it back, and discovers that he has killed Polonius. It was at this point that the thing happened. Auldearn had just called out when his voice was drowned by the report of the revolver.'

'And why', said Appleby, 'should one shoot Lord Auldearn?'

Thirty minutes ago the Duke had been listening to the Prime Minister authenticating this young man with some enthusiasm from a public telephone-box in Guildford. Nevertheless he looked at him warily now. 'I thought', he said, 'that somebody might be after something he might have. That was why I shut up the hall and held on to the whole gathering.'

'But later you let the audience go?'

The Duke's wariness modulated imperceptibly into weariness. 'In the particular aspect I imagined – it was a mare's nest.'

'Agents after a document?'

'Yes. We found it.'

'Found it?'

'Just at midnight. On him – in a manner of speaking.' And the Duke produced a slender roll of paper from the folds of King Claudius's raiment – produced it and put it away again.

But Appleby in his turn brought out a fountain-pen. 'I'll give you a receipt,' he said briefly.

'I beg your pardon?'

'May it please your Grace, a receipt.'

There was enough of Macdonald's technique in this to make the Duke blink. A receipt and the portentous document – *Pike and Perch Joint Scheme* – changed hands. 'Please go on, sir,' said Appleby politely.

'Not on; back,' said the Duke a trifle pettishly – and thought for a moment. 'Auldearn was just calling out when the shot was fired. I made for the sound and came on the rear stage from behind. My kinsman, Gervase Crispin, was kneeling on the floor, with Auldearn's head on his lap. Clay – Melville Clay, that is, who has been playing Hamlet – was standing beyond, his rapier in his hand; I think he had just come through from the front stage. And a Mr Bose was standing a little to one side. Gervase said "Dead, I think"; and at that I hurried behind scenes again and stopped some of the other players who were running up from coming in. Then I called for Dr Biddle – he's our family doctor, and was in the play – and for Sir Richard Nave; he too is a doctor, but taken to something eccentric, I believe. Then I crossed the rear stage again, passed through the curtain and spoke to the audience of a serious accident, asking them to keep quiet. When I turned back to the rear stage, both Nave and Biddle were beside the body, and both said "Dead." Auldearn, as you saw, had simply been shot through the heart at close range. He was one of our oldest friends.'

The Duke paused on this and Appleby said nothing. The Prime Minister and his fire-engine, the mysterious Captain Hilfers, the grim talk of documents that might be levers and engines towards war – these things had receded, it seemed, and in front lay plain police-work. And Appleby was relieved; in plain police-work you could usually go straight for the truth, whereas in work with political implications a halt was often mysteriously called when the truth was in sight. But now the Duke continued, edging away from the hinted personal aspect of the catastrophe by way of momentary generalization.

'When somebody dies in this way – is shot, murdered – one's first feeling is not of mystery, but of alarm. One looks round for a maniac brandishing a revolver and threatening further lives. There's a young man upstairs who might bear that in mind when he next writes up that sort of thing.' The Duke did not stop to elucidate this. 'But there was no maniac. My second thought was of robbery, robbery of no common sort. I seized the most reliable fellow beside me and sent him to secure the door behind the audience. There is only one other door – behind the green-room here – and I went straight to that and locked it myself. We had had a telephone put in so that we could communicate easily with the house. I went to it and was through to the Prime Minister by eleven o'clock, within five minutes of the shooting. Then I rang up the local police at Horton. Then somebody suggested that Auldearn's bedroom should be guarded and I agreed; I was for every precaution. I let my cousin Gervase and the man I'd sent to the farther door – a kinsman of my wife's – out by this door here and locked it after them. The next important thing was to prevent the audience and the players from mingling. Behind the scenes I had a manageable crowd, and a crowd I could take drastic measures with if necessary. But the audience was a mob and it included one or two diplomatic people; one can't go through an ambassador's pockets can one?'

Appleby agreed monosyllabically. He was equally fascinated by the efficiency of the proceedings narrated and by some indefinable remoteness in the narrator. The Duke, he was almost inclined to put it to himself, was not interested.

'If something were gone, you know, and there was a possibility of it having been successfully conveyed to a confederate in the audience, I should have had the responsibility of deciding for or against the scandal of a general search – a thing I can imagine Cabinet debating for a day, can't you?'

Appleby did not admit to any vision of His Majesty's ministers in council. Instead, he made a shorthand note.

'Be that as it may,' continued the Duke, 'there was every chance of preventing anything of the sort. We were isolated from the audience and could remain so. I went out upon the front stage again, crossed it and jumped down to break the news gently to my mother; she is a very old lady and was sitting alone in the front row. Then I climbed back and announced straight out that Auldearn had been killed. And nobody, I said, must either leave the hall or attempt to come behind the scenes.'

'What control had you on that?' asked Appleby.

'As it happened – complete control. There are only three avenues of communication: across the open stage in full view of everybody or by the curtained entrances at one or other side of the stage. And by each of these entrances we had a fireman. Players and audience were as cut off from one another as could be.

'At eleven-twelve my cousin Gervase came back from Auldearn's room and I let him into the hall. He had startling news. The room had been burgled. Professionally it would seem, for the safe had been cracked.'

'I see,' said Appleby.

'I beg your pardon?'

'Please go on. Is a safe, by the way, a regular feature of your bedroom furniture?'

'People come sometimes with foolish quantities of jewels. We have found small wall-safes in some of the rooms the least bothersome way to cope with them. Well, the news was, I say, startling – if after murder anything can be called startling. I knew very well that Auldearn had this ticklish paper.'

'He had shown it to you?'

'No. But he had mentioned it. And mentioned a joke about it: it is endorsed *Pike and Perch Conciliation Board*, or something of the sort. Well, here in Auldearn's room was evidence of at least attempted robbery. And this attempt could scarcely have been made by the murderer *after* the shooting, for nobody could have got out of the hall – nor would there have been time to crack a safe in the seven or eight minutes that elapsed between the shot and Gervase's reaching the bedroom. I concluded that – unless there was a gang at work – the shooting had taken place because the burglary and safe-breaking had been unsuccessful; that what had been sought for in vain in the bedroom had later been sought for on a person, a person who had been murdered to facilitate the seeking. One sees objections, of course – but that was my first thought.'

If the Duke was rather weary now he was also very lucid. And lucidity is something that one does not often get hard after violent death; now it was saving Appleby hours.

'There was an obvious thing to do. With Dr Biddle I searched the body. There was nothing there.'

'I understood you to say –'

'Wait. There was nothing there. Then it seemed to me that the situation was grave and I knew that I must hang on, continue to hang on to everybody not merely until the local police arrived but until somebody came down who had been in touch with London. I wondered what I could best do in the interval. I thought of the weapon.'

The Duke took a restless turn about the green-room and came to a stand before a long table littered with theatrical debris – wigs, swords, a crown, the Ghost's helmet. Aimlessly he picked something up and Appleby saw, not without a start that it was a skull – Yorick's skull.

'It seemed unlikely that anyone should have ventured to retain a revolver about him and it could not have been got right away. So I cast round. But I found no trace ... dear me!'

The exclamation was a mild one. For with a little clatter

94

there had fallen from skull to table a tiny revolver. 'Dear me,' said the Duke, 'Giles would like that. Well, so much for the weapon. Might it have finger-prints, do you think?'

Appleby stared – not at the weapon but at the man. In this moment he discovered what Scamnum had now known for some time: the Duke of Horton was a born actor. No man could be other than startled at so queer a coincidence of word and event. But the Duke – for no conceivable reason, surely, save the pleasure of the thing – had given a bizarre display of impassivity. And now in a moment he was proceeding with his narrative. It would be easy, Appleby decided, to become too interested in the Duke – for here was a man with some suppressed instinct to hold the centre of the stage.

'Nothing more happened – barring a little subdued and uneasy discussion and moving about on this side, and a little uneasy shifting on hard seats on the other – until just after half past eleven. Then your local colleagues arrived. I have some faith in specialists; so I immobolized them.'

To immobilize country policemen is no doubt one of the privileges of a master of Scamnum. But Appleby, who had as yet seen only a stolid constable guarding the body and a nervous constable who had met him under Scamnum's *porte cochère*, felt that he might himself come in for some species of recoil. 'Immobilized them,' he echoed courteously.

'To be precise, I told them of the burglary and they have gone after that. There is a sergeant and he said something about questioning the servants. You know, he'll find a devilish lot of them.'

Appleby doubted if his rural colleagues were as simple as they were pictured; the picture seemed to merge with a discernible ducal taste for conventional sub-humorous effects. But he said nothing.

'So again we marked time, though I got down on paper as complete a list as I could of people's whereabouts behind stage for the relevant period.' The Duke smiled tenuously as he thus jerked Appleby back to the fact of Crispin efficiency. 'And then I thought of our unfortunate audience. I consulted my wife and she said "Feed them" and telephoned to the house for coffee and sandwiches. Her organization is always remarkable; the stuff was thrust through the bars, so to speak, within ten minutes. And then Mr Bose discovered the document.'

'You mentioned Mr Bose as on the rear stage when you first entered it. He was a player?'

'Prompter. An intelligent Hindu. My wife, you know. And he found the document.' The implication was plainly that intelligent Hindus – even Hindus intelligent enough to find vital documents – were more in the Duchess's line than the Duke's. But in the tone of the final sentence Appleby thought that he detected something more. The words rang with a curious finality. The safety of this document once established, they seemed to say, Scamnum's special responsibilities ended; blood-hunting was for others.

'Mr Bose found the document by accident. Just on midnight I became aware of him standing beside me – one never notices him approach – and looking miserable. It occurred to me he wanted to be helpful; he's a friendly little person enough. So I asked him to find my daughter Elizabeth; I meant to send her forward to my mother, about whom I was a little anxious. He went through the species of curtained corridor you will find behind the rear stage, and in doing so he nearly slipped on something that had apparently rolled off the rear stage itself. It was a little parchment scroll which Polonius was designed to carry throughout the play; part of his stage business was that of referring to it from time to time in a slightly fussy manner. Well, Mr Bose picked it up – and noticed a different coloured paper inside. He is an alert and subtle creature and he brought it to me at once. That is what I meant by saying that it had, in a manner of speaking, been on Auldearn all the time. And at that I let the audience go. If there had been an attempt on the document Auldearn had outwitted it. Perhaps he knew there was to be an attempt. Perhaps the inexplicable messages had warned him.'

'Messages?'

'*Hamlet, revenge!*' said the Duke mildly – and explained.

*

It was now twenty to two and the hall was still a sort of discreet gaol. The prisoners had by this time some right, perhaps, to murmur – but Appleby would make no move with them until he had a stronger grip of the case. The spy-story seemed to be fading fast into the realm of fantasy; emissaries of foreign powers do not commonly advertise themselves by clamours for revenge, and of the burglary in Lord Auldearn's bedroom Appleby had his own opinion. But there seemed to be one further cruicial test: the time-element which the Duke had already hinted at as a difficulty in the spy theory. No calculating criminal would shoot in order to steal unless there would be reasonable time for the stealing. Had there been this? Almost certainly not; the shooting itself had been an extraordinary hazardous action and only the peculiar construction of the rear stage had given the criminal even a fifty-fifty chance of escape.

The rear stage was simply a large rectangular curtained recess into which one could slip through a parting on any of its sides. But because the single curtain had been found insufficient to deaden green-room noises, further curtains had been hung on the three back-stage sides, giving the effect of a corridor with two right-angled turns. This multiplicity of thick and in places overlapping drapery would have given a bold man a chance to slip into hiding unobserved at some favourable moment, and a less substantial chance of so manoeuvring after the shot as to escape discovery. And it seemed that this must, indeed, have happened. Suspicions might yet be reported, but had anything damning been observed there would surely have been denunciations long ago. Diligent ferreting, such as the Duke claimed to have begun, lay ahead if the movements or whereabouts of some thirty people were to be pinned down for the fatal minutes round ten fifty-five.

But Appleby's preliminary problem was simpler. Who first got to the rear stage after the shot, and how long after it? On how many seconds could the assailant reckon for an attempted theft, and for escape? Appleby picked up the weapon that had so dramatically revealed itself, dropped it – wrapped in a handkerchief – into his pocket, and together with the Duke made his way to the other part of the hall. He was now to confront more at leisure the main body of players whom he had glimpsed on coming in.

The scene was reminiscent of a species of abrupted revelry with which he was professionally familiar – of one of those dismal occasions on which, in the midst of frolic, certain stalwart and hitherto most frolicsome gentlemen disentangle themselves from false noses, paper caps, balloons, and streamers, bar the available exits and admit a bevy of uniformed colleagues to count the bottles, sniff at the glasses, and take down the names and addresses. Three more constables had been sent into the hall by that sergeant who was still obstinately engaged elsewhere: one was standing shyly in a corner, apparently scanning the rafters for concealed gunmen; one was grudgingly permitting Bagot to replace an exhausted coffee-urn by a full one; and the third, being the fortunate possessor of a tape-measure, was solemnly taking the dimensions of the front stage. The company sat huddled in groups, half-heartedly consuming further coffee and beginning, Appleby surmised, to regard one another with some dislike. Several he recognized at once. Gervase Crispin, that high-priest of the Golden Calf, was covertly playing noughts and crosses with a young man of vaguely Crispin appearance. Melville Clay, still in Hamlet's black beneath an enveloping dressing-gown, was unmistakable. The Duchess of Horton, very pale, was plainly engaged in looking after the young women; one of the young women, evidently her daughter, was equally plainly engaged in looking after her. Lord Traherne was wandering about with a plate of sandwiches, as if at one of his 'homely' colonial parties – but was failing to offer them to anyone. The black man had withdrawn into a corner and seemed engaged in meditation, or perhaps purification and penance. Everybody looked up as Appleby appeared.

'I want to know, please, who was first on the scene of Lord Auldearn's death, and how soon after the shot.'

At this the black man called out very softly, but so as to be clearly heard from the corner from which he now advanced: 'It was I.'

'A moment before I got through the front rear stage curtain,' said Clay.

'Mr Bose? Will you come up, please?'

Appleby turned back towards the rear stage and after a few paces halted under the impression that Mr Bose had failed to follow. Whereupon Mr Bose, who had been just behind, bumped into him and there were apologies. It was Appleby's introduction to the movement which the Duchess had described as 'not earthly'.

'He is ... quite dead?' asked Mr Bose gently.

'He died instantly.'

Mr Bose made a gesture of resignation – a queer, expressive gesture which Appleby could not afterwards fix – and said: 'And now ... I must tell you?'

'Please.'

'My place was here.' Mr Bose led the way off the rear stage and into the curtained corridor behind. At the extreme end of one of its shorter sides was a stool. 'My place was here, because from here I could see both the front stage and the rear stage.'

'You could *see* the rear stage?'

Mr Bose looked obscurely troubled, but answered readily. 'Why, yes. It is most necessary sometimes. Here is a slit through which I see the front stage and here is one by which I see the rear stage too.'

Appleby considered for a moment in some perplexity. 'But you saw nothing strange?'

'Remember, please, I was prompter. The eye must be on the text – though I know the text *very* well. Occasionally I look through the curtain – but to where the suffering is.'

'The suffering?'

'The drama – action. And at this time I glance perhaps at the front stage where there are Hamlet and the Queen and much action; but on the rear stage is only Polonius alone, waiting.'

Mr Bose appeared somewhat obliquely inclined, but what he meant to say seemed clear. And here was remarkable information. Anyone slipping through the rear-stage curtain with intent to murder and steal did so under the known and substantial risk of being observed by the prompter through his spy-hole. The possibility seemed to Appleby to double again the already remarkable hazardousness of the deed.

'And after the shot, Mr Bose – did you not at once look then?'

'I started to my feet in alarm. For a moment I stood still. Then I caught at the curtain to pull it aside and enter. But I was confused and pulled the wrong way. When I broke through to the rear stage it was – save for the body and gunpowder smoke – empty. But a moment later Mr Clay came from the front stage.'

'And then?'

'I ran out, in great fear for the life of Lord Auldearn, and called for the Duke. Mr Gervase came first and then the Duke. Then the physicians came.'

Before Mr Bose Appleby felt curiously baffled. He had a sense of subterraneous processes beneath these answers – processes perhaps profoundly deceitful, perhaps merely profoundly strange. But then it might be that this was a stock response; that one confronted the Oriental mind with such a sense ready-made.

'Mr Bose, this now is the important question. Between the shot and your breaking in upon the rear stage – how many seconds?'

The black man considered. 'With *very* great accuracy?'

'Please.'

The black man produced a watch. Then he meditated. Then he looked at the watch and at the same time began to murmur some fragmentary text. Then he looked at his watch again. 'Five seconds.'

Appleby rather supposed the procedure employed to be intelligent and reliable; Mr Bose's sense of time was bound up, no doubt, with ritual recitation. 'And then Mr Clay –?'

This time Mr Bose simply studied the second hand of his watch with concentration. 'Two seconds.'

'Thank you. And can you give me any further information?'

Mr Bose looked at Appleby in discernible perturbation; made an equally perturbed gesture. 'It is a *very* evil thing!' he said

Perhaps the Western world still seemed to Mr Bose – despite an advancing familiarity with the works of Mr James Juice – a morally unaccountable place; perhaps he felt that he was really giving Appleby information. Or perhaps the odd answer represented evasion. At the moment Appleby was held less by the words than by the glance that accompanied them. It is easy, looking at a dark face, to speak of a flashing eye; but Mr Bose's eye held at this moment more than a common fire. He was, indeed, an almost unearthly creature, the youthful raw material, surely, of a character wholly contemplative, wholly spiritual. But Appleby, if he saw the saint, suspected too the tiger. He felt it would be useful to know something of Mr Bose's way and rule of life. 'You are a Brahmin, Mr Bose?'

'I am a Warrior!'

The reply, given with a sudden lift of the head, was more than a simple statement of caste. It acknowledged the implications of the question it answered, was perhaps a threat – or a promise or a challenge. And a second later it might have been none of these things – and here merely a scared expatriated Oriental.

Appleby resolved that his next questions should be public, so he proceeded to the front stage, strode down it like a player about to deliver a soliloquy, and surveyed the company at large. 'Mr Clay, what interval elapsed between your hearing the shot and entering the rear stage?'

Clay answered promptly. 'Seven seconds.'

This tallied remarkably with Mr Bose's estimate. But Appleby expressed surprise. 'You are sure it was not less? It seems a long time.'

'A second's pause on the shot. Something under four seconds across the stage; I was making time until it was clear the scene must be broken. Something under two seconds in front of the curtain, making time still. Then a fraction of a second getting through.'

'Mr Clay,' said the Duchess, as if anxious to substantiate her guest's credit, 'has an uncanny sense of time on the stage. I believe the interval was just as he says.'

The Duchess's impression, for what it was worth, was the only substantiation that could be got from the players; all the others had been behind the scenes. But now a severe person, sitting hand to forehead beside the Duchess, made a suggestion. 'What of Dr Bunney's contrivance? Was it not making some sort of record?'

'Sir Richard Nave – Mr Appleby,' said the Duke, apparently feeling an introduction desirable.

Appleby pounced on this. 'The machine that gave one of the messages? It was here recording?' Whereupon Bunney, with an incongruous mingling of pride and alarm, produced the black box. 'Science', he began ponderously, 'never knows to what uses –'

Nave interrupted brusquely. 'What may be useful is the recorded interval between the shot and the next succeeding audible words: Mr Bose's calling out "My Lord!" No doubt he was summoning the Duke.'

Mr Bose nodded vigorously. He had been summoning the Duke. Appleby promptly took charge of the black box – though without much faith in its detective qualities. Then he considered.

Anyone entering the rear stage to shoot Auldearn had had five seconds to make good the first part of his get-away – behind the curtains. But all the time he might have been under the fatal observation of Mr Bose. Would any man wishing to steal a document adopt such a method? He thought not – or not in the case of a document of the kind involved. It was possible to conceive of a document – an unopened letter, for example, giving information on a grave crime – which might be worth securing on such bloody and dangerous terms. But a state document is stolen neither in passion nor as a last desperate act of self-preservation; it is stolen, almost certainly, for mere gain – a little, perhaps, for excitement. And – as the Prime Minister had observed – the sort of person involved in such things does not kill; certainly not when the chances are heavily in favour of instant detection. Auldearn's murder, with its dramatic *locale* and theatrical preliminary warnings, represented – Appleby was persuaded – an altogether different kind of affair. And the spy story was fantasy, fantasy evoked by the mere fact that the dead man was known to have possessed an important document and to have safeguarded it in a somewhat eccentric yet rational way.

And looking round the shocked and jaded people in the hall Appleby doubted if an attempt to grapple with such a large company in the remaining small hours would be useful. Common sense and the facts of the case as they stood counselled him to send them all off to bed without more ado. But there still remained a doubt, a doubt that the thread before him might not be single. And he knew well enough that his whole reputation was going to stand or fall on his handling of an affair with which, in a few hours, all England would be ringing. And he determined to be utterly cautious – which meant being uncommonly bold. He spoke briefly to the Duke and then turned to the company.

'I am going to require something which some of you may judge unnecessary. Please remember that Lord Auldearn's death is inevitably going to cause a tremendous sensation. Everything that has happened tonight – everything concerning the preliminary handling of the situation by the Duke of Horton and myself – may be debated and criticized by thousands of people with no very marked ability to see their way through a complicated set of facts. They will ask certain stock questions; there are newspapers that take up such things with clamour. Because of this – and for other reasons – I believe that it is in the general interest here that each one of you should submit to a search before leaving the hall – as I hope you may shortly do – for the night. There are several magistrates here to whom I could go, but I think perhaps you will not stand on any form.'

It was a successful speech. Some of the company felt that by going through an unpleasant formality they would in some way avoid scandal; the more perceptive were put in good humour by the consciousness of being more perceptive and of so appreciating this young policeman's wiliness. Only Bunney protested, but he was assured by Malloch – confidentially and as between scholars – that in good society in England one never objected to being searched by the police. Peter Marryat, who had been beguiling the time by trying – *sotto voce* and with the assistance of Tommy Potts – to get the abandoned Norwegian Captain right at last, interjected an intrigued rather than an indignant 'I say!' The Duke expressed curt and slightly absent agreement and the Duchess, knowing the next move to be with her and seeming to recognize herself as still too shaken for effective action, murmured to Mrs Terborg. And Mrs Terborg promptly took charge: if the police had a respectable woman there would be no difficulty.

This gained, Appleby made discreet haste to another point. 'After leaving the hall nobody, I hope, will be disturbed again for the night. But a constable will be in the green-room and you will please go in one by one as you leave and give names; I must have a record, I think, in that form. And one other thing. It may be that some of you have something to say that you feel

103

should be said soon, but which is too indefinite for other than the most confidential communication to the police. You will all understand me. While Lord Auldearn's death remains a mystery there must be suspicion, weighing of doubtful circumstances, possibly significant recollections. And any matter of that sort with the least substance it is your duty to advance. A word to the constable will bring me at once.' And having with these words baited a traditional but often-successful trap, Appleby gave certain further directions to the constables and then turned to the Duke. 'And now, sir, I must find the sergeant and the missing guest – the one who stayed guarding Lord Auldearn's room.'

'Ah yes,' said the Duke. 'Yes: Giles Gott.'

Appleby's response had just that quality of vehemence which made Stella Terborg jump.

'Giles Gott!'

3

'HULLO,' said Gott – whom, when excited, nothing could surprise.

'Hullo,' said Appleby. The two men looked at each other in silence and with profound satisfaction – a proceeding which Sergeant Trumpet, who was versed in the literature of crime, interpreted as that intent matching of swords proper to the first meeting of fated antagonists.

'My eye's been on him,' said Sergeant Trumpet heavily.

Appleby nodded gravely. 'Quite right, sergeant. The man Gott has planned many a murder before tonight.'

'Has he now!' said Sergeant Trumpet, deeply gratified and edging a little nearer to his suspect.

Gott spread himself more comfortably in Lord Auldearn's easy chair. 'The sergeant thinks I must be the central figure because I alone have broken away from the pack. He has given it out that he's sleuthing the third boot-boy, but actually he's been hanging on to me grimly.' He looked at Appleby lazily. 'And what may this mean that thou, dear corse, again, in complete steel, revisit'st thus the glimpses of the moon? Whence comest thou, shade?'

Sergeant Trumpet frowned. Appleby sighed – he thought he knew this mood. '*Les Présages*,' he answered absently. 'Sergeant, a word.' He led his colleague from the room and presently returned alone. 'That better?' he asked.

'Inspector Buxton', said Gott, 'has chicken-pox and Inspector Lucas has gone on holiday as far as Bridlington, where his late wife's sister keeps a boarding-house not far from the front. I had it all from the sergeant while his eye was on me, but during the last half-hour it palled. ... Well, here's a mess ... what's happening below?'

'Search. Which has at last lured away your sergeant. Now talk. Better than the Duke if you can – and he's not bad.'

'On the Duke's suggestion I came up here with Gervase Crispin. The room was, of course, unlocked. Nothing seemed disturbed. But Gervase knew of a safe – behind the Walcot dry-point there – and it was cracked. Gervase went back and I sat down on guard, and to think – if I could. Presently the sergeant came and sat down to guard the guard. In the intervals of strained conversation I continued to attempt to think.'

'Good,' said Appleby. 'Results, please.'

'The shooting has to do with the play. It's been thought out in the context of the play. They'll have told you of the messages? Someone with a real sense of effect. Motive: perhaps just effect.'

'At least, not documents of state?'

'I don't know.'

Appleby had been inspecting the safe. Now something in his friend's voice made him turn round. 'Giles! –' He was interrupted by a question – and by the knowledge that Gott, despite his lazy way, was as much in earnest as himself.

'Have they found this damned thing, John? You forget I don't know what's happened down there. I only know there was something, and that this safe's cracked.'

'Yes, they found it. Auldearn was keeping an eye on it, though in a precious queer way. He'd stowed it in a sort of scroll he was due to hang on to, apparently, throughout the show.'

'I see. And you've decided the spies are moonshine?'

'It seems very probable that they are.'

'Materials for sensational fiction, not dealt in by Messrs Appleby and Gott?'

'Clearer-headed reasons than that, I hope. Everything points to quite a different sort of affair.'

'Everything except what Elizabeth – the daughter, that is: by the way, John, I want to marry her – everything except what Elizabeth and I saw in the garden.'

'Good luck to you. . . . What?'

Gott told of the flitting figure in the moonlight and of the mysterious something tossed over the wall. Appleby shook his head. 'I think Lady Elizabeth jumped to conclusions, though I know there has been spy-activity here before. I suspect I know something about this safe-cracking business that might interpret what you saw. Briefly, there's circumstantial evidence that a certain cracksman and jewel-thief, one Happy Hutton by name, has been operating hereabouts. And what you saw was not improbably Happy making contact with his inside stand. I shouldn't be surprised to find some of the other safes like this one cracked too, and that it has nothing to do with the nasty business downstairs. And why should spy-business be thought out, as you say, in the context of *Hamlet*?'

'Why indeed. But you believe, don't you, in the delicate processes we lump together as feeling something in the air?'

'Yes. And so, no doubt, does the sergeant. But talk about the people first, the whole bewildering crowd of them.'

For a moment Gott looked querulous. 'But I'm still trying to think. And why aren't you superintending your search?'

'Because I'm hoping that when left to the simple and unintimidating rural bobby somebody may be moved to drop dark – and misleading – hints. I've left half an invitation that way. And as for thinking, think as you go.'

'Very well, I'll talk. I'll talk like Marlow in *Lord Jim*, who made a habit of delivering a hundred thousand words – uncommonly well – to casual after-dinner audiences while contriving to smoke a succession of cigars.' During this empty prologue Gott kicked off the Dumb-show King's slippers and undid his ruff. Then he plunged, slightly eccentrically, into exposition.

'Talking of Conrad, I hope you read Wodehouse. If so, you will have realized that the Duke cultivates the part of Lord

Emsworth – you remember? Mark him, and you expect to mark that immortal porker, the Empress of Blandings, round the corner. The man cultivates ineffectiveness and it is moderately amusing. Obviously enough, he is able; and his hobby-horse is the first thing, no doubt, that gives one the feeling of Scamnum's keeping a good deal below the surface.

'The Duchess, who is a sort of relation of mine, is clever, charming, and oddly determined to have me for a son in-law. In that ultimately, I suspect, lies the genesis of *Hamlet* played at Scamnum Court – and so of this old man's death.' Gott paused. 'Auldearn was her friend chiefly and – I believe – part of her past, in a respectable way. In fact Auldearn was to the Duchess what I, with bad luck, may be to the Duchess's daughter – but that is by the by.

'In the present generation Gervase, as you probably know, is the centre of all things Crispin. He controls a big whack of the planet; too big, I imagine, for him to deal in miching mallecho and mean mischief. Scamnum is, as it has always been, simply the Crispin show-case, dukedom and all. And the Duke has a show-case role. He's an Elder Statesman. When the public shows signs of getting worked up about something the Prime Minister and such-like come down and consult him. Scamnum is put on the picture-page with an inset of the Duke in knickerbockers – faintly evocative of the Empress – or at his desk writing a monograph on trout-fishing. The effect is soothing and England stands firm. One has some respect for the technique. But whether the Duke is actually deep in the counsels of our rulers I don't know. Gervase, of course, is a junior minister from time to time but doesn't much exert himself along those lines.

'Kincrae – the heir, that is – is eccentric and has gone to govern a Crown Colony. He writes fish-monographs rebutting his father. Then there is Elizabeth. Elizabeth is twenty-one, serious, romantic, practical, childlike, mature, passionate, detached, ironical, and baffling.'

'Quite so,' said Appleby. As Gott talked he was systematically examining the dead man's bedroom. 'Now go on to the mob,' he directed.

'It's rather a large order. Shall I begin alphabetically? A's for Auldearn, the man who was shot. B is for Bunney, the man who was not. Very little to say about Bunney. He's rather like yourself – same policemanly figure and something of a detective mind. C is for Clay –'

'It might be better', said Appleby, 'if you didn't go right through but simply picked out the type of the amazingly foolhardy murderer.'

'You think he – or she – must have been that?'

Appleby nodded. 'He walked out on the rear stage, shot Auldearn almost point-blank in what might have been full view of the prompter, was lucky in having five seconds to get off and amazingly lucky in manoeuvring into some uncompromising position thereafter without exciting remark. I call him foolhardy.'

'But I think', said Gott, suddenly serious again, 'none of the conditions you have been describing necessarily holds'

Appleby stopped exploring and sat down. 'Explain,' he said.

'Well, begin this way. You must thoroughly explore from a likely premise before you go on to one less likely. Now a likely premise is: The murderer exposes himself to as little risk as possible; he is *not* foolhardy. Take that and base a question on it. Why did the murderer, being resolved to expose himself to as little risk as possible, choose for his act the precise place and time that he did?'

'Why indeed.'

'Because, John, he could foresee your mind moving on the level on which it has actually begun to move. Literally, *level*. Did you look up when you were on the rear stage?'

'Yes,' said Appleby, 'and I see what you mean. And it didn't occur to me. And I hope the reason that it didn't occur to me was that it won't do.'

'Immediately above the rear stage there's what is called the upper stage. It has a trap-door. And in a shadowy corner of the upper stage was an old gentleman painting a picture. And anyone lying flat on the upper stage would be invisible to the audience –'

'It won't do,' said Appleby. 'Auldearn, as it happens, was shot from floor level. I'm almost certain of that at this moment, and I think the medical report will prove it. And I doubt if the distance could be more than six feet – though that's for experts too.' He looked at Gott and added: 'Giles, you have another shot in the locker!'

'I think I have. It comes from having produced the play. I suggest that Auldearn might have been shot *where* he was because one would immediately begin to think in terms of someone coming through the rear-stage curtains; of an "amazingly foolhardy murderer", as you said, who would half-announce his intention in sinister messages and so forth. But I think there's another *Why*. *Why* was Auldearn shot *when* he was? Conceivably because he had just lain down, preparatory to being discovered "dead" after Hamlet had stabbed through the curtain. And a shot from above when he was *prone* would carry on the suggestion that he had been shot from a level *when standing*. And the distance would be about eight feet.'

There was a little silence – and then Appleby smiled. 'Round One to you,' he said. And getting up he resumed his inspection of the room.

'So you have one suspect,' continued Gott, ' "aloft". And you have a possible maximum of – let me see – twenty-seven suspects "within".'

'Twenty-seven,' said Appleby. 'Excellent.' He was examining a bowler hat. 'By the way, had Auldearn a man with him, do you know?'

'He had no man – and kept nothing of the sort, I understand, in town. He lived very simply in a service-flat. His only establishment was in Scotland somewhere. But I'm giving you the biographies – by express invitation – of twenty-seven suspects.'

Appleby had turned to examine the contents of the dead man's wardrobe. He seemed to consider the process as of some importance, for he delayed Gott's further narrative with absent-minded banter. 'I say, Giles – what if you were all in it together? Twenty-seven conspirators getting up all this *Hamlet* stuff. But why should twenty-seven people wish away a Lord Chancellor?'

'Because', said Gott sadly, 'the Lord Chancellor is a wholesale blackmailer and keeps twenty-seven micro-photographs of compromising documents permanently secreted beneath a wig and false skull. . . . Are you ready?'

'Where were the originals?' asked Appleby seriously; he was peering inside an old and shabby deer-stalking hat. 'Well, never mind; I'm ready.'

'There were thirty-one behind-stage folk. Subtract Auldearn – thirty; the Duchess and Clay, visible on the front stage – twenty-eight; old Cope, the suspect "aloft" if you like – twenty-seven. Twenty-seven suspects "within". And beyond that it's a matter of which of them can swear to which. Elizabeth, Noel Gylby, a girl called Stella Terborg, and myself you will find swearing to each other; we were in a group. And I can swear to one of the two footmen; I had him in the corner of my eye when the pistol went off. You will probably find other more or less authenticated alibis; but you will find too that people will be remarkably confused. Quite apart from the notion of a Royal Academician sniping from the heavens. I'm really not convinced of any absolute foolhardiness. The man knew his bloody game. On an occasion of this sort – for acting, you know, is a curiously exacting business even to the least nervous amateur – its remarkable to what an extent each individual off-stage is wrapped up in himself. One would almost hazard that the criminal had a developed sense of crowd psychology – like the fellow Nave or the advertising girl, Sandys.'

'Suspicions', said Appleby, 'crowd thick and fast upon us. Nave I remarked; the advertising girl, not yet.'

'I don't know that it's much use my talking about the people in detail before you've more than glimpsed them. But I was going to say something of the party in general, and of feelings in the air. I find I have two conflicting impressions about the party. First, it was particularly pleasant and well-contrived – one of those socially skilful mixtures in which each element finds the other charming, and so on. Secondly – and quite contradictorily, I'm afraid – it was on edge from the first. And the messages ... well, worked something up. If I say another word I shall be dealing with things so tenuous as to appear fanciful. It's best, perhaps, to go back to the statement that everything was bound up with the play – the first thing it occurred to me to say to you. The murder has been woven somehow· into the play – and the play had woven itself into the party. Not the mere fact that we were play-acting, though that did at times engender a curious self-consciousness. I mean the particular atmosphere aimed at – by men, heaven help me! – in this particular production of the play *Hamlet*. The conflicts which are in the play were present with us as we sat at dinner; that sort of thing.'

'I see,' said Appleby; and there was no fear that Gott should feel him to be taking this difficult exploration lightly even when he added briskly : 'Well – to seize on something more concrete – I think there's no doubt that friend Happy has been present with us too. In fact I suspect this of being his hat.' And Appleby poked the bowler that had interested him.

'Happy's? Why not Auldearn's? It's a gentleman's hat, as they say.'

'Oh, for that matter Happy is quite the gentleman. He comported himself in a most gentlemanlike way – and with a hat – the last time I saw him. But not Auldearn's hat because not size of Auldearn's hats. See wardrobe. And probably Happy's because I see what Happy's been doing – gate-crashing. When I met him making a get-away some hours ago he was wearing a high hat – but of the collapsible sort. You see, Giles?'

Giles didn't altogether see.

'He specializes in raiding houses when there's a big affair on. And to get at the bedrooms his best chance would be to pass as a valet; half a dozen people have probably brought men-servants – some quite strangers to the Scamnum staff. Dark coat, appropriate sort of scarf, bowler discreetly in hand, upper-servant walk – and Happy might successfully make this bedroom or that. Business in bedrooms over, he abandons bowler, produces opera-hat – a thing easily concealed – puts scarf in pocket, opens dark overcoat on immaculate tails – and stands an excellent chance of snooping round usefully among the sahibs before being politely asked to leave.'

Gott sighed. 'You certainly know the habits of your friends. Round Two to you. But are you not jumping about more than your habit was?'

'Perhaps because there looks to be an uncommon lot to jump about between. But the likelihoods about Happy are part of my main drive at the moment – eliminating the spy-notion finally. Point is that this safe was cracked by a professional person in the way of ordinary business, and with no thought of secret documents.'

'Yes, I think the spy-scare is out of court.' Gott paused in sudden perplexity. 'But there was some other reference to spies, if I could remember; besides Elizabeth's in the garden, I mean.' His brow cleared. 'Oh, it was just an earlier joke of hers, or perhaps of Noel's. That Bunney was the spy in black; his black box must have suggested the phrase. A lot of blacks we were bandying; spy in black, black box, black hand, black man –'

'Meaning the Indian who found the document?'

'Mr Bose. It was Bose who found the document? Curious; he was first with the body too.' Gott's eyes suddenly narrowed. 'John – *when*? *When* did he find it?'

'Midnight,' said Appleby quietly. 'Remember, they have all been searched.'

'An hour after the killing! Well, there's something I should have been at the lodge gates to tell you, and it's come to me only now. Searched! Did you get Nave or Biddle to do a little trepanning – to look inside their skulls?'

'Out with it, Giles.'

'The black man's memory. It's like a photographic plate. If he could contrive to read through a longish document once – even in covert snatches – I believe it would be in his head next to *verbatim*.'

'And so – just conceivably – re-enter the spies.' If Appleby's tone was sceptical his action was decided. He strode to the telephone by the bed-head. And just as his hand went out to it it rang. He picked up the receiver.

'*Les Présages*,' said Appleby presently, causing Gott to stare. And after a longer interval he said steadily and formally: 'I am aware of a probable channel and have a good chance of getting the situation under control.' A moment later he had rung off and swung round. 'Giles, is the house isolatable?'

'Yes. Designed by a rectangular mind. Foursquare with two wings and broad terraces on all four sides, even towards the offices. And you can floodlight them.'

Appleby snatched up the telephone again. 'The green-room, please. ... Sergeant? ... Is the search over ... all gone? How many men have you? ... Good ... turn them all out on the terraces this instant, light up and patrol. And if anyone tries to make a getaway they can hit hard. ... Yes, of course.' Rapidly he added some further instructions. 'Hurry.' Again he rang off.

'*Les Présages?*' queried Gott, taking up the first point of bafflement.

'Sort of pass-word – as used in sensational fiction when there are spies about. And they *are* about; right back in the centre of the picture. That was one Hilfers, a spy-fancier. Somebody in your respectable audience celebrated his release by sending a wire from a local call-box: the thing had been worked and the goods would shortly be despatched. A dark message but intercepted, Hilfers says, on its way to a recipient that puts the thing beyond doubt. There has been miching mallecho with that document, all right. But if your playbox was as tight shut as is made out we have half a grip on the thing yet. And now we'll find the little black chap.'

He strode to the door and opened it – and then Gott heard an oath he had never heard from Appleby before. In a moment he discovered the reason. The little black chap had not been far to seek. His corpse lay across the threshold.

4

LOOKING back upon this stage of the Scamnum affair Appleby was to ponder, in unprofessional perplexity, on the vagaries of human emotion. Lord Auldearn had died full of years, dignity, and achievement; almost the last of a line of scholar-statesmen whom he profoundly respected. The books which represented the dead man's incursions into literature and theology were on his shelves in the little Westminster flat; and in the midst of a world dipping towards chaos Auldearn's name had stood out, for him as for many others, as a point of resistance and of sanity. If the Duke of Horton were a show-case Elder Statesman Auldearn had been the real thing.

Auldearn had been murdered; and within an hour Appleby had heard talk of confusion and craziness drawing nearer as a result. It seemed as if the Scamnum *Hamlet* had yielded a full measure of irony; that on the make-believe Elizabethan stage

Auldearn had died amid tragedy actual and profound – died guarding a wretched paper which, philosopher as he was, he must have believed to represent no more than the organizing of madness against madness. And these things – brutal murder, murder followed by the distant murmur (baseless, perhaps, as many such murmurs are, and yet, perhaps *not* baseless) of unimaginable calamity – these things had left Appleby almost unmoved. As a policeman he had been excited and as a policeman he had worked like a machine; he had debated with the unexpectedly-discovered Gott with the elaborate detachment which had established itself long ago as a convention between them. But now an unknown black man, a waif from the Orient, a murderer it might be and a fomenter of mischief, had been tumbled lifeless before that other dead man's door. And Appleby, who had seen a score of violent deaths, was shaken profoundly. He stood up, pale to the lips, and said not quite steadily: 'Another dead man.'

It was steadily enough that Gott responded, but he responded with a single word: 'Nightmare'. And Appleby knew that Gott at least, collected as he was, had been facing nightmare for hours. Amid this general horror he had his own distress. These things had happened in the house in which – perhaps on the night on which – he had thought to speak to the Lady Elizabeth Crispin of marriage.

An instant more and Appleby was speaking with decision. 'The sergeant is on the rear stage; he must stop there until the ambulance comes. And the others are inside. I want you to come with me. Go and get somebody reliable to stay here, Giles. And get one of the doctors.'

Gott stepped carefully over the body – stretched like some slumbering guard before an eastern monarch's chamber – and departed silently down the dimly-lit corridor. Once more Appleby knelt down. There was no question but that Mr Bose was dead: the thin lips were drawn back over the perfect teeth in a grimace of sudden overwhelming agony; the lustre of the dark complexion had turned to livid in irregular smears, as if here were a player who had hastily begun to swab off his make-up. Death had come from a dagger-thrust hard below the left shoulder-blade. And the weapon stood – horribly – in the wound still. Appleby scrutinized it coolly enough, rapidly searched the body. Then he stood up and half-murmured in perplexity: 'I could have been almost sure ...' And then he shook his head. 'Far, far too remote!'

A minute later Gott came back, bringing Noel and Nave. Although fashionable Harley Street psychiatrists are not commonly called to examine two violent deaths in a night, Nave's perturbation seemed no more than a convention of distress conceded to lay bystanders. He knelt for a long time, perhaps a full minute. Then he got up. 'He is dead,' he said, 'and he was instantly killed. A blow from behind.'

'A skilled blow?'

Nave's eyes went again to the dagger. 'It might be an anatomist's blow,' he said gravely, 'or it might be an evil chance.' There was silence for a moment and he added: 'Shall I stay here ... or take any message?'

Appleby shook his head. 'There is nothing to be gained by your staying. Mr Gylby is going to stay for a time.'

Nave glanced dubiously – perhaps with a sort of masked kindliness – at Noel, who looked strained and more than usually young. Then he nodded and went away. Noel looked resolutely at the body. He felt sorry for Mr Bose and wanted to say something restrainedly distressed. But a trial of his voice told him it would be risky and he found safety in being practical. 'Mr Appleby, must it stay here? Could we move it into the bedroom? These other rooms are occupied ... any of the women might come along.'

Appleby nodded. 'We can move the body. He wasn't killed here.' With Gott he stooped to the burden – it was strangely light – and bore it into what had been Lord Auldearn's room. Then for a moment they hesitated.

'On the bed,' said Noel with the sudden authority of Scamnum. He threw off the upper coverings and they laid the body face downwards. Noel picked up the fine linen of the counterpane. 'It won't ... damage anything on the knife?' Appleby made a negative sign and they shrouded the body. For a moment they looked at the grim little pyramid which concealed the haft. Then Noel offered something practical again. 'That dagger – I don't know if you know – it hangs with some stuff on the wall outside the ... the black man's room. Medieval French, I think.'

'Is his room next door?' asked Appleby.

'Lord, no. Some way off, round a couple of corners.'

'And these rooms are nearly all occupied?'

'Yes. Most people have gone straight to bed – or at least to their rooms – after the search. A curiously shaming process it was. But a few have been fluttering about to jabber.'

Appleby shook his head in plain bewilderment – a habit, it occurred to Noel, never indulged in by Gott's fictional sleuths. And then, almost as if he had read Noel's glance, he smiled. 'Decidedly the time-honoured stage at which nothing fits!' But his voice instantly went hard. 'And we can't give our time to sitting back and thinking, Giles; some crazy logic of events is working itself out around us now. Come.' He strode back to the door and turned to Noel. 'Mr Gylby, do you mind – for an hour, perhaps?'

'I shan't doze off,' said Noel drily. 'Don't bang the door.'

In the corridor Appleby paused. 'He wasn't killed where he lay; there would have been a nasty sound we should have heard.' He walked half a dozen yards down the corridor and called softly. 'He was killed – where we'll presently discover. There is blood as far as this that we can probably track. But here it stops, and here I take it the body was simply picked up, rushed the last six yards, and set gently down on our doorstep – and Auldearn's. Now follow the trail, probably to his room.'

'Intimidating scale the place is on,' said Gott absently. The corridor along which they were walking was some eighteen feet wide; dark parquetry with six feet of patternless cream carpet down the centre.

'Somebody wasn't intimidated – nor concerned to avoid a mess.' Appleby's eyes were on the carpet; on the two clearly discernible furrows made in the deep pile by the dead man's heels and on the steady sequence of congealing gouts of blood. 'You see, Giles, how the evidence points different ways. The *show* of violence. . . .'

Gott started, made a gesture at Scamnum flitting past in the subdued light: vistas of dark panelling and soft enamels; the basic design elegant everywhere and a little dry, but relieved by the glow of rich stuffs, the gleam of fine cabinet-work; the whole eloquent of tranquillity and a large security – the Peace of the Augustans.

> 'We do it wrong, being so majestical,
> To offer it the show of violence. ....

The play is impressing itself on you too, John. Here is Bose's room.'

Mr Bose's room was dominated, startlingly and appropriately, by a Gaugin : dusky figures crouched in a vibrant shade, a hot, dark composition that seemed to cast its tropical glow far into the cool greys and greens of the lofty room. And the apple-green carpet was flecked with blood; it was as if the mangoes that made fiery points in the picture had tumbled out and been crushed to an ooze about the floor. Gott sat down abruptly, almost as if he had been hit in the stomach. 'It's Elizabeth's room,' he said, 'she moved out when this mob came – there's a limit even to Scamnum's resources.' And then he said – and with bitterness – something that Appleby had said to himself in the Prime Minister's car : 'Death at Scamnum Court !'

Appleby, who had already begun a swift exploration, paused. 'Yes?'

'It would be a learned joke. Perhaps somebody's having a learned joke ... Scamnum.'

'Scamnum?' Appleby frowned in perplexity. 'A bench?'

'Yes; it was arrogantly named after old Roger Crippen's usurious counter. But it's the same word as something else.'

Appleby shook his head.

'Shambles, John. For God's sake let's get something done !'

Appleby was on the point of saying : 'Steady !' Instead he said quietly : 'Come and look at the bureau.'

The bureau stood to one side of the outer wall beneath a cur-tained window – a slender Chippendale piece. Near at hand, and overturned on the floor, was a low-backed mahogany chair. Appleby looked back at the door by which they had entered and then at another door in the side wall close at hand. Gott fol-lowed his glance. 'A bathroom, I think, converted from a dressing-room and with a second door giving direct on the corridor.' He moved swiftly across, disappeared, and returned in a moment. 'Yes.'

'Then that is how he entered. Coming through the bathroom door he had only to take two strides – and stab. And he stabbed while the black man was –'

'Writing!' said Gott softly. They both stared at the narrow writing space of the bureau. A fountain-pen lay in the corner, amid a splash of ink suggesting that it had tumbled there from a surprised hand. The Scamnum notepaper was undisturbed in its place; Mr Bose had been writing on a common scribbling-block. And from this block some pages had been hastily ripped away. The exposed surface was blank; nevertheless Appleby picked up the block delicately and studied it with infinite care. 'If things are as they seem,' he said, 'we're both beaten. As a policeman I'm out-witted and as a fantasy-weaver you're blown clean out of the water. Just cast about the floor, Giles, for the stub of the unique cigarette or the accidentally dropped scarab.' But as he spoke Appleby himself was casting about the floor in a search that was wholly serious. And Gott, instead, cast about in the air.

'Little Bose – Emissary *A* – kills Auldearn, snatches the damned paper, contrives to commit it to memory and then "discovers" it. As soon as the search is over he comes up to his room and gets it down on paper. Then an unknown *B* – a rival Emissary – stabs Bose. . . .' He buried his head in his hands. 'John, it's not *impossible*; it's not even *unlikely* merely because it's grotesque. The document is grotesque in itself – and yet there it is, with hard-headed people in London worrying their heads off over it. I suppose that there are scoundrels and scoundrels at the game; and that Bose, being one, should be stabbed and robbed by another seems likely enough.'

'And yet', said Appleby, 'you get a feeling from the air that Auldearn's death is basically a piece of theatrical effect, and mysteriously bound up with *Hamlet*. And what did you think of Bose, anyway? He's in the middle of the picture now. Describe him.'

Gott – avoiding the area between bureau and doors – strode up and down the room. 'Like most of the Duchess's finds he was charming. But there's nothing easier, I suppose, than to find a charming and unearthly black man, and perhaps the process is just one of being taken in. If it had fallen on me to pronounce an emergency Last Judgement on Bose I should have sent him straight among the Saints, though he would have found their beliefs and proceedings absurd. But one can only have confidence in sizing up one's own sort. The little man was far too remote . . .'

'Exactly,' said Appleby. He drew back the window-curtain, threw open the window on the summer night and leaned far out. Below was a brightly-lit terrace with two constables constituting a very adequate patrol. He turned back into the room, locked the bathroom door, picked up the writing block once more and moved towards the door by which they had come. And then he paused to repeat the burden of his thoughts. 'If the substance of the document has really passed from Bose to unknown hands I'm next to beaten – and not all the constables in the home counties can help me.' He opened the door and transferred the key to the outside. 'Come along, Giles. There's some hope. There was the way we dealt with Bose's body – and there is the Duchess. I promised not to disturb people again tonight but you must take me to her all the same – now.'

Nevertheless Appleby stood a moment longer, his eye steadily on the further wall. And Gott realized with a start that in this, the crisis of his career, his friend – unobtrusively enough – was pausing to give proper attention to a noble picture. And for some reason his spirits rose.

Carefully, Appleby locked the door of what had been the Lady Elizabeth Crispin's room. Now it was to hold a ghost, a dusky presence that would hover before the uncertain shelter of that equatorial leafage, the half-recognition of those glancing eyes, the dubious kinship of those brown and glistening limbs.

5

MOVING about Scamnum at night, it seemed to Appleby, was like moving in a dream through some monstrously overgrown issue of *Country Life*. Great cubes of space, disconcertingly indeterminate in function – were they rooms or passages? –

flowed past in the half-darkness with the intermittent coherence of distant music, now composed into order and proportion, now a vague and raw material for the architectonics of the imagination. Here and there a light glowed still over a picture – on this floor pastel copies of family portraits scattered elsewhere : gentlemen extravagantly robust for the fragile medium into which they had been translated, ladies arbitrarily endowed with the too-heavy features of Anne and with dresses cut low over low, vaguely-defined breasts. And the scale of things wavered as in some hypnogogic trance. A low chair in the distance started into a randomly disposed grand piano at one's elbow. A hand extended to a door-knob fell upon air; the door was a door of unnatural size ten paces away. Appleby tried to imagine himself feeling at home amid this vastness and signally failed; he felt an inexpungeable bourgeois impression of being in a picture-gallery or museum – a well-contrived museum in which each 'piece' had air and space in which to assert its own integrity and uniqueness. He recalled the great palaces – now for the most part tenantless – which the eighteenth century had seen rise, all weirdly of a piece, about Europe. Scamnum, he knew, was to be a different pattern; would reveal itself in the morning as being – however augustly – the home of an English gentleman and a familiar being. But now it was less a human dwelling than a dream-symbol of centuries of rule, a fantasy created from the tribute of ten thousand cottages long perished from the land.

Thus Appleby reflected as he was piloted about Scamnum by Gott in search of the Duchess of Horton. And the nocturnal prowl so tinged his consciousness that he would not have been surprised to find in the Duchess – though he had eyed her attentively enough in the hall – a lady who had sat in Marlborough's tent or drunk chocolate with Bolingbroke in the seclusion of Chanteloup in Touraine.

The Duchess had not gone to bed. She was writing letters in a minute apartment which she had made peculiarly her own, a sort of porch-closet in Vanbrugh's manner, enshrining a bewildering display of photographs such as the most refined of the middle classes – it occurred to Gott – no longer think Good Form. The Duchess indicated two not very comfortable knob-chairs, looked very attentively at Appleby and laid down her pen.

'I've written twelve out of twenty,' she said, counting rapidly. 'We shall do no more entertaining until Scotland, and people must be let know. I've used the same formula twelve times and perhaps at the twentieth it will make me weep; if one could charm oneself into being the weepy sort it would be easier. But it's some good having something to do.'

'And Elizabeth?' asked Gott.

'I hope she is asleep. When she came up to her room her maid decided to be rather hysterical. Elizabeth quieted her, got her to bed and then went to bed herself.' The Duchess turned to Appleby. 'Have you seen the Duke again?'

'No, madam.'

The Duchess smiled – a smile which it would have been accurate, if banal, to call sweet. 'He won't join in the hunt much, I am afraid; far less for Ian's murderer than if the victim had been a mere acquaintance. It was different when he thought there was this secret – the paper – at stake. I can't explain it; his particular vision of good and evil drives that way. I suppose it is that there are people who, when the spectacle of evil opens at their feet, will stand insulated and immobile before that black pit. It appears as a sort of fatalism in face of personal calamity.' The Duchess sighed. 'Teddy is Hamlet,' she said. 'Which is why he made such a capital Claudius on the stage: Mask and Image.'

This was a glimpse of what had once made Anne Dillon more than a mere beauty in Edwardian drawing-rooms. It was fascinating and penetrating – but why was it offered? Appleby did not pause to speculate, but it would have been the answer, perhaps, that the Duchess possessed a genius for establishing personal relations. She had discerned in Appleby a certain temper of mind; someone to whom it would be best to present her own mind in its natural movement and colour. 'I very much hope', she said, that *I* can help. I am not Prince Hamlet.' And she shivered. She had not failed – Gott supposed – to notice her last allusive utterance as a trick bred of long acquaintance with Lord Auldearn.

Appleby recognized the quotation but not the cause of the

shiver. He plunged straight at his matter. And the straightness of the plunge indicated, perhaps, that the Duchess had established herself where she would have wished. 'You can help at once by telling me about Mr Bose. He too – it is very bad news – has been murdered.'

For a long moment the Duchess sat quite still and silent. And then it became very clear that if she was without tears she was not without passion. Her eyes blazed. 'Vile,' she said, 'oh ... *vile!*' Then she controlled herself and added quietly: 'But, Mr Appleby, this means ... a maniac? There is still danger? ... you have adequate men? And where did this happen – when?'

Appleby answered slowly. 'I do not think that Mr Bose was killed in mere madness and without reason. He was killed – stabbed – not more than half an hour ago in his bedroom.'

The Duchess's thought was what Gott's had been. 'In Elizabeth's room!'

'It is very necessary – urgently necessary, which is why I have disturbed you – that I should know about your acquaintance with Mr Bose, in detail and from the beginning. Would it be too much to ask you to attempt that now? And I will put off an explanation of the importance of the matter until afterwards, if I may.'

'You are asking almost for a story.' Perhaps, despite her real distress, there was a faint undertone of eagerness in the Duchess's voice, for a story was something she loved. 'But I will be as brief as I can; you must ask me if I don't mention the relevant things.

'I first came across him in the British Musuem. You see, Nevil – my son, that is, who is abroad – is interested in fish.' The Duchess paused rather challengingly, as if to assert that fish were a perfectly rational object of interest. 'And quite often I look things up for him in the library here. But a couple of years ago he became involved in a controversy in something called *Zeitschrift für Ichthyologie und tropische Tiefseekunde* – you will know it, Giles.' The Duchess had boundless faith in the universality of the learned of her circle.

'So then, when we were in town, I used to go to the British Museum sometimes and look things up there. I noticed Mr Bose the very first time. There are so many queer-looking people in the Reading Room – sandals, you know, and bearded sages in semi-religious robes and muddled women doing Higher Thought – that anybody who is remarkable rather than queer strikes one at once. And, of course, Mr Bose was remarkable. He used to drift about, very shy and looking rather lost. I don't know what his work was exactly, but I think it was all half-mysterious to him – a ritual that would bring him at last to the secret of the astounding and alarming West. One thought of the Reading Room as a temple whenever one looked at him; and – as you will hear – he thought of it as a temple himself.' The Duchess paused a little dubiously, as if aware of an incongruity in these reminiscences at three o'clock in the morning. 'But you cannot want all this, really?'

'Please. Just as it comes to you, cutting nothing out.'

'He worked for the most part in the room behind the Reading Room, where they give you the older books. It is quite a small place, no bigger than an ordinary library like our own here,' Gott, who was himself a frequenter of the twin vastness of 'the room behind the Reading Room' and of Scamnum's library, smiled at this description, but the Duchess continued unnoticing. 'Sometimes I went in there myself to look at the big monographs that need a whole great table to lay them on. There was one enormous and lovely thing by a man called Bloch – lovely plates of the most unbelievable creatures – and one day like a fool I tried to carry it back from table to counter myself. And, of course, I dropped it – two great volumes. It was more than rather dreadful! There is a superintendent who sits in a sort of pulpit and he stopped writing and put on an extra pair of glasses and *looked* at me. And an old gentleman with one of those French ribbons in his buttonhole got up and walked very quietly up and down, waving his hands – quite restrainedly – above his head; I suppose I had broken an important train of thought. I hadn't felt so bad since I made a perfectly thunderous mistake once, visiting Elizabeth at Cheltenham.' The Duchess plainly controlled an impulse to diverge on this and continued. 'Professor Malloch was there and he began to come across at a sort of modified, courteous trot. But the little black man was before him and gathered up Bloch – though I'm sure Bloch was far too heavy for him – and carried it to the counter. After that I felt entitled to get to know him if I could. I thought he might be interesting.'

The Duchess smiled as she touched on this foible. 'Unfortunately other people had thought the same thing. One of the Higher Thought women – I discovered afterwards – had invited him to tea and had prepared a room all draped in purple – and with joss-sticks, I think – and asked all her friends to share the mysteries. So he was naturally rather shy. Then one day I happened to take sandwiches, thinking it would be pleasing to eat them on the steps as I did long ago, when I used to take – go with my father for a day with the marbles. You know how people sit on the steps and under the portico and colonnade and feed the pigeons. Well, I noticed Mr Bose and he seemed to be *wanting* to feed the pigeons. He had sandwiches with him himself – a very small packet – and he seemed several times to be on the point of throwing something to the pigeons and then to think better of it. I went and joined him and I am afraid my interpretation of his actions was primitive, really gross! I really thought he hadn't brought enough and was hesitating between his own maw and the birds'. So I said – like a fool – "I have too much here; let's feed the pigeons." He was dreadfully worried at having to demur and made a great business of explaining. He regarded the Museum as a holy place and the pigeons were surely sacred birds. And he believed that the Higher Thought ladies who were sitting about, scattering crumbs, had it as a sort of ritual charge to care for them. And because these were not his rites he rather doubted the admissibility of joining in – though he wanted to feed the pigeons. He would have to consult his father, he said, who gave him various dispensations from time to time such as were necessary for moving in Western society.'

'Like the egg!' said Gott. 'Do you remember? When winter came he had his father's permission to eat an egg, if constitutionally necessary.'

The Duchess nodded. 'And then he talked to me very simply about caste and about his family – very old landowners, it seemed – and finally he told me that I was like his mother. At that I felt the horrid triumph of the successful collector; just like Mrs Leo Hunter, no doubt, when she had secured the exotic Count Smorltork. But I was mistaken. Mr Bose led me a long dance after that.'

'You mean,' said Appleby, 'that you had great difficulty in ... in carrying the acquaintance further?'

The Duchess raised a whimsical eyebrow. 'It wasn't quite a matter of pestering him; indeed, Mr Appleby, I would try not to do that. He liked me, I believe, and was always pleased when we met and he would talk very much as if I had been truly his mother. But afterwards he would retreat slightly and I had to begin all over again. He had learnt that I was what he called a ranee and perhaps he felt that I ought to make all the advances. So it was slow and difficult. You see, I didn't just want to trap him in a room with purple curtains and flummery.

'But we finally cemented our friendship one afternoon in Rumpelmayer's. I felt it as rather tragic at the time that his Achilles' heel was, so to speak, his stomach after all. It was when I had introduced him to that paradise of sweet and sticky delights – and particularly to the chestnut things that Elizabeth became so fond of in Vienna, Giles – that he finally opened his heart to me.' The Duchess pulled herself up. 'But his heart is not part of the story. Well, even later it was extraordinarily difficult to get him to come down and stay here. And when he came it was to his death. Invading him as I did seems terribly wanton now. He enjoyed himself, I think, and it was because I knew he would that I brought him. But now –'

The Duchess, despite the animation of her narrative, was clearly exhausted and only by an effort remaining other than distraught. Appleby rose. 'You have told me all I wanted to know. And if you will excuse me? ... Minutes may be valuable now.'

'Then go at once. Servants will be up all night; coffee, anything you may require, they will bring. And there will be a man continuously in the telephone-exchange; anybody in the house you will be able to rouse instantly from such sleep as they are likely to get. And now, I will finish my letters.' The Duchess, seeing that Appleby wanted to waste no more time with her, wasted no more time on him.

'Now ... the terrace.' Appleby, as he made his way down the great staircase with Gott, appeared lost in thought. Presently he roused himself. 'It makes the position no better; what do you think, Giles?'

'Once more, that the spies are a fable. Bose was no spy. That was not the story of how a spy worms himself into a house.'

'Quite so. That was the first fact I wanted; that the Duchess went after Bose and not Bose after the Duchess. And – you know – we had an instinct that Bose was all right when we were getting his body decently on Auldearn's bed.'

Gott gave a sort of sigh of relief. 'Not a Bath Mat Oriental' – and without pausing to explain – 'I'm glad.'

'And we have learnt why he was killed.'

'Yes.' Gott had no flair for being a Dr Watson. 'He was sending the whole story of murder to his father – thousands of miles away – and imploring guidance. But it seems pretty mad.'

Appleby shook his head. 'Not mad. Only – as we said – very remote. I thought he evaded a question of mine; he would not, I think, tell a direct lie. We were a very queer people to him, I suspect – despite his labours in the British Museum. He was not sure if I realized that the prime fact of the matter was that something evil had been done. And imagine yourself in a rajah's palace, Giles – a rajah's palace in a rajah-ruled world. You peer through a curtain in the middle of certain crazy proceedings and you see A wipe out B. I think you would be in some doubt. And Bose may have had fundamental philosophical difficulties; rather like those the Duchess attributes to the Duke, but more so. With what ought one to meet a particular sort of evil, and in particular circumstances as a guest? – and so on. If his code required him to consult paternal authority before feeding a pigeon or eating an egg, one can imagine its requiring something of the sort in the face of bloodshed. And so the murderer, who knew Bose knew, got his chance.'

'And Bose memorized nothing; that was just my novelist's fancy. And the spies are a fable.'

They had emerged on the terrace – to be pounced on by a constable. He recognized and saluted Appleby. 'Your photographers are in the theatre, sir – in the little stage place, with the sergeant. And the ambulance has come and we've sent it into the court. All been quiet apart from that, sir.'

They walked the breadth of the upper terrace and turned to

look back at the house. It rose before them, a great expanse of stone still fretted with half a score of lights, colossal and mysterious as a liner looming out of the night – the soft line of encircling illumination bathing the terraces like foam. But Gott, watching the steady pace of the patrolling police, had another image in mind. 'A platform before the castle,' he said. 'Quiet guard ... not a mouse stirring. .... The play haunts us still.'

Appleby laughed harshly. 'Hamlet? ... Spy-stuff off a bookstall. Sprung to life with God knows what ingenuity.' They made the long round of Scamnum, verifying the efficiency of the cordon, before he spoke again. 'I may have been too late with this guard,' he said, 'and it may be all over now. Or I may be losing the game this moment through having an insufficiently elastic mind. Giles, do you know anything about wireless?'

Gott exclaimed: 'It doesn't fit ... it's nonsense! We're faced with some private, passional thing.'

Appleby shook his head. 'You forget –' He broke off to stare into the darkness and then back at the house, his gaze travelling between the twin bulks of Scamnum and Horton Hill. 'Do you see any light – any flicker of light – on that hill?' He called up a sergeant – the place seemed now swarming with police – and spoke rapidly.

'We thought of it, sir,' said the man, stolidly but with pride. 'There's a man far out to each quarter watching the house and others on the roof looking the other way. If they see anything but steady lights they'll report.'

Appleby moved off a few paces with Gott and sighed with satisfaction. 'And the Duke thinks the county police should be immobilized! Perhaps they're not quite adequately energetic in the matter of poachers. But it may all be too late. Back to your play-box now.'

'Are you not putting rather a lot of faith in your telephone friend? His report stands alone now against all appearance; and I suspect that sort of person is oftener wrong than right.'

'No doubt. Read unvarnished accounts of spy-work and you see that muddle's it's middle name. And I have no doubt that if Auldearn were being stalked with the object of theft and then this killing happened, a spy in the audience might jump to the conclusion that his friends had acted a little more vigorously than expected and send off a rash promise from the first callbox. In fact Auldearn's death may have been, as you say, a private affair and the document never got at all. But I can take no chances. And so, back to your theatre.' He looked at his watch. 'Three o'clock.'

6

THE door of the hall, thrown open by a discreetly impassive constable, became – disconcertingly – a valve for the release of exceedingly angry voices. 'Hamlet and Laertes,' said Gott, 'quarrelling by Ophelia's grave.'

And certainly the scene revealed looked like a quarrel in a play. Dr Biddle and Sir Richard Nave, undeterred by the dubious glances of another constable in a distant corner, were standing plumb centre of the front stage, under the full glare of the still burning arc-lamps, and only too evidently very much displeased with one another indeed.

'Clearly the localized form,' Nave was vociferating. Recently so cool among the corpses, he was now quivering like an athlete on his mark. '*Leontiasis Ossium* –'

'*Leontiasis* fiddlestick!' Dr Biddle, an amiable little old gentleman to all normal seeming, was dancing – dancing in something grotesquely like a low-comedy convention of indignation. 'Simple, generalized Paget's – plain as a pikestaff! If Harley Street ideologues –'

'Sir,' thundered Nave, 'you are impertinent!'

Appleby nudged Gott briskly forward. 'What they call consultation, no doubt,' he murmured, 'but of whom this honourable interest in diagnostic minutiae?' When Appleby fell to sarcasm it was a sign of outrage; and indeed the scene was more indecent than funny. A few yards away, behind the rear-stage curtain from which there came a low murmur of voices, lay the body of Lord Auldearn, with a bullet in his heart and surrounded by police photographers. High words in such a presence were sharp exemplification of something Appleby knew well enough; that the shock of violent death will obliterate and transform social responses in a very remarkable way. But now both men made an effort to control themselves, and it was in his normal manner that Navé addressed Appleby.

'Dr Biddle, who is police-surgeon, has done me the honour to include my signature on the preliminary report that must be signed, it seems, before the body is moved. That is why we are here. But Dr Biddle proposes, I understand, to offer a contribution to knowledge as well.'

The tone insinuated that country doctors – even those who attend on dukes – do not commonly make contributions to knowledge and it almost sent Biddle off his balance again. He contented himself with a frown – but the anger was there, and apparently it was going to unleash itself on the police. 'I wish to say', said Biddle belligerently, 'that it would have been proper in you to consult me at once on the cause of death.'

'The cause of death!' said Appleby in genuine astonishment.

'Tcha! The manner of death, if you prefer it. Suicide. I am convinced that Lord Auldearn committed suicide and that this intensive police investigation is unnecessary and ... and highly indecorous.'

'Suicide ... unnecessary ... indecorous!' It was Navé who broke in, and for a moment he seemed angrier even than before. Was it, Appleby wondered, the common enough irritation of an able man before a donkey-colleague? And was Biddle a donkey?

Biddle continued resolutely. 'Suicide, I say. Lord Auldearn was a sick man; a dying man, in fact. He was suffering from a not common but nevertheless unmistakable' – he shot a venemous glance at Navé – 'unmistakable disease which has only one end. And he took a quick way out.'

Appleby glanced at Navé. 'You disagree about his having been mortally ill?'

'Most certainly I do not. But clearly –'

Appleby interrupted smoothly. 'I see, you were discussing the technical details when we came in. But, Dr Biddle, have you any reason to suggest for Lord Auldearn's choosing such – well – such a striking occasion for his deed?'

'He had a damned queer humour,' retorted Biddle. And beneath the competent and humane, if momentarily upset, old practitioner Appleby seemed to see for a moment a raw medical student to whom most sophisticated attitudes would be inexplicable.

Nave said drily: 'And so – if it was suicide – must other people have had – damned queer. Somebody, for instance, picked up the revolver and humorously hid it in Yorick's skull –'

Appleby whirled on him. *'How do you know that?'*

Nave looked mildly surprised. 'The Duke told me –my good sir!' He turned back to Biddle. *'Your* skull, by the way, Dr Biddle. And then that somebody, or another somebody, fell into the spirit of the evening and stabbed the unfortunate little Indian.' He looked blandly from the startled Biddle to Appleby. 'Dr Biddle and I were so absorbed in scientific talk that I forgot to tell him. Somebody has thrust a dagger into Mr Bose's heart. And I have come to the conclusion – mere student of the mind that I am – that the result has been death.'

Biddle, shocked apparently by the news and goaded afresh by Nave's irony, again exploded against the police. 'If there has been another death I should have been sent for at once. I shall speak to the Chief Constable. And I want to know if I am to be detained throughout the night. I have had a message that a bedroom has been got ready for me. I don't want a bedroom! I want to go home! In fact I demand to leave! I have my practice to attend to. I don't even know what urgent calls there may have been.'

The first rumpus, thought Gott – and said aloud: 'Hadn't you better stay? Then you can be led to the deaths as they occur.'

Biddle jumped. 'Deaths?'

'There is an unknown person, callous of human life and apparently utterly reckless, at large in this house. I don't know what may happen but I do know that in such a situation it is – well – highly indecorous to badger the police. Unfortunately by this time we are all thoroughly tired and on edge.'

'Mr Gott is right,' said Nave. 'And – Dr Biddle – we have been hasty. I apologize.'

Appleby seized upon this favourable moment. 'I am afraid, Dr Biddle, that it may be necessary to detain everybody for some time. I am very sorry. Any urgent messages would have come through by telephone and been referred to you at once. And any message you wish to send out may be sent out through the police.' It was not a generous concession but Appleby made the most of it. And presently, sure enough, Biddle was wooed to something like amiability. But he reiterated his conviction of suicide. Auldearn's choosing to shoot himself in the middle of the Scamnum theatricals was queer; but sick men do queer things. Whereas murder would be sensational and appalling; and the sensational and the appalling simply had no place at Scamnum. As for the violent death of Mr Bose, Biddle was obviously unprepared to believe in it without the evidence of his own senses. And to acquire this, and make appropriate official memoranda, he was presently successfully despatched under the guidance of a now courteous and remotely amused Nave.

Appleby moved towards the rear stage looking faintly perplexed. 'I suppose', he said, 'that Harley Street ideologues and Sussex G.P.s are naturally a sort of pike and perch. But it seems to have been an unnecessary flare-up.'

'I suspect Nave of having forgotten a good deal that lies outside the psychiatry he makes his money by. And if he was simultaneously cocky and hazy that would infuriate Biddle.'

'What was Biddle in the play?'

'He petitioned to come in at the last minute. We made him an attendant lord.'

'Well, he seems just such a minor figure. Only not very strong, perhaps, in the courtier's patience and self-control. And now, Giles, for the constabulary's star turn; scientific detection. But I'm afraid you'll find it lacking in novelty.'

The rear stage was certainly a highly-conventional effect. In one corner a lounging young man stood amid a litter of those large glass bulbs, filled with a gleaming silver-foil, used by press photographers; he was loosing them off in a bored way for two muttering and exclaiming persons with large cameras. Looking up, Gott saw a third camera peering down from the trap-door of the upper stage, and the head of a third muttering and exclaiming person bobbing about behind it. A severe little man with glasses and a bald head, very like a distinguished scientist discoursing on shaving-soap in one of Diana Sandys's advertisements, was industriously and impassively applying a miniature vacuum-cleaner to the surroundings of the corpse. In the background a brother scientist was puffing some sort of powder through a machine at the faldstool. To one side stood Sergeant Trumpet and two local constables, impressed, respectful but latently antagonistic. It was nothing if not a highly-coloured scene. Gott ran an agitated hand through his hair, indicated the manipulator of the vacuum-cleaner with a polite little-finger. 'John – I say – is that Dr Thorndyke?'

'It must be,' said Appleby.

Dr Thorndyke switched off his machine and addressed Gott with a disturbing fusion of American *camaraderie* and London accent. 'There was an old girl once thought her husband a bit dusty-like. Laid him down on the mat just like this 'ere' – Dr Thorndyke jerked a thumb innocent of irreverence at the body – 'and vacuumed him proper. Twisted all his po'r bleeding inside and he had to go into 'orspital. Almost knocked him off. Yes, siree.'

This was presumably Dr Thorndyke's favourite semi-professional anecdote; all his colleagues had plainly heard it before. 'You see,' murmured Appleby, faintly apologetic, 'they go to study these things in New York.' But Gott had turned to the person puffing at the faldstool. 'And I take it', he said, 'that this contrivance is . . . is what I call an insufflator?'

Appleby looked with subdued irony at his friend. 'I suppose it is rather macabre; the Gott *genera* coming alive, so to speak.'

'It's like stepping through the looking-glass,' said Gott morosely. He had never seen Appleby in this full professional setting before.

Appleby raised his voice. 'Nearly through?' There were affirmative noises. The young man with the flashlights draped himself in flex and departed. The faldstool was carried out to be photographed elsewhere. The army of criminologists melted away.

'Is all that useful?' asked Gott.

'Your insufflator's useful; finger-prints still catch criminals by the pint. And an expert gunsmith is useful. And good photographs serve sometimes to hold the attention of a tired jury.

The rest's hooey, more or less. But I have to think of the fuss there's going to be if we're held up for long. Questions in Parliament: was such-and-such attempted and does the Home Secretary know of the advanced methods of the Kamchatkan police? I've been caught before by scamping the window-dressing. But now I must have a word with them and then we can look round.'

When Appleby returned he was carrying the heavy iron cross that the Duchess had obtained along with the faldstool from Hutton Beechings. 'Found on the floor,' he said. 'It was part of the rear-stage set?'

Gott nodded. 'Yes. Standing on the little ledge of the faldstool.'

'Then it just conceivably suggests a slight scuffle – or it may have been knocked over during the get-away. They thought Auldearn might have snatched it up to defend himself. But it's clear of finger-prints.' Appleby paused to pace out the dimensions of the rear stage. 'They agree with me about the shot. Getting on for close-up but distinctly outside suicide range – nothing in Biddle's theory. And certainly not from as far as the shelter of the curtains. But just conceivably from as far as the trap immediately above.'

They both looked up to where the trap-door had been left open. 'Still the spot, then,' said Gott, 'from which a venerable Royal Academician may have committed the first of two imbecile and beastly murders. Shall we go up?'

They went behind scenes and climbed to the upper stage. Cope's easel and canvas were still in position in a corner and his palette and a wooden box, with about a dozen very large tubes of paint, lay on the floor. Appleby took up a position behind the easel and looked out over the body of the hall. 'Was the lighting like this? He could be seen, surely, by the audience?'

'Yes, just like this – a half-light representing the battlements at night. The true Elizabethan upper-stage must, I think, have been pretty shadowy. But even so, he could, as you say, be seen. He wanted to paint from here and I felt that his presence, just discernible in the shadow, wouldn't spoil the play.'

'The question then would be whether he could get to this

trap-door in the middle without being detected. I'll give the fellow at the far end of the hall there a shout. It would be from the back that he could be seen, if from anywhere. Just get behind the easel, Giles, move about a bit and then make for the trap-door as well as you can.' Appleby advanced to the low balustrade of the upper stage and called out to a constable at the extreme end of the hall : 'Just look up here, will you, and tell me what you can see besides myself in the next two minutes.'

The constable looked – open-mouthed but keen-eyed. Gott stood behind the easel; moved right and left of it once or twice; withdrew behind it; got cautiously down on his knees, on his stomach; squirmed towards the trap. Gaining it, he paused a moment, wriggled round, returned as he had gone and in a moment was appearing right and left of the easel again as if studying the composition before him.

'Well?' called Appleby.

The constable lumbered up the hall and climbed on the front stage. 'I saw the gentleman dodging about behind the picture,' he said. 'Then he disappeared for a bit like, and then he showed up again, dodging about as before.'

'What do you mean – disappeared for a bit?'

'Well, sir, happen he were just standing still behind the picture. It's all in shadow and hard to tell.'

Appleby nodded. 'Well, that's all right; quite possible. So tell me about Cope.'

Gott hesitated. 'He's imbecile, or thereabout. Which need not suggest the perpetration of imbecile crime. It's simply that the age is in and the wits are out. And there is a sense in which one feels that he might do any crazy thing. One's not a considerable artist without plenty of inner stress, and when one's mind and control begin to break up conceivably the stress may let fly in a perfectly helter-skelter way.'

Appleby looked dismayed. 'This latest tendency to psychologize your fictions, Giles. It sounds well, but I don't know that there's much record of considerable artists embracing the straight-jacket by way of multiple homicide.'

But Gott was pursuing his thought soberly. 'No, but there are plenty of suicides recorded among them. And the two mechanisms are not altogether remote. However, it's the Bose factor that seems vital.'

'Quite so, Cope could have shot the recumbent Auldearn from here and nothing neater. But could Bose have known? You must do that reconstruction all over again, Giles. When I say Go.'

Appleby descended from the upper stage and took up Bose's position on the prompter's stool between the two thicknesses of heavy curtain. Applying his eye to the peep-hole commanding the rear stage he cried: 'Go!' And within a few seconds something significant happened; he was conscious of a stealthy slithering noise from above – Gott crawling cautiously over the boards. So far good; Bose, who as prompter would be giving his whole consciousness to sound, might well have had his attention attracted in this way to the upper stage – and so, by a natural transition, have directed his glance through the peep-hole and upwards. So he peered in and up. And in a moment he saw some movement in the shadows – it was the trap-door sliding back – then, clearly, a pointing hand. It was Gott's, a finger extended as if aiming to shoot. Bose, then, could have known. What was more important, as explaining his presumed reluctance to speak, he could have suspected without knowing positively. A revolver thrust through the trap from the upper stage must *almost* certainly have been in the hands of Cope. Bose could have almost known. But how could Cope have known that Bose almost knew?

'How,' said Gott, coming down, 'how could Cope have known Bose knew – supposing, I mean, it was so?'

'Exactly. But the answer is simple enough if you psychologize. A single glance between the two afterwards would have told him.'

'Yes, a look could no doubt tell all. But the Cope theory, remember, is another thrust towards oblivion for the spy theory. I don't know Cope's subsequent movements, access to Auldearn's body and so on; but if one shot to grab, one would hardly shoot from another storey.'

'Perhaps the grabbing is another story, very little connected with the shooting? And though the Cope theory is beguiling it's the grabbing I must hold on to now. And for that the vital point is the hermetic sealing.' And on the hermetic sealing, Appleby went to work. The structure of the hall, the floor, the doors, the windows; the chance of throwing something through a window, of thrusting something through a ventilator, of catapulting something through the darkness of the rafters to the far end of the hall – everything was considered. It was plain, to begin with, that nobody could have got away. There were only two exits from the hall. That behind the green-room had, as it happened, been under the observation of Gott, Noel, Elizabeth, and Stella Terborg at the moment the shot was heard and Gott had stood by it until the Duke arrived, locked it, and sent him to see to the other door – that behind the audience. And at this second door there had been a fireman, who could speak absolutely to nobody's having come or gone. Until the Duke dismissed the audience, therefore, nobody had left the hall except Gott and Gervase Crispin when they went to Auldearn's room:

'It seems a hundred to one', said Appleby – and to Gott he appeared almost restless – 'that it's as you say. Either this Hilfers person has made the merest muddle or there really were people after the document and one of them, being in the audience and seeing what happened, jumped to conclusions and sent an over-confident message to his pals. And yet –'

'But any *danger* is gone, surely. The thing is in your pocket; Bose turns out overwhelmingly unlike a spy and so it's irrelevant that he had a memory like a photographic plate –'

'And so', said Appleby, 'we might turn to this: Sergeant Trumpet's instinct was sound.'

Gott frowned – and started. 'To hang on to anyone who had left the hall! John, have you got your eye on me?'

'I have not. But there was also –'

He paused at the startled look on Gott's face and then swung round to confront the advancing figure of the Duke. And the Duke, who had been so impassive in the contemplation of murder, was moving in something between daze and distraction. He walked straight up to Appleby and spoke as if out of a trance. 'Mr Appleby, I have just been to my cousin Gervase Crispin's room. I happened to go in quietly by the dressing-room and he failed to notice me. I came away at once. He failed to notice me because he was sitting at a desk manipulating ...

an instrument.' For a moment the Duke's knees seemed to sway beneath him.

'It was a little camera,' he said.

＊

There was only one question on which to pause. And the answer to it was uncompromising: it had certainly been Gervase's suggestion that Auldearn's room should be inspected and guarded. At this Appleby hurried behind-stage with directions; half a minute later he and Gott were running upstairs. Neither said a word but Appleby noticed that Gott was almost as disturbed as the Duke. In a night that had included two murders and the rumour of more than private calamity there had been nothing as simply dark as this. That an enigmatical Indian should have a memory like a photographic plate and employ it in mischief-making had been one suggestion; that Gervase Crispin might have been about the same job with an actual camera was another. It belonged to a different world of blackness. And to the quick imagination of Appleby the dimly lit vistas of Scamnum, as they flowed past once more, took on a new unsteadiness, as if the foundations of the place were rocking above a subterraneously exploded mine. But Gott, as he ran up the great staircase, was hearing again the frantic bell that had pealed so wildly there just twenty-four hours before and the voice that had rung out in sequel:

> '. . . there shall be done
> A deed of dreadful note.'

The words had been from *Macbeth*. And the deed had been treason.

'Better knock,' said Appleby, pausing coolly before Gervase's door. He knocked; there was no answer. He turned the handle and walked in. Darkness. He flicked on the light. There was no sign of Gervase Crispin in the bedroom; the dressing-room and bathroom were empty too. Without wasting a moment, and perfectly methodically, he began to search the room. 'Perhaps the Duke's gone queer in the head,' he said presently. But his search was ruthless and the remark – half whimsical, perhaps, and half apologetic in intention – rang harshly when it was uttered. And then he put the case plainly. 'Gervase Crispin shoots Auldearn, gets the document, suggests searching Auldearn's room, leaves you there, and hurries to his own. He takes the photograph – perhaps gets the plate off to a confederate – and then returns to the hall and manages to get the document into the scroll. It seems to hold.'

Gott was analysing this in a flash. 'It won't hold. If he had a confederate waiting somewhere up here, he would surely give him camera and all: it couldn't be got away too soon. And he would have no reason to be fiddling with the camera afterwards when Scamnum was teeming with policemen. And if he had no confederate to get the thing away he would be taking a frightful risk. If the search in the hall had been followed by a search in his room – and there was half a pointer that way, for he had been out – he would have been caught.'

'There was more than half a pointer, Giles. And – Lord help me! – I missed it. As for frightful risk, frightful risks enough have been taken in Scamnum tonight; think of trundling Bose's body past all these bedroom doors! But tell me about Gervase straight, while I finish this rummage. Then, if he doesn't return, we must be after him.'

'If there's anything in this, then when I spoke of nightmare I spoke too soon. He's a Crispin. Indeed, as I said, he's *the* Crispin. And they're at the heart of England. It's fantastic.'

Suddenly, and while still searching like an automaton, Appleby spoke with something like passion. 'York's the heart of England – and Stratford and Preston, perhaps, and Huddersfield. Scamnum! ... didn't you say yourself it was a show-case – and the Duke and his fish and his pigs show-case stuff, too? And what's the real Crispin, this Gervase's Crispin? We were talking about grab – isn't that him? The honourable history of grab. First hundred years – grab in England and Holland; second hundred years – grab about Europe, India, and the Levant; third hundred years – grab round the planet! Gervase is big at his game – really big, I grant – and that's where something of the incredible comes in. But the heart of England is sob-stuff. Gervase is money, the root and heart of money. And for all I know his home and his allegiance may be wherever money spawns quickest at the moment. I've no more reason to trust him than I have a labourer out in the Crispin fields – less, in fact.'

'I didn't know you were a Jacobin, John.'

'No more I am. I'm probably violently reactionary. Even when *Hamlet* was being written Crispin was still Crippen, pushing a trade honest men didn't favour. But all that's irrelevant. Here's my point, though. I know almost nothing about this document that's in my pocket now, and I probably wouldn't learn much more if I sat straight down to study it. It's about international industrial organization, as far as I can gather, and it may be far more a matter just of Grab than of the Union Jack. It was put to me in terms of this country and that, and with rumours of conflict in the background. But I know that once one touches the fringes of an affair like this, one is fated to work half in the dark. For all I know it may be just a racket that's going to cripple Gervase in Germany or Gervase in North Africa – that sort of thing. And you can't deny that the Duke, having been smart enough to see the significance of a camera, was sufficiently impressed to come forward – rather heroically – with the story. He may know that the document is in some way connected with Gervase's interests, which would be a reason for his instant extreme concern. And I'm not sure that I wasn't given half a hint not to trust ... well, the family.'
Appleby was thinking of the Prime Minister's remark about not trusting even the Archbishop of Canterbury.

'But mightn't Gervase be in on the document-business anyway?'

'Not necessarily. He's not in the Cabinet, for instance. But tell me about him – as a private person, I mean – while I prod this sybaritic spring-mattress.'

Gott considered gloomily. 'Gervase has the family feeling for a role,' he said. 'In the play he took Osric and the second Grave-digger, and that more or less represents what the Terborg girl calls his *persona*: something midway between the fantastic and the buffoon. His jokes have deliberately no sense to them; you know the sort? But one is aware all the time that he is the able banker and all the rest of it; one would be aware of something of the kind at a first meeting and without knowing anything about him. As for the rest, the Russian woman is his mistress –'

'Ah, the heart of England again. Go on.'

Gott smiled. 'Certainly it adds a neat touch to the cosmopolitan-villain picture. It's a recent affair, but I believe honourable enough or she wouldn't be here. The Duchess is ironical about it but actually approves. They can't marry I understand, because she has a husband in a mad-house.'

'It looks rather as if she had a lover in one too. Tell me more about them, if you can.'

'There's something a little puzzling about their relationship. Nave, for instance, was questioning it the other day. He has a nose for the psychopathic that he would do better to keep for his consulting-room. And – though I knew the story – I didn't discuss it with him. The point is, I understand, that Gervase doesn't in any sense keep the Merkalova. She's an independent creature, contriving to make some sort of living out of fashionable journalism, and she's temperamentally a virginal creature as well, so that it is one of these affairs that are laced with long-term platonics. It was the feel of that, perhaps, that baffled Nave.'

For a moment Appleby had looked startled. 'It's just possible –' He checked himself as if before a hazy speculation. 'But it's interesting about Nave. After all, he's a professional observer. What exactly did he think about them?'

Gott hesitated. 'It may have been his idea that they had less the air of lovers than of colleagues. But –'

'But you think – being full of reactionary prejudice yourself – that Nave would be baffled before anything outside farmyard relations. Maybe so. And here, surely, is friend Gervase returning.' Appleby punched the mattress and looked calmly round the ransacked room. 'I'm afraid that – like Wilkie Collins's traveller – he's going to find a Terribly Strange Bed.'

Footsteps had made themselves heard in the corridor. They ceased and there came a half-hearted – almost an inattentive – rat-tat. Appleby wrinkled his nose in disgust. And then the door opened and admitted Max Cope. 'I'm seeking Gervase,' he said placidly and with something of the North Country idiom it had always pleased him to retain. 'It's Gervase I'm seeking. Have you seen him, Gott? Is he about?' He advanced into the room and stopped to contemplate the cascading pile of rifled bed-clothes in the middle of the floor. 'How very, very pretty!' he said – and sat down and nodded his own lovely and cascading white beard.

For a moment it seemed as if this irruption of another Scamnum exhibit was too much for Appleby. Then he spoke briskly. 'I'm glad you like it; it's the lighting, no doubt, that gives the effect. Did you know that Mr Bose is dead?'

Cope looked dreadfully upset. 'Bose – the little dusky fellow who moved so well? Dear me, how dreadfully sudden!'

'Bose was murdered – *too*.'

'Worse and worse,' said Max Cope; 'worse and worse. It makes it much more dreadful. One wonders could a girl ... could a girl, one asks oneself ...' He paused doubtfully, looked very seriously at Appleby. 'You see, before I say anything to the police I feel I should consult Gervase. I should ask Gervase, I think, before speaking to the police. Don't you think, Mr –?'

'Appleby,' said Appleby.

'Appleby,' said Cope. 'Appleby – quite so.' His eyes strayed to Gott – and lit up. He wagged a cunning finger. 'The oyster-wife, you see. I kept the oyster-wife in mind. And then there she was!' He gave what in another man would have been a leer – for beauty still hung oddly over all Max Cope's gestures – and then he chuckled crazily. Suddenly he stopped, his eyes widening on Appleby. 'But didn't you arrange that search? The search – wasn't it you –'

'Yes,' said Appleby.

'I *see*.' Cope turned to Gott. 'Gott, this is a policeman. And little Bose is dead ... where's Gervase?'

'Missing but not, we hope, very far away.' Gott felt as baffled before Cope as Nave had felt before his problematical lovers. He wondered if this quasi-lunatic discussion was evoking in Appleby the irrational irritation that it was evoking in himself. Nevertheless he continued civilly: 'You wanted him very much?'

'He seemed the best person. Gervase seemed best. One must be so careful these days. I mean, there's just a suspicion of a thing and then they write about it. The mere suspicion might ruin the girl. The girl might be ruined –'

'What girl?' asked Gott – positively sternly.

Cope stared. 'Diana Sandys, of course. Gervase seemed –'

Appleby made a big effort to control the proceedings. 'Diana Sandys – one of the players? Mr Cope, tell me please, what is this about Diana Sandys? *What about her?*'

For a moment Cope seemed scared by the concentration behind the question; scared or simply, perhaps, lost and confused. 'Diana Sandys? Oh, no bone – don't you feel? No interesting bony structure. Pretty and illustrative ... determination or something of the sort. Pressure about the mouth...' And as Appleby was on the point of giving up Cope seemed suddenly to emerge. Quite simply he said: 'She burnt something, you see.'

In the little silence that followed Appleby was aware that this rambling old person, as he made his announcement, was eyeing him intently. And as if to avoid reciprocal scrutiny Cope now ambled across the room and into shadow, to sit down and fidget by Gervase's rummaged desk. 'Burnt something,' he repeated with a species of gently imbecile guile. The child burnt something. And what, we wonder, did the child burn?'

How many of the pleasant people who had gathered at Scamnum – it suddenly came to Gott – were going to be pleasant no longer? Twelve hours ago Max Cope had been crazy and wholly amusing; now he appeared crazy and not a little nasty. Perhaps the nastiness was not in Cope; perhaps it was a poison in the air, a distorting medium that would soon people these stately rooms with knaves, a destructive element that would overwhelm all normal human confidence and make honest people eye each other with suspicion and fear. An exclamation of impatience was on his lips when he was prevented by Appleby – and by Appleby's favourite phrase.

'Tell me about it, will you?'

And ramblingly, repetitively Cope told. While the players had been waiting about the hall and shortly before the arrival of Appleby, one of the Terborg twins – he couldn't remember which, not that they were in the least indistinguishable as people maintained – one of the twins had remarked that there was sure to be a thorough police search. Whereupon Diana

Sandys had said, 'I simply must have a cigarette,' and – though nobody was smoking – had gone off to one of the dressing-rooms to get her cigarette-case. And Cope had followed – followed, as he said, simply because it would be kind to hint that nobody had thought it proper to smoke. But on sticking his head round the corner of a curtain he had observed her applying a match not to a cigarette but to several small sheets of paper. And on this it had come to Cope, apparently, that Miss Sandys was what he called the oyster-wife, the person who had been responsible for the 'Hamlet, Revenge!' messages. The notion of a police search having been suggested to her she was hastening, he supposed, to rid herself of a little stock of similar messages. What it had to do with Auldearn's death he didn't know. But there it was.

'You thought it was messages?' asked Appleby – and continued evenly: 'It didn't occur to you that she might be burning notes made from the document?'

Cope's eye, he felt, was again narrowing upon him. But Cope's voice came out of the shadows in helpless bewilderment. 'Document, Mr –?'

Appleby sighed. 'And you thought you must speak to Mr Gervase Crispin about it? You hadn't by any chance an appointment with him?' The question was shot out.

'An appointment with Gervase? Dear me, no. I thought it would be wise to speak to him. If the poor girl had been perpetrating this joke ... and then if this had happened ...' Cope, fidgeting still at the desk, allowed his voice to falter into bewilderment and silence.

'I see. But Mr Crispin doesn't seem to be coming back. I think, Mr Cope, you should stop worrying now and go to your room for a little sleep. You will be able to consult him in the morning.'

And he humoured the aged painter like a tired child from the room. But when he turned back it was to exclaim: 'I wonder!' He took a turn about the room. 'A fresh trail? A red herring? A deep game of some sort? Giles, is the old rascal as daft as he appears?'

'I think he's daft all right. But he might be up to a deep game all the same. But what? Is he telling lies about this girl?'

'And in with Gervase? You know while he was rambling

away I thought he was sizing me up with a pretty queer concentration.'

Gott started. 'I rather imagine –' He crossed over to the desk and came back holding a piece of paper. 'A habit of Cope's,' he said, 'and accounts for the calculating eye. And it's worth about thirty guineas, so hold on to it.'

Appleby stared dumbfounded at the vigorous pencil impression of John Appleby. He read the inscription: 'With best wishes for good hunting – M. C.'

'Oh my God!' said Appleby, swearing for the second time in Gott's knowledge. 'Of all the nights.'

Gott crossed to the window and drew back the curtain.

'Getting on for dawn,' he said. 'The dawn, ah God, the dawn – it comes too soon.'

7

APPLEBY caught at a suggestion from the *aubade*. 'I suppose that's where Gervase is,' he said. 'With the lady.'

'Perhaps. But as I said –'

'Quite so. And they may be just colleagues. But in any case we must try to get hold of him. He's the centre of the picture still, despite this story of Cope's. Question is – who's to fetch him?'

Gott considered. 'You might use the telephone. "Mme Merkalova? – may I speak to Mr Gervase Crispin?" But it seems indelicate. The obvious person to send is the Duke, but I think the Duke might be spared contact with Gervase at the moment. After all, he has practically suggested he be put in gaol. And the next most obvious person is the other member of the family – Noel.'

The proprieties must be preserved, even in nightmare. 'Then,' said Appleby, 'will you find him – once more? He'll long since have been relieved of his lyke-wake.'

Gott fetched Noel, whose sleepy eyes grew round as he surveyed Gervase's devastated room. 'I say,' said Noel, 'is this affair entirely non-stop, Mr Appleby – a sort of detective marathon? Do we feed you through a pipe as you sleuth?' He was a charming youth, tall, slim, obstinately pink and white, and now enfolded in beautiful green silk. And a murder seemed to have approximately as much effect on him as an aspirin tablet; there was a slightly depressant action lasting about an hour.

'There is something rather difficult I want you to do,' said Appleby. 'It's to get Mr Gervase Crispin here at once.'

'To be sure. And I don't suppose it's just in order to see him to bed. Have you got an eye on old Gervase for the shooting and stabbing?'

'He's got himself suspected,' said Appleby abruptly, 'of tampering with a document of state.'

'My good sir!' Noel's expostulation was as immediate as a reflex action.

'And the person who first suspected him was the Duke.'

Noel's eyebrows went up. 'Giles, it isn't that Mr Appleby's ... feeling the strain?'

'It is not.'

Noel sat down on the bed. 'Friends,' he said soberly, 'give me your instructions.'

Appleby thought for a moment. 'We think Mr Crispin may be talking things over with Mme Merkalova. Go to her room –'

'Oh Lord!'

'Go to her room, knock, and call for him. If he reveals himself as being there – or if he doesn't, for that matter – say this.' Appleby paused to consider Noel's conversational style. 'Say: *"Gervase, will you come and deal with this detective? He has turned your room upside down and now he wants to convict you of stealing the secret treaty with Ruritania."* And –'

Mildly, Gott made as if to protest. 'Isn't that rather dangerously giving away –'

'And be sure', said Appleby, 'that the lady hears every word. Then come back; a member of the family won't be amiss. And now hurry. The night's gone and we've no grip of this business yet.'

Noel departed. Appleby was still prodding about the room. Gott sat down beside Gervase's spacious fireplace and stared thoughtfully at the soot which had been the sole result of Appleby's explorations there. His inner eye kept turning back to the rear stage in the hall, tenanting it anew with that fairy-tale squad of detective-officers photographing and vacuum-cleaning round the body of a Lord Chancellor of England. They were a symbol of the clamant fact: a pistol-shot – still utterly mysterious – had tossed Scamnum into a world as fantastic as any in the whole domain of his own Elizabethan drama. His mind switched to the bloody carpet in Elizabeth's room; that, he felt, had been less a symbol than a menace, a portent of danger lurking no one knew where. And remotely but convincingly before him he discerned the possibility of a reaction to experience that he had never thought to know – the reaction of panic. 'John,' he said, 'I think I'm going to be panicky.'

'You mean you're anxious about Lady Elizabeth. I hope we'll be too busy presently to be envisaging unlikely dangers.'

It was not a very sympathetic speech, perhaps because it had been absently framed. Appleby's mind too was on the rear stage, a rear stage that kept presenting itself in disconcerting fusion with that other and vaster stage on which he had watched Massine's obscurely struggling destinies. A queer cinematographic cross-cutting of *Hamlet* and *Les Présages* ... he dismissed it as the muddle of a brain beginning to grow tired.

Noel returned. 'Coming,' he said. 'He started like a guilty thing upon a fearful summons – I don't think.' He paused with relish on the vulgarism and then added: 'If you ask me, he's annoyed.' And Noel sat down on the bed with something the air of an expectant *habitué* of the National Sporting Club.

Half a minute went by. There was a brisk but deliberate tread in the corridor. The door opened and Gervase entered. He took an unhurried glance round the room and said: 'May I have an explanation of this extravagant proceeding?' It was true that he did not look guilty. But neither did he appear angry – until quite quietly he added: '... you imbecile baboon?'

Noel wriggled luxuriously on the bed. Gott made a deprecatory noise which immediately struck him as donnish and ineffectual to a degree. And Appleby said: 'Sit down.'

Gervase's eyebrows went up, much as Noel's had done some time before. But his person went down, ponderously into the most comfortable chair. 'Mr Inspector,' he said, 'I don't mind your gambolling among my things a bit. It's a comparatively harmless employment until we can get you taken away. But I object extremely to being hunted about the house as I have just been hunted. And my resentment is less with you than with my cousin here, who behaves like a bell-boy while presumably claiming the character of a gentleman. And now, what do you want?'

'The camera,' said Appleby.

Gervase's eyes narrowed. 'My dear man,' he said, 'you're wasting your time.'

Imbecile baboon or dear man appeared all one to Appleby. He said: 'As you probably know, the house is now very efficiently isolated. Go back, please, and bring the camera.'

What, it occurred to Gott, if the Duke had made a mistake? One cannot tackle the Gervase Crispins of the world like this and escape unpleasant consequences if one's ground gives way beneath one. But Appleby seemed perfectly assured.

'I have told you that you are wasting your time.' Gervase paused and shifted his ground slightly. 'Will you explain just what is in your head?'

'That you brought a document out of the hall, secured a photographic reproduction of it after you had left Mr Gott in Lord Auldearn's room, and then deposited it where it was eventually found on the stage.'

It would have been difficult to affirm that Gervase was not dumbfounded. And certainly he was angry; Appleby scarcely remembered an angrier man. He turned on Noel. 'So that's what you meant by Ruritanian treaties!' He turned back to Appleby. 'Apart from this fantasy about myself, have you any reason whatever to believe that the document has been tampered with at all?'

'Yes.'

'And you have no other line to work on except this that you are putting over on me?'

'At present, nothing so circumstantial.'

'And you've been here for – what – four hours?'

'About that.' Appleby's resentment in face of this inquisitorial method was all assumed. Let the other man take the lead and there is always the chance of his heading in a significant direction. 'About that,' said Appleby in grudging admission.

'And a document – of importance apparently – has been

tapped. And your net progress consists in turning this bedroom upside down and asking me fool questions about – a camera, did you say?'

'Yes,' said Appleby. 'The camera. Will you go and get it, please?'

Noel chuckled audibly. Gervase raised his hands to his head in a sort of despair. 'And it hasn't occurred to you that you are building wildly on next to nothing? That against this story of a camera that you've got hold of stands the solid blank unlikeliness of my having shot a guest and old friend of the family in order to pick his pocket? Had you not better at least *begin* with something less improbable and come back to me, you know, if all else fails?'

'I have to begin with what first significantly presents itself. And you rather pile on the unlikeliness. The murder of Lord Auldearn and the tapping or attempted tapping of the document may be matters essentially unconnected.'

Gervase stiffened. 'No doubt. And you want me for the tapping?'

'I want that camera. And if you don't fetch it I must fetch it myself.'

Gervase sprang to his feet in so evident a passion that Appleby found himself involuntarily bunching his fists. But there was no attack; with a noise that Noel likened to that of a sealion diving Gervase steadied himself. He walked to the far end of the room, turned, and spoke on the first stride back. 'Mr Appleby, on my coming in I spoke to you offensively. You're not a fool.' There was something about Gervase that made this admission an almost adequate apology for apostrophe as an imbecile baboon. 'No doubt you know your job and what you must go for. And surely you see that the ... matter you wish to discuss is probably irrelevant? Will you take my word as a gentleman that it is so?'

'Mr Crispin, you're wasting my time. I am aware of the probabilities but I can't deal in them yet. If I were investigating the loss of my own cheque-book I'd take your word at once. As it is –'

The sentence was never finished. Without warning the door flew open and Anna Merkalova swept into the room. 'Gervase,' she demanded tragically, 'have they found out?' And she tossed a small metallic object upon the bed.

Gott wondered if too much concentration on the Scamnum *Hamlet* was inclining him unwarrantably to assess things in terms of stage effect. The Merkalova's entrance had been excellent theatre. Noel, who had apparently decided for the time being to contemplate the distressing and confusing events of the night with all the aesthetic detachment which an editor of *Crucible* could command – Noel was obviously gratified by the turn the proceedings had taken. He twisted his neck to contemplate the exhibit which the Merkalova had cast on the bed and then straightened it to observe the more compelling exhibit of the Merkalova herself. She was not very adequately clothed. Perhaps she was content with the garment of psychic virginity piously attributed to her by Gott. But she had none of the appearance of one riven between Artemis and Aphrodite; she was a maturely and unambiguously attractive female, her Russian eye (thought Noel, quoting the poet) underlined for emphasis, and lit up, at the moment, with the most lovely intimations of passion. The lady, he said to himself, is about to throw a temperament.

'It's a sort of camera,' said Noel placidly into the momentary silence that had fallen upon the room.

What followed was not without its perplexities. The Merkalova's language – addressed to Appleby – was fortunately obscure; or obscure to all but Appleby, who happened to know some Russian. And the camera-business was obscure; Appleby took one step towards the bed, looked at the instrument – and smiled rather wryly. He turned to Gervase. 'Mr Crispin, I half-suspected this – until I felt no man would be obstinate enough to conceal anything so trivial. If my time has been wasted it has been wasted by you. You have played the donkey, sir.'

Noel sighed happily. Gott listened in some surprise to the urbane Appleby's apparently joining a slanging match. But in a moment he saw that the attitude turned on some shrewd reading of character. Gervase, after one indignant shout, was no longer an angry man. He gave a low guffaw of laughter and tumbled into a vein of extravagant humour. 'In fact, the fable of the donkey, the baboon, and' – his glance went to the still voluble lady – 'the humming-bird. ... Anna, for God's sake be quiet.'

Perhaps Gervase was brusque because he had been caught in what was essentially a chivalrous action, or perhaps that was the suggestion which – amid much *outré* humour – he was now contriving to establish. Gott, noting these alternatives for future consideration and wondering if Appleby were doing the same, eyed the tiny camera and listened to the chivalrous story. And certainly the two fitted together. The camera might be presumed capable of photographing documents, but that certainly was not the purpose for which it had been designed. The Duke had called it 'small'; actually – while being obviously an instrument of precision – it was a mere matchbox of a thing. In fact it was a spy's camera in a very special sense : the sort of camera with which audacious persons obtain for public gratification pictures of occasions too intimate, awful, or exalted for overt recording. Gott remembered a recent batch of such snapshots in a magazine : surprising glimpses of what had been called a 'cheery party for sub-debs'. And the smart journalizing Merkalova, desiring doubtless with laudable independence to earn her own guineas, had apparently adopted the not-laudable plan of introducing such a machine to profane the wholly decorous, but intriguing mysteries of the Scamnum *Hamlet*. There would be a handsome cheque in it and no particular mischief beyond a gross abuse of hospitality. So it was a likely enough tale. And so was Gervase's account of subsequent events. The Merkalova, thoroughly scared after the pistol-shot, had thrust the embarrassing apparatus upon him and begged him to get it away. He had realized what she had been about, foreseen the possibility of search, and taken the opportunity, incidental to his suggestion of visiting Auldearn's room, to throw the mildly incriminating object into his own. Later – and this was what the unfortunate Duke must have happened upon – he had thought it discreet to remove the film pack from the camera, chop it up, and put the fragments down a drain.

Thus Gervase's story, which he concluded with the vigorous symbolism of pulling an imaginary plug. And plainly the story had to be accepted, as Appleby had ingeniously accepted it before it was told. It covered the facts. And, as Gervase went on to point out in his own peculiar idiom, it covered the facts in a probable and almost prosaic way. 'I'm afraid, Mr Appleby,' he said with a grotesque gesture over his face, 'that it strips away the false whiskers and the sinister leer of the unscrupulous magnate. I suppose unscrupulous magnate was the phrase in your head? Well, well – the melodrama turns limp comedy. A pity ... such a damned good story it would have made – eh, Giles? But elderly back-benchers with drab City backgrounds just don't cut out for that sort of part. The whiskers sit awry on the blunt and honest face and the leer turns out to have been all in your own mind. And though Anna is quite the sinister Roosian –'

'She is nevertheless', Appleby took him up with a polite inclination to the lady, 'as English as you are; is that it?'

Evidently, it was not it. Gervase's expostulation was brief, the Merkalova's was sustained – but the indignation of both was extreme. Appleby made apologetic murmurs. He had been quite wrong in this as in the major issue, the matter was irrelevant anyway, everything had been explained. He made tentative movements as if to gather up Gott and Noel and leave the room. But the Merkalova had been touched in the vitals – with a nice economy, Gott felt – and now, very decidedly, she had something to work off. What it was emerged in a variety of the languages of Europe. But it was not philological interest in a virtuoso display of cosmopolitanism that caused Appleby to give some attention as the harangue progressed. It was the matter. How infamous – so ran the gist – and that the police should waste their energies trumping up a tale about Gervase carrying off a document and photographing it when a little inquiry would satisfy them of the guilt of somebody else. Whom else? Whom, of course, but the Sandys – *cette saligaude*! ... *Búrlak!*

A diversity of responses followed this outburst. In Gervase there was uncomfortableness and impatience, as if the wrong coda were being clapped on a hitherto well-constructed piece. Noel manifested rage as extreme as Gervase had been displaying some time before. Gott felt mild distress and traced it down to resolutely romantic views on what Bunney, he unjustly suspected, would call Woman's Higher Moral Number. But

Appleby's reaction was to frame particularly careful questions. 'Ah, yes,' he said: 'now we come to something important. Can you remember, please, exactly what Mr Cope said?'

It pulled the Merkalova up. 'Cope? ... *ce radoteur-là!* I know nothing of Cope, *Isprávink-Mudr'yónui.*'

'Then you saw the burning yourself?'

'*Akh! Bozhe moï!* Burning? *Aber geh ... n'en sais rein.* She was writing – she. Scribbling ... *no? Deprisa, ligera, heimlich, in piccolo ... no-no?* Secret writing – *bátiushki moi!* ... *Voilà la conduite qu'elle tient,* the smug pug, *salope!*' The Merkalova turned passionately to Gervase. '*Golubchik – próshol! ... Proshtchaï!*'

And having delivered herself of this reckless linguistic grand tour the Merkalova swept from the room with a final '*Ukh!*' followed by a dubious Gervase and a resolved Noel. Gott and Appleby were left as they had been – lords of Gervase's ravished apartment.

Gott looked at his watch. 'A grain of comfort', he said, 'lies in the unfaltering approach of the Scamnum breakfast. But what do you make of all that? And why was the lady so angry when you doubted her true-blue hyperborean blood?'

Appleby got up. 'As you say, breakfast. Now I wonder –?' He disappeared into the bathroom and emerged a minute later lathering his face with two fingers and brandishing one of Gervase's razors. 'Must keep smart for your friends, Giles. Well, as we were saying – did you look at the lady's legs?'

Gott raised an austere eyebrow. 'They were certainly there to be looked at,' he said.

'You didn't find them suggestive?'

'My dear John!'

'Think of Degas, Giles. And moonlight and muslin.'

'Ballet!'

'Yes. The Merkalova's past is in ballet. You remember the only juryman to laugh at Serjeant Buzfuz's joke about greasing the defendant's wheels in *Bardell Against Pickwick*?' Appleby could be like this when excited – or baffled. 'He laughed because he'd greased his own chaise-cart that morning. I spotted the Merkalova – that turned-out stance of hers – because I've just come from ballet. And I happen to have enough Russian to notice that her Russian is just two streets ahead of mine. I expect she was in the Imperial Schools for a bit before the war. And – as a point of minor psychological curiosity – I expect her profession explains old Sir Richard What's-his-name's puzzlement over the happy couple's love-life. Ballet people are a species by themselves, getting all the common relations of life a bit odd.' Carefully – for strange razors are tricky things – Appleby finished shaving. 'But where are we, Giles? Where are we now?'

Gott looked at his watch again. 'For one thing, we're at five-fifteen. And our other whereabouts are up to you. I should put them at the moment as somewhere between pillar and post. Where are we, indeed, with Gervase and the Sandys and Cope and Happy Hutton and Timothy Tucker –'

'Who's Timothy Tucker?'

'One of the dozen or so exhibits not yet shown.'

Appleby waved Mr Timothy Tucker aside. 'Order,' he said; 'method; the little grey cells! Or in other words we are where we are and have to begin from there. Now Gervase –'

'Haven't we moved – or been moved – on to the Sandys? Are you not hurrying after her at once?'

'I think that's what your Noel's doing, and she'll keep for a little as far as I'm concerned. Hold on to Gervase for a moment and give me your estimate. Imagine yourself editing a text in your own learned way. There's a disputed reading. One variant is: "Gervase's story of the Merkalova sneaking photographs of Scamnum celebrities for gossip-papers is true." And the other variant is: "Gervase was after the document either with this camera or another, and his story represents either a planned get-away or a brilliant improvisation." Now bring all your knowledge to bear and attempt a numerical estimate of the probabilities involved.' Appleby, though putting the matter in this odd way, was obviously wholly serious.

Gott considered. 'Allowing pretty generous weight to everything against Gervase – a certain pat quality about the Merkalova's appearance, for instance, that may well have been fortuitous – allowing that I should still put the odds at about forty to one in favour of Gervase's story being the true reading.'

'I was going to say fifteen. But it's impressive odds at either estimate, particularly if you remember the first effect on us of the Duke's disclosure about the camera. Anyway, as soon as I saw that snapshot-snooping toy I knew there was no further pushing that way; the story would be watertight. The long chance remains and all we can do is to note it and look elsewhere. But pushing the spies into limbo again, what about an estimate of Gervase simply as a murderer?'

'An impossible question. Almost anyone *might* murder. Ten to one against might be a rough assessment of my feelings. But if, as you say, we shelve the long chance of Gervase doing spy-work and still look for spy-work *somewhere* it seems to me we are up against the Sandys as a last chance? But the situation's safe. The evidence suggests that she contrived to scribble an abstract of the document – a desperately difficult thing to manage, I should imagine – and was then forced to destroy it under threat of search.'

'That's the story. But – without knowing the Sandys – I'm inclined to see her less as a possible principal than as a possible inspiration.'

'Possible what?'

'Inspiration,' repeated Appleby innocently. 'And that would, of course, lead us back to recasting the odds.'

Gott sighed. 'I think', he said, 'I'll go and have a bath.'

'You'll be the brighter for it,' said Appleby cheerily.

8

RESOLVED but apprehensive, Noel paused for respite at the first turning of the stair. He flung up a window and surveyed the world. It was undeniably the familiar world – the world on which, rising early to canter on Horton Down, he had flung up his own bedroom window just twenty-four hours before. In the farther park two textures of moving grey were sorting themselves out: mist drifting, eddying, dispersing; sheep beginning to move in the dewy feed. Already the day declared its season; already the scent of the syringas, heavy as orange-blossom, was blowing up from the gardens. The hubbub dawn-chorus had thinned to distinguishable notes: willow-warblers monotonously tumbling downstairs, chaffinches as unvaryingly revving-up, and suspense provided only by the wrens, who pleased themselves as to whether or not they should add answer to question. And dominating and insistent, as if he were aware that a fortnight, a week now might command him to silence, the cuckoo called from the oak woods. To Noel, who associated birds – a few moorland varieties apart – with clerkly nature-lovers and girl-guides, these effects came confusedly. But as mere massive sensation their familiarity disturbed him and he looked round almost anxiously for sign of change.

It was there. It was there in a curl of smoke rising – a full hour early – in the middle distance: Mrs Manley at the south lodge, aware that the skies had fallen and determined to face the unknown with the day's routine well forward. It was there – more obviously – in patrolling policemen. It was there in a little group of people toiling hastily up the brow of Horton Hill: a gesticulating person in front and behind a knot of persons with impedimenta – cameras, this time, of the cinematographic and telescopic sort. And it was there – had Noel known it – in the couple of cars that flashed over the visible rise of the Horton road: the press making hell-for-leather for Scamnum Court. And it was there – again if he had known it – in the farthest puff of white on the horizon. For that was the express hurtling the London dailies south and west, all with the Scamnum story in two inches of smeared red – or all save the *Despatch-Record*, whose news editor, having pushed his stop-press button with some extra minutes to spare before going to bed, had built in a flaming streamer that became Fleet Street talk for days.

Noel leant out further inches, automatically estimated the possibility of spitting on a policeman's helmet below, and then turned his eyes sharp right along the east façade. In the remote distance he could just discern a fugitive line of blue. 'The sea', he chanted, 'lay laughing at a distance. . . .' He waved to the astonished constable below. 'And in the meadows and the lower grounds was all the sweetness of a common dawn.' And having keyed himself up in this fashion Noel slammed down the window, bounded up the remaining stairs and knocked briskly at Diana Sandys's door.

' 'Llo,' said Diana. She was sitting up in bed with a gold pencil behind her ear, and eating chocolates. 'Come in.' She looked rather uncertainly at her visitor. 'You can climb on the bed,' she said firmly.

Noel climbed on the foot of the bed. There was a pause that would have been embarrassing if both Noel and Diana had not known that one was *not* embarrassed. 'I'll call it a night,' said Noel presently.

'One helluva night.' Diana's idiom was at times affected. The Terborgs would have disliked it.

'Hasn't etiolated you, though,' said Noel politely.

'Hasn't *what*? Have a chocolate.'

'Give sickly hue to person.' Noel took a large chocolate and bit into it. 'I say, Diana –' Then he changed his mind and returned to the chocolates. 'I've always been told that women devoured these things in secret – particularly the ethereal kind that shudders away from the honest thrice-daily public trough. But wenches naturally tending to plump out –'

'They're nauseous things!' said Diana fretfully. With her right hand she stretched out for another; with her left she beat out a tattoo on the soles of Noel's beautiful green slippers. 'It's only that I've got to sell them.'

'Sell them?'

'They're coming out in August and I've *got* to sell them. And I've got three boxes here and before the rumpus I meant to get one of those Terborg girls in a sunny corner and eat them all with her. To get the feel of it.'

Noel stared at her blankly. 'Feel of it – and wouldn't I do?'

'No, you wouldn't,' said Diana, becoming animated. 'Not the way I'm analysing it out. Do you know the chief difference between chocolates and tobacco?'

'If it's a riddle I give it up. But look here, Diana. Something frightfully –'

'It's like this. Tobacco – except snob-cigarettes – is nearly always sold homosexually – Chaps Together, you know. Or occasionally one builds on the over-compensated Oedipus – Dad Advises Sonny-boy. But chocolates are quite invariably sold heterosexually – Boy Brings Girl Box. But with these I'm going to try Women Together. Women stuffing them after *tête à tête* teas, women clutching half-pounds at chummy matinées. And I'm going to have them called the Sappho Assortment. A good name, I think; splashy and prodigal associations, exotic word, and yet difficult to mispronounce –'

'First rate,' said Noel with dubious heartiness. Noel thought Diana wonderful. Part of him thought the wonder to consist specifically in her adherence to the Newer Womanhood; but part of him – the part representing, perhaps, the tutelage of Mr Gott – sometimes saw this as being on the contrary the snag And, finding this business-as-usual attitude disturbing, he canalized his dubieties into a minor channel and said: 'But I don't know about pronouncing. I rather think you'll have female dons – all tense and arm in arm, no doubt, as you want – going to their favourite sweet-shop and asking for *Sap-foh*.'

Diana made a note. 'I'll go into it. But there will have to be snob-appeal too. Boy Brings Girl Box runs much further down the income-levels than Women Stuff Box Together. I shall be going for the eight-room-upwards public, which means they must sell at a higher price than they intended. Have one of the twirly ones.'

'If they charge more will they improve the quality?' Noel was interested in this irrelevant business of the Sappho Assortment despite himself.

'Cut down on it, possibly.'

'Oh,' said Noel – and added: 'Not very honest?'

'Most contrariwise. And not good policy. Half our troubles come from pious Victorian-minded manufacturers who think they can take the quality out of the product if they're putting it into the advertising. But that sort eliminates itself. It's inefficient.'

'Good,' said Noel. It sounded like a sort of feeble moral fervour. There was an awkward pause, during which Diana ceased fiddling with the slippers. 'Sleep well after the shambles?' Noel asked.

'Didn't have a shot at it. I've been trying to remember something and get it down on paper ... what are you jumping at?'

'Jumping? Dunno. Pretty awful end to the play, wasn't it?'

'Bloody. I can't bear to think of it. And I can't even get my mind to planning out these dam' chocolates.'

Diana, it occurred to Noel, was in her present phase remarkably a person of one idea. And suddenly he seemed to see, very far away, possible light. Carefully, he located Diana's big-toe beneath the blanket and secured it firmly between finger and thumb. 'I say,' he said, 'how do you really like it?'

'Nix – it's marzipan. And I've told you they're *all* nauseous. But one has to discover what it feels like to be full of Sappho Assortment –'

'I don't mean that. I mean all the racket; the lone girl's career.'

'Oh!' Diana turned up a childlike but resolute chin. 'It's no sort of Sweet Seventeen affair. And it's not like being a duke or a don or a black-beetle; you don't stretch down comfortable roots into the job. And the line of talk you deal in wouldn't make the best illustrative matter for a treatise on the Beautiful and the True. In fact it would be a poor life if the pace weren't so snappy; that's what makes it fun. It's a dog-fight and you're on top only as long as you produce tip-top copy six days a week. No room for amiable inefficiency in national advertising – it costs too much per inch. If you go stale and your copy turns lousy – out you go.' Diana scrutinized Noel's face and was prompted to add: 'I'm not out yet. And remember I was kept in hygienic wrappers at expensive schools until I was twenty and now I'm twenty-two and pulling twelve pounds a week. While you're a twenty-three-year-old caterpillar on the commonwealth still. So there.'

Noel after some search found the companion big-toe. 'Get on top of you ever?' he asked cautiously. 'Ruling passion, fixed idea – that sort of thing?'

Diana regarded him apprehensively. 'Please stop playing at being a crab – two crabs,' she said; 'I suspect it of being a morbid form of Bedside Manner. And why this indecorous visit at all?'

Unhappily, Noel let go the toes. 'Well, you see, I thought I'd better tell you. You know there was something missing – or thought missing – or tapped or something? And that that's why there was a search? Well, there's a story got about – the police have it – that you –'

'Noel,' said Diana abruptly, 'draw the curtains and let in Sol.'

Noel did as he was told and returned chanting with unreal ease:

> *'Busy old fool, unruly Sun,*
> *Why dost thou thus,*
> *Through windows, and through curtains call on us?*
> *Must to thy motions lovers' seasons ...'*

'Why, Diana!'

Diana was crying. And Noel was as alarmed as if he had been confronted with a woman in process of cutting her throat, or one fallen suddenly into childbirth. 'Oh, I say ...' he mumbled.

Between sobs Diana said: 'Such a helluva show-down ... up ... down. I wish I was beastly dead!'

'Diana – Diana darling. . . .'

But Diana's extravagant woe had to spend itself. Presently she stopped and without pausing for handkerchief or powder-puff asked: 'Noel, will these awful policemen know about my job ... will they?'

'Well, I expect so. You see Appleby – that's the man from London – is getting case-histories and thumb-nail sketches from Grandpa Gott.'

'And they'll want to know ... what it was?'

'Perhaps – in general terms. It was suspicious, you see. Writing and then consigning to flames when search impended. Quite *à la manière de la main noire*. And the police mind –' He floundered unhappily. 'Let me wipe your eyes. . . . Perhaps if you told me – vaguely, I mean – and I passed it on quietly. This Appleby's a decent chap – gentleman – and it appears quite a familiar of Gott's. And, for that matter, he's likely enough to have guessed. Alpha brain.'

Diana took no comfort in the quality of Mr Appleby's breeding or brain. But she said: 'Yes, I'll tell you, Noel ... emetic process ... probably good for the system. Get a bit of scribbling paper from the table.

Diana scribbled. And as the scribble grew Noel firmly improved on the toes. 'I see,' he said at last. 'Quite enormously ingenious – Diana, you're frightfully clever! But certainly not comfortable to be found with amid the sorrowing friends afterwards. . . . Never mind.'

'You see,' said Diana miserably, 'one learns to squeeze an idea out of everything. It's a rule that just everything that happens must be squeezed. ... Of course that poor old man doesn't come into it. It was just the general idea of violent death that gave me the notion ... and it *is* a new tie-up ... with gangster magazines, action fiction ... just the public for the product, too! And I felt I just *had* to get it down. But of all foul inspirations to be caught having –' She paused at the sound of footsteps in the corridor. 'Noel, is that the flatties?'

'I expect it is.'

'Lock the door.'

Noel obeyed. A moment later there was a knock and Diana called out: 'Is that the policeman?'

'Yes, madam.'

'You can't come in. It's indecorous. Besides' – Diana felt Noel's arm about her and her spirits rose outrageously – 'I have a gentleman here already.'

'Madam, I would not presume. One question only: last night – did you happen to engage in any abortive professional activity?'

Diana gritted her teeth. 'Yes,' she said, 'I certainly did.'

'Thank you.'

The footsteps retreated. 'He's gone!' said Diana.

Noel scrambled to the floor. He crumpled up the scribbling paper. 'Must be pushing too. No hacking about today, I'm afraid; looks like being prisoners within the moated grange. But there's always squash.'

•

In the corridor outside the hall Murdo Macdonald had sat, motionless and vigilant, for a space of hours. Now he stiffened. The door had opened from within; the constable on guard stood aside; a little procession emerged – stretcher-bearers, under the directions of a sergeant, bringing out the body of Lord Auldearn. Macdonald stood up, drew into what remained of early-morning shadow in an alcove and bent his head as bearers and burden went slowly past. His lowered eyes were watchful beneath their heavy brows. Some yards down the corridor the sergeant halted and called back to the constable by the door; the constable moved towards him as if to receive a message. Macdonald glided into noiseless and rapid motion. Though elderly he was spare and agile; in a moment he had darted from shadow to shadow and gained the hall. He looked rapidly round. No one was visible; only the constable outside, returning to the door, might look inside as he closed it. Macdonald ran to the front stage, clambered up, and had gone to earth down the Ghost's trap before he heard the door shut on the apparently untenanted hall. So far – good.

For a full minute Macdonald crouched unmoving in the darkness beneath the low stage. Then he began to make the laborious progress which Dr Crump had rejected – subterraneously behind-scenes. He emerged close by the back curtains of the rear stage – again undetected – and slipped within the double folds. 'Dinna fash,' he murmured to himself. 'A wee bittock luck an' ye'll get awa' wi' it in a' preevacy!' He tiptoed to a parting of the curtains and peered through to the rear stage. A constable was standing guard, wearily but efficiently. Macdonald's eye roved over the little stage. Then he retreated and looked out the other way. There appeared to be a clear field to the green-room – a rectangular, match-boarded structure a dozen paces away. He emerged, stepped out towards it boldly and was presently surveying it from the somewhat precarious shelter of a curtained doorway. The green-room too was guarded by a constable. Macdonald eyed him warily and then once more began to cast about, scanning the litter of properties and effects scattered around the room. Presently his gaze concentrated itself in a corner, and then turned to the guardian policeman again with something like desperation. 'Ten to yin it's either that or the Assize,' he muttered in perplexity – and felt a tap on the shoulder.

'Now then, what are you after and how did you get here?'

Macdonald turned round to confront a highly suspicious Sergeant Trumpet. But he seemed at no loss. 'Get here? I walkit in by the faur door.'

'The far door . . . nonsense! It's guarded.'

Macdonald shook his impressive head. 'Yin o' you laddies was clacking wi' your sairgint up the corridor a wee. But the door was open and I walkit in. I'm for my horrn.'

'Your what?'

'I'm for my snuff-horrn. Somebody coupt a cup of coffee when I had the horrn in my haun' and I put the horrn by tae tak up the coupit cup and disremembered it.'

Sergeant Trumpet was incensed. 'And you think you can come skulking about after a peck of snuff as though there hadn't been murder done? Don't you know that murder –'

'Laddie,' said Macdonald, 'Murdo Macdonald needs no sairmon frae you on the weight o' the Sixth Commaun'ment. But twa' oonces o' Kendal Broon bides twa' oonces o' Kendal Broon. And in my graun'-faither's horrn foreby! We'll look th'gither.'

They looked together. But no snuff-horn was found.

*

Charles Piper, towelling after an early shower, had retreated hastily from the bathroom on hearing the approaching footsteps of Giles Gott. Now he was doing his exercises in the security of his own room and feeling – as active young novelists must often feel – the want of several brains to pursue simultaneously the variety of thoughts which battled for the single organ he possessed. Pursue one idea with concentration and you so easily lose all the others for good – hundreds of potential words, proper for elegant embodiment in Timothy Tucker's characteristic fount, whirled fatally into limbo.

First, he had a thought – a chronic thought this – about thinking during the exercises. If you don't (he thought) concentrate on the exercises they don't work. Labourers, though they exercise their muscles all day, fail to develop beautiful bodies because they don't concentrate their minds on the idea of harmonious muscular development. Then stop thinking (thought Piper to himself) during the deep breathing; concentrate on the breathing *qua* breathing; picture, perhaps, the mysterious cavities of the lungs – spongy, soot-lined, slowly filling out, slowly sinking. Perhaps one could really see them if one tried very hard; hysterical people could see their insides ... and the surrealists. But let the mind rest. Simply contemplate through the open window the fluid line of Horton Hill – itself rhythmical as a good exercise – and count: *one – two – three*.

There was a crowd of people up there, a crowd that was an

abrupt reminder of the gruesome term that had been put to the Scamnum *Hamlet* ... Gott's *Hamlet*. And Gott offered another train of thought. What reason could be put forward to himself for retreating from Gott in the bathroom? Perhaps he felt uneasy now at having discussed the man's absurd hobby with him the other morning. It must, when one thought of it, be an uncomfortable position, this finding himself involved in an extravagant actualization of his own species of fantasy. Rather like a surprised Pygmalion receiving undesired advances from his Galatea ... the image was not bad. Or perhaps he had retreated from the bathroom because he felt a little awkward on his own account? Had he not made rather naïve remarks about his own willingness to plunge into a sort of blood and thunder existence if it should turn up in real life – to accept a stray embrace from the other man's Galatea, in fact? Something about being ready to play pass-the-buck if confronted with a corpse and something about a hankering after picturesque international intrigue – that was what he had said. And it had been very foolish; such conversation was quite embarrassingly foolish in retrospect – reminiscent of the vaguely sinister remarks which everyone had to make in turn, no doubt, near the beginning of *Murder at the Zoo*. Piper swung up and down – touching his toes, sometimes getting the palms of his hands almost flat on the floor – and Horton Hill swung up and down outside like a green sea across a rolling port-hole.

There was a knock at the door.

It had been Melville Clay's habit to stroll across the corridor while dressing and consume, amid desultory talk, Piper's neglected and tepid morning tea. But this morning tea was still an hour off and Clay, like Piper, was newly bathed. He was in beautiful black and white: white slippers, black pyjamas, black dressing-gown with an exaggeratedly robust white cord – and his face almost hidden behind a mass of white lather. 'How now, Horatio!' he articulated with odd clarity through the soap, 'you tremble and look pale: is not this something more than fantasy?'

'Pale?' said Piper pettishly but apprehensively – his face was red from the toe-touching – 'nonsense! Though I've had a shocking night.'

'Never mind. Good copy. Do Gott's stuff straight from life now. As they say – more than fantasy.'

This sentiment – delivered somewhat in the manner of Clay's departed colleague, Mr Jingle – hit disconcertingly on one of the thoughts. The reactions of all these people to sensational and mysterious murder would make good watching in the immediate future. But Piper felt the suggestion of copy must be snubbed as unseemly. He continued doggedly at a gesticulating exercise by the window and allowed a minute to elapse before he said briefly : 'A horrid business.'

'Horrid.' Clay had moved over to the other window and begun to shave. He was, Piper thought, a beautiful creature – with the proud bodily beauty that comes from heaven and not from a system of exercises. Perhaps he had a feminine streak – the little silver mirror he had taken from his pocket was too elegant; his deft movement as he caught the light with it under chin and nostril was too much that of a conscious beauty. Piper reflected rather jealously that he had no feminine streak himself – an invaluably informative thing to have.

'You know, you are quite extraordinarily beautiful,' said Piper, by way of conscientious experiment.

As experiment it was ill-timed; Clay might have blushed like a girl or he might not – the lather still obscured him. 'Ah, yes,' he said indifferently, 'one grows that way when one's bread and butter's in it. And rather showy too. Public means which public manners breeds. I'd as soon be out of it.'

Piper eyed him curiously. 'You haven't been in it long. You've risen like a rocket.'

'Soon to decline, perhaps, like a falling star. There may be copy in me too.'

Piper ignored the reiterated jest. 'But what', he said, 'do you think of all this?'

'I think' – Clay had finished shaving and turned to look out of the window – 'it's already a first-class sensation, if one may judge by that crowd on the hill.'

'Pretty morbid, isn't it – turning out just to stare? And they've been mighty quick.'

'Oh, that's not what they're about; that lot's still to come. I guess these are Press people, training all sorts of ingenious cameras on us at this moment. Good publicity – Mr Charles Piper doing remedial exercises at his window shortly after the fatality.'

Piper drew hastily back. 'Disgusting!' he said – with some reminiscence of Mrs Platt-Hunter-Platt. 'But I've hardly got the hang of what's happened yet. What was the search supposed to be about? Was someone supposed to be hiding a revolver?'

'I think something had been stolen – from the body.'

'Robbery!'

'I rather gathered from something the Duke let fall – robbery of a special sort. A secret document – that sort of thing.'

'Spies!'

'Exactly.' Clay looked lazily at Piper. 'Again not in your line, I suppose? The missing treaty. Sort of contemporary version of cloak and sword adventure, you know.'

Piper almost jumped. It was the identical silly phrase he had used to Gott. Slightly fussily he began to get out his own shaving things. 'I wonder', he said vaguely, 'who did it?'

'I didn't,' said Clay.

•

David Malloch lowered stiff legs from footstool to floor as the little tray was set down beside him. The footman looked without curiosity at the unruffled bed – there was nothing remarkable in anyone's having done without sleep that night – crossed to the window, drew back curtains, raised the blind. He went out at the other door; in a moment there was the sound of running water; an eddy of steam drifted into the bedroom. Still Malloch did not move. His hands, fingers extended, lay Pharaoh-like along the arms of his chair; his mouth might have been hewn in basalt; his eyes were fixed and sightless as eyes that gaze out over Karnac or Memphis.

The man came out of the bathroom, moved towards the door. 'There is no change in the hour of breakfast, sir.'

Malloch inclined his head and the man went away. For a long time there was neither sound nor movement in the room; next door the water ran unchecked. Presently Malloch's eyes, staring through the window as if across some vista of desert, faltered and changed focus. He got painfully to his feet – it was breaking the posture of hours – and moved slowly across the room. From the centre of the white blind, in silhouette against the light, hung a slender cord and silken tassel. He took the cord in his hands, looped it, thrust the head of the tassel within the loop. The head tilted to a macabre angle: it was a manikin that he held suspended in a little silken noose. For a moment his mouth tightened another shade; then he tossed the tassel lightly in the air and it fell to its normal position, straight and free. He turned and hurried to his bath.

3

DÉNOUEMENT

See you now;
Your bait of falsehood take this carp of truth:
And thus do we of wisdom and of reach,
With windlasses and with assays of bias,
By indirections find directions out.

1

ONCE more Appleby stood on the rear stage. Here, he knew, lurked the heart of the mystery; as often as he moved from this spot, so often he was in danger of losing himself in a maze of irrelevant or subsidiary detail. Here, during Act Three, Scene Four of an amateur performance of *Hamlet*, Lord Auldearn had died. This was the one fact; as yet all else was speculation. And the fact was of an extraordinary fascination. To begin with, it was bizarre – almost as bizarre as any criminal act he could remember. And the place and the victim – Scamnum, a Lord Chancellor of England – gave it a colouring alien to mere police news, threw over it a half-light of history that was not without its own beguilement for an imaginative mind.

But it was the technical problem that was absorbing. What could one get from the specific way in which the thing had happened? The odd locale, the dramatic moment – were these things a structural part, so to speak, of Auldearn's murder, or were they decorative merely? Gott had talked of feeling behind the catastrophe the working of a mind theatrically obsessed; a mind outlandishly absorbed, over and above any practical motive for murder, in the contriving of an astonishing effect. And certainly it would be hard to deny at least an element of mere display in the circumstances surrounding the deed. The threatening messages of the preceding days could only be interpreted as a preliminary flourish of melodrama, a prologue to the melodrama being prepared within the framework of the Scamnum *Hamlet*. And that framework had been itself more simply melodramatic, apparently, than modern *Hamlets* commonly are. The show of violence ... and then a show of violence within the show.

The show of violence ... in the small hours Gott had quoted the context of that – a speech by Marcellus when the guard had tried to stay the Ghost:

> *We do it wrong, being so majestical,*
> *To offer it the show of violence;*
> *For it is, as the air, invulnerable,*
> *And our vain blows malicious mockery.*

You can't beat Shakespeare, thought Appleby irrelevantly – and for a minute his mind strayed over what he could remember of that tremendous opening scene – the scene in which they bring the sceptical young student Horatio to confront the uncanny thing that walks the battlements of Elsinore at night:

> *How now, Horatio! you tremble and look pale:*
> *Is not this something more than fantasy?*

More than fantasy ... that was the next point. Was there something more than a mere effort after fantastic effect behind the manner of Auldearn's murder? Had it been exactly so because, for some reason, it had to be exactly so? By every conceivable theory save one – the theory implicating Cope 'aloft' – the deed had been extraordinarily hazardous. Was that hazardousness gratuitous – something accepted, it might be said, for fun – or had it been accepted after calculation as necessary to some specific end? The murder of Bose was evidence here. For Bose's murderer had dragged the body of his victim with a crazy bravado down a long corridor, known to be tenanted, in order to pitch it wantonly on Auldearn's threshold – and Appleby's. Bose had been murdered, almost certainly, because he *knew* – or almost knew; his murder was a crime of calculation and prudence. But to swift and efficient action had been added this grace-note of pure sensationalism: the body had been moved, at great risk, for the single pleasure, apparently, of securing a momentary effect. Might there be a similar mingling of motive, then, in Auldearn's murder? Had the deed itself been rational, directed to some practical end, and the hazards accompanying the specific manner of its accomplishment been accepted for the sake of added melodramatic colour? Or had – conceivably – the melodrama been all, an end in itself; had the effect been the sole motive; had the whole thing been the resultant of some ghastly perversion of aesthetic instinct?

Or – third and final possibility – was Auldearn's murder rational through and through; had there been – once again – cold reason for every hazard? These were the questions, it seemed to Appleby, which lay at the centre of the case. What, then, of the business of the document?

It was very difficult to connect the facts he had been considering with any designs upon the Pike and Perch paper. Spies, he had agreed with Gott, do not go about their work to an accompaniment of threatening messages. They rarely shoot; they very rarely shoot eminent statesmen; positively, they do not shoot in circumstances which make their chances of subsequent successful theft exceedingly tenuous. Even if spies had broken into the safe in Auldearn's room and, having drawn blank, concluded that the paper they wanted was on his person – even so, and even supposing them prepared for desperate measures, they would hardly have chosen to shoot when and where Auldearn had been shot – at excessive risk and in a hall that could instantly be sealed like a strong-room. And there was no reason to suppose that it had been spies who cracked Auldearn's safe. Three safes in all, it had turned out, had been cracked and Happy Hutton was in all probability responsible. Indeed – once more Appleby came back to this – there was no reason to suppose the presence of spies at all – except for the intercepted message which Hilfers had reported. Save for that the spy-theory had its sole origin in the Duke's first alarm. That alarm had been reasonable, but it had been based on no positive evidence beyond the cracked safe and the unsuccessful search of Auldearn's body. And when the document had turned up – in a sufficiently ingenious hiding-place – that alarm had been allayed. Gott had revived it with his startling leap upon the possible significance of Bose's photographic brain. Then the Duchess had dissipated that possibility; Bose was *not* a spy, nor the kind that makes a spy. After that there had been two further alarms: the Duke's alarm over Gervase, Cope's and the Merkalova's alarm over Diana Sandys. But if Miss Sandys – and it seemed next to impossible – had contrived to copy the document before Bose discovered it, she had subsequently had to destroy her notes and no harm was done. Besides, which, there was a perfectly reasonable explanation of her conduct to which Appleby, who knew something of advertising people, had jumped at once. And Gervase and the Merkalova, similarly, had a perfectly reasonable if equally embarrassing story. Only one thing gave Appleby pause here; he had mentioned it – with a mischievous obliqueness – to Gott.

There was a slightly disturbing coincidence between the two

stories – the Merkalova's and Diana's. Both ladies had been pursuing an essentially innocent, but nevertheless uncomfortable professional activity: the Merkalova taking press-photographs on the quiet; Diana getting down a commercially-useful suggestion which had been prompted, presumably, by some aspect of the murder in the hall. It was not a startling coincidence; nevertheless it was something on which to pause. Suppose that Gervase or the Merkalova had detected Diana making professional hay, so to speak, by the lurid glow of Auldearn's murder: might this not have suggested to them their own story when they came to feel that a story might have to be put up? But at most this was to say that to Gervase and the Merkalova there still clung some fragment of suspicion: with the Merkalova's or another camera the document might have been photographed after all. And it seemed to Appleby that while this one conceivable channel did remain, he must maintain his blockade of Scamnum; or maintain it, at least, until he had positive orders from the Prime Minister himself to desist. Again there was no evidence; nothing but suspicion – and his suspicions of Gervase Crispin as a spy continued to be tenuous. If the Merkalova had appeared at moments to be putting up a set show – and this was the only point of significance he could find – that might well be because she was, just as much as Melville Clay, a creature of the stage.

All of which was not to say that the spies had no probable existence. Appleby was less disposed than Gott had been to dismiss Hilfers's report as unreliable. That there had been spies about he believed – and one of them had doubtless sent away an over-sanguine message. But the spies represented a different thread from the murder – just as there was a third thread in Happy Hutton. These three threads might not be tied up with each other at all; were probably quite without significant interconnexions. Happy Hutton, indeed, appeared the merest sideshow. He had wormed himself into Scamnum, cracked three safes, left a bowler-hat – and left no other mark on the case. But the spies, though their presence might have been ineffective in the end, had complicated the whole affair – had already given a peculiar twist to the conduct of it.

Appleby had abundantly gathered that for the Prime Minister

the safety of the document was an issue to which even the apprehending of Auldearn's murderer came second. And he had placed it first himself; was still proposing to maintain elaborate precautions over it. But, in point of the murder, it was a distorting factor in the investigation, a red herring. And now Scamnum spies were fading fast into ineffectiveness – and six hours were gone since Appleby had arrived on the scene. On the business of the document he had gone – as Gott had hinted – from pillar to post and it was impossible to tell what he had missed that he would not have missed had his attention been concentrated on the single issue of murder. Now, given the maintenance of the blockade and a careful watch on Gervase and the Merkalova, he could concentrate on that issue in security. And the first step to the finding of Auldearn's and Bose's murderer would be a careful sifting of movements among that unwieldy crowd of backstage suspects – Gott's twenty-seven suspects together with old Max Cope 'aloft'.

So Appleby paced the little stage, reviewing a tolerable confusion of materials and planning the morning's attack upon them. He was interrupted by Sergeant Trumpet, who brought news of difficulty with Scamnum's awakening domestic staff. You may isolate some two hundred people without much inconvenience during the hours of the night, but in the morning what of the butter, the milk, and the eggs; what of those outdoor servants who came into the servants' hall for meals; what of the bevy of chauffeurs at the Scamnum Arms who would expect breakfast in the steward's room; what of the guests, not involved in the play, who would presently be proposing to pack? The last question, obviously, was one for the Duke when he should be available : the others Appleby resolved to turn to the solution of himself. He would hold the blockade rigidly if possible till noon, by which time he should be able to report comprehensively to, and get further instructions from, London. Meantime it was simply a matter of organization; butter and eggs and chauffeurs must come in and nothing must go out. Appleby went in search of Bagot, whom he supposed the fountain-head of authority of Scamnum's menial affairs.

Bagot was already performing his first duty of the day – superintending the arrangement of a little ocean of silver on the breakfast-table. He was a silvery and ineffective old person – rather more like a domestic chaplain, Appleby thought, than a butler – and extremely bewildered. And in his bewilderment he was inclined to retreat on an anxious maintenance of Scamnum customs and forms. Of course he could go round with Appleby and arrange effective police supervision of all comings and goings in the offices. But he ventured to think it might really be Mr Rauth's province. Would the inspector see Mr Rauth? Mr Rauth had risen; indeed, Bagot had just seen him in his room – Mr Rauth never, of course, left his room – and he was very upset, exceedingly so. The inspector had better, perhaps, remember that Mr Rauth was exceedingly upset.

Very naturally, agreed Appleby – and asked to be directed to Mr Rauth, whom he conjectured to be someone in the exalted position of a house-steward or major-domo. A footman conducted him; nothing easier than to find old Mr Rauth, he said, because Mr Rauth *never* left his room – had never been known to. But everyone had his own idea of what you might call a life, he supposed – and tapped respectfully on a door.

Mr Rauth, certainly, had all the appearance of a picturesque recluse: he was lank and dim and dusty, with a sort of peering stoop and the gentle voice of one who for long has communed only with abstractions. But he was distinguished, suggesting a librarian, perhaps, or an eminent antiquarian bookseller. And somehow one guessed that here was the very hub of Scamnum and that in the extreme neatness of the clerical paraphernalia by which he was surrounded was symbolized that virtuoso efficiency which made Scamnum among other things a great smooth-running machine. Behind Mr Rauth – around Mr Rauth – one sensed the accumulated experience of generations on the job.

'Yes?' said Mr Rauth. 'Yes. . . .?' He shambled forward, peering up at the visitor. Then he shook his head. 'No, sir, no. I really couldn't do it. Science may be science, sir, and cooperation cooperation; but this morning No. I am too upset.'

Having an active mind, Appleby presently realized that he was being taken for the philologically zealous Dr Bunney – doubtless notorious below stairs since his treatment of Bagot. Laboriously he explained himself and Mr Rauth at length understood. But the only immediate result was that Mr Rauth removed his glasses, polished them, and reiterated: 'I am very Upset.' The voice was gentle but its weight was great. Mysteriously, every sentence of Mr Rauth's had an august and solemn close.

'A great shock,' said Appleby, paying a timely tribute to the proprieties before getting on.

Mr Rauth at last looked at his visitor approvingly. 'As you say, a great Shock. Such a thing has not happened here – if my memory is sound – 'for Years.' He returned his glasses to his nose – or rather his nose to his glasses, with a disconcerting ducking motion. 'Of course,' he said, 'I know that it is often Done. I know that sort of thing Occurs. As a general thing, we cannot Deny It.'

Appleby looked at Mr Rauth a little blankly. He hardly seemed a helpful ally; one might almost suspect that he had indulged the whim of never leaving his room to a point which had endangered his sanity. 'Of course,' said Mr Rauth, 'it is the younger people who Do These Things. One hears Stories. There was the venison party at Hutton Beechings. There was the grassy corner pudding at poor Sir Hubert Tiplady's. One acknowledges the Fact.'

'The fact?' said Appleby. Scamnum, it seemed, always had a trick up its sleeve with which to overwhelm one. This was more unnerving by a long way than Max Cope.

'But,' said Mr Rauth, his voice mysteriously diminishing in volume as it gained in emphasis, 'here there is always ample provision made. Two bath olivers, two rich tea, and two digestive in every room. Replenished daily and changed three times a week. The bath olivers go to Mr Bagot – he has a Partiality for Them – and the others to the servants' hall. I am Dumbfounded. And at the very moment when there has been a death almost in the Family! I am more than dumbfounded; I am Aghast.'

'And all despite the fact', said the now enlightened Appleby gravely, 'that an ample variety of sandwiches was served shortly after the late Lord Auldearn's death – decease.'

Mr Rauth looked at Appleby as if he had at last found an embodiment of Perfect Comprehension. That an unknown reprobate – certainly a guest – should asperse the hospitality of Scamnum by breaking into a pantry in the night and purloining half a tin of biscuits – this was very terrible to Mr Rauth. But there was something comforting – soothing indeed – in the ready understanding of this sympathetic stranger. 'But let that Pass,' said Mr Rauth, with a friendly peer at Appleby and returning to his interrogative manner. 'Yes ... ?' And in a couple of minutes he was being a most effective ally after all. He flicked out a plan of Scamnum, telephoned to the lodges, the bailiff, the home-farm, the kitchens, the King's Arms; directed the locking and unlocking of doors. In ten minutes the complicated traffic of the Scamnum offices was reorganized on a basis of easy and adequate police supervision. Perhaps Mr Rauth had a hope that it would all lead to the unmasking of the violator of the pantry; certainly, he worked with a will. And Appleby got away from him under twenty minutes all told – the morning's last fragment of time to be sacrificed to the ghostly suspicion of spying that still clung to Gervase and the Merkalova.

Very soon the unwieldy household would be beginning to assemble for breakfast. Appleby wished he could observe their reactions to each other but failed to see how this could comfortably be managed; no doubt Giles would report. So he went to the green-room and set about organizing it as a sort of headquarters. He made various routine arrangements with the local men. He sent off several telegrams; one of these it rather pleased him to hand to Sergeant Trumpet – for it read with a fine mysteriousness: *advise h huttons size in hats*. If Happy, that very minor fish, could be proved an illicit swimmer in the waters of Scamnum he might as well be caught. And then Appleby returned obstinately to the rear stage. Here – he reiterated perserveringly – lurked the heart of the mystery. On this place – on all the implications of this place as the site of the murder – he must concentrate his mind. And suddenly Appleby felt enormously hungry.

He had enjoyed a not particularly substantial dinner just thirteen hours before. Since then there had been various excitements: ballet, a ride behind a fire-engine with the Prime Minister, murder, spy-hunting, and a number of interviews, all of a more or less exacting and lively kind. During this time he had had no sandwiches, neither had he broken into any pantry for biscuits – and he was just allowing his thoughts to stray a little anxiously to the problem of how Scamnum was likely to treat detective-inspectors within the gates when he heard a gentle but unmistakable rattle in the green-room. He hurried. An expansive breakfast was being wheeled in on a series of trollies – and under the superintendence not of Bagot but of an ugly and cheerful person in tweeds. Sergeant Trumpet was looking doubtfully at the ugly and cheerful person; much less doubtfully at the breakfast. And the ugly and cheerful person gave the advancing Appleby a friendly wave. 'I'm Timothy Tucker – late Guildenstern, of Rosencrantz and Guildenstern, twisters,' he said amiably. 'It occurred to me you might like to be in advance of the pack and I dropped a hint to Bagot and here we are. And I'm uncommonly hungry myself; I wonder if I might join in? Gott may come, but family ties are around him – if only by adumbration, you know.... Obviously, there are kidneys.'

Gott, it was presumably indicated, was going to breakfast with his Lady Elizabeth. And Appleby was in no mood to reject the appositely named Mr Tucker. 'I shall be very glad,' he said. 'My name is Appleby. I'm frightfully hungry.'

The long tables – already cleared of the properties which the police had removed, searched, and inventoried – were spread with a magnificent meal. There was a table for a little shifting army of constables, a table for Appleby's men now returning from labours in Auldearn's room, a table that was a species of sergeants' mess and a table for Appleby himself, Tucker, and Gott if he came. And Appleby surveyed the scene wryly; it suggested that a riot rather than a murder-investigation was the business in hand. When he got rid of this crowd he would begin to feel the possibility of getting on.

Timothy Tucker swallowed much tomato juice, buried much butter in the warm heart of a roll, and halted a descending fish-slice to point at the group of burly constabulary. 'And are those', he innocently enquired, 'what you call the Flying Squad?'

"County police, Mr Tucker. I have a great many men at the moment patrolling the outside of the house. When there has been murder, you see, it is always possible that someone is thinking of slipping quietly away.'

'Come, come!' Tucker, imitating the Duke, smiled inoffensively.

Appleby smiled too. 'Have you come to pump the police?'

Tucker shook his head. 'Oh, no,' he said. 'Not that at all. Egg?' He waved a hand in the direction of the sergeants. 'They stopped me telephoning a telegram – or rather they censored it. *Ultra vires* I'm sure, Mr Appleby. Not that I complain – nor am curious about that side of it, rumours of missing papers and so on. But I expect you've been sending telegrams or telephone messages yourself?'

'Yes,' said Appleby, wondering where this led.

'People's careers, interconnexions, all particulars; that sort of thing?'

'Just that,' said Appleby. Tucker, he noticed, was no longer exuding easy cheerfulness; he had thrust away his fish and was stabbing half-heartedly at Scamnum's celebrated pork cheese as if some considerable weight were on his mind.

'Last night,' said Tucker, 'you said something about speaking up. I rather took it to be a walk-into-my-parlour move. Inviting the criminal to pass the buck.'

'Possibly so,' said Appleby.

'But, of course, one must speak up all the same. I don't mean that I saw anything in particular last night – not that at all. Do you know Spandrel?'

'The publisher?' Appleby shook his head.

'Yes, the publisher. I'm one too. Spandrel and I both do a fair amount in the way of memoirs; mismemoirs, a good many of them – but all the thing just now. You know: *Recollections of a Political Scene-Shifter* and *My Long Life of Love*.' Mr Tucker shook his head mournfully – presumably over the depravity of the reading public. 'Well now, about a year ago an old gentleman called Anderson sent me a manuscript called *A Waft from Auld Reekie* – an excellent title, for it was a distinctly highly-flavoured book. I don't know that there was anything positively actionable in it when it came to me, but it was plainly full of lies. So I sent it back.' Tucker paused over his modestly insinuated glimpse of virtue and then added with some complacence: 'After that, of course, Anderson had a shot at Spandrel.' He paused again, this time to reach for a bone and investigate the Devil sauce; once launched on the process of speaking up he seemed to have recovered his spirits. 'Spandrel, as you may know, is a rash young man. He agreed to publish the book. Whereupon old Mr Anderson died – and exchanged Edinburgh, I don't doubt, for all the sad variety of hell. And that didn't leave Spandrel in too good a position. He was contracted with Anderson's spawn, administrators, assigns, and so forth, and he was left, of course, to stand any racket himself. So he cut a bit and delayed a bit – and the result is that the book is coming out next week. In other words there are scores of advance copies floating about England at this moment.' Tucker took more coffee. 'So you will understand my position. If I had refused the book and it had then gone into limbo I should be the possessor of confidential information of a sort and in a difficult position. As it is, I am merely telling you of what you can read for yourself in a day or two. Because whatever Spandrel has cut out I think it very unlikely that he will have cut out all the business of Auldearn and our good Professor Malloch.'

'Ah!' said Appleby with a becoming inscrutability. He reached for the marmalade – a beautiful dark kind with whole quarters of peel.

'One needn't suppose', Tucker went on, 'that Malloch knows about the book yet. And if he doesn't it will be a bit of a jolt – and would have been for Auldearn too. This Anderson had a flair for the ridiculous and he succeeded in making something quite tolerably diverting out of the relations of these people getting on for fifty years ago.'

Appleby looked curiously at Tucker. 'Fifty-year-old stuff? And ridiculous and diverting merely?'

'In the main, ridiculous and diverting merely. But shading off finally into hints of darker matter – matter that might smoulder till the end of a lifetime. That's what I didn't like about friend Anderson; his dropping hints. The courts don't like it, you know.'

'Quite so. But failing a copy of *A Waft from Auld Reekie* will you give me some details?'

'Sure Auldearn – Ian Stewart, as he was then – and Malloch were contemporaries at Edinburgh University. Auldearn was by some years the older; had been three or four years, I think, in a country solicitor's office first. Anyway, they both started square and on the same line – the grand old fortifying classical curriculum. One doesn't know how much' – said Tucker with the placid assumptions of the Cambridge man – 'of how these Caledonian academies conduct themselves. But I gather there is a great deal of top-boy feeling all through. No waiting three or four years to see who is the better man but much importance given to the results of Professor Macgonigal's fortnightly test.'

'Dear me!' said Appleby.

'Yes. Well, Ian Stewart and David Malloch were twin top-boys from the start and remained so all the way through. And – what didn't necessarily follow – they were rivals – and enemies. Not real enemies from early on, I suppose, or they would probably have ignored each other. They were friendly rivals at first, but with a real and deepening spirit of antagonism between them which they cloaked for a time in various boisterous ways. Both, as it happened, were distinguished in the primitive sports of the day, and were rivals there too. And that helped to make their rivalry a matter of public concern to the whole student body. There were two factions: the Jacobites, supporting Stewart; and the Mallets.'

'Mallets?'

'Yes. It was a joke, apparently, thought of by Stewart. Some time in the eighteenth century there had been a person called David Malloch occupying an obscure position in the Edinburgh High School; he went to London and set up as a literary man and changed his name to Mallet. And Dr Johnson, it seems, objecting to disguised Scots, made fun of him and his name in the *Lives of the Poets* and elsewhere. It was just the sort of little literary joke to annoy David Malloch the younger. Anyway, the Jacobites and the Mallets were famous in their day. There were wild doings – both between the factions and between the principals themselves. Malloch captured Stewart and hung him in chains – not by the neck, fortunately – over something called the Dean bridge. Later Stewart captured Malloch and succeeded in conducting him, tied head to tail on a donkey, a good way down Princes Street. Later still, there were rumours of a duel. And then their time was over and Stewart came straight to read for the English Bar and that was an end to it.'

Tucker was filling his pipe. Appleby regarded him curiously. 'And you are putting forward these events, which happened nearly half a century ago, as a possible motive for murder?'

'I am putting them forward', said Tucker placidly, 'as a subject for laudable curiosity in policemen. But when I said that was an end of it I meant that was an end – or all but an end – in friend Anderson's narrative. Anderson writes all this up and then leaves off with a hint: so much for the amusing doings of these wild young men; how sad that a darker turn to it all was to follow – that sort of thing. Well, I went after a little information on my own and it was partly what I came on that made me finally turn down Anderson's book. All this talk of wild students now grown to eminence one could get away with. But if there had been anything serious, anything that this gossip and hinting might tend to rake up, then the thing would be highly offensive and it would be mug's work to touch it. So I found a Modern Athenian of enormous age who had been in on the doings of that time and he told me a lot – without vouching for the truth of what he was telling me. Anderson's stuff was more or less true, if a bit coloured up. But beyond that there was rumour of matters that had been kept very dark. A girl had come into the affair and complicated it. Or rather she had simplified it, making the rather involved, half make-believe enmity wholly deadly. The two men fought a solemn duel by moonlight on Cramond sands – it was the period of R. L. Stevenson come to think of it – and Malloch got the bullet and Stewart got the girl. And after that Stewart came south in a hurry – which is why he ended his days as Lord Chancellor and not as Lord Justice General. So there you are. And if Spandrel knew there was this lurid legend on the fringes of this book he's putting out he wouldn't be at all happy.' Tucker smiled comfortably.

Appleby was silent for a minute, contemplating the extraordinary motive for murder which Tucker – wasting little time – had presented to the policemanly curiosity. Revenge delayed through almost a lifetime: it was a thing fantastic enough to contemplate – and yet not unknown to criminal science. But revenge, when it was long delayed, was commonly delayed because of some physical barrier, some long-standing practical obstacle. Men had paid off old scores after ten years in prison; emigrants, after far longer periods overseas, had come home and rekindled within themselves the lust for some half-remembered rival's blood. But in such a case as was here to be supposed delay would be inexplicable, unmotivated. . . .

'Mr Tucker' – Tucker almost started at something subtle that had happened to the young policeman – 'Mr Tucker, what of the relations of these two people as you have observed them? They have been together, I suppose, rehearsing? And – if you will give me your opinion – what sort of a person is Malloch?'

Tucker set himself to answer the last question first, and with precision. 'Malloch is what they call a systematic scholar – and of tremendous eminence, I believe, in his own line. Clear, retentive brain – very retentive – and has had his jacket off working hard for sixty years. Crawls over texts comma by comma, you know, and coaxes surprisingly interesting results out of the process.'

'Rather Gott's line.'

'Yes. But Malloch is positively an *Ober-Gott*. Better brain.'

'I see.' Appleby was rather dubious. He knew how Giles's mind could leap.

'But that's not all that's to Malloch. These people usually pay for their concentration in narrowness, it's said. Illiterate after 1870; never buy a new book.' Tucker shook a gloomy head. 'But Malloch's informed all round and lives quite in the world. Not that his learning's so relevant as his character, which I don't know much about. He's a correct, tartly courteous person, but showing an occasional streak of savage brilliance that suggests those old Edinburgh days. And that comes out in his writing, which can be very good – particularly in a destructive way. I'd like to have him on my list.' This was obviously Mr Tucker's furtherest word in intellectual commendation.

'And his relations with Lord Auldearn?'

'I don't know much about that. Malloch only came down on Friday night and I didn't see them much in each other's company – not that I have any impression that they avoided each other. And I've never stopped in a house with the two of them before, though I seem to remember their passing the time of day at stray parties. The Duchess would know most about all that.'

'Yes,' said Appleby. 'Yes. . . .' He rose with the polite finality of the Prime Minister himself pronouncing brief valediction on a deputation. 'Thank you very much. Now I must get hold of the document in the case.'

'Anderson's book?'

Appleby opened innocent eyes. 'Dear me, no. Shakespeare's play.'

2

'IT came into my head,' said Piper to Gott, speaking across Elizabeth and not very amiably – for like most of the people scattered round the breakfast table he was feeling uncomfortable and frayed – 'it came into my head that in this business you must feel rather like Pygmalion when his statue came alive. You think out these things – and here you are.'

'A most felicitous idea. And what about the story of Frankenstein? – there is some possible application to be worked out there too. You might elaborate something good.'

Elizabeth, setting an example in the eating of an unagitated and adequate meal, frowned at her plate over this passage of arms. And Mrs Platt-Hunter-Platt, who had been explaining to the Duke how essential it was that she should be allowed to leave Scamnum when she pleased, did not improve matters by attempting a discussion on the dangerous influence of the cinema on the lower classes – so many films full of stuff that was a standing incitement to crime!

Nave injudiciously rallied her. 'And what, my dear lady, of the play you came to see? Does that not, according to the argument you suggest, invite us to adultery, incest, parricide, fratricide, murder, and revolution – to say nothing of going off our heads? No, no, these things, films of criminal life, stories of ingenious homicide – they are all safety-valves, madam, safety valves.'

Gott cracked an egg in gloomy silence.

'But Shakespeare,' said Mrs Platt-Hunter-Platt – with some obscure sense, apparently, of sustaining an argument – 'Shakespeare was a poet.' And this failing to provoke comment she added: 'And in my opinion the Duke should send for a detective.'

'A detective?' said Noel politely from across the table. 'You mean a real detective – not like the police?'

'Exactly – a real detective. There is a very good man whose name I forget; a foreigner and very conceited – but, they say, thoroughly reliable.'

Gott made the little hair-rumpling gesture which he resorted to when the world seemed peculiarly mad. And unexpectedly Elizabeth murmured: 'Giles, couldn't you clear it up – solve it?'

Gott looked at her with something like alarm.

'I mean that they're right, in a way. What they're getting at. It is rather your sort of thing.'

'You mean inspired by sensational fiction?'

Elizabeth considered. 'No. Murder is obviously inspired by something more solid than that. But the way the thing was done, the setting, the technique – it seems the product of the same sort of mind that writes a complicated story. You might have an insight into it.'

'Not the insight Appleby will have. I don't think I'd make a very good real-life detective. I'm not foreign and ... but come and meet Appleby.'

They had reached the door when they were arrested by Clay, who had snapped his fingers impulsively and addressed the Duke and the company at large. 'I say, it occurs to me there is something that ought to have been put to the police. About your apparatus, Dr Bunney. Did anyone explain to them its extreme accuracy? I mean the chance of identifying the voice that used it to deliver one of the messages – "I will not cry Hamlet, revenge," wasn't it? Do you believe you could really do that? I remember Miss Terborg suggested something of the sort at the time.'

Bunney, who had been the dimmest of figures during breakfast, brightened at once. 'I am sure I could,' he said eagerly. 'You see, it's impossible to disguise the human voice against modern phonometric tests – *my* phonometric tests. Not even you, Mr Clay, could defeat them. All I should need would be control recordings.'

It had become a convention at Scamnum to consider Dr Bunney and his black box as a mild joke – which was doubtless why nobody had pursued this possibility before. But Bunney's confidence had something impressive in it now. Even the Duke was interested. 'And you've kept the cylinder – record, whatever it is – of that message?'

'It's in my room now.'

'And the machine?' asked Malloch.

'The officers have that.'

Gott struck in. All this seemed to him more for Appleby than for the company at large. 'Then will you come along now? I think this should be put to Mr Appleby at once.'

Bunney had not thus been in the centre of the picture since the notable occasion on which he had proposed to switch on the Lord's Prayer. He joined Gott and Elizabeth with alacrity. At the door they met the Duchess, always a late arrival at breakfast. 'Has anything been discovered, Giles? And what are their plans?' Gott was already the recognized intermediary between Scamnum and the new power so disconcertingly planted in its midst.

'Nothing startling, I believe. All of us back-stage people will be questioned this morning – and meanwhile we and everybody else are fast prisoners. I don't know what would happen if anybody rebelled, but so far there is only a little grumbling from Mrs Platt-Hunter-Platt.'

'And from me.' Nave had come up behind. 'But if Mr Appleby will despatch a telegram for me to an exalted patient who must be tactfully put off I shall be placid enough. I will come and see him now if I may.' Nave plainly liked it to be known that he had exalted patients.

They found Appleby, who had abandoned the still-populous green-room, sitting dangling his legs over the front stage and absorbed in the prompt-copy of *Hamlet*. Elizabeth wondered if Mrs Platt-Hunter-Platt would have been impressed; it was somehow distinctly reminiscent of the reliable foreigner. But Gott broke in upon these studies abruptly, anxious to get ahead of Nave and the pother about a telegram. 'Dr Bunney believes he could identify the voice that used his dictaphone for one of the Revenge messages.'

Appleby looked at Bunney in surprise. 'I had hoped we might narrow down the possible access to your instrument, and to the other means by which messages were given. But I understood the Duke to say that the voice was disguised? And surely a carefully disguised voice, coming through the medium of a dictaphone –'

Bunney broke in impatiently. 'You don't understand. This is not a commercial dictaphone. It is an instrument of precision for the scientific study of the minutiae of speech. I should like to explain it to you if you will have it brought here. I have shown several people how it works: it is very easy to understand. It *measures*, you see – measures relative intervals, stress, which nobody could disguise. Of course one would make no show with such a thing in a court of law: it would be ridiculed. But for us – for you – it can point. All I need is control speeches from everybody concerned. Come to reckon on it, I have got them all already. It is just a matter of comparing each minutely with the cylinder which has the message and the job is done – you see? It's not a quick business, though, rather a long one. But the cylinders are all up in my room. I may get them? And you have the machine?'

Bunney's eye was gleaming. He was a detective in his own line and now the instinct was up in him. His slightly comical pomposity was gone; the words tumbled out impressively. And Appleby was prepared to suspend disbelief. 'Get them by all means,' he said. 'It's something wholly new in criminology – at least in England.' And at this gracious speech, Bunney bounded away like a schoolboy.

'It seems worth Dr Bunney's working on,' said Appleby candidly to the others, 'while the very laborious business of sifting movements – both in relation to the messages and the murders – goes forward. For we are up against a long job, I am afraid, and people must be patient.'

Gott looked curiously at his friend during this speech and the subsequent negotiations over the telegram. He had told the Duchess that nothing startling had been discovered; now he was not so sure. He suspected that something had turned up sufficiently odd to catch at Appleby's imagination. And Appleby's next words scarcely seemed to lead directly to the laborious investigation he had promised. 'Giles, what would you say was the chief problem in *Hamlet*; the thing one puzzles over when one begins to analyse the play?'

'I suppose one is chiefly troubled to account for Hamlet's delay in revenging himself upon King Claudius. There seems no reason for it. That was almost the first difficulty raised by early critics of the play. And it has been discussed ever since.'

'Delayed revenge.' Appleby swung upon Nave. 'Now what if Lord Auldearn was murdered as he was murdered – right in the heart of *Hamlet* – in order to make the statement: "Thus dies Lord Auldearn, by a long-delayed revenge"?'

Nave's eyelids drooped over alert eyes. 'Are these professional consultations that you are holding? Are Mr Gott and I going to unite our crafts and work the thing out together?'

'Perhaps something of the sort. I feel that Lord Auldearn's death and the play *Hamlet* may be in some way implicated with each other, and that the manner of death constitutes a statement, a statement intelligible and satisfactory to the murderer though necessarily enigmatic to us. And conceivably the statement is just this: "At last, long-delayed revenge!"'

'This is much better than turning our pockets out and so on last night; it should get you much further!' Nave was obviously stirred to interest. He leant against the stage, hands deep in pockets, and knit his brows at the floor. 'A statement, yes: nearly every homicide has its aspect as a statement, a manifesto. And here that seems to be pronounced. At once pronounced and enigmatic; a clamant riddle. There really is matter for a psychological approach.' He glanced keenly up at Appleby as if assessing the policeman's ability to conduct anything of the sort. 'A riddle to which the solution lies deep within an unknown mind – it is an interesting idea. Not an affair as in your stories, Gott; no footprints, no flakes of that unique East Loamshire clay.'

Appleby smiled. 'You are behind the times in that sort of thing, sir. Stories of the kind always have a psychological drift now.' He looked mischievously at Gott and added mendaciously: 'For instance the elaborate analysis of the gorilla-mind in *Murder at the Zoo* –'

Nave turned to Gott. 'Dear me – I had no idea! Another use, it seems, for psychology; just as with the advertising.' This was a neat retort upon a joke now some days old and it seemed to put Nave in good humour. 'But what exactly is the problem for the psychologist here? The likelihood, I presume, Mr Appleby, of the sort of "statement" you suggest. "At last, long-delayed revenge!" I don't know if you have some particular suspicion in mind – but I see the general idea as possible enough. Suppose someone with a lust for murder; suppose him directing it on a particular victim and crediting himself with a motive which he calls "revenge". His head is full of revenge and he nurses the idea. He thinks of himself as delaying his vengeance and finds pleasure in that. He is playing cat and mouse –'

'Which', interjected Elizabeth, 'is one interpretation of Hamlet's conduct.'

'Very true, my dear Lady Elizabeth; perhaps an important point. In any case, the delay has been part of his pleasure; his sense of power is implicated with it; he could strike but he has delayed. And then remember, as I said, that nearly every murder is a manifesto – and nearly always a manifesto – so to speak – of self, a piece of exhibitionism. The criminal looks forward to his appearance in the dock as the martyr to his martyrdom – and for exactly the same reason: it is limelight, it is a supreme manifesto of self – nothing more.' For a moment there was a fanatical gleam in Nave's eye – but he came back to his reasoning swiftly enough. 'He is proud of the power, the control that has gone to his delay. And so the delay must go into the statement. It may be gloried in in the dock or – better – it may be declared doubly in the way of the killing itself. *Hamlet, revenge!* And Hamlet procrastinates – and then at length kills.'

'But', Gott objected, 'here it was Polonius who was killed, whereas in the play Hamlet is out for the blood of the king – it is there the revenge lies – and the killing of Polonius is merely an accident.'

'Yes,' said Nave vigorously. 'Yes! But in acts like this, remember, it is not wholly the rational waking mind that is in control. The primitive is at work. And the primitive uses – just as dreams use – rough and ready symbols – and uses them *illogically*. Here, it would be quite enough for the purpose of statement, of manifesto, that the murder should take place in a context of delay; in the middle of a play the main problem of which is procrastination.' Nave made an excited and nervous gesture; obviously he had a pleasurable feeling of power himself in this analysis. 'Yes; I believe you may be on it, Mr Appleby!'

Appleby was drumming a finger on his copy of the play. 'But can we come down to types, Sir Richard? What sort of person nurses thoughts of revenge – and for how long – or about what? Lord Auldearn has been shot by someone of whom we know only one thing: that he or she is what ordinary people call "normal". There was nobody in the hall who is not commonly regarded as a responsible agent. Very well –'

'What', Nave put in drily, 'of the eminent Mr Cope?'

'An old man grown eccentric, no doubt. But what I am trying to put is this. Here are so many people we may suspect and all of them are – within certain elastic limits doubtless – normal people with normal lives behind them. How does our idea of darkly declaring a nursed revenge and so on accord with this very rough limitation of types that we can establish? Would you expect to find such a thing only in subjects patently unbalanced?'

'Certainly not. A very normal-seeming type might, I believe, do just such a thing. Strange things bubble up even in the godly, you know – uncommonly strange things.'

'No doubt. But can you imagine this: a normal-seeming person – indeed, an intellectually-distinguished person – nursing the idea of revenge for some passional injury over a very long period of time; husbanding up murder and finally producing it from hiding-places more than forty years deep?'

Nave looked startled, and so did Gott and Elizabeth. Plainly, Appleby was not intending to use a mere figure of speech. And to look for a motive for Auldearn's death more than forty years back, was drastically to narrow the field. Nave straightened himself. 'You have some specific thing in mind,' he said, 'and it would not do to give any sort of scientific opinion rashly. I don't know. But I should venture that murder voluntarily delayed over forty years, and by such a type as you describe, would be disconcerting even to a morbid psychologist – and, believe me, we are not disconcerted readily. But do not misunderstand. I am speaking of a murder in which the motive centres wholly in a remote past. One can imagine a long-standing, but still present motive – some stolen thing still flaunted, some deadly and irreconcilable ideological conflict even, which might span a great stretch of years. But such speculation is worthless; we have nothing sufficiently precise before us. Here is Bunney.'

The approaching footsteps, however, were those of Sergeant Trumpet. The Prime Minister was on the telephone.

Appleby had already sent a message that the document was in safe keeping. And now, excusing himself, he hurried to the green-room without enthusiasm. During the last hour he had been feeling that the hunt was up – and it was a hunt that had nothing to do with Pike, Perch, or Prime Ministers. Despite the continuing blockade the whole spy-business had been becoming progressively unreal.

'Well,' came the Prime Minister's voice, 'you've got it and so far good. Hilfers is going down for it straight away. Can we be easy in our minds? From this second intercepted message I rather suppose we can.'

'I haven't had any second intercepted message,' said Appleby.

'Haven't? Then I suppose Hilfers is bringing it down to you. It says something like this: "Regret premature advice have to report failure and no further opportunity probable." Some fool, you see, thought that because a shot was fired his friend had certainly got what they were after. Surprisingly stupid some of them are. Not like the police, Mr Appleby.'

'Thank you, sir,' said Appleby gravely.

'But it shows there was mischief afoot – that sort of mischief. Some precious scoundrel down there with you still. Don't let him hit you on the head before you hand over to Hilfers.'

'No sir.' Appleby might have been Trumpet.

'And you've still got everyone stoppered up? No remaining chance of the thing's having been tapped after all during the excitement, I suppose?'

The Prime Minister, Appleby realized, was thorough. And he replied: 'There were one or two false trails of that sort, sir, that took up time. But now I can see only one slight possibility that way; otherwise we're safe.'

'One possibility?'

'Yes, sir. One person was in a position in which he might have secured something.'

'I see.' The Prime Minister's voice was anxious again. 'Who?'

Appleby hesitated. But the line, he knew, would be well secured. 'Mr Gervase Crispin.'

Disconcertingly, what must have been a guffaw of laughter wafted itself over the wire from Downing Street. 'If that's all, Mr Appleby, you can unstopper. Gervase! – well, well. Suspect the Duke if you like; I've never got to the bottom of him. But Gervase, you see – though it's a great secret – well, he drafted the document for me. Did you catch that? ... drafted the document.'

'Oh,' said Appleby.

'After all and come to think of it, who else could, you know, who else could? Well, get the brute who murdered Auldearn. Good-bye.'

And the Prime Minister rang off.

Appleby cursed the Prime Minister, cursed the muddle-headed Scamnum spies, and cursed in particular Gervase Crispin. His vision of Gervase as what Gervase himself had mockingly called the unscrupulous magnate had certainly been – and again in Gervase's own words – a waste of time. And Gervase had most irresponsibly let him waste time for a mere freak of fancy; he had denied, implicitly or explicitly, any intimate knowledge of the document. But perhaps he was pledged that way; certainly, not even the Duke had known that his kinsman was privy to it. About the whole business there was something peculiarly annoying. It was annoying – basically annoying – that the world should concoct, stalk, and tremble over Pike and Perch schemes. Not a soul involved, probably, but knew that; and yet – there it was. And to one minded like Appleby it was equally annoying that nobody concerned seemed wholly efficient – everyone had muddle, as it were, round the corner.

But at least the path was now cleared to the murders. Appleby gave orders to take the men off the terraces and then turned back to the front of the hall. So far, three avenues had opened before him. There was a laborious study of the where-abouts of many people – in point both of the murders and of the messages. There was the strange path which Tucker had indicated as leading to Malloch, and which had prompted his recent conversation with Nave. And there was Bunney.

And here a new thought came to Appleby. Bunney's contrivance, although a veil of fun had apparently been cast over it, had nevertheless been known to Scamnum as an instrument of sober, if not very fruitfully-directed, science. Bunney had demonstrated it; shown people how it worked eagerly and freely. And it made particularly accurate records of the human voice. The innocent – with the exception of the clever Miss Terborg – had been slow to see the possibility of this, but it could hardly have escaped a wary sender of the sinister messages. However well one could disguise one's voice, recording it on Bunney's apparatus was risky. Then here again, surely, was the now familiar theme of hazard; once more – as with the shooting of Auldearn and the dragging of Bose's body through the house – there seemed to be deliberate courting of danger. And twice the criminal had got away with it. Was it possible that on this third, and actually anterior venture he would fall down? It was not impossible. Bunney must get to work at once.

Appleby stepped back into the hall to find Nave, Gott, and Elizabeth where he had left them – the two former engaged in some sort of verbal duel; Elizabeth looking on with a pucker of amusement. But Bunney had not yet returned. Appleby looked at his watch in surprise. 'I wonder –'

The far door burst open and Noel came breathlessly up the hall. 'Mr Appleby, Nave – will you come? Bunney has been attacked just outside his room. I think he may be dead.'

*

Bunney had been hit on the head from behind while in a darkish stretch of corridor. He was not dead – only on the verge of death. Nave and Biddle were of the opinion that he might pull through but that his position would be critical for some hours: the toll of the Scamnum murders, as Nave grimly put it, was at the moment uncertain. And it was hard to believe that wanton murder had not been intended, for a far less severe blow would have cleared the way to the theft which seemed the criminal's rational objective. Theft there had certainly been. In a corner of Bunney's room stood a large suitcase, elaborately fitted with an arrangement of pigeon-holes. And in each pigeon-hole was a hollow metal cylinder coated with some waxen substance; that and a little descriptive card. Only one was missing, but the corresponding card was still there. It bore simply a date and the significant words: '*The curious message*'.

They had taken Bunney into another bedroom. Appleby, pacing up and down with a set jaw, was alone with Gott. He stopped in his stride. 'The swift, ruthless devil! Tell me, Giles, how did this come up? – before you came with Bunney to the hall, I mean. Was there a sort of public canvass of the possibility of identifying the voice?'

Gott nodded. 'Yes. Clay brought it up at breakfast. It suddenly came into his head and he came out with it. And at that Bunney said yes, he believed he could collate the cylinder bearing the message with known recordings of our voices and so identify the perpetrator. And at that I brought him along to you.'

Appleby made a slight, uncontrollable gesture of bafflement. 'And it gave the alarm and the murderer decided to act on the spot! I should have thought of it. I should have known that from that moment Bunney was running a risk – poor devil. Who was there, Giles? Who was at breakfast?'

'At that moment, I should think about half the house-party. I could give you a good many names, but not a complete list. It would be another case of laborious inquiry.'

'Yes. But it gives a control on all the other alibi-occasions we shall come to. Opportunity to send the messages, to shoot Auldearn, to stab Bose, to overhear Bunney's plan and attack him: when I tabulate everybody on all that I shall begin to get somewhere – perhaps. And it looks the quickest road now the Bunney hope has gone.'

Briskly, Appleby made for the door. And Gott felt that he was becoming an angry man.

3

THE unwanted guests – those who had been staying at Scamnum merely to be spectators at the play – were gone. In silence, or discreetly murmuring premeditated words, or mumbling whatever came into their heads, they had shaken hands with the Duke and Duchess and been bowled away to freedom and importance: once back in town they would be in the greatest demand for weeks. Pamela Hogg had departed in tears, the morning post having brought news of Armageddon that was very bad indeed. Mrs Platt-Hunter-Platt had offered to interview either the Home Secretary or the reliable foreign detective – whichever the Duke pleased. And the Dowager Duchess had returned to Horton Ladies' without ever knowing that an American philologist, now just edging away from death's threshold upstairs, had wanted to compare her linguistic habits with Lady Lucy Lumpkin's as reported by the learned Odger. They were all gone and Scamnum, with less than a score of remaining guests, seemed for a time like a great school when only the holiday boarders are left.

In the green-room Appleby, Bunney's possible short-cut having been snatched out of reach, was taking the long and laborious way. He was as yet without any eye-witness evidence; as far as the murders went no one had reported seeing a sinister thing. And, a common type of revolver apart, he was without material clues; nothing of the footprints and unique Loamshire clay variety had turned up. What he had was an isolated motive – pitched abruptly at him by Timothy Tucker – and a number of significant places and times. On the basis of these last, he had suggested to Gott, it should be possible to elaborate a table of eliminations – to prove that this person and that could not have done all that the criminal had done. Of course it was theoretically possible – quite apart from what was almost certainly a parallel activity in the spy or spies – that many hands were involved. The two murders might be unconnected. The person responsible for the messages might not be responsible for the deaths. Each of the five known messages, even, might have a source independent of the others. But all these were fantastic hypotheses, to be neglected until the likely hypothesis had been explored. And the likely hypothesis was that in these messages and murders one hand was at work. One hand had shot Auldearn, stabbed Bose, stunned Bunney, and contrived five messages.

In these circumstances as they lay before him, Appleby

thought that he detected a familiar thing: almost reckless daring. The murderer had wantonly multipled the dangers he must run; and always for dramatic effect.

(i) He had shot Auldearn under the possible eye of Bose. Even if he proved to be old Max Cope he had done that. For Bose, as a simple experiment had made it clear, had only to look up at the vital moment to see enough of what was happening through the trap-door to know that the shot came from the upper stage – the upper stage of which Cope was in possession.

(ii) He had risked carrying his weapon, a revolver, with him from the rear stage. And this was a big risk in itself. Without it, he might have been detected emerging from the curtains after the shot and yet – for lack of positive evidence – been tolerably safe. But with the revolver on him, he had only to be resolutely challenged by an observer, held; and searched and his fate would be sealed. And this risk, again, he had taken for a small, but startling effect: that of secreting the little weapon in the grisliest possible place, Yorick's skull.

(iii) He had dragged Bose's body past a dozen tenanted rooms. And for an effect again – a sort of gesture of defiance.

(iv) He had contrived, by one means and another, five threatening or sinister messages. And in these, it seemed to Appleby, a new factor appeared. Here again was risk: five cumulative risks. Each message might conceivably be traced; and even a doubtful or inconclusive association with a given person would become formidable if made in the case of three, or even two messages. There had been cumulative risk; had there been cumulative effect? For the murderer's eye for effect was, in its own peculiar way, excellent; it was a master of the startling and the macabre that was at work. Had not there been something superfluous in the management of the messages? Wholly effective in the light of subsequent events had been the one found by Gott in Auldearn's car: the lines on the fatal entrance of Duncan under Macbeth's battlements found at the very moment of Auldearn's arrival at Scamnum. And wholly effective had been that other passage from *Macbeth*, ringing through the sleeping house its warning of an imminent deed of dreadful note. And effective too, if only because of the oddity and ingenuity of the method of communication, was the message delivered through what Scamnum had light-heartedly called Bunney's black box. After that, however, there was a drop into comparative pointlessness. Noel had been sent a message through the post and Gervase had been sent a telegram. And about neither of these did there seem to be any special appropriateness or force. From the point of view of the artist – and as an artist the murderer had, strangely, to be regarded – these two messages marred a certain pleasing economy in the contriving of sensation.

But (said Appleby to himself) look at it this way: look at the *method* employed for each communication. And he made a list: (*a*) *by hand*, (*b*) *by radio-gramophone*, (*c*) *by dictaphone*, (*d*) *by post*, (*e*) *by telegram*. Was this not what Nave would call a manifesto; was it not the action of the boxer who, sure of his invulnerability, amuses himself by tapping systematically now here, now there? One might say that only radio proper was missing – the Black Hand could scarcely capture the air – radio proper and the telephone. And Appleby wondered if a sixth message by telephone had actually been sent to someone who chose to remain silent. Or – conceivably – if a telephone message were yet to come.

The messages, then, served two purposes. They created sensation and they were a challenge. Look – the Black Hand said in effect – at the variety of channels I can use – use and get away with. A piece of typescript through the post may be hard to get a line on; but what of a telegram, a note delivered in an eminent statesman's car, dealings with other people's gramophones and black boxes? Appleby felt that even if an investigation into the origins of the messages yielded nothing, the mere fact of their being so clearly a challenge was not without its light.

He decided to make this investigation his first concern. His assistant, Sergeant Mason, who had arrived from London with Captain Hilfers some time after the attack on Bunney, could meanwhile begin sifting people's movements at the time of the two murders – a vital business to which Appleby himself would turn as soon as preliminary data had been collected. In this way he hoped to save himself time on blind-alley interviews with people who could produce clear alibis.

The first point about the messages, he reflected, was that out of all five there survived the physical vehicle of only two. The note tossed into Auldearn's car, the note posted to Noel Gylby, the telegraph form received by Gervase – all these had been destroyed. At the time of their reception they had been no more than imbecile anonymous communications and they had passed by way of the wastepaper basket to limbo. The dictaphone cylinder which had so signally failed to offer up the Lord's Prayer had been successfully stolen – it was a hard thought – from under the very nose of the police. What survived was two gramophone records and – possibly – the original of the telegram sent to Gervase. Even if the telegraph message had been telephoned to the post office at Scamnum Ducis, so that no written original existed, a date and hour of transmission would still be on the post-office files.

As well begin with Auldearn's message. Appleby got hold of Gott, one of the available witnesses, and went with him to find the other, Auldearn's chauffeur. The man was grimly polishing his dead employer's car; he was bewildered, angry, and anxious to help.

The message, Gott said, had been in typescript on a quarto page of common paper. He had noticed it, a crumpled ball, in a corner of the car a few minutes after getting in and just before drawing up at Scamnum. The chauffeur, Williams, who had looked at the clock on his dashboard on arrival in order to time the run, could name the minute: four-twenty-two. By about four-twenty on the Friday afternoon, then, the message had been in the car. What of an anterior limit? When had it certainly *not* been in the car? It had not been in the car, Williams could swear, when Lord Auldearn got in outside his London house; had it been there he, Williams, would have spotted it when arranging the rugs. And that had been at two-five. But it might have been tossed in within the next five minutes, when he had gone to his place at the wheel and they were waiting for a stray suitcase to be brought out. Would Lord Auldearn not have noticed it himself if it had been in the car throughout the journey? And would he not have been likely to notice its being tossed in? No, said Williams; his Lordship was distinctly short-sighted and often failed to notice more conspicuous things than a ball of paper. If they had not picked up Mr Gott he would certainly have found it himself sooner or later; probably on handing out to the footmen on arrival. And, of course, he would have given it to his lordship; he would not take the responsibility of destroying what might be of consequence. When one was with a Lord Chancellor –

Quite so, said Appleby – and turned to the next point. After starting from town what opportunities would there have been? Williams looked doubtful. Anywhere until clear of London, perhaps, when going slow or in a block; but how could the fellow know just where to reckon on that? From another car it might be possible – with skill. But once they had got clear of London he doubted if it could have been managed.

'And when you got to Scamnum?'

'Well, I went very slowly up the drive, as Mr Gott knows. Gentlemen who have deer are sometimes very touchy about pace through their parks.'

'I see. But was there anyone on the drive?'

'There was Macdonald, the head gardener,' Gott struck in. 'I remember him touching his cap to us as we went past.'

'Macdonald?' Appleby was about to mention that curious behaviour of Macdonald as reported by Trumpet but checked himself before the chauffeur. 'You would have noticed if anyone had thrown the message in while you were in the car, Giles?'

'Probably. But not certainly,' said Gott cautiously. Then a thought struck him. 'You came by the south lodge?' he asked Williams.

'Yes, sir.'

'That's a possibility.' Gott turned to Appleby. 'There are twin lodges there, joined by a sort of mock-battlemented bridge you drive under. And there's an outside staircase and anyone is allowed up. There's a view.'

'I was going very slow there,' said Williams.

And that was all that was to be discovered. Two-five to two-ten in town was a likely time; two-ten to four-ten on the route was possible but not probable; four-ten at the south lodge was likely again. A suspected person would have to be cleared in relation to these times. Going back to the house, Appleby tried another line. Gott didn't remember anything special about the text of the message – any sign, say, of its having been taken from a particular edition? Gott smiled at the ingenuity of this, but remembered nothing of the sort. The message had been in modern spelling, as most Shakespeares so deplorably were, and might have come, say, from the old Cambridge text – of which there was a copy in every fifth house in England.

And that was that. Valuable times had been fixed, and yet Appleby felt that on the whole here was one up to the Black Hand. There was opportunity in London and opportunity near Scamnum – a point all in favour of the unknown.

Next came Noel's letter. No time need be wasted on it – nor could; there was nothing whatever to be done. It had been posted in the West End on Friday morning; Noel remembered that. But it requires only the most moderate ingenuity to arrange for the posting of a letter where one pleases. There was no road that way.

Appleby turned to the gramophone records and the opportunities of access to the radio-gramophone at about two-thirty on the previous morning. If the records were new there would be some chance of wringing information from them. Neither the carillon nor Clay's reading from *Macbeth* would be big-selling recordings and the manufacturing company's files would show what retailers could usefully be questioned. Appleby sent for the records; they were much scratched disks and both recordings were old. If the Black Hand had bought them when new, the transaction probably lay too far in the past to get any line on. And if he had picked them up recently and second-hand there would be needed a very elaborate net indeed, if there was to be even a slender chance of successful inquiry. Nevertheless, Appleby communicated with London at once. He then considered the matter of access to the machine and found no progress was to be made. It stood in a small ante-drawing-room, close to a service door. Anyone could have gone down in the middle of the night, set the machine going, slipped through the door, and returned to an upper corridor by more than one pair of service stairs. Scamnum was a building made for such tricks. And in the alarm, occasioned by the pealing bell, nobody had been on the look-out for suspicious movements. From all this there was derivable only one inference: the Black Hand had a fair familiarity with the house. Which told one really nothing. So far, Appleby said to himself, the enemy was winning all along the line.

An understanding of Bunney's box and private access to it some time before breakfast on the Saturday morning, were the next points. The most important witness here was not available; it would be some time before Bunney could again be on speaking terms with the world. But significant facts were to be gleaned. Bunney had arrived after luncheon on Friday and had lost no time in bringing his machine into play – as Gott had discovered on the terrace before dinner. Mysterious phonetic nicety apart, there was nothing particularly novel about the machine, except that it combined recording and reproducing units in an unusually compact way. But Bunney, being proud of it, hawked it round. Late on Friday night he had been demonstrating to all comers in the library; in the library just short of midnight, the somewhat reluctant Bagot had repeated the Lord's Prayer; and in the library, finally, the machine had been left for the night. The Black Hand had merely to walk in. Which was not helpful, thought Appleby – and turned to his last chance.

Gervase's telegram seemed more hopeful. It was the earliest of the messages, having been received at the House of Commons on the Monday afternoon – a week before the play. And the office of origin was Scamnum Ducis. In other words the telegram had been sent from a hamlet within a mile of Scamnum Court – and sent some days before the majority of the house-party was assembled. And Appleby doubted if it could very readily have been telephoned. You can dictate telegrams from the right sort of public telephone-box. And there was such a one, he discovered, some miles along the Horton Road. But from there, it appeared, you would get not Scamnum Ducis but King's Horton as the office of origin. Another possibility was that a telegram could be telephoned in fair secrecy from Scamnum itself. That depended on just what the domestic arrangements in such matters were and for a moment Appleby debated another interview with the alarming but efficient Mr Rauth. But it occurred to him that the local post office would have to be tackled in any case; and moreover that thirty minutes given to walking there and back might serve instead of the night's sleep he had missed. So he got his directions and set out briskly through the park, challenged occasionally by one of his own local auxiliaries. He had withdrawn the men from the terraces but was going to make sure, all the same, that nobody now at Scamnum should quit without formal farewells.

Appleby drew deep breaths of June air as he went briskly down the drive. The summer was advanced in this southland country; from somewhere came the scent of the first hay and already the oak-leaves were darkening. Over his left shoulder he looked up at Horton Hill. Across the crown there must be some right-of-way, for no attempt had been made to eject the people gathering there. It was quite a crowd now: idlers in the neighbouring towns, reading the stimulating news in their morning paper, had hurried to get out the car and motor over to see what they could. And soon there would be similar arrivals from London; people 'running down for the day'. And portents these, thought Appleby, of a society running down in another sense: clogged by its own mass-production of individuals who, let loose from a day's or a lifetime's specialized routine, will neither think nor read nor practise any craft, but only gape. Hence an unstable world, in which Pike and Perch Documents can have a real and horrid power.

But his immediate concern with that was over. Appleby's eye, travelling along the hill, rested on a red and white object moving towards the crowd on the summit. It puzzled him for a moment; then he saw that it was an ice-cream barrow. Commerce follows sensation.

Scamnum Ducis is a tiny village; the cubic space of all its buildings put together would go several times into one of the wings of Scamnum Court. A queer proportion of things, thought Appleby, still in sociological vein and yet not so blighting as the constant proportion of biggish villa and smallish villa that now makes up most of presentable England. He looked about him. There was – inevitably – a Crispin Arms: he noticed in a quartering the three balls that told how an early Crispin had married a decayed Medici. There was no church, for the church was within the park; it was more convenient for the family so. There was an institute erected by the belatedly romantic duke, with a bas-relief of Shakespeare, Milton, Wordsworth, and Lord Macaulay holding a committee-meeting. And there was a post office, the sort of post office that is also a general shop. There were picture postcards of Scamnum and cardboard boxes of slowly melting sweets in the window and the whole was of such modest proportions that Appleby, who remembered the classics of his nursery, would scarcely have been disturbed to find it presided over by Ginger and Pickles or Mrs Tabitha Twitchit. But it wasn't. It was presided over by a young girl most start-lingly like the Duke of Horton.

Genetic law makes no scruple to confront you with embar-rassing memorials of your ancestors, thought Appleby – and introduced himself. But the girl, on learning that she was in the presence of Scotland Yard, gave out a scared, gulping sound unworthy of the Crispin spirit and disappeared into the recesses of the shop. Her place was presently taken by a venerable but sharp-eyed woman who studied Appleby with the greatest con-centration. And Appleby regarded her in turn with considerable hope. A knife-like and restlessly-curious old body, she might just possibly represent the sudden downfall of the Black Hand. 'I'm tracing the sending of a telegram,' he told her; 'a telegram sent from this office not very long ago. I'm going to ask ques-tions. But I don't want anyone to begin thinking they remember what they don't remember. I've come in just on the off chance – you see?' Appleby had found this a useful technique in the past; people's memories are better when they don't feel some-thing urgently expected of them. But the sharp-eyed old person looked at him with some indignation. 'There's not many tele-grams come into this office that *I* don't remember,' she said firmly.

This was excellent – though scarcely an attitude that would have been endorsed by the Postmaster General. 'It's rather a curious telegram, too,' said Appleby. 'It was just two words: "*Hamlet revenge.*" '

'Ah,' said the old person; 'there's been plenty like that.'

Appleby was taken aback. He had been hoping a good deal from the wording of Gervase's message; it should have held attention in transmission. But he had forgotten something which the Black Hand had not: for some weeks past Scamnum had been sending out telegrams about the play with all the prodigality of a great house. And in these, as often as not, the word 'Hamlet' had occurred. As the old woman said, there had been 'plenty like that' and the message *'Hamlet revenge'* would not in itself attract particular attention.

'Plenty like that,' said the old woman. 'A fortnight come tomorrow, now, Mr Rauth himself came in with two. One was to Jolce and Burnet, St Martin's Lane: *'Reference Hamlet duelling properties not delivered please check despatch – Gott.'* And the other was to Miles, Oxford Street: *'Despatch ten copies New Cambridge Hamlet by return – Horton.'* And the same afternoon a stranger came in – a tall gentleman in a grey suit and a green tie, just the height of our Tim, who's six foot exactly, with grey eyes and one or two freckles across his nose like a girl – and he stood over there making up his telegram and putting his hand through his hair. And then he brought it across. It was to Malloch, Rankine Lodge, Aberdeen: *'Hamlet revived and Hamlet revised stop our motto back to Kyd exclamation looking forward discussion – Gott.'* Then the next morning . . .'

Appleby regarded the sharp-eyed old person, thus steadily forging through a fortnight's telegrams, with something like professional envy. Her description of Gott was only a shade less miraculous than her verbatim memory of a piece of academic banter that must have been incomprehensible to her. His hopes soared once more, Even if there had been 'plenty like that' the old person seemed to have a virtuoso gossip's grip of the whole corpus. 'Then', he said, 'you may remember this telegram, *"Hamlet revenge"*, and its sender.' But a puzzled, almost cheated look had come over the old person's face; she shook her head sombrely. 'It's not long ago,' he said encouragingly; 'just eight days – a week ago yesterday.'

'Monday!' The old person was extremely indignant. 'You expect me to remember anything about a telegram handed in here on the Monday? Have you never heard of Horton Races?'

So that was it. That was why Gervase had received his message when he did. There was one day in the year on which anybody could send off a telegram from the little post office of Scamnum Ducis without the slightest chance of being remembered. And that was on the day of the local race-meeting, when the village became an artery for streams of cars, and when scores of these stopped hourly at the post office to enable their owners to wire or telephone bets. Not only could anyone have driven down from London or anywhere else and sent the telegram in perfect safety; anyone from Scamnum could safely have sent it too. For there had been two strange assistants working hard, and the Duke himself could have handed a telegram to one of these without anyone being the wiser. And, finally, the message had been handed over the counter, not telephoned. The old person found it without difficulty, duly endorsed as having been despatched at two-fifteen p.m. It was a common telegraph-form with the message pencilled in neat block capitals – a thing with which nothing could be done outside a fairy-story.

Appleby walked back to Scamnum with the feeling that in the matter of the messages he had come off second-best. All he had gained was certain exiguous facts of time and place. Setting aside the thoughts of agents and accomplices, he had it that the Black Hand had been in Scamnum Ducis post office at two-fifteen on the Monday before the murders and that a few days later – on the Friday – he had been *either* outside Auldearn's London home just after two *or* in the neighbourhood of the Scamnum south lodge just after four or – less probably – some-where on the route between these places at the time of the passing of Auldearn's car. But this information, if slight, was not valueless; it might serve to eliminate – at least in a tentative way – this person and that from what was an alarmingly large body of suspects. And in conjunction with the other similar tests a good deal of progress might be made. Take, for example, Malloch as a suspect. One would ask could he, on his verifiable movements, have (a) thrown the message into the car, (b) sent the telegram, (c) shot Auldearn, (d) stabbed Bose, and (e) at-tacked Bunney. By this means, laborious as it would be to apply to over a score of people, one should get a long way. And this was a fact that the murderer must have reckoned on; it was his rashness again. And suddenly Appleby halted in his stride; he thought it likely that he had got somewhere already – and not where he wanted to be.

He had taken Malloch as an example – involuntarily. Tucker's story had been extraordinary; quite extraordinary enough to make him, in the almost complete obscurity in which the case was still enveloped, eye the subject of it as a benighted traveller eyes a glimmer of light in the east. At the moment he would be sorry to see Malloch go. And Malloch, it suddenly came to him, lived in Aberdeen. He was said to have arrived from Aberdeen late in the evening of the Friday on which the message had been pitched into the car. Unless he had faked his movements – and to do so beyond the likelihood of detection would be difficult – he must have been hurtling through the midlands in an express train at the moment when Gott was smoothing out the crumpled message in Auldearn's car. And what about the previous Monday afternoon – the relevant time for Gervase's telegram? Would Malloch prove to have been south of the Tweed? Appleby – rather regretfully, rather irrationally – doubted it. Here was the technique of elimination beginning to work – and to dispel what hope of light there had seemed to be.

There was one further immediate inquiry to make in connexion with the messages. Appleby made a detour and visited the south lodge. It was, as Gott said, a curious twin affair, bridged across on the upper storey – one dwelling, apparently constructed on this fantastically inconvenient plan to gratify a melancholy taste for symmetry. And there were two pairs of twin staircases: a pair going up from within the park walls and a pair going up from the public road. Anyone who wished could go up and prance on the lodge-keeper's roof. Appleby, whom ill-success was making more and more radical-minded, felt that he could work out this gesture as a pretty symbol of what Crispins offer the world. But instead he ran up the steps and pranced on the roof himself – or at least walked round it and lay down on it. The bridge-affair had a three-foot parapet; by simply sitting down and appearing to sun oneself against the wall one could lie in wait, concealed from the road. It was the ideal place from which to launch Auldearn's message.

Appleby went down to the lodge and made inquiries about the Friday afternoon. But nothing had been observed. The gates stood open all day and when a car drove through it was not, it seemed, part of the lodge-keeper's duties to appear. You could hear people on the roof sometimes – walking-folk mostly – if you were in the upper rooms. But nobody would carry such a recollection in his head; there might have been somebody up there on the Friday or there might not. So Appleby came away not much wiser. That, for a moment at least, was the end of the messages.

And now to take up what Mason had been beginning to attack: the accounts people could give of their own or others' whereabouts at the time of the murders. And there was a considerable difference between the two. For the shooting of Auldearn there was an exact moment fixed; for the stabbing of Bose there was no such precision. Auldearn had been shot when everybody concerned was confined within the restricted area of the back-stage part of the hall; Bose had been stabbed when these same people had scattered to their rooms. The crucial moment, then, was the moment of the shooting. Who had been there – with whom – seen what? And here, Appleby felt, one might reasonably suppose oneself to be on extraordinarily promising ground. But he had a doubt. And he was canvassing this doubt in his mind when, approaching the house, he noticed Nave pacing moodily about the upper terrace. With a sudden thought he ran up the shallow steps and joined him. 'I wonder if you would allow me another professional consultation?'

For a second Nave looked at Appleby vacantly, as if the question had broken in upon some more than commonly absorbing train of thought. And for that second it seemed to Appleby that he saw more in those eyes than vacancy – he saw what might have been the hint of some intolerable strain. But Nave was alert in a moment. 'I will help if I can,' he said quietly.

'I have just been reflecting on the moment of the murder – Lord Auldearn's murder. There were nearly thirty people in the comparatively restricted area round about. And the murderer, even if he had been lurking within the curtains for some time before the shot, must have slipped away from them immediately after. He must have slipped out of them immediately after the murder had announced itself resoundingly. And yet nobody appears to have seen any suspicious movement – or at least nobody has come forward with anything of the sort. That seems to me strange. Surely the murderer was taking a tremendous risk? Or rather two risks: the risk of being immediately detected and the risk of the other people being able to vouch for each other's whereabouts so readily that one could come down to him by a process of elimination? What I am wondering about, you see, is the quality of people's attention and memory. Here was this shattering event. Would not the moment, the visible scene, be vividly printed upon every consciousness present?'

Nave took time to consider. 'It is an interesting point. And the answer depends entirely on the magnitude of the shock. If something interesting, surprising, or even thoroughly disconcerting happens one tends to remember the setting, the concomitant circumstances, more or less detailedly and vividly. That is true of everyone almost without exception. But it is a different matter when one comes to a substantially traumatic event – an event, I mean, involving a very considerable degree of shock. When that happens we are found to be split into types. Take being run over by a bus in the street. Some will have afterwards a complete picture of the occurrence down to the position, looks, gestures of the bystanders, and so on. Others will come from the same experience either in a state of amnesia about the whole affair – completely without memory of it, that is – or, what is more common, with a memory for it which is distinctly confused and unreliable. It is venturesome to attempt a numerical estimate, for there has really been no reliable statistical work done. But the people who remember vividly are certainly a minority.'

'This unexpected and shattering pistol-shot in the hall : would you class that, Sir Richard, as a substantially traumatic event – an event following upon which most people's minds would be confused?'

Nave appeared to consider almost anxiously. 'That again is interesting – very interesting indeed. I will tell you why. If the shot had been fired on some other occasion – say when we were all seated at dinner – the effect would have been startling, of course – but not, I believe, shocking in a technical sense. In the middle of the play it was different. I don't know if you have experience of the atmosphere of amateur theatricals; it is distinctive and peculiar. Everyone is oddly wrapped up in himself and his part. One seems to attend to other people without in fact attending to them. In making your inquiries about what was happening before the shot you will, I imagine, be surprised to find how vague everybody is about everybody else.'

Appleby nodded. This agreed significantly with something Gott had said.

Nave continued. 'And it was upon this absorbed company that the pistol-shot irrupted. The effect upon most of us present behind the scenes may not have been incomparable with the effect of being run over. Certainly I should expect a good deal of blurring and confusion of memory.'

'The murderer could have counted on that?'

'If the murderer has a flair for psychology – yes.'

'He has a flair for display,' said Appleby.

'That', said Nave, 'is abundantly clear.'

•

Noel Gylby and Diana Sandys walked round and round the lily pond. And conversation would not take the straight line it ought; it went round and round like the path. Partly it was because the gardens were without their usual privacy. Policemen – some meditative amid the beauties of Scamnum, others awkward before its splendours – still haunted the middle distance with unobtrusive efficiency. And partly it was because Noel and Diana had their minds on different things. Noel wanted Diana's view on the universe – but was shy on the job. Diana wanted Noel's explanation of the Scamnum murders – and was persistent. Irritation was just round the next curve.

'It's absurd,' said Diana. 'Here's almost a whole day gone and nothing seems to have happened at all. I don't believe they know anything. Who do you think did it?'

'Some silly ass,' said Noel with exasperating vagueness. 'Silly-ass thing to do.'

'It all seems to me remarkably smart. Everybody baffled.'

'Yes, just as you'd be baffled by some kid's trick that you can't get the hang of because it's simply too silly. Murders are done by people with kids' minds. Arrested development. Peter Pans – have you ever thought what a sinister affair that is? And if I had to pick among the people here for the murders I'd pick the prime silly ass, Peter Marryat. But I don't know that it's interesting. The poor devils are dead – and let the police do what they can about the loonie responsible.'

'That's just the air that the Duke has,' said Diana. 'I suppose it's Crispin hauteur.'

'Oh, come, Diana –'

'Exactly. "Come, come." And as for Silly-ass Marryat I don't know that he's more arrested than anyone else – though his mental age *is* about eight. If you were going sleuthing on those principles you'd have to tip almost the whole distinguished company.'

'All half-wits, you mean?'

'No. Just kids. All – or nearly all – with the motives of kids just underneath. Peter Marryat simply lacks a protective covering of conventional adulthood – that's all.'

'Isn't that rather a desperate view – average mental age human race eight?'

'I don't know. But you can't sell soap and toothpaste without knowing that people in general are sub-adult. Perhaps it's just in our time – a sort of progressive dotage. That's what I thought when I was doing Woman's-page before I got to copy-writing. The average mental age seemed to drop every week. In fact, we had a rule. If a thing was just too steep to put over – too unfathomably childish and imbecile – we simply put it in a drawer for a month or six weeks. Then folk were ripe for it. I suppose that's what's called history.'

'Yes,' said Noel hesitantly. He had got his discussion of the universe after all – and it rather alarmed him. 'Then what's to be done? Let the eight-year-olds and homicidal adolescents rip and look out for oneself?'

'Well, isn't that what you were putting over? The deaths of Auldearn and the little nigger man not interesting: let's talk about Life and Woman and Art and –'

'I meant –' began Noel, aggrieved.

'Never mind. But when one's sold soap and written up Woman's-page and seen people such trapped helpless mutts one feels that if one knew an honest, no-gup uplift one would go for it all out.'

'Yes,' said Noel – more happily. He was a fundamentally

serious youth and much concerned to establish Diana's seriousness.

'Or perhaps just do a good mop-up where one happens to
stand. Hunt out this public nuisance of a murderer, for instance.'

'Yes,' said Noel – with only a hint of doubt. This basing of a
pertinacious interest in Lord Auldearn's murder on impressive
if sketchy ground of high moral principle was not perhaps altogether consistent with Diana's first reactions to the same event
in the hall. But it would have been a maturer Noel who could
have reflected on this. 'Oh yes,' he said. 'Certainly he should be
hunted out. Appleby's job, though.'

'That,' said Diana, 'is what the Duke thinks.'

'You don't suppose we could take a hand ourselves? We
haven't any of the information that the police have – and I can't
see that we should have a single advantage over them.'

'I'm not sure. For instance, Noel, take people in the most
general categories you can think of. And begin placing the type
of the criminal that way.'

Noel considered dubiously. 'Oh well – to begin with I suppose
it's a man's crime –'

'Exactly!' said Diana, at once triumphant and indignant.

'I say, have I been tactless? Women's rights and all?'

'No. Just over-confident – as this policeman will be. Too much
guts in the affair to think of a woman.'

'I doubt if Appleby will take for granted –'

'He thinks he won't but he will,' said Diana firmly. 'And,
anyway, you and I are going to canvass the ladies.' She glanced
at Noel, saw that she had gained her point, and promptly added:
'*Please*, Noel.' To study the masculine temperament was – after
all – part of her job.

4

IT was late afternoon. Appleby and Sergeant Mason, sitting in
the green-room with pencil and paper before them as if playing
a parlour game, had been joined by Gott.

'I never thought we'd get as far,' said Mason soberly.

'It's not far enough,' said Appleby, looking at the lengthening
shadows on the floor.

Gott looked restlessly from one to the other. 'Are you on a sound track?' he asked. 'I should imagine that if you work purely on eliminations the evidence will almost certainly stop before it becomes useful. How many do you reckon left now?'

'Four,' said Mason. He had little enthusiasm for amateurs.

'That's impressive. But even so –'

'We may get something more yet,' said Appleby. 'And anyway, Giles, do you see any other method open to us at present – *any* other way of getting at the truth?'

'I think we've got it.'

Mason sighed. 'You mean you *know*, sir?' he asked gently.

Gott looked doubtfully from one professional to the other. 'Yes,' he said, 'in a sense that one knows where the kettle is – at the bottom of the sea.' He frowned at the tips of his fingers. 'It sounds very absurd, no doubt. But I feel that at the bottom of my mind, I *know*. And it's just a matter of getting it up to the surface.'

'I see, sir,' said Mason.

But Appleby was really interested. 'In other words, we have sufficient evidence before us – if we could see it. May be so. But surely, Giles, it's not a merely intuitive feeling you've got – a vague sensation in the back of the head? You must feel that your feeling comes – so to speak – from *this* and *that*?'

Gott nodded. 'Yes, indeed. And first and foremost is the strong impression one has of the dramatic aspect of the affair. In the light of that alone we should see our way farther than by all this alibi business.'

Mason, an intelligent man, reacted unexpectedly to this. 'I think you have a line, sir; I don't think it's impossible that you may get there first just by fishing in the depths of your own mind. I wouldn't like to be short with a thing merely because it's not my own way. But what about summing up our facts first – alibis and everything else? It might give you the start you want.'

Gott nodded. 'By all means. And perhaps my innings later.'

Appleby looked at his friend attentively. From Gott's mind, he believed, something really was going to emerge. He recognized in him just the same excitement that he had himself felt earlier in the day on making the significant link between

Tucker's Malloch-Auldearn story and the delay-theme in *Hamlet*. Such starts of mind may be will-o'-the-wisps – or they may be arrows to a mark. But now he turned to Mason. 'Go ahead,' he said briefly.

'Yes, sir. I'll begin with the first murder, although there are earlier events to be considered. Lord Auldearn was shot through the heart just on eleven o'clock last night. Owing to the construction of what they call the rear stage no one could see what happened, with the probable exception of the prompter – the Indian gentleman – who seems to have paid for his knowledge with his life. But we have a certain amount of evidence as to what occurred, nevertheless. There is the remarkable fact that the shot was not fired from the shelter of the double curtains : the experts swear to that on the strength of the powder-marks. Just conceivably the shot might have come from above when Lord Auldearn was in the act of lying down; in other words, just conceivably the shot might have come from the painter, Mr Cope. But it seems more likely that the shot was fired by a person who walked straight across the rear stage to effect it – risking the observation of the prompter in doing so. There may have been a moment's struggle or flurried movement, because an iron cross was knocked off what they call, I think, the faldstool; or this may have happened when the murderer was making his hurried escape back to the curtains. We must notice that the revolver – a small foreign weapon which it will not be easy to trace – was carried off the scene of the shooting and hidden in a very odd spot in this green-room here. And there's a point where I differ from you a little, sir. You see that as evidence of deliberate hardihood – one of a number of such pieces of evidence. But whatever we may think of placing the gun in the skull, I feel that carrying it away would be automatic. Calculation would no doubt tell the murderer to drop it before attempting his getaway through the curtains – I admit that. But calcution may not have come in. It isn't a man's instinct to drop a gun after firing; he makes off, gun and all.'

'A good point,' said Appleby quietly. 'Perhaps I was astray.'

'Well, sir, the next point is : No finger-prints, no material clues. And nobody saw anything; at least nobody had anything to report. At this stage – except for what's coming in the matter of Mr Bose – we seem to be faced with a perfectly successfully accomplished crime. We know that it must be the work of one of a defined but large group of people – the behind-stage people – and we know nothing else.'

Mason paused for a minute to take his bearings. 'The next point – or rather *not* the next point – is the presence of spies who are concerned to steal a document from Lord Auldearn. I say they are *not* a point in our case. They are distinct from it, run parallel to it, and by tackling them we won't get nearer Lord Auldearn's murderer. For a time it seemed that they might have succeeded in taking advantage of the murder. But that supposition is now dissipated. One of the spies – we presume there was a little gang of them – at first sent his principals a hopeful message: he thought either that the shooting had been a successful stroke of a confederate's or that a confederate had successfully taken advantage of it. But later he corrected himself, reporting that Auldearn's death was another affair altogether, and that their chance was gone. We take the spies, therefore, as having been present, but ineffective. They merely lead away from our business now.'

'No doubt true,' said Gott, who had been following Mason's methodical recapitulation with considerable respect. 'But nevertheless it seems likely that there is a spy among us still. It would be satisfactory to know who he or she is.'

'Yes, sir. But we must have concentration on the vital object before indulging miscellaneous curiosity.'

It was a crushing reply and Gott acknowledged it as such with a gesture. Mason plodded on.

'Next and as a matter of routine we look for bad characters. And we find reason to believe that a cracksman called Happy Hutton has been on the premises and has broken into three safes. Conceivably, he may later have insinuated himself among the audience during the interval. But after the interval he would be as cut off from behind-scenes as anyone else. Therefore, like the spies, he is irrelevant. We have his hat, it seems. But we can't jug him on that. Happy fades out.'

Appleby interrupted. 'Sorry; there's been a telegram you haven't seen.' He rummaged for a form on the table. 'It wasn't Happy's hat after all – not his size. So we've got nothing on him whatever except that I saw him scuttling for town like a scared rabbit some eight miles from Scamnum – and that the safe-work was his technique. That hat is another guest's as like as not.'

Gott chuckled. 'And how you crowed over it, John! Happy Hutton's habit with high hats and the vivid account you gave of them – well, well!'

Mason, possibly not without amusement, looked stolidly at his own large fingers. 'Happy fades out,' he repeated. 'And next we come to the second murder, that of Mr Bose. It seems next to certain that Mr Bose, as prompter, saw enough of what happened to be a mortal danger to the murderer. But instead of coming out with the story he went off in an outlandish heathen way to write home about it – as the custom was with him, it seems. And so he was killed too. His death has just two points of significance for us: it gives us – though much less precisely – another place and time at which the criminal was active; and it gives another of the evidences – undoubted this time – of something like foolhardiness in the criminal's conduct of the affair: he dragged the body about the house just for display. And the theme of display, as we all seem to be agreed, is a crux.'

Gott was stirring slightly impatiently again. His mind was too rapid for this stolid march; it wanted to leap about. But Mason, who felt there had been enough leaping about, went steadily on. 'This murder was planned, deliberately and at obvious risk, to take place bang in the middle of Shakespeare's *Hamlet*. And it was preceded by various more or less lurid messages, the burden of which was the idea of revenge. The point there, then, is clear. Vengeance – and vengeance in highly theatrical and sensational circumstances – is either the *real* motive or a *fake* motive for Auldearn's murder. For there is always the possibility that this *Hamlet revenge* business is a screen and that some quite different motive is at work. When we come to the people concerned – the definite number of people who *could* have killed Auldearn – we have to look about both for one sort of motive and the other. And we do come to the people now, after just one minute more with the messages.

'The messages, although they were launched with great cunning, give us certain further places and times. And one of them turned out to be dangerous to the sender – dangerous because Bunney's machine is an instrument, as it happens, of such phonetic precision that a voice recording for it would not be secure against identification however disguised. Hence the attack on Bunney and the stealing of that particular record from his collection.

'And now we come to the thirty-one people who were concerned one way or another with the play. We have to scrutinize their movements and – if we can – their minds and their pasts. In other words, we have to look for the cardinal things in a murder investigation : opportunity and motive. But we needn't trouble over motive where there was no opportunity whatever.'

Mason, Gott was thinking, was unafraid of the obvious. And yet Mason, may be, was the type of the successful policeman; beside him John Appleby seemed to have something of a lingering and speculative mind – a mind of which the true territory lay, possibly, elsewhere. But now Appleby interrupted with a hard saying: 'That depends entirely on the class of motive involved.'

Mason looked at him dubiously. 'I don't quite see –'

'What I say applies both to the shooting and to the sending of the messages. Take the point you're on now, the actual shooting. You say we needn't trouble over motive where there was no opportunity whatever. That holds, I say, only if a particular sort of motive is involved, the sort of motive that practically rules out conspiracy. If we were certain that the motive here were what it seems – a matter of private passion and long-cherished revenge – we would be justified in hunting only among the persons who had an opportunity to commit the crime. But suppose the sort of motive that is compatible with conspiracy to murder – murder for the sake of great gain, political murder, murder resulting from some anarchist or terrorist ideology, and so on – then what you say wouldn't hold. We might find the motive most readily in the mind or past of somebody who had not the opportunity, and go on from that to establish the fact of conspiracy with someone who had the opportunity. And again, there is the possibility of an actual murderer who is not so much a confederate as an agent or creature – who might himself be unaware of the ultimate motive behind his deed. And, obviously, the same considerations apply to the messages. Grant the possibility of the sort of murder to effect which men combine and the whole business of eliminations takes on a different aspect. To clear anyone of Auldearn's murder it will then not be enough to show that he could not have murdered Bose or attacked Bunney or been concerned with this or that message; his confederate may have dealt with these.'

Gott was about to come rather indignantly to the assistance of Mason when Appleby forestalled him with a nod. 'Yes, I know. It's not Mason's summary I'm attacking but my own earlier position. And even at that it may be I'm no more than making an academic point – or if academic is an ill-used word, say pedantic.' He smiled at Gott. 'I can't see any room for conspiracy. But let us say two things : we look for opportunity and motive alike just where we can find them; and we remember, as a theory to fall back on if necessary, that more than one hand may have been at work. And now, Mason – go on.'

'We come', said Mason patiently, 'to thirty-one people and begin to eliminate. And I suggest we begin by eliminating Lord Auldearn.'

Gott thought he might be pedantic as well as Appleby. 'It's quite certain he didn't shoot himself?'

'If he did,' replied Mason tartly, 'it's quite impossible to find sense or coherence in any of the previous or subsequent events; that's all.'

'It's not all – fortunately,' said Appleby. 'Mr Gott here could spin a yarn in which Auldearn shot himself and yet all these other things – Bose, the messages, Bunney – would have some sort of coherence and plausibility imposed upon them. Couldn't you, Giles?'

'I'm afraid', said Gott morosely, 'I could.'

'No, we've better ground than that. There was only one wound; the bullet came from the gun we possess, and we have expert evidence that it was fired at not less than two nor more than five paces. Quite apart from the weapon's having been removed, the evidence against suicide is conclusive. Eliminate Auldearn.'

'Having eliminated Auldearn, then,' Mason continued, 'I take it we can go on to the next victim and eliminate Bose.'

'Suppose', said Appleby, 'that Bose sent the messages and shot Auldearn – a sort of political or ideological crime. And suppose that the Duke, say, found out and killed Bose. The Duke, after all, is a curious creature. In the business of the document – when he conceived something like national danger to be involved – he reacted normally and efficiently. But his attitude to the murder is enigmatic – except in one point. He has clearly no enthusiasm for policemen and formal justice.' Appleby looked apologetically at Gott. 'You may think that fantastic and gratuitous. We are both convinced that Bose was not that sort of person, and no doubt you have – quite justly – the same conviction about the Duke. It's simply that we mustn't think we're locking doors when actually we're not. The theoretical possibility remains.'

'That the Duke stabbed Bose in the back in his own daughter's bedroom, and then hauled the body about Scamnum Court for the sake of a sort of wild justice', said Gott, 'is not my idea of a theoretical possibility. It's a laborious absurdity. And it still leaves you with Bunney on your hands. If Bose sent the messages, then only Bose would have an interest in attacking Bunney and getting the dangerous cylinder. And Bose was dead long before Bunney was hit on the head.'

'Very well,' said Appleby briefly – and gave Mason a nod.

'If we count Bose out,' said Mason, 'we're down to twenty-nine. The next people we eliminate are the Duchess and Mr Clay. They were on the front stage, in full view of the audience, and yards and yards from the rear stage. In a story, of course, it would *have* to be one of these two, just because they were where they were. Mr Gott' – Mason added with friendly irony – 'will know just how it could be done.'

'It would need', said Appleby, 'a revolver previously trained and released from a distance. A sort of infernal machine, in fact – and that never writes up convincingly.'

Gott meditated for a moment. 'Oh, no it wouldn't. You've forgotten something – or rather you've failed to guess at something which hasn't perhaps been mentioned. When that shot was fired in the hall it echoed and re-echoed about the place like a little salvo. All Clay, say, would have needed was an exceptionally loud one-bang firework on a time-fuse. That would go off when he was approaching the rear-stage curtains; he would pause for a second and then dash through and shoot Auldearn with a small pistol. The actual shot the audience would take to be one of the final echoes. What they would take for the actual shot would be just a squib, the remains of which Clay would promptly pocket.'

The impassive Mason was shaken at last. He stared at Gott round-eyed. 'But isn't that just what may have happened?'

Appleby interposed. 'No, it's very ingenious – but it won't fit this case. Clay was too long in getting through the curtain for the reverberations to be anything but very faint. Indeed, they must have been quite over. He was marking time because he didn't want to break the scene.'

Mason got out a large handkerchief and blew into it vigorously. 'I haven't come across anything so ingenious since I read a crazy thing called *Murder at the Zoo* –'

'Clay and the Duchess out,' said Gott hastily. 'Twenty-seven.'

'And I suppose twenty-seven more battles,' said Mason. 'At which rate we'll be talking here till midnight.'

'The battles are healthy,' said Appleby. 'We can't have too much of them. Twenty-seven. Go ahead.'

'Well, sir, at this point – keeping in mind what you have said about possible confederates – we have to make a distinction. We have to put people in three classes: those who are vouched for by other people at the moment of the shooting (though there again conspiracy might come in); those who could not have stabbed Bose or attacked Bunney or been concerned with one or more of the messages; and those who have no alibi for any of the relevant matter at all.

'I'll take first the people who are vouched for by other people. And there is, as it happens, a simplifying factor there – one that seems to rule out conspiracy in that regard. People were in groups. Wherever a person is vouched for he is vouched for by two or more companions. That is the greatest luck we've had; and I'm inclined to say the only luck we've had. It means that these people – a wild improbability of multiple conspiracy apart – really do go out. And here they are.

'The two dressers and the Duke's valet were together by the dressing cubicles and they had just called up one of the two footmen. That's a group of four. And the other footman was under the eye of Mr Gott and one of the American ladies, Miss Stella Terborg – vouched for by two. Mr Gott himself, this Miss Stella Terborg, Mr Noel Gylby, and Lady Elizabeth Crispin were all together – a group of four. Mr Piper, Mr Potts, and Lord Traherne were together – group of three – and Lord Traherne says he saw the parson, Dr Crump, and Miss Sandys a little way off. And as these two vouch for each other, each of them is thus vouched for by two. Finally, there were Mr Tucker, Dr Bunney, and the other Miss Terborg – Miss Vanessa. In a way that group is a special case, Bunney's testimony not being available. But I think we can accept it all the same. And that is as far as we have been able to get. As I say, we've been lucky to get so far. We might have had impressions and doubts to weigh up and we haven't; the evidence as far as it goes is decided and clear cut. When you allow for the confusion and shock we counted on it's good going. Twenty-one people are eliminated outright. Ten are left for the other categories.'

'I can't see', said Gott, 'that it's really good going. I was prepared for confusion – and yet it seems to me quite extraordinary that at the moment the shot was fired there should have been ten people in that back-stage area, each invisible to the other or to anyone else. *And* each, it seems, able to give a plausible account of his or her whereabouts.'

Mason shook his head doggedly. 'It followed partly from the lighting, sir, and partly from the rather elaborate way the area had been partitioned off – the number of little cubicles and so on – and partly just from flurry and confusion. And they do all give a reasonable account of themselves; I haven't been able really to rattle a single one of the ten.' He turned to Appleby, 'Shall I go over that ground?'

Appleby nodded.

'The Duke, when he came off after the prayer scene, went straight to the little telephone hutch behind the green-room. He had remembered some instructions he wanted to give about the calling round of people's cars after the show. He was just about to pick up the instrument, he says, when he heard the shot and hurried to the rear stage. Nothing shaky there. Mrs Terborg was alone in her cubicle; Macdonald and Dr Biddle the same; Mr

Marryat was alone in the sort of general men's room that the men's cubicles give upon. So far, there are two points to make. All these people account for themselves perfectly naturally; and all profess to have been at a considerable distance from the stage. But that last point is not conclusive: a sharp person could, I believe, have slipped about fairly freely. Still, these people were in considerably less interesting positions than the remaining five to whom I am coming.'

Mason, it seemed to Gott, was a man resolved to get somewhere – confident that he was getting somewhere minute by minute. Beside him Appleby, very still and absorbed, seemed a personification of wary doubt. They made, unquestionably, a formidable combination. Gott began to feel his own imaginative tinkering with the case a very ineffective method of attack indeed.

'Five people,' said Mason. 'Mr Cope, Sir Richard Nave, Professor Malloch, Mr Gervase Crispin, and Mme Merkalova. Cope, we know, was on what is called the upper stage – immediately above the scene of the crime; he was alone and if he shot Auldearn he shot through the little trap. So much for him – he was close enough anyway. And so was Malloch. Malloch affirms that at the moment of the shot, he was climbing up the little staircase to the upper stage; it had come into his head, he says, to take a glance at Cope. Again, it's a likely enough story, I suppose; and he could easily be there without being seen, for the staircase is quite elaborately match-boarded in. But there he is too, as close to the scene of action as could be. And next Nave. Nave had been close to the back curtains of the rear stage, listening to the prayer-scene. At the close of it he lingered a minute or so and then turned round and walked towards the green-room. He was a little more than half-way when he heard the shot. So he also was warm. And finally Mr Gervase Crispin and the Russian lady. They were together in the green-room when it occurred to them to have a look at the audience – again a likely enough story, particularly in the light of the affair of the snap-shot camera: no doubt the lady wanted to see who was where. Well, they came out of the green-room and moved towards the stage. But at the back of the rear stage, they separated, Mr Crispin going to the left and the lady to the right, so that they were hidden from each other by the rear stage itself. Each, that is to say, was going to peer through one of the entrances to the front stage – the entrances that flank the rear stage on either side. Once more, it is perfectly reasonable – and yet one could see it as the first movement in a concerted attack. There they were, both free from observation, and in a dead line between them – and separated from each merely by the double curtains that form the rear stage – was Lord Auldearn.'

Appleby stirred. 'Bose,' he said. 'Within these double curtains, close by where Gervase Crispin went to stand, was Bose, the one man who might have had an eye on the rear stage.'

Mason nodded. 'That carries on the idea of a concerted attack. Mme Merkalova, say, was to shoot Lord Auldearn while Gervase Crispin somehow distracted Bose's attention. Only Gervase Crispin failed.'

'That's a theory,' said Appleby; 'or a bit of one. And now let's have the last batch of facts.'

'Yes, sir. The final facts concern the movements, at the other significant times, of those ten people who are unvouched for at the time of Auldearn's murder. They relate to the messages, to the stabbing of Bose and to the attack on Bunney. And they are facts, we are agreed, which may be considered as positively carrying the eliminative process further only if we neglect the possibility of conspiracy. Here they are as far as they go – for we haven't yet finished checking up. I needn't go into details, I think. I'll just sum up:

'The Duke could not have got the message into Auldearn's car either in town or subsequently. He could not have attacked Bose; he could not have attacked Bunney; he could not have been at the post office in Scamnum Ducis within two hours of the time endorsed on Mr Gervase Crispin's telegram. And the same holds of Mr Marryat: he could have done none of these things. Mme Merkalova has not a set of alibis like that but she has one. She cannot account for herself throughout the periods within which occurred the attacks on Bose and Bunney: on both these occasions she claims to have been alone in her room. Nor can it be shown that it was impossible for her to have sent the telegram; she was already staying here on Monday and she had gone out for a longish walk in the park, alone. But she could not have got the message into Auldearn's car. Dr Biddle has a similar partial alibi – one similarly conclusive on one point. He could not have stabbed Bose : we have that on the authority of our own local men – he was down here, fussing round them, all the time. But he seems unable to bring evidence that he wasn't lurking on the roof of the south lodge, or that he didn't send the telegram or that he didn't go upstairs after breakfast and hit Bunney on the head. Nave is in the same position as Biddle. He can clear himself on one point only – the attack on Bunney. He was in the hall with yourselves and Lady Elizabeth during the whole period at which that could have happened. And Gervase Crispin, finally, has an alibi on all counts but one. He couldn't have run down and sent himself the telegram; he couldn't have attacked either Bose or Bunney : but he could have been up on the south lodge pitching a message into Auldearn's car. And that is as far as we have got, the remaining four people not yet having been fully questioned. At the moment it comes down to this : if we allow the possibility of conspiracy we have ten suspects for Auldearn's murder and no very clear means of getting further : if we rule out conspiracy we are down to these four people who remain to be questioned – and it may be possible to eliminate some of them. Notice that there is nobody who has failed to produce an alibi – sound alibi, I guarantee – for at least one event yet. And the four people left are Macdonald, Mrs Terborg, Cope, and Malloch.'

There was a little silence. Mason sat back in the consciousness of honest work accomplished. It was Gott who spoke first. 'It would be uncommonly injudicious to abandon the notion of conspiracy while it stares one in the face.'

'Two things stare us in the face,' said Appleby. 'And one involves conspiracy and the other virtually excludes it. You are back on the old ground of Gervase and the Merkalova, Giles – and certainly here they are again in startling enough concert. They bear down on the flanks of the rear stage at the critical moment with more than a suggestion of deliberate manoeuvre. And then when we come to study people's movements in relation to the other events, we find their alibis over the series coming together like the pieces of a puzzle. The one thing the

Merkalova couldn't do – get the message into Auldearn's car – is the one thing Gervase could do. As you say, it stares us in the face. But what of a motive – a motive of a conspiratorial sort? They weren't after a document of Gervase's own composition. Then what were they after? At the moment one sees no glimmer of motive. The only motive that one sees anywhere is the motive one can attribute to Malloch. That, of course, is the other thing that stares us in the face. And it takes us right away from conspiracy: we agree, I suppose, that if the motive is a stored-up revenge from the remote past the notion of confederates and so on is an unlikely one.'

'It comes to this,' said Mason. 'If there was no conspiracy we have four suspects: Macdonald, Mrs Terborg, Cope, and Malloch – with a strong line on Malloch. If there was conspiracy we must add to these as possible murderers of Auldearn: the Duke, Marryat, Biddle, Nave, Gervase Crispin, and Mme Merkalova. With a line, in that case, on the last two. But not, I put it, a strong line. The interlocked alibis and the movements at the time of the shooting are startling at first, I admit. But they're a good deal less impressive after you've had a steady look at them. You were impressed, Mr Gott, because you had these two people linked in your head earlier on, when the document was on the carpet.'

This sound observation Mason apparently designed as his last word for the moment. He applied himself to stuffing a pipe and looked expectantly at Gott, as if awaiting the promised innings. Logic had got as far as it could: if imagination could get further – let it. But Gott, too, was filling his pipe; and having lit it he puffed silently until prompted by Appleby. 'What do you think, Giles: have we got anywhere?'

'I'm bound to think you have. I don't see Auldearn's death as a conspiratorial affair. And that being so, and taking your eliminations as valid step by step, I admit that you are confronted by four suspects: Macdonald, Mrs Terborg, Cope, and Malloch. But they don't impress me as I feel they should.' He looked apologetically at the impassive Mason. 'In fact, as suspects they don't appeal to me.'

But Mason was not to be drawn. And Appleby's formula came as usual: 'Go on.'

'Just consider them. Macdonald has worked in the gardens here – man and laddie as he would say – for something like forty years. You've gathered his type: severe, steady, dignified, and a bit of a tartar – a compendium, in fact, of all the most uncompromising Scottish virtues. It's simply unbelievable that he should break out into murders and murderous assaults. And there is nothing whatever against him except the local sergeant's story that early this morning he was found lurking about the hall. Somehow I can't attach much importance to that.'

'Quite so,' said Appleby.

'It needs explaining, all the same,' said Mason.

'Then Mrs Terborg. Isn't she another type one just *knows* about? Polite New England with a lot of Europe on top. And we're to suppose her guilty of two murders, a murderous assault and miscellaneous activities including dragging a dead body about the house in the small hours. I don't see it.'

'Quite so,' said Appleby. 'She and Macdonald, in fact, belong to the two most inflexibly virtuous traditions that the Western World has produced. The kind who might, perhaps, commit a crime under some severe provocation, but who would *not* embark on a series of consequential crimes to save themselves. It's an impressive psychological argument. Go ahead.'

'Max Cope. One can just conceive a crazy old man determining to kill Auldearn because of some mortal grievance buried in the past. And one can conceive Cope sending the messages. He knew the sources of Gervase's message: *Hamlet, revenge!* And I remember his asking the Duchess if there was to be a detective in the house: you might consider that suspicious. And he's a cunning old man – and perhaps malevolent. But I can't see him as having the drive to put through the whole series of events. I've seen quite a lot of him and unless he has been simulating a failing brain for years he just doesn't possess the intellectual grasp and tenacity to proceed, move by move, as the criminal has done. For you'll agree, I think, that there has been more than just cunning at work. There has been something like incisive intellect.'

'Quite so,' said Appleby. 'And now Malloch – the last man in.'

'Don't forget', said Mason, 'that even these four are in only negatively, so to speak. They're just the four that are left over at the moment and to be questioned by Inspector Appleby presently. It may be possible to eliminate more of them.'

'It may be possible', said Gott, 'to eliminate them all.'

'Malloch,' interposed Appleby invitingly : 'the great scholar. And you can't say, Giles, that scholars don't at times behave in a distinctly curious way.'

'No. I've no psychological arguments to advance about Malloch. And if Tucker's story is true it's impressive.'

'It's true all right,' said Appleby, 'as far as the stuff being in Anderson's book goes. It's all here – the whole story of the Jacobites and the Mallets.' And he tapped a book on the table.

'You've wasted no time. But my point about Malloch is simply that he will probably eliminate himself out of hand on our no-conspiracy basis. He came straight from Aberdeen on the Friday.'

Appleby nodded. 'Yes, I know. And we'll be certain soon. But I'm leaving him to the very last – to cook.' He looked at his watch. 'Which reminds me : we're not going to be left entirely in peace much longer. The local Chief Constable's on his way here now. He's come pelting over from Ireland.'

'What sort?' asked Mason.

'A very gallant officer. And quite new to the job.'

'Ah,' said Mason darkly – and added after a moment : 'But Mr Gott hasn't given us those ideas of his yet.'

Gott shook his head. 'I haven't exactly got ideas. I just think there are other possible lines to take up – that material is before us which might lead straight to a solution. I think we want to know just why Auldearn was killed when and where he was. That it was simply to set his death in a context of *Hamlet* and so make an enigmatic statement or manifesto about delayed revenge – the Malloch theory in short – seems to me ingenious but not quite adequate. The circumstances of the murder were not merely decorative but structural – you understand me? That is my first feeling.'

'Yes,' said Appleby; 'I did some thinking along that path too.

It was so because it had to be so. I find that satisfactory as a general proposition; I mean I feel the criminal to be the sort of person who would like it that way. But at the moment I can't drive the idea further.'

'That is my one point,' said Gott. 'And the other is this. Something went wrong.'

Mason stirred in his seat. 'Wrong, sir?'

'With the showmanship – the producing. Even if the dramatic manner of the thing served some practical purpose which we can't at present place – even so, the dramatic manner of the thing was something that the murderer delighted in for itself. And there was a hitch. Something went wrong.'

Appleby was tidying accumulated papers on the table. Mason looked at Gott with a sort of perplexed respect. 'How do you make that out, sir? I mean, how do you know?'

'I'm quite prepared to believe I'm making an ass of myself. Or perhaps something canine – believing I can usefully work by smell. But I seem to know out of a dramatic sense – akin to the murderer's, I suppose – that has been sharpened at the moment by the business of producing the play. But you mustn't attend to me too seriously. I know how much it is something in the air.'

Appleby finished straightening his papers. 'The Chief Constable', he said, 'will find our dockets on the table even if our ideas *are* in the air. And I've had sufficiently airy beckonings in this case too, goodness knows. For one thing, I should like to spot why I'm so constantly beckoned by Fate in *Les Présages* –' He stopped to stare at Gott. 'Giles, what on earth –?'

Gott's eye had fallen on the topmost paper of one of the little piles. And now he had sprung up, seized the pile, and was beating the air with it like a maniac.

'Giles – for heaven's sake! It's only the telegrams sent out for people this morning. What's come over you?'

But Gott was pacing about in a blaze of excitement that made even Mason's eyes grow round. 'Yes,' he cried presently. 'Yes ... yes ... and yes!' He whirled about on Appleby. 'I will *not* cry Hamlet, revenge!' He paced about the room again; stopped. 'There's a snag – of course there's a snag.' He flung out an arm, snapped a finger in extravagant bafflement. Decidedly, thought Appleby, Giles had never behaved like this before. 'There's a snag – a horrid snag. But there it is – *there it is*!' And he swung round the green-room, chanting :

> '*Come, seeling night,*
> *Scarf up the tender eye of pitiful day,*
> *And with thy bloody and invisible hand –*'

From the door of the green-room came a respectful but desperate cough.

'The Chief Constable,' announced Sergeant Trumpet.

5

'SANDFORD'S come,' the Duke announced. Sandford was the Chief Constable – but from the tone he might have been the Last Straw. Took it upon himself to hurry back from a holiday in Ireland. When we were getting on very nicely with that unobtrusive young man.'

The Duchess looked at her watch. 'How rather awkward! Will he stop to dinner?'

'And take a short view of the suspects over the soup?' suggested Noel.

'You can't have murders without these awkwardnesses turning up,' said Mrs Terborg placidly. 'Perhaps, Anne, he will like to dine with the detective – and confer, don't you think? The detective seems quite –'

'Yes,' said the Duchess. 'But I don't know that I could just suggest it.'

'The last time Sandford came here to dinner', said the Duke, he began by talking nonsense on dry-fly, went on to a boring description of the Harrow match, and ended by being impertinent about the port. Nevertheless, Anne, you must ask him – and let him have a view of us as Noel says. Go along.'

The Duchess rose with a sigh. 'Teddy,' she said, 'they don't suspect you by any chance – or you, Noel? And they can't suspect Elizabeth?'

The Duke shook his head. 'I don't think they can reasonably suspect any of us.' He glanced in surprise at his wife's troubled face. 'And I don't know that we need exactly commiserate ourselves over it. I've no desire to be gossiped about as Ian's possible murderer.'

'No, of course not.' The Duchess crushed out a cigarette. 'But I wish I hadn't been sitting in sober innocence on the front stage. And I wish the family *weren't* clean out of it. We ask a lot of people down and Ian and Mr Bose are murdered. And we keep well clear and have Colonel Sandford in to suspect the poor wretches round the dinner-table. It's rather mean.'

'There's still Gervase,' said Noel cheerfully. 'I'm not sure they're not hot after him still. So there's a chance for the family yet. Bear up, Aunt Anne.'

Mrs Terborg interposed briskly. 'This is great nonsense. To begin with the poor wretches take the police and so on as quite in the day's round. This horrid thing has happened and we must expect to be badgered. And for another thing, Anne, you don't care twopence for the poor wretches. You care only for what's been and done with – and anxiety for the feelings of your guests is merely defensive social disguisement. And for a final thing I'm sure they can't suspect Mr Crispin. They're much more likely to suspect his –'

'Friend,' said the Duchess firmly. 'Perhaps you're right, Lucy – and you're a great comfort. And now for Colonel Sandford.'

The Duke got up. 'I'm coming too. Bagot must go down and find a bad Bordeaux. I promised myself never to give that man Scamnum port again.'

Noel was left on the terrace with Mrs Terborg. He eyed her warily, misliking his job. But the exigent Diana stood behind him in the spirit, as ineluctable as some invisible Homeric goddess commanding the hero to engage. For a few minutes they conversed indifferently. Then Mrs Terborg prepared to rise. 'Almost time to go up,' she said.

Noel did not like to contemplate what would happen if he missed his chance. 'I say,' he said, 'did you ever go round to Peter's Gothic pavilion, Mrs Terborg?'

'Gothic pavilion?'

'Yes.' Noel was guardedly eager. 'Everybody doesn't know

of it; it's tucked away beyond the rock-gardens. I'd like to show it to you.'

Mrs Terborg may have been shrewdly surprised at the attention, but all she displayed was mild gratification. 'How interesting – such an interesting man Peter must have been! If we have time –'

'Oh, yes,' said Noel. 'Do come.' And artfully he held out to Mrs Terborg the bait of polite learning: 'A Gothic pavilion convertible into a greenhouse. I believe it was taken from Repton's *Theory and Practice of Landscape Gardening*. Long afterwards, of course, because Repton died – didn't he? – quite early in the century. We go round this way.' And he led Mrs Terborg through the gardens.

Diana had prepared a questionnaire; getting it skilfully across, she had said, would be good diplomatic training. Noel rather wished he had it before him in black and white. It had run so smoothly when rehearsed by Diana – was such an innocent excess of friendly curiosity. But now it went so badly that Noel felt that, like Peter Marryat with the Norwegian Captain, he must be muddling it all up. Or perhaps it was just that Mrs Terborg's responses didn't end where they ought, so that there was difficult steering to the next point. Still, Mrs Terborg seemed unaware of guile, and by the time he had got to Question Six Noel was beginning to have some confidence in his ability to extemporize approaches.

'What magnificent Dorothy Perkins!' said Mrs Terborg.

Noel leapt at an opportunity for Question Seven; he didn't understand it but Diana thought it particularly important. 'Frightfully prickly, though,' he replied. 'You need gardening gloves before you think of touching them. By the way, did you happen to leave a pair of kid gloves in the hall last night?'

'I'm sure I didn't,' said Mrs Terborg firmly – and gave Noel what might have been described as a long look.

Noel felt a little trickle of sweat down his spine. The thing was like a horrible drawing-room game in which you have to insinuate outlandish words into your conversation undetected. And that last attempt had been almost fatally clumsy and precipitate; he must go slow and strive for the authentic Crispin finesse. So he abandoned the questionnaire during the inspection of the Gothic pavilion and talked glibly about Repton and Capability Brown.

> At Scamnum, Croome, and Caversham we trace
> Salvator's wildness, Claude's enlivening grace,
> Cascades and Lakes as fine as Risdale drew,
> While Nature's vary'd in each charming view.

The Rise and Progress of the Present Taste in Planting Parks – you know it? Very amusing?'

This was what Mrs Terborg liked; the expedition to the convertible greenhouse became for a time a great success. 'Mason,' Noel continued easily, 'in his *English Gardens* – a romantic tragedy of landscape gardening, you know – Mason is thought to describe one of the Scamnum conservatories; not this one but the classical one beyond the orangery:

> High on Ionic shafts he bade it tower
> A proud rotunda; to its sides conjoin'd
> Two broad piazzas in theatric curve,
> Ending in equal porticos sublime.
> Glass roofed the whole. . . .

Odd to bring a design for a greenhouse back from the Grand Tour. Have you been in Greece much?'

Mrs Terborg had been in Greece, knew Turkey – and yes, she had been in Russia several times. This, on the other hand, was perhaps an over-ingenious approach to the groups of questions dealing with Movements and Interests, but eminently it had finesse. Noel was once more rather pleased with himself and all went well until, when they were again in the rock-gardens, he got to Question Fifteen, which was almost the last. But at Question Fifteen, although Noel considered it particularly adroitly introduced, Mrs Terborg halted.

'Mind you own business,' said Mrs Terborg.

Noel was overwhelmed. 'Oh, I say, I'm most frightfully –'

But Mrs Terborg had stooped down to the border. 'This one with the tiny flat leaves,' she said. 'Such a quaint name: mind your own business! And everything is here: elecampane, birthwort, lovage, rosemary, clary. . . .' And she held to her own favourite species of polite learning until they reached the house. Noel made no attempt to deflect her; he concluded – as he presently explained to Diana – that there had been a Hint.

*

But still Diana would not be put off. 'We're getting on,' she said.

'Getting on! I've been getting on Mother Terborg's nerves, if that's any good. And I don't see that the women offer any field at all. There's only the Merkalova that's fishy –'

'She's a wrong 'un, all right,' said Diana viciously.

'And we're only down on her, really, because she spat out nasty about you. In fact – I think this is where we stop.'

'The next thing', said Diana, 'is to get into the hall. Do you think we can? I want to nose round.'

'Nose round?'

'Just that. *Nose*, Noel. Noel, *do* get me in – *please*!'

'Well,' said Noel, melting but judicial, 'as long as there's no more Terborg-stalking stuff, and provided the heavies aren't still lurking there after dinner, I expect we could reconnoitre.'

'Oh, good. But, Noel, there *is* more on the Terborgs. Think of the twins.'

'I have in the past. But at the moment I'm not promiscuously minded.'

'Thanks. But *think* of them.'

Noel made a resigned gesture. 'I suppose this to be the way my unmellowed Aunt Anne treated the young Teddy. All right; I'm thinking of them. Then what?'

'Don't you see –' Diana paused as Gott came out on the terrace and stood looking at them dreamily. 'But here's an authority. Please, Giles Gott, if you were writing a mystery story – one all about x being here while y was over there – wouldn't you find two people who might pass for one another uncommonly useful?'

For a full ten seconds Gott stared at her.

'Invaluable,' he said, 'Miss Sandys – invaluable.'

*

Colonel Sandford put down the telephone with a clatter. 'That was the Home Secretary,' he said. 'Inspector! – the Home Secretary. We must act.'

'Did he say we must act, sir?' asked Appleby mildly.

'No, no. Not that. But he is concerned – gravely concerned.'

'We're all concerned, sir,' said the sober Mason.

'Quite so. But we must prepare to move in this affair – to move, you know. Now, Inspector, where are we? I have great confidence in you – confidence. Now what grasp have you? Grasp on it – grasp.'

Appleby did not think the pompously agitated Chief Constable too bad a fellow. He replied carefully. 'At the moment it's like this, sir. We're trying to get people into three groups. The first group comprises those who could not have shot Lord Auldearn. The second group comprises those who could have shot Lord Auldearn but who could not have committed one or more of the other acts: sending messages, stabbing Bose, attacking Bunney. The third group – one we're trying to establish – comprises people who could *both* have shot Auldearn *and* done everything else. And shortly before you arrived we had four people left to deal with. These were the only four people left who *might* have done everything. So you see where we were. We had, so to speak, four chances left of proving the possibility of its having been a one-man affair. If all those four people could prove that they belonged to the second group – the group of those who could have shot Auldearn but not done something else – then we should be faced with the certainty of a conspiracy; the certainty that a criminal and one or more accomplices must be involved.'

'I see, I see. In fact if these four establish themselves as in the second group you're back nowhere.'

'Not at all, sir,' said Appleby patiently. 'We should merely be back with a larger group of people – ten, to be precise – who might have shot Auldearn but who could not have done one or more of the other things; for whom, in fact, we should have to find an accomplice or accomplices.'

'Yes, I see. You mustn't expect me to be as quick as you are. I see. But, if these four make their get-away to the second group, at least it's a set-back?'

'Quite so, sir. And we're now at our last chance. The four remaining people were the head-gardener, Macdonald; old Mr Cope; the American lady, Mrs Terborg; and Professor Malloch.'

'Cope – that old fellow? He painted my grandfather – deuced well.'

'Yes, sir,' said Appleby politely. 'Well, we were interested in Macdonald because he behaved in a suspicious way early this morning – he was found prowling about the hall and invented some story of looking for a snuff-box. But I hadn't much hope of him because of the message that was thrown into Lord Auldearn's car. He could only have had an opportunity for that when he passed the car some way up the south drive and it would have been exceedingly difficult. And, in fact, Macdonald routed us. He couldn't have murdered Bose; he couldn't even have sent the telegram from Scamnum Ducis. So he goes very clearly into Group Two.'

'But still suspect of something? What about this business of skulking about the hall?'

'I got an explanation out of him about that – though with a good deal of difficulty. It's odd – quaint indeed – but I feel inclined to accept it. A few days ago Macdonald was induced, it appears, to repeat the shorter Catechism and one of Burns's poems for the American philologist, Dr Bunney. And he discovered afterwards, to his great annoyance, that these recitations had been recorded by Bunney's apparatus – the machine, as you know, sir, through which one of the messages was delivered. And when Macdonald heard about that – about Bunney's machine being mixed up with the messages – he got really worked up. For he believed that we would try to trace the perpetrator by means of Bunney's record – which is just what we were going to attempt when Bunney was attacked – and that everything about the machine would inevitably be exhibited in court. Well, he wasn't going to stand for the outrage of his versions of Burns and the Catechism being reproduced at the Assizes and he determined to get possession of the relevant cylinder – which he conceived to be still in the machine. The machine was in the green-room and that was what he was stalking. As I say, it's odd. But it's true to character, it seems to me, and I don't disbelieve it.'

'Well I'm dashed,' said Sandford. 'I suppose he ought to be prosecuted. But if that's all there was to it, I think we'll let it alone. I don't altogether blame him.'

'No, sir. And the immediate point was that as a single-handed criminal Macdonald was out. And – to be brief – Cope and Mrs Terborg have established themselves clearly enough in Group Two as well. So it's a case of one beer-bottle sitting on a wall.'

The Chief Constable meditated the proprieties for a moment and decided to laugh. He laughed loudly. 'And if *that* beer-bottle has an accidental fall – well, there was more than one person in the game. Malloch, you say? Is he any more hopeful than the rest?'

'Yes, sir – in a way. I've left him till the end on the chance that it may rattle him. He's in a special position – the only person against whom there's any suggestion of motive so far.'

'Ah, motive!' said Sandford eagerly. 'Motive; yes, of course – enormously important. Glad you've been on to motive. I'd forgotten it. Shocking thing – my mind hadn't turned that way. Motive.'

'Yes, sir. There is a story – with considerable foundation apparently – of something like deadly enmity between Malloch and Auldearn. Something dating from their student days.'

'I say!' said Sandford. 'Better have Malloch in. Embarrassing, chivvying gentlemen – but it must be done. I'll keep quite quiet, you know – just sit by. Better have him in.'

'Yes, sir.'

*

Nave entered his bedroom and closed the door. A sunbeam, dropping towards the horizontal, broke upon the dress-clothes laid out on chairs; the man had been and gone.

He moved to the window and looked out for a moment abstractedly; then his gaze travelled to the summit of Horton Hill. The crowd, the ice-cream barrows – they were there still. He smiled grimly at the distant audience, smiled as the student may smile at a predicted result. Then he turned and paced the room – up and down in some mounting agitation : it might have been anxiety, bewilderment, some ungovernable impulse from within. He halted as if to steady himself, undressed deliberately, went into his bathroom, and turned on the bath. He came back.

Standing in the middle of the bedroom he let his eye travel – but reluctantly, mesmerically – to a far corner. Resolutely, he brought it back to the business of cuff-links; uncontrollably it strayed again.

He strode to the bookshelf. And warily, as if it were a forbidden act, he took down a book.

*

With serious politeness Mason set a chair.

'Professor Mallet?' said Appleby.

'Malloch.' Malloch was not more severe than an eminent savant should normally be. And he did not seem disturbed.

'Malloch – I beg your pardon. And I am sorry to have left you till the last – and so near dinner-time. We have asked people to come in and discuss matters in quite a random order, I am afraid.'

'No doubt,' said Malloch. And he looked square at Appleby across the table. It was to be a real duel – this Appleby instantly knew, and knew that Malloch had deliberately given away that fact to him. It was a declared duel, with buried deep in it the strange enjoyment that such things can have.

'Mr Malloch, you have particularly interested yourself in *Hamlet*, and came to Scamnum to take part in the late production for that reason?'

Malloch considered this line of attack carefully. Appleby wondered if he would protest at once, as he well might. It was an opening more proper to a barrister in a court of law than to a policeman soliciting statements from possible witnesses. But Malloch replied deliberately and fully. 'Yes, I have published a study of the play called *The Show of Violence* – chiefly in the province of literary criticism.' Literary criticism, the tone implied, was a scholar's relaxation from severer things. 'And when I was invited to come up I was very glad to accept. Mr Gott, though chiefly a textual worker, has stimulating ideas about the drama generally. I welcomed talk with him.'

There was a pause. It was rather – Sandford reflected – like the opening of a test-match : slow and infinitely cautious. And, forgetting his conviction that the Home Secretary expected immediate action, he settled down to listen.

'And, like most of the other people, you had agreed actually to take part in the play before you came?'

Malloch answered both question and implication. 'Yes, I did not think I should feel awkward in it. There was to be sober company enough.' Which was true. There could be no ground for saying that he had shown a suspiciously unprofessorial levity in getting himself where Auldearn's murderer had been – in the play.

'By the way, you knew the family?'

'I knew the Duchess slightly. But I came, as I have said, chiefly through the instrumentality of Mr Gott.'

'You knew Lord Auldearn?'

'We were students together at Edinburgh. And we have met fairly frequently since.'

'And you know Mr Cope well?'

'Cope? Only by reputation. I am not aware of having met him before.'

'I see. I thought you might be friends, since you were going up to visit him on the upper stage, it seems, almost at the moment of Lord Auldearn's death. Might your visit to him not have disturbed the play?'

'I was merely going to stand in the shadow for a moment and glance at his canvas. He had invited me to do that earlier, when we were having some talk on the progress he could make during the performance.'

Appleby knew this to be true and that it was one of Malloch's strongest cards. But it was wholly without emphasis that Malloch laid it on the table.

'But you did not actually go up?'

'No. I was half-way up the little staircase – I suppose there are no more than a dozen steps – when I heard the shot. I stood still for a few seconds wondering what could have happened. Then I smelt gunpowder and guessed it was something serious. I turned back and got down just as a number of people were hurrying up. I understand that none of them noticed me come down the staircase. There was a good deal of confusion.'

'Quite so,' said Appleby. 'But here you were, sir, remarkably close to the actual crime; closer perhaps than anyone except Mr Bose. You cannot help us in any way; you have no information, nothing to suggest?'

Malloch took time. 'I have no special information or you would have had it despite our delayed interview' – he smiled gravely at Appleby – 'long ago. And my thinking on the subject is unlikely to have done more than parallel your own – if that. Primarily, I should conceive that the number of spaced-out acts committed by the criminal would be a great factor in his detection.'

This sounded like confidence – but it might be bluff. 'Yes, we must come to that presently. But my mind is on *Hamlet*; on the fact that Lord Auldearn died in the middle of *Hamlet*. I wondered if, with your knowledge of the play, you could help us there?'

'I don't think I can,' said Malloch.

'I was thinking particularly of motive. Here is an imaginative criminal –'

'A gratuitous assumption, inspector. Say a fanciful criminal.'

Appleby accepted this academic correction smoothly. 'Here then is a criminal of fanciful or fantastic mind. He kills Lord Auldearn in fanciful or fantastic circumstances; accepts a good deal of risk in order to do so. Why?'

'Conceivably because the criminal, like Hamlet, thinks of himself as in pursuit of vengeance. To kill his man in the middle of the play would be – in a rough and ready and a fantastic way – to say so.'

There was a silence. Then Appleby renewed: 'Thinking along those lines – which I confess have occurred to me – can one get any further? Can one qualify, for instance, the sort of vengeance with which Hamlet – and thus conceivably our criminal – is concerned?'

Malloch responded slowly but without hesitation. 'It is a tenuous line, perhaps, but certainly one can carry further – and in more than one direction. There is, for instance, the motive of Hamlet's vengeance: the theme of fractricide, incest, and usurpation punished. In the criminal here you might look for something equivalent to that. Or you might neglect the motive of Hamlet's vengeance and consider its character. Predominantly, it is a procrastinated revenge. That is what has always been debated about *Hamlet*: why the delay?'

This time there was a longer silence. Malloch was as steady as a rock. It was clear that he had the whole case against himself in his mind and had deliberately made the discussion of it inevitable. Had he some power in reserve? Appleby greatly feared he had: an unshakable alibi in Aberdeen. He took up another line.

'Mr Malloch, the safest way to commit murder is colourlessly: a shot in a lonely place, a knife in a crowd. When a murder takes place in curious circumstances – as Lord Auldearn's has done – there are two likely explanations. One we have touched on. The criminal, a person perhaps of unbalanced mind, wishes to actualize some fantasy, to kill startlingly or grotesquely. The other explanation of a murder accompanied by odd and striking circumstances is that there has been an attempt to involve an innocent person – a plant or frame up. The marked peculiarities of circumstance are there because they point at somebody. You follow me?'

'I suspect,' said Malloch, 'that I precede you.'

Colonel Sandford blinked at the grimly facetious repartee; Mason stolidly took notes; Appleby said, 'I believe you do.' And there was another silence.

'If you are inviting my opinion,' Malloch continued presently, 'on the likelihoods of an attempted plot to incriminate an innocent man, I will give it. I think it unlikely.'

This was too cool. Appleby came abruptly into the open. 'I suggest that some unknown person – having read Anderson's book or being possessed of other information – shot Auldearn after having concocted all this *Hamlet, revenge!* business in order to incriminate yourself, Professor Malloch. You think that unlikely?'

Malloch inclined his head gravely. 'You no doubt wish to suggest that it is a theory that should have its attractions for me. Maybe so. But as one a good deal accustomed to weigh evidence I cannot accept it.'

'Will you tell us why?'

'Certainly. My first reason is that it is nonsense. There is nobody – knowing Anderson's forthcoming folly or not – who would wish to incriminate me in a murder charge. That is a thing which a man may be presumed to know. Secondly – and this will impress you more – the suggestion will not stand logical examination. In contriving the messages and shooting Auldearn as he did the criminal incurred grave risks. Before he did so he would, we may be sure, want to be reasonably certain of his object – that of incriminating me. Could he be reasonably certain of a situation in which he would be safe and I would be compromised? I think not. And – more conclusively by a long way – his method of incriminating me as you suggest it would be the very way – almost certainly – to let me out. The messages – which are, after all, only a feeble pointer in my direction – would actually be, in all human probability, fatal to the plan. It is inconceivable that he should be so minutely familiar with my movements, minute by minute and hour by hour, as to be certain that for one or more of these messages I had not a solid alibi. And on a single solid alibi the whole risky and laborious plot would break at once. Your kindly suggestion won't hold.'

'I am inclined to agree,' said Appleby. Inwardly, he was contemplating a wall without beer-bottles – and the remote and stony streets of Aberdeen. Neatly enough Malloch had come round to what would be Appleby's breaking-point as well – alibis on the early messages.

'And the fact', said Malloch quietly, 'that I am possibly uncovered for any of the relevant times is a remarkable circumstance on which your supposed criminal could not conceivably reckon.'

For an instant the words rang meaninglessly in Appleby's ears; then he realized their bearing. 'Ah yes,' he said equally quietly, 'we must come to that now. You will understand that questions intended to establish alibis are of a routine nature and put to everyone.'

'No doubt,' said Malloch.

'That the information with which you are volunteering to help us you may if you wish withhold, or defer until you have taken legal advice.'

'Quite so,' said Malloch.

'And that anything you say will be taken down and may be presented in evidence against you or otherwise.'

'No doubt,' said Malloch.

'And now, if you will be so good, we will work backwards. The attack upon Dr Bunney between nine-thirty and ten o'clock this morning. Nobody has mentioned you as in their company, so I presume –'

'Immediately after breakfast I went to the library and stayed there, alone.'

'Thank you. Did you meet anyone going or coming?'

'No.'

'The murder of Mr Bose between one-forty and two this morning.'

'Shortly after the search in the hall I went to my room and stayed there.'

'Thank you. Most people, of course, did just that. And the time of Lord Auldearn's murder we have discussed. So now we come to the messages. I understand that you came from Aberdeen –'

Malloch calmly took out his watch and looked at it. 'I would not wish', he said, 'not to change. Perhaps it will shorten matters if I explain that I was in London for over a week before I came down to Scamnum.'

Appleby looked at him very gravely. 'There is a general impression –'

'Quite so. It is a matter of social prevarication. I was pressed to come earlier but, although I looked forward to the play itself, I rather fought shy of long preliminaries. So I pleaded pressure of work in Aberdeen and arranged to come south on the Friday, arriving here after dinner. That was the course of things I actually expected. But I found myself able to get away a week earlier and took the opportunity to go to London and put in the time at the Museum. I then came here on the Friday evening as arranged. And I judged it not necessary to explain my previous movements.'

'In fact you gave it out that you had come straight from Aberdeen?'

'By implication – possibly so.' Malloch was unperturbed.

'There were five messages that we know of. Working backwards again, there was the message on the radio-gramophone early on Sunday morning. I do not suppose that you, more than anybody else sleeping in the house that night, have an alibi for the effecting of that?'

'I am sure I have not.'

'Nor for the message that came through Dr Bunney's apparatus at breakfast on Saturday? I think you had the apparatus explained to you shortly after your arrival on Friday night?'

'Yes. No alibi.'

'Nor – again like everybody else – for the letter posted in the West End to Mr Gylby on Friday?'

'No alibi. And anybody could arrange for such a thing.'

'Quite so. And now, can you detail your movements on Friday – everything before your arrival here?'

'I was at the Museum at ten and worked, under the frequent observation of people who know me, till half past twelve. Then I took a cab to the Athenaeum and kept a luncheon appointment with the Provost of Cudworth – an erratic scholar but a credible witness. He had only an hour; we parted at a quarter to two and then the fine afternoon tempted me to walk in St James's and the Green Park. I took a cab back to the Museum a little after three.'

'You met nobody you knew during this walk?'

'Nobody.'

'You could have been outside Lord Auldearn's flat off Piccadilly a little before two o'clock and tossed a message into his car?'

'If I had known Auldearn's car was standing off Piccadilly I could no doubt have kept an appointment with it.'

'Thank you. There is only one other relevant time, that concerning the telegram sent to Mr Gervase Crispin from Scamnum Ducis. Can you take your mind back to the Monday of that week – eight days ago?'

'Yes,' said Malloch. 'That was the day I went down to Horton races.'

The lead of Mason's pencil snapped on the page: it might have been a revolver shot. Then Appleby said: 'And you still reject the idea of a plant?'

'Yes. No danger of drowning would make me clutch at it. I am convinced that nothing but coincidence is involved.'

'Will you give us an account of your racegoing experiences?'

But Malloch was not to be shaken by sarcasm. 'Certainly. I like – perhaps because I am a man of the people – to mingle with common life. It is not a matter of curiosity and observation; it is just that I like a vulgar crowd. I keep it a private foible – a matter of occasionally slipping away. And on the Monday I simply went down with the crush on the excursion train, mingled with the crowd on the course, and returned as I went.'

'And you met, of course, no one whom you knew?'

'Fortunately not. Or perhaps unfortunately not. For I take it I really am one of those who fulfil all the conditions you want – who could, in fact, have done everything?' Malloch was stony still but pale.

'Professor Malloch, supposing all these acts to be by one hand, you are the only person who could be responsible.' Appleby paused. Then, in a deadly stillness, he enumerated: 'The two murders, the assault on Bunney, the five messages –'

Sharply, the house-telephone interrupted: an urgent buzzing at his side. Appleby picked up the instrument. 'Hullo –' His chair fell backwards with a crash; he sprung to his feet. He depressed the receiver-arm, released it, was calling urgently: 'House-exchange ... where was that call from ... where ...?'

He put the instrument down, looked at his companions. 'The sixth message,' he said; 'another line from *Hamlet* and again about revenge: *"The croaking raven doth bellow for revenge."* It looks as if there may be miching mallecho still.'

Mason put his notebook in his pocket; Sandford swore. 'Where from?' he cried. 'In heaven's name – did they know?'

Appleby hesitated. 'Well, sir,' he said, 'plainly not from Professor Malloch.'

And he ran from the room.

*

Ten minutes later Appleby came downstairs and ran into a gracefully dinner-jacketed Gott.

'Now that Sandford's here I daren't approach,' said Gott. 'How are things?'

'Backwards. No beer-bottles sitting on the wall. Malloch was the last and he's just had his accidental fall. So it's as you prophesied. As far as a one-man show goes everybody is eliminated. Conspiracy is now the word.'

Gott shook his head. 'If I prophesied that I was wrong. And I don't think I did. My point was that in all this eliminating business there were too many quirks. One might trip. And one has. I can find you a single-handed murderer yet.'

Appleby stared at his friend. 'The dickens you can! And, I suppose, tell me all about the sixth message?'

'There's been a sixth message? Perhaps I can tell you what it was. "*The croaking raven doth bellow for revenge.*" '

Appleby fairly jumped. 'Giles! how did you know?'

'By applying your own favourite method, John. Elimination.'

Appleby took him by the arm. 'This', he said, 'is where the shy scholar has a quiet talk with the police.'

6

'I am sure', said Colonel Sandford, square before the fireplace and speaking in a politely diffident yet discreetly fatherly way, 'that it has been a very trying time for you all – very trying indeed.'

The arrest had been made; the news had gone round; the first stupefaction was abated, and in its place was dawning an enormous relief : the nightmare of uncertainty and suspense was over. And now at half past nine the Chief Constable had collected a small group of people in the little drawing-room. Plainly he was pleased – exultant in the knowledge that he had taken action and that there was calm in Whitehall. But he was decently subdued, semi-official to just that degree which becomes a soldier playing policeman at Scamnum Court – in fact altogether correct. The Duke might have repented about his dispositions in the matter of port.

'A time of bewilderment and anxiety,' amplified Colonel Sandford, 'and I think you are entitled to some explanation of how the matter has been cleared up.' He considered for a moment. 'That is perhaps a prejudical expression – let me say rather – entitled to an explanation of how we have reached our present position. And as all of you here will, in the nature of the thing, be required as witnesses I don't think I ought to risk the appearance of laying down the police case to you now. It might not be quite correct – not *quite* correct. But I am going to ask Mr Gott – who pieced things together, you know, pieced them together – to give you his own brief outline of the affair. If you would be so good, Mr Gott.'

Mr Gott looked as if he had very little impulse to be so good. But around the room was a little circle of expectant faces from which there was no decent escape; to decline would be the part of a conjuror who walks off the stage with a much-advertised trick still in his pocket. Gott edged himself a little further into the shadow of a generous chair and began cautiously and informally.

'The affair has been full of contradictions; even now it's difficult to thread one's way through them. For instance, there was all the appearance of premeditated murder – and of murder heralded, almost literally, by a blast of trumpets. But I don't know that murder was intended. And I am quite certain that there was no intention of shooting Lord Auldearn. It was when one had a first suspicion of that, indeed, that one might have seen a first gleam of positive light.'

A murmur, discreet and fragile as the Ming and 'Tang about the walls, ran round the little drawing-room – a muted version of the expectant buzz that greets the entrance of the Disappearing Lady.

'Again, the mystery appeared baffling. But in a sense it wasn't meant to be that. And it was when one got the idea that it wasn't meant to be baffling that there was a chance of its ceasing to baffle. If that is rather enigmatic I will put it this way. The thing was theatrical. It had, as we all felt from the first, an element of showmanship or display. Just what was being displayed? On that question I was present at an interesting conversation between Mr Appleby and Sir Richard Nave. We explored the notion that a motive was being displayed, that the peculiar circumstances in which Lord Auldearn died constituted a cryptic but very real manifesto of motive. Well, there was the motive – already declared in the messages – of revenge. And taking the central problem of *Hamlet* into account we hit on the conception of a delayed revenge. We were not altogether astray there, for that notion did, I think, come in. Nevertheless the pursuit of a displayed motive was, in a way, an obscuring factor. It obscured the question: Was anything else displayed?

'And failing an answer to that question, a solution was, I believe, a very long way off. Mr Appleby, after analysing the entire series of events with which he had been confronted, came to the conclusion that an element of conspiracy was essential in the case. And he was finally faced with a considerable number of people – I think ten – any one of whom might have been Auldearn's murderer, but each one of whom would have required a confederate to carry out one or more of the other actions which appeared to be bound up with the case. Now, inquiry strictly along those lines would eventually have exhausted itself – for the simple reason that there *was* no conspiracy. And after that it would have been natural to inquire by what device the criminal succeeded in doing everything himself while making it appear impossible that he could have done everything without a confederate. But that inquiry would have been unsuccessful too, because it would have been wrongly grounded. The facts are these: it appeared to Mr Appleby that no one of the persons involved could have done everything; actually one of the persons involved could have done everything; but the appearance to the contrary was something not devised by the criminal but fortuitous.

'I say, then, that a solution was far off – failing an answer to that obscured question: Was anything else besides motive deliberately displayed? And that question was not adequately pursued; it just happened that at a certain stage an answer to it thrust itself under my own nose. You will see the point that I am making here – though to make it is really to anticipate. There has been in this affair an element of deliberate duel. The criminal displayed certain things which one might or might not spot – introduced, in fact, a perverted sporting element. And in the whole conduct of the affair the criminal made no mistake: only where a clue was offered has a clue been found.

'But now let me take up certain questions in the order in which they presented themselves.

'Why was Lord Auldearn killed in the middle of *Hamlet*? That was the first question and one couldn't look at it long before feeling it to be insufficiently precise. It was better altered to: Why was Lord Auldearn killed at Act III, Scene iv, line 23 of the Scamnum *Hamlet*? For then there was an obvious answer: Because Lord Auldearn was alone in a small enclosed space, and because at that moment he was expected by everyone within ear-shot to act in a particular way. *He was expected to call for help.*

'Now, from technical evidence – a matter, I believe, of slight powder marks – we know that Lord Auldearn was shot at fairly close range. Barring a suggestion that he was shot from above, it is certain that the murderer walked out to the middle of the rear stage. That gave a second question. Why did the murderer do this? Why forsake the safety of the curtains, from the shelter of which it would be possible to shoot, and walk out under the possible observation of the prompter? Three things suggested an answer: the messages; the answer to the first question; and a certain haunting memory, confessed to by Mr Appleby, of the ballet called *Les Présages*. Mr Appleby's memory was of Fate or Destiny, a figure of whom one suddenly becomes aware as standing, threatening, on the edge of the stage. Fate, retribution, revenge – you see how Mr Appleby's mind had moved. And you see, too, what was designed to happen on the rear stage. The avenger, who had already so explicitly threatened Auldearn in the message thrown into the car, was to step boldly out – at whatever substantial risk of observation by Mr Bose – and confront the victim. And you see the peculiar pleasure proposed. In those agonized seconds in which Auldearn recognized his attacker and his attacker's intention he would be helpless. He might cry out for assistance in the instinctive words that would come on such an occasion – and not a soul in all the hall would take it to be other than as Polonius that he was calling. "What, ho! Help, help, help!" That, structurally, was why the murder occurred where it did in *Hamlet*, and to that any decorative notion of a manifesto of motive inhering in the play was secondary. It was a diabolically-conceived thing.'

Gott paused – and paused amid a dead silence. For a moment the nightmare had darkened even as it was being dissipated. But presently the quiet, almost reluctant voice continued.

'I believe that Mr Appleby – though he will say nothing about it – had arrived at all this long before I had. But the next point was peculiarly my opportunity. Just as he had an obstinate sense of that fleeting parallelism with *Les Présages*, so I had an obstinate sense that – somehow and in terms of our own show – the thing hadn't gone right. The effect had not been as it should be. I puzzled over this and could make no headway with it for a considerable time. As directed against Lord Auldearn the thing had been perfectly effective. And then I saw that there was something lacking to it in another aspect – its aspect as something presented to the audience. For something was assuredly being presented to the audience; we are all certain of the sense of showmanship involved. An artist was at work and I felt – being keyed up, I suppose, in matters of theatrical effect – that something had fallen out as this very formidable mind could not have designed. And I hunted it down at last. It was the way the murder announced itself in a pistol-shot. The pistol-shot was startling enough – but how much more effective if Hamlet had simply drawn back the curtain in the normal course of the play and found Polonius – Auldearn – really dead! Why was Auldearn killed so noisily – why not, for instance, quietly stabbed and left for Hamlet to reveal to the audience? I looked at that question for a time and thought I found it, as you may find it, fanciful – a mere imaginative refinement. So I put it by. I didn't realize that in contemplating it I was contemplating the heart of the case.' Gott paused again. 'I didn't realize', he added – absorbed and wholly unconscious of contriving a grotesque effect – 'the essential connexion between Auldearn's having been shot and Mr Appleby's friend Happy Hutton's not having left a hat at Scamnum after all.'

There was another silence. Somewhere at the back of the room Peter Marryat, who had slipped in uninvited, sighed in perplexity. All this was running away from him.

'I don't know that one could have hit on the truth at that point. But in the early hours of this morning I overheard a conversation which really should have given a key. If either Mr Appleby or I had contrived to leap upon that we should have solved the mystery in something like a dramatic manner – and not, as it has been solved, on evidence which the murderer, in that pervertedly sporting manner, has deliberately provided.

'Now let me turn for a moment to motive. The pursuit of

motive, I have said, in a sense obscured one question – the question of other things that the murderer might have built into the manifesto, the display. Nevertheless the pursuit of motive did take us somewhere. The crime – the original murder of Auldearn to which the subsequent murder of Bose was merely consequential – seemed to be a passional crime; one, likely enough, of revenge or retribution such as the face-value of the messages suggested. Revenge or retribution over what? And, if one of the implications of the *Hamlet* situation was to be accepted, delayed or suspended revenge over what?

'I think Mr Appleby, though conscious of the structural reason for Auldearn's death taking place where it did – the getting the victim, I mean, in a situation in which he could call for help in vain – retained some faith in what may be called the manifesto-significance of the situation. He took as dominant in the play the notion of delay and then tried to interpret the crime as an act of vengeance for a certain personal injury that occurred a very long time ago indeed. But, for my part, I was impressed by something said by Sir Richard Nave in a conversation I have already mentioned. He implied, I took it, that a very long-delayed revenge would be – at least at a certain intellectual level – surprising, unless the cause of the supposed injury were still in some way present: he instanced a stolen thing still flaunted. Now, in the case Mr Appleby was tentatively constructing, and which I need not particularize, there had been – according to a legend that came his way from Mr Tucker – a stolen thing. But there was every reason to suppose that this stolen thing had disappeared from the picture long ago. So I was inclined to ponder another suggestion Nave put forward. Delayed revenge, he suggested, might be the consequence of some deadly and irreconcilable ideological conflict which had extended over many years. I say that interested me. For whereas Mr Appleby's theory involved a young and passionate Ian Stewart from very long ago – too long ago, it seemed to me – this other suggestion might involve the contemporary Lord Auldearn – I mean the statesman, the philosopher – and the man who sometimes invoked his power as a statesman to enforce his philosophy in its practical implications. In fact I felt that, seeking some such motive as this, I was approaching – if only approaching – psychological probability in respect of the intellectually and speculatively inclined people gathered in this house. You will say that men do not commit murder to defend an ideological position – much less as a sort of demonstration in its favour; they commit murder out of fear or cupidity or some variety of sexual passion. But perhaps that is not fully to take account of our time.'

Gott hesitated, as if seeking some brief expression of what lay in his mind. 'All over the world today are we not facing a rising tide of ideological intolerance, and are not violence and terrorism more and more in men's thoughts? And this dressing-up of the lawless and the primitive as a ruthless-because-right philosophy or world-picture or ideology that must and will prevail – is this not something to haunt and hold naturally unstable men, whatever their particular belief may be? The modern world is full of unwholesome armies of martyrs and inquisitors. We bind ourselves together by the million and sixty million to hate and kill – kill, as we persuade ourselves, for an idea. Are we to be surprised if here and there an individual kills simply because he hates – and simply because he hates an idea?

'At this point it would I believe have been possible, granted a good enough brain, to solve the mystery. But I was far from having such a brain and Mr Appleby, all this time, was preoccupied with an alien, but very grave matter on which I shall presently have to touch. And so the solution came not dramatically but by chance. I say chance without exaggerating one iota. It so happens that the criminal has a certain relative. That relative does not impinge upon the case in the least. But if that relative did not exist, we might never have discovered – and it is a humiliating thought – that the criminal had boldly signed to the murder, not once, but again and again.'

*

Slowly, the little drawing-room was dissolving into shadow; the last glow from the west had climbed to touch the shoulders of Whistler's Anne Dillon by the piano and disappeared; the blue and silver nocturnes, the early *pointillist* Copes, the hot and flashing Dillons were swimming together on the walls. A cooler breeze stirred at the open window, whispered through a great bowl of flowers, caused somebody to slip timidly from the window-seat to a warmer place. And Gott's voice talked on, remote, growing colder. . . .

'If Sir Richard Nave, I say, did not have a brother – a brother who like himself practices medicine – he would be unsuspected still.

'He invited suspicion. I believe that he knew his own craziness; that the sporting chance he gave represented his own sane self, looking with his own scientific ruthlessness at his own growing madness and endeavouring to ensure that the madman should not escape. Perhaps that is too subtle, too much one of the quiddities of his own craft. We shall never know. And I do not forget that in a legal sense Nave is not mad, is very far from mad; I don't deny that in the last issue he is not a criminal lunatic, but a criminal.

'He invited suspicion in a series of displays, not insinuating his motive cryptically but declaring his identity almost outright. These displays – I mean, of course, the messages – were investigated diligently enough. But that very diligence tended to hide the key they contained. The questions Mr Appleby asked about the messages were: *When?* and *How?* When were they sent? In what manner? Which one of the possibly suspect persons could have contrived this message and that? There was, of course, another question: *Why* the messages? But the answer seemed so obvious that one didn't pause over this aspect long. The messages were simply the showman-criminal's way of announcing his purpose. *Hamlet, revenge!* That was the first message – the one sent to Mr Crispin at the House of Commons – and there seems nothing to pause over. It is simple and appropriate, conjoining menace and the projected play. Next Lord Auldearn's message is seen, in the light of later events, to add to this a grim dramatic appropriateness; in the car that brought him beneath the walls of Scamnum were found Lady Macbeth's words on another fated victim:

> *The raven himself is hoarser,*
> *That croaks the fatal entrance of Duncan*
> *Under my battlements.*

'The next message, that to Mr Gylby, was a couple of lines from *Titus Andronicus* – lines which did no more than reiterate the idea of revenge:

> *And in their ears tell them my dreadful name,*
> *Revenge, which makes the foul offender quake.*

' "Foul offender" gave perhaps something more. Nevertheless it was at this message, I think, that Mr Appleby paused to ask a very acute question: Why *all* these messages? They were not all equally effective; why should this criminal, so careful of his effects, send as many as five messages of varying effectiveness? Mr Appleby's answer was certainly accurate: the diversity of messages was a challenge. The criminal was saying in effect: "See how many messages I can send – each in a different way – and get away with." But there was another question besides the question: Why so many messages? There was the question: Why just *these* messages?

'And this question should have become clamant with the next message – the message that came through Dr Bunney's philological box: *I will not cry Hamlet Revenge.* The method of delivering the message was effective but the message itself seems pointless. What point, again in the light of subsequent events, could be thought to attach to that recantation? And at this stage I must say that I am ashamed of myself. My mind failed to go at once to the source of this message. And with a sort of obstinacy with which Professor Malloch, perhaps, will sympathize, I avoided looking it up. I didn't see the matter as significant and I wasn't going to be beaten over something I certainly new. Actually, the phrase *I will not cry Hamlet Revenge* comes from Rowland's *The Night Raven.* The fact came back to me in the instant that I happened to glance at Nave's telegram – a telegram he had despatched through the police this morning, putting off a patient. Commonly one signs a telegram with one's surname only; but because Nave has a brother, also a practising physician, he has a different habit. And I looked at the signature 'R. Nave' and saw the anagram at once.'

There was a little pause. Peter Marryat, too enthralled to be diffident, called out: 'I say – please – what's an anagram?'

'When you take the letters constituting "*R. Nave*",' said Gott soberly, 'and form from them the word "*Raven*", you make an anagram. In other words, Nave had – if in the rather tortuous way that is characteristic of the modern medical psychologist's mind – set his signature to two of the original five messages – indeed to three. The raven was hoarser; *The Night Raven* was quoted; and the second passage from Macbeth – the one that came through the radio-gramophone in the night – was cut off by me just before it spoke – if not actually of the raven again – of the *crow* and the *rooky* wood. When Mr Appleby told me this evening that a sixth message had been received I was able to guess the very words. For there was one message, the most pat of all, that had not come – a passage in which the raven and revenge and *Hamlet* are all bound up together. Most of you will remember what I mean – Hamlet's exclamation in the play-scene: *The croaking raven doth bellow for revenge*. Mr Appleby had half-expected a further message. And these words of Hamlet's were actually spoken to him over the telephone a few hours ago – and spoken, as the man in the house-exchange was able to tell him, from Nave's own room. When Mr Appleby hurried up there he found Nave's own Shakespeare beside the telephone and open at the page. And a fraction of an inch below the line in question treatment revealed the fresh imprint of the index-finger of Nave's right hand. Which was the end – or all but the end – of the affair. There was something in Nave, I repeat, that would not let the murderer get away. He gave the police their clue and then, when they appeared to be making no headway, he gave it them again. *The croaking raven doth bellow for revenge*.'

*

Gott stirred in his chair. 'I said all but the end of the case. Even at this stage there was a snag. But before I come to that let me put briefly what I think occurred, and bring in some important matters which I haven't yet mentioned: for instance the iron cross.

'But for the iron cross there might, I believe, have been no murders. And but for the iron cross there would not have been that hitch to the affair in its aspect as something presented to the audience. But I must begin at the beginning.

'Here, then, is Lord Auldearn, a veritable symbol of a certain old order of things. He is, I say, a statesman, a philosopher, and a theologian. His writings are famous; to be found on most thoughtful people's shelves – including I know, Mr Appleby's. And here again is Sir Richard Nave, another typical figure – a scientist, a hard-boiled nominalist, an aggressive atheist – as many of you know who have conversed with him – and a life-long contemner of superstition, priests, priestcraft, and all the rest of it. What then happens? Does Nave decide to make away with this symbol of all that stands against him? I think not. But he does something else. Partly from some necessity of his own inner nature and partly – I have suggested – worked upon by the ideological terrorisms of our time, he begins to weave a fantasy of destruction round the figure of Auldearn. Two phrases of his stick in my head – I think they were spoken with reference to crime stories and crime films: "a healthy resolving of suppressed criminal tendencies in fantasy" and "safety-valves". Now it may be possible that inventing imaginary crimes is a "healthy resolving" and the rest of it – I don't know. But what Nave did was something different: he began envisaging a crime against a real person whom he really hated. To imagine that that was a safety-valve was just bad psychology. And the moment came when the impulse stepped outside the borders of fantasy and began to actualize itself – actualized itself by degrees.

'This is what I meant by saying that the murder was, in a sense, not premeditated. Even when the messages were sent the position was no more than this: that the fantasy had got ominously out of hand. I don't know when Nave provided himself with a revolver, but it would be to that action that I should point if I had to indicate the moment at which unreason got the upper hand. He was arming himself against eventualities.

'But – as I have said – he didn't mean to shoot Auldearn; the revolver was a precaution. What held him, and now impelled him forward, was the unique dramatic opportunity, the opportunity to confront Auldearn in the very character of Nemesis and kill him in the moment that he was calling in vain for help. I think he meant to stab Auldearn, just as Bose was stabbed; to stab him, and leave the body for Hamlet to find. It was a compelling fantasy; you may say that the circumstances were conspiring to unbalance him finally. But even yet it might have remained fantasy merely and the messages a harmless folly that would never have been explained. It was the arrival of the cross that was fatal.

'Here, ready to hand on the faldstool, was to stand a heavy iron cross. To what a terrific power would the representative, the ritual power of the act be raised if he should snatch up this symbol and with it dash out his victim's brains! So he abandoned whatever dagger he had meant to use – but the revolver he retained against emergency.

'Why, then, did the plan miscarry? Why the shot? Ideally, it would have been possible to arrive at the answer – and in consequence to get very near to the identity of the criminal – on the strength of two things I have mentioned: an overheard conversation; and the hat that was not Happy Hutton's hat. Briefly, Mr Appleby found a hat in Lord Auldearn's room and concluded it was not Auldearn's because it was bigger than Auldearn's other hats. But there is a certain condition in which one's new hat will be bigger than one's old: it is if one happens to suffer from Paget's disease.'

If Gott relished the odd turn his narrative was taking he gave no sign. His voice flowed on without emphasis. 'Lord Auldearn was gravely ill. But why was there such passion behind a technical diagnostic discussion between Nave and Dr Biddle – a conversation overheard by Mr Appleby and myself in the hall? I can remember what they said. "Clearly the localized form," Nave said, "*Leontiasis Ossium*." And Dr Biddle replied "*Leontiasis* fiddlestick ... simple generalized Paget's." And over that Nave was passionately angry. Why? Well, I need not and cannot be technical. Put it this way. What, in effect, Nave was saying was, "At the moment I was going to strike my rather rusty general medicine came back to me; I saw that I was proposing to crack a morbidly thick, morbidly hard, and ivory-like skull: as I couldn't risk failing to kill I dropped the cross and shot instead." And what Dr Biddle replied was, in effect, "You were wrong; the skull was certainly abnormally thick; but it was far from being abnormally hard – rather the reverse." In other words, Nave used the revolver as he did, and in doing so marred his intended effect, because, suddenly becoming conscious of Auldearn's morbid condition, more precise knowledge failed him in the sort of lightning diagnosis he then made. He supposed himself to be in the act of hitting at something like a billiard-ball. Actually it was not so; he might have hit out effectually enough. And his vanity was injured by the mistake. Dr Biddle tells me that if Nave's general medicine had not been distinctly in disrepair he would have recognized the significance of Auldearn's bowed walk and other symptoms long ago.

'This matter of the changed plan is the most remarkable feature of the case. It is the one point at which the criminal came up against the unexpected and the one point at which he might have been caught on ground – so to speak – other than that which he voluntarily gave away. The right man – an acute medical jurist, I suppose – hearing this technical conversation in the hall, might just conceivably have got somewhere on the strength of it. At any rate, it is the point at which the sheerly bizarre is most evident in the case; in telling a story for effect one would stop at it. Nevertheless, there is another matter of some importance that I must explain.

'Even with all this there was a snag – a hitch in the case against Nave. Mr Appleby, you remember, had got to a stage in his investigations at which he had ruled out the possibility of single-handed crime. Reviewing the events linked up with Auldearn's death in relation to what was known and provable about people's movements, he found that nobody could have done everything. The murderer must have had an accomplice. Had Nave, then, an accomplice? The sort of crime which we are imputing to him – a crime actualizing a private fantasy – is not the sort of crime in which one would expect conspiracy. What, then, was the exact position? It could not be shown that Nave was unable to send any of the messages. It could not be shown that he was unable to murder Auldearn. It could not be shown that he was unable to murder Bose. But it could be conclusively shown that he was unable to attack Dr Bunney. At the moment that attack was made Nave was talking with Lady Elizabeth, Mr Appleby, and myself in the hall. It would seem at first logical to look for the accomplice that Nave must have had. But he had no accomplice.

'Consider the relationship of all these events on which Mr Appleby was relying in his eliminative process. The messages, plainly, hold together among themselves and cohere with Auldearn's murder. Unmistakably, the person who sent them was directly concerned in that murder. Next take the death of Mr Bose. Of that only one explanation was found to be reasonably tenable: he was killed because he knew something about Auldearn's killing. But now we come to the attack on Dr Bunney.

'Was this attack, equally with the other events, bound up with the original murder? The accepted version took it that this was so. At breakfast this morning Mr Clay happened to suggest that Bunney's apparatus, being a phonetic instrument of unusual precision, might hold a clue. It might be possible to identify the voice which, carefully disguised, had delivered through it the message *I will not cry Hamlet Revenge*. And at this – it was suggested – the murderer took alarm and shortly afterwards attacked Dr Bunney in order to obtain the potentially incriminating cylinder. To support this interpretation is the fact that after the attack the cylinder in question, indexed as "The curious message", was found to have disappeared. But it has to be asked whether this is the only conceivable explanation of the attack on Bunney, whether it is the best explanation one can suggest, whether it is a good, or even possible explanation. Why, for instance, half-murder a man in order to filch from his room something that might have been stolen without violence? There was plenty of time for such a theft between Mr Clay's remark at breakfast and Bunney's going to his room. Well, I think it can be shown that the attack upon Bunney was no part of the murderer's work, nor of an accomplice's; that it belongs to another affair altogether.

'It is common knowledge now that the events we have experienced have been complicated by an alarm of espionage. Lord Auldearn had in his possession an important paper, the safety of which was feared for. Actually, the paper was not in danger; nevertheless, the alarm was not baseless. Spies – and spies indeed seeking that paper – there have been amongst us; their possible activities formed that grave preoccupation of Mr Appleby's of which I spoke. They were ineffective, however, at their job; they had nothing to do with the murders; and they have been thought of as having dropped out of the story. But they do make this one and not altogether ineffective appearance at the end. For the attack on Dr Bunney represents their last attempt to get the paper.

'Let me ask two questions. Exactly how was Bunney attacked? He was hit on the head from behind in a darkish corridor outside his room. Where was this paper when he was attacked? In Mr Appleby's pocket. Please look at Mr Appleby.'

Electric lights snapped on. Everybody stared at Appleby. It was an eminently successful if slightly flamboyant effect that Gott had allowed himself at the end of his recital.

'You see what I mean at once. The first thing I casually mentioned to Mr Appleby when speaking of Bunney was the fact of a certain resemblance to himself. And the same thing, Mr Appleby tells me, misled Rauth, the steward, this morning. The spies, then, guessing that the document had been transferred to Mr Appleby's possession, made one last throw. But the person they thought was Mr Appleby going to Bunney's room to investigate the business of the cylinder was actually Bunney himself. And when they found that their plan had miscarried they very adroitly stole the "curious message" cylinder, thus removing suspicion of the attack from themselves and transferring it to the murderer. With the realization of this simple sequence of events Nave's last defence breaks down.'

A long silence in the little drawing-room was presently broken by an advancing tinkling sound from without.

'Ah,' said the Duke. 'Whisky? Well – come, come.'

4

EPILOGUE

What, has this thing appear'd again tonight?

'YES, they've gone all right,' said Noel, peering through. 'And very naturally too. It's all settled now except for the chaplain's final snuffle over the fallen infidel.'

'*Get on!*' said Diana fiercely. And she thrust Noel before her into the hall.

*

Gott stared at Appleby. 'You mean you would have held your hand? You didn't find it convincing?'

Appleby wandered restlessly – oddly expectantly – about the room. 'There was no holding my hand when you'd spilt Sandford all that. And, of course, it was convincing – overwhelmingly so. Only, my dear Giles, you were having it all your own way. One thing was lacking.'

'That being?'

'A competent criminal lawyer to laugh you out of court.' Appleby's tone was dry but without rancour.

'It's as bad as that?'

'Well, consider the business of Auldearn's skull. Is that going to be convincing – convincing in court, with a subtle mind working against it?'

'It all fits.'

'Quite so. I think it is a triumph. But do you think they'll miss the point that it's a triumph of your own craft – a bit of ingenious fiction? It *may* have been so. It sounds beautiful. But there is just no shred of evidence that Nave ever picked up that cross or thought about the consistency of Auldearn's skull or spoilt a dramatic effect by outing with a revolver. Counsel wouldn't be at it for ten minutes before it was just a lovely picture in the air.'

'You don't believe –'

'But never mind about me! It's my job to think of a judge and jury. And when I do that in this business I'm scared. Say I want evidence.'

'The messages.'

'Planted.'

'Nave's fresh finger-print on the line "*the croaking raven doth bellow for revenge*". You find that three minutes after the message had come from his room. It's that that's conclusive. As you said yourself : finger-prints still catch criminals by the pint. Nave knew to leave nothing on the revolver or cross; but running his finger down a page of Shakespeare – he never thought.'

'Yes, that finger-print' – Appleby was kicking absently at an imaginary object on the carpet – 'it was on the strength of that finger-print that I gave a sort of agreement to Sandford's acting. To put it ignobly : if Nave is tried and acquitted that finger-print will save me from ignominy.' He stood stockstill. 'He says he was in his bath.'

'At the moment of the sixth message? But what does he say about the print?'

Appleby shook an almost indulgent head. 'Bless us, he doesn't know of that yet. That's to keep a bit. And I promise you it needs adding to. Evidence needed – that's the word. By the way, Giles, about the motive – you don't think you were a bit carried away?'

'Perhaps I ran it up a bit.'

'Quite so. What an unstable world we live in nowadays. And therefore did one Richard Nave, Knight, having one set of convictions, feloniously kill one Ian Stewart, Baron Auldearn, having –'

'Really, John.'

'All right. But I'm only putting what will be put in court. They will boil it down to look just like that. And what evidence have we? With Malloch we had at least an actual deadly feud about which we could have brought witnesses. But with Nave we have no single specific record of his having cherished one fleeting impulse of hatred for Auldearn from the moment of his birth to this. What you say about the power of impersonal, ideological hatreds may be abundantly true. But the jury aren't going to be what you called "intellectually and speculatively inclined men". They're going to be butchers and bakers – perhaps fortunately so. And they're going to be thoroughly disconcerted when they're told that there is no personal or private element in the affair and that Nave is a murderer because he is a hard-boiled nominalist who rejects the validity of the subjectively apprehended epistemological problem of –'

'I don't –'

'But that's what they'll say! And I put it to you myself that the motive's weak. It came partly from your own habit of mind, Giles. For talking of hatred, nobody hates a forthright, aggressive atheist like Nave so much as a muzzy and apologetic agnostic, consciously steeped in the benefits of Christian tradition, like yourself.'

Gott ran quick fingers through his hair. 'That's fair enough,' he said. 'I believe you could presently persuade me that I've made an unholy ass of myself.'

'It's a matter of us, not you. But the point is – evidence. Just put it at that at present : we're short of evidence.'

'Yes, but I want your own conviction now, John. Taking the case against Nave as I outlined it, is there anything you blankly disbelieve?'

'Yes, there is – and it's what makes me feel that we're not through yet – certainly that without more evidence we shall be lost in court. I don't think you really got round to the snag – the business of Bunney, I mean, and Nave's undoubted alibi for that, I admit the full force of your main position there : Why a murderous attack when a simple theft was possible? But beyond that I can't go. I don't see these spies tracking me about Scamnum. And whatever you and your precious, short-sighted Rauth may say, I don't see myself as that Bunney's double. If it were a case of real doubles – like the Terborg girls, for instance – I could swallow the story. But the fact that there is a resemblance is not good enough. Before hitting a man on the head like that, one makes sure. It's what counsel would detect as another tinge of fiction about your version. I want a better explanation of Bunney. As it stands, I know it's going to be a weakness in the story.'

Gott looked at Appleby thoughtfully. 'I believe you distrust the story altogether.'

'No.' Appleby spoke very carefully. 'If I had distrusted the story altogether, I would have opposed the arrest – as a matter of principle if not of policy. There is a case against Nave too strong to distrust altogether. His arrest was justified. But I have certain doubts. And at the back of them – to some extent at least – is the fact that the case is yours, Giles – is so brilliantly yours. Don't misunderstand. I'm simply scared by a sense of your extraordinary facility in these matters. You created a magnificent case – or at least a magnificent effect. But some people would say that you could have done the same with half a dozen other suspects.'

'In fact, the irresponsible romancer. It wasn't just like that, you know.'

'I don't say it was. I'm sure you weighed up the probabilities responsibly enough before you let me lead you off to Sandford. But you know what I *do* mean.'

'You mean that my wretched fancy will work on anything. Give it a start and off it goes. Which is true enough. But I've rejected a good many starts because they were plainly nothing more than an invitation to fancy. I've dredged through everything that happened in the past week and all sorts of notions have started up as I did so. Things that this or that person said which the romancer – I suppose – could build on.'

Appleby was still restless – roaming about while pulling heavily at a pipe. 'Yes ... yes. Such as?'

'Well – Piper; I told you about that. Piper displaying a dark and yearning zest for miching mallecho. One might build on that.'

'Anything else?'

Gott made an irritated gesture. 'Futile fancies,' he said. 'The Duchess, for instance. Coming up the drive in his car, Auldearn said something about the Duchess that might have been a beautiful dramatic irony. The Duchess was one who would work underground for weeks to contrive a minute's perfect effect. And a little later Elizabeth said something equally dark about Bunney: that he was the Spy in Black, black-boxing secrets of state.'

Something snapped. Appleby caught at his pipe as it fell, took the bitten-off mouth-piece from his lips and looked at it. Then he looked at Gott. And then he moved towards the door.

'John, what on earth is it? And where are you off to?'

'It's the truth – the first glimmer of the truth. And I'm off to chum up with Nave. It will be only discreet.'

The door opened as he approached it. Mr Gylby's head appeared. 'I say, may we come in? Diana thinks she's busted the *auto-da-fé.*'

'She's *what?*'

'Spiked the chivvying of infidel Nave. You see –'

'*Get on!*' said Diana from behind. A moment later she was in the room and had thrust a limp white object at Appleby. 'There!' she said.

Appleby looked at it. 'Yes. But everything, you know, has been examined –'

'Examined!' said Diana. 'Well the examiners haven't got no noses. Smell it.'

Appleby smelt it. 'Yes,' he said – and handed it to Gott. Gott sniffed and shook his head. Appleby turned to Noel. 'And you?' Noel, too, shook his head. Appleby tossed the object on a table. 'As one would expect,' he said, 'very faint indeed. And, though Miss Sandys and I detect it, it isn't evidence. But it's a clue.' He turned to Diana. 'It is Mme Merkalova's?'

'It is,' said Diana with deep satisfaction.

'And the confederate' – Appleby made some effort of memory – 'is one of five persons: the Duke, Gervase Crispin, Dr Biddle, Clay, Cope.'

Gott stared at him. 'Why, in heaven's name, these?'

'Because they were the five back-stage people who had some conversation with the Dowager Duchess of Horton.'

*

Clay and Elizabeth were walking down the long corridor together towards their bedrooms. 'I've been feeling glad it's over,' said Clay; 'but really, of course, it's not over yet. The police-court and the trial and so forth will all be rather horrible.'

'It seems a pity they can't quietly shut him up. It seems the rational thing to do.'

Clay shook his head. 'Possibly so – but only after a trial. Mad or sane, he must have his chance. But mad or sane he's dangerous and – I suppose – tormented. Better dead. I for one will be glad when he's hanged.'

Elizabeth shivered slightly. They had paused at Clay's door.

'I'm afraid', said Clay, 'you must feel a bit shaken after it all? While there's mystery the tension keeps one going. But afterwards one finds one is badly shocked.'

'No,' said Elizabeth – firmly and with something of Diana's reaction – for Clay's 'one' seemed directed at her sex. 'It hasn't left me shocked. Only distinctly hungry.'

'Bless us! Well, have a biscuit.' And Clay dodged through his door and reappeared with a little silver bedside box.

Elizabeth took a biscuit; then stared in surprise. There were at least a dozen biscuits left. 'Why,' she cried, amused, 'it was you who rifled the pantry and upset Rauth!'

'I know nothing about that,' said Clay.

'But there are never more than six –' Elizabeth glanced at Clay; their eyes met; she stopped. He had made a mistake – the first, perhaps, in the whole affair – and he knew it. And she knew it. And he knew that too.

Elizabeth took a heroic bite at her biscuit. 'Stupid of me,' she said – hardly knowing what the words were. 'And thank you. Good night.' And unhurryingly but with a whirling head she went on to her room.

She closed the door and leant against it, waiting for her brain to stop rotating and come clear. She knew that she had no new knowledge. All along – or ever since Clay had performed those dazzling tricks in the little drawing-room – she had known – something. Now it was simply that her knowledge had been revealed to her. ...

'Silly!' said Elizabeth aloud, and conscious of herself as watchful against hysteria. Then, regardless of her astonished maid, she opened the door and went out again into the corridor. It might be a mere brainstorm. Anyway, she was going to see it through.

Down the corridor and round a corner; once more she was outside Clay's room. She had a momentary impulse to knock at Charles Piper's door opposite. But she suppressed it and raised her hand to knock on Clay's door instead. A voice was speaking within and something – something perhaps in its quality as conveyed in mere murmur through the solid wood – made her pause again. She was suddenly aware that she was on the verge of veritable danger, that common decencies were suspended, that there was a job of work she could do. Her hand, raised against the panel, fell to the door-knob, turned it, gently opened the door a fraction of an inch. And Clay's voice, guarded but vibrant at the house-telephone, came clearly.

'Anna ... are you alone? Listen. In fifteen minutes – ten perhaps – they'll have it all worked out. Can you make the cow-house straight away ... you know? Take nothing ... no ... there first ... it's hidden there. Over the wall they'll be cruising round ... quick now. ...'

Softly, Elizabeth closed the door. *The cow-house straight away ... hidden there ... they'll be cruising round. ...* She turned and ran back to her own room, burst in. 'Jean, find the police, Mr Gott, Mr Gylby. Tell them to come to the cow-house at once. *At once* – you understand? Go ... now!'

Anything might happen at Scamnum in these days. And Jean was from Kincrae; she had been unnerved once by these strange events and was determined not to be so again. 'Yes, my lady,' she said and ran from the room.

Elizabeth kicked off evening slippers and thrust on shoes. Then she ran out and along the corridor, going left to avoid the route by Clay's room. In a minute she was downstairs and out by a side door.

'Run, girls, run!' murmured Elizabeth. Her views on female athletics were Dillon and satiric. But her spirits as she plunged down the terraces were Dillon and Crispin both. She took the final steps with a leap. Her heart was pounding as she ran: *it's hidden there ... it's hidden there.*

*

Charles Piper sat in his room and made notes on the events of the day. Having his own ideas of what was interesting and what was not, he was far from giving his attention exclusively to the queer and deporable affair of Sir Richard Nave. He had enjoyed some conversation with Vanessa Terborg – an interesting type – and he made notes on that. He thought out a short story set in Venice for someone rather like the Duchess, and then changed Venice to Pienza as less hackneyed. And then he thought of Melville Clay.

Of all the people at Scamnum, Clay interested him most. It

was not Clay's meteoric career, appearing from nowhere and rising to eminence in a few years; rather it was something integral to the man himself. There was, for instance, that feminine streak .. the way he had stood that very morning, posed with his back to the window, tilting the little shaving-mirror now here, now there on his face.

Piper frowned; the frown gave place to something startled. In the hall after the murder, when he had glimpsed Clay through the curtain talking to the Dowager Duchess ... surely there had been some similar impression connected with that? A contrived ease – that was it! an ease of poise and movement that was actually, to a more than commonly sensitive eye, the result of terrific concentration. Why? ... *why?* And then something further about that fleeting picture in the hall; something that had registered itself just off the focus of consciousness in Piper's then agitated mind ... something surprising ... a surprising appearance. *Surely the old lady had been asleep.*

And that mirror. ... Piper leapt to his feet with something like a shout, looked round as if in search of a weapon, then ran out and across the corridor to Clay's door. He paused before it for a moment. Then he opened it and walked straight in – straight into a world of melodrama. Clay was gone. But a lady's maid – Elizabeth's maid – lay bound and gagged upon the carpet.

And Piper whirled into action. He got the girl free, he got the story, he telephoned, he sent her to the police. And then he leapt to the window and vaulted to the sill. He dropped to an architrave, to the *porte cochère*, to the colonnade, to the ground. And ran. His pumps were split and his feet were bruised – but undoubtedly one saved thirty seconds that way.

He ran steadily and well, as people who practise deep breathing are able to do.

2

ELIZABETH paused cautiously on the threshold of Duke Peter's picturesque cow-house. It was utterly silent. She was here before them. And with luck the police would be here before them too – catch them in ambush; unless – it was an ugly thought –

they were already here in a kind of ambush themselves. And Elizabeth realized that she was standing in idiotic silhouette under the arched doorway. Hastily, she slipped into shadow.

The cow-house, commonly so pleasing an absurdity, was eerie now. A low-riding sliver of moon was fleeting amid gathering clouds; the uncertain light came and went about the bogus ruin, gliding up the steps so ingeniously hollowed as if by generations of pious feet, playing on the crisply chiselled draperies of saints who stood as they had been fashioned without heads or arms. The mouldering tower, no more mouldering than on the day it was built, rose with an impressive appearance of insecurity overhead; the pale ivy stirring about it in the night breeze like myriad-tongued green flame, the bats flitting round, a single owl hooting from some crenellated fastness. All, Elizabeth thought, as Peter would have liked, but unnerving on the present occasion. For a moment the moon went; she slipped inside. It was wholly dark. In a sudden impulse of panic she whirled round on herself, as if a dagger threatened her where a dagger threatened Bose. Nothing. But she pressed her back against the wall and stood quite still, palms pricking. The little wind rustled in the ivy. The moon came again; she searched the dissolving darkness, the outlines of the forming shadows; suppressed a cry. Close to her feet the pale stone floor was flecked with drops of red.

But queerly luminous red. And her breath went out in a wary sigh of relief; she looked up to the fictively shattered traceries of a rose-window – and to the ruby-coloured lights of fictively shattered stained glass. 'Oh, Peter,' she breathed to herself, 'you did give me a truly Gothic thrill!' And she moved boldly forward again. In this Radcliffean world you took your courage in both hands and all was well; no mystery too horrid to plumb. But let go and you would outyelp Stella Terborg.

It was hidden here. If she knew just what the hidden thing was she would have some idea where best to look for it. And she wanted to get it. Somebody, something – a car perhaps – was cruising round – waiting for Clay and the woman over the wall. And if Clay were here, say, within two minutes he might conceivably be ahead still of the police. And get away – get away with *it*.

The cow-house was used as a store for garden things; shelves had been built round the old cattle stalls to take flower-pots, bags of lime and manure, miscellaneous implements. She crossed rapidly to the end stall and her eye, as if abnormally acute, went in an instant to the upper shelf. There stood a row of little sacks – uniform, but from one a little trickle of whitish stuff had fallen to the floor. She reached for it. The mouth was folded under, but unstitched. She plunged in her hand. 'Got it!' Elizabeth was exultant in her swift success. And in the same instant she heard a sound outside, a sound that was neither wind-stirred ivy nor bat nor owl.

In a flash she scrambled over into the next stall and crouched down. The moon vanished. When it came again she saw a raised arm – no, the shadow of a raised arm – groping for the rifled sack; a second later came Clay's subdued curse. Elizabeth crouched very still, not three feet away. Her heart, she thought, must make Duke Peter's well-cemented ruin quiver like a mill-house. And she recalled – it was less a recollection than something probing to a nerve – the sheer sensory acuteness of the man near her, his every-day effortless vigilance, his perfectly coordinated ear, eye, and hand. And now he was very still too, listening. His picture rose up before her as he had been in the nunnery-scene – Hamlet, tense, straining his senses towards his concealed enemies. He had only to search and she was done for. Where were Giles, Noel, the police? They must have had Jean's message long since.

He was searching the stalls. And always, searching the stalls, he would be between her and the door. So she was done for. With some idea of finding a weapon her fingers groped, touched something, explored. It was only an empty paint tin, but it gave her a plan. Above the door was a trefoil aperture unglazed. If she could get the tin through she might have a long chance yet; if she failed she would be no worse off than staying still.

It was dark again. She waited for the ivy to rustle and cover the sound of slight movement; then she lobbed at the scarcely distinguishable target. And the tin went through. From outside the cow-house came a splendid rattle – suggesting, she rather deliciously thought, the true Radcliffean ghost in chains. In a flash Clay was outside and in a flash Elizabeth was after him and pressed behind a buttress.

The wind was rising; the moon was playing hide-and-seek with little, heavy scudding clouds; the moonlight was coming and going – a mild lunar lightning – about the gardens. She saw Clay standing, a revolver in his hand, some ten yards away; his eye swept round and past her; he turned and ran back into the cow-house. But she was not safe yet. Straight before her lay the long path to the house – a furlong and a half between towering hedges and oblivious deities. Down that path she must go. Up that path help must presently come – but there was no sign of it yet. And in seconds Clay would be out again. And not till she was a hundred yards or more down the path would she have some chance of escaping unnoticed.

To her left was a little track leading only through and round a shrubbery. Could she – conceivably – trick him a second time precisely as she had tricked him the first? Elizabeth made no pause to weigh up the unlikelihood. She picked up two heavy stones from Duke Peter's carefully dumped rubble; she gave a little panicky cry; she hurled the stones in rapid succession as far as she could into the shrubbery. It *might* have been somebody blundering a way through – but to Elizabeth it sounded just like two stones falling. She could hardly trust her eyes when Clay ran out and flashed past her in pursuit of the sound. He moved beautifully – like a panther. Nevertheless, Elizabeth reflected, to be taken in like that he must be rattled – more rattled than she was. And she picked up the skirts of her trailing frock once more and ran. The great dark cliff-like hedges, the pale deities dimly outlined against them, flowed past.

She was half-way, more than half-way. And then Clay's voice came from far behind her, carrying clearly through the night in a long-drawn call of warning:

'A – nna! Com – ing!'

Almost in the same instant a flicker of moonlight passed over the end of the path for which she was running and for a second she saw a figure standing there, waiting. It must be the woman – the Merkalova. And she would be armed. And behind, Elizabeth could now hear Clay approaching – searching as he came. On either side of her were the impenetrable, soaring hedges. Of help there was as yet no sign.

She was trapped.

*

Appleby dashed back from his garaged Bentley; slipped as he ran the safety-catch of the heavy revolver he had snatched from it. The others were fifty yards ahead ... forty ... thirty-five. ...

*

Clay turned on the Merkalova. 'You've let her through!'

'No! But does it matter? You have it?' She seized his arm. 'Quickly, back and over the wall.'

Clay swore, scanned the shadows. '*She* has it ... and you let her through ... you must have!' He stopped abruptly. From somewhere in the darkness came the sound of running feet. 'All right ... back.' He swung round – and as he did so the moon came out full. '*God!*' He raised his arm and aimed – upwards. And in the same instant a figure rose from the dark base of the hedge, like a Red Indian from the earth, and swung a blow at his jaw.

Clay staggered; Charles Piper leaped at him; the Merkalova ran at Piper to shoot point-blank – and took Clay's bullet as she ran.

For a shocked moment the two men looked at each other across the body. Then again Clay took aim. 'Turn round', he said, 'and go back.' And again Piper leapt at him. There was a flash, a report, and Piper staggered, only half-dazed from a graze on the temple.

'Damn you,' said Piper very seriously – and again advanced. This time Clay took his time. His revolver dropped to the line of Piper's heart; his face – calm, intent – was held by a shaft of moonlight that might have been limelight on a stage. And then from forty yards away came a deeper report. The heavy bullet took him square in the forehead, lifted him perhaps half an inch from the ground, tumbled him backwards like a felled tree.

*

Appleby stood up. 'Both dead.'

There was a silence. The moon had almost disappeared. Noel flashed an electric torch, measured with his eye. 'Lord, Mr Appleby, what a shot!' The beam of the torch, playing at random on the ground, flitted across what had been the face of Melville Clay. Rather abruptly, Noel leant against the pedestal of a dimly outlined goddess – looked again at the bodies. 'Even at the base of Pompey's statue,' he said a little crazily.

Again there was silence. And then the statue spoke from the darkness. 'I should like to get dressed now,' it said firmly.

Everyone jumped. Noel exclaimed. 'Who on earth –'

'The Pandemian Venus,' said Elizabeth mildly from her pedestal.

3

BUNNEY sat up in bed, his head swathed in bandages, his eyes sparkling with excitement. 'Science never knows,' he said, 'to what uses –' He paused as if realizing that he must conserve his strength, picked up the cylinder. 'And Lady Elizabeth brought it perfectly unimpaired through all her adventures!' He slipped it into the black box and flicked a switch.

... what wilt thou do thou wilt not murder me help help ho help help my lord there has been a serious misadventure please all stay where you are there is very bad news mother about Ian I am just going to tell them he has been shot I have bad news the pistol-shot you all heard was aimed at Lord Auldearn he is dead for the moment nobody must leave the hall ...

... sit still Aunt Elizabeth Biddle is coming across in a moment thank you Gervase I have no desire to run about Biddle may come if he wants to this is very sad very sad we must not be too agitated drink this then my dear lady presently we shall be able to get away I hope you will be all right if I go back now a very great shock memorandum of cabinet emergency organization basic chemical industries date two six thirty –

'Thank you,' said Appleby.

Happily, Bunney switched off.

*

'And so,' said the Duchess to Appleby, 'it was a spy-story after all – every atom of it!'

'Every atom; but designed to bear a very different appearance.'

The Duchess placed delicate hands on the stone of the balustrade, already warm in the morning sun. She looked from Appleby to the Duke and from the Duke to Appleby. Then she looked away to the crown of Horton Hill. 'Iain is dead, and poor Bose. And Elizabeth is alive only because of Piper's courage, and Piper only because of your marksmanship, Mr Appleby. Perhaps I should wish never to hear another word about it all. But I am curious and I want you to tell it as a story; if only in return for the story – Bose's story – I told in the small hours.'

'Yes,' said the Duke, 'interesting to hear it all cleared up – a second time tóo. But I'm afraid I can't stop. Must see Macdonald – wreaths and things, you know. Extraordinary shot that of yours, Mr Appleby. Extraordinary. You must come to Kincrae some time. Good-bye, good-bye.'

The Duchess watched her husband disappear. 'He will never speak of it again,' she said. 'But I am different, I fear. Now, Mr Appleby.' She tapped the balustrade.

Obediently, Appleby sat down.

'The story begins with the Merkalova. She was the original spy; she became familiar with Mr Crispin, I am afraid, simply because in doing so she came very close to the sources of power and information. It is interesting that Nave detected something out of the way in their relationship and that several of the ladies– less tolerant than yourself – thought, well, unfavourably of her.'

'Gervase regarded himself as having married her,' said the Duchess briefly.

'Which makes it extraordinary that she elected to continue prosecuting her profession, if one may call it that. But there she was; and she – I suspect – brought Clay in. And Clay was bloody, bold, resolute, and an artist. An artist chiefly: one must believe that he took to the game simply because it offered new and incomparably exciting scope for his craft. Certainly there was no money in it comparable to what he made on the stage. And that is all the good – if it be good – that can be said of him.

'These two converged on Scamnum, probably with no very definite mischief in mind; the Merkalova because Mr Crispin brought her and Clay because it was at least a promising field for this most exciting of all games – espionage.'

The Duchess raised forlorn hands. 'And I thought I had exercised such skill in getting him!'

'But presently a less indefinite prospect showed. Auldearn was coming; to Auldearn the gravest matters were constantly being referred; and – it may be – Auldearn's slightly eccentric habits of taking important papers about with him and so forth were known. It was at this point that Clay thought it worth while to make preliminary plans. He was an imaginative and a ruthless, reckless man – qualities which spies, contrary to popular opinion, do not commonly possess. And these qualities went into his plan, to our very great confusion – I am ashamed to say – in the early stages of the investigation. I must confess that we were caught saying: "Spies don't work this way" – which was just what Clay designed that we should say.

'Everything was to be violent, catastrophic, and – in the word Giles found so early – theatrical. And this was to serve two purposes: it was to give the affair an atmosphere remote from espionage except in the wildest fiction; and at the same time it was to satisfy Clay's real craving for theatre – for dramatic effect. Long before there was a definite prospect of anything important being with Auldearn he amused himself with envisaging murder. And he and the Merkalova began to send the messages.'

'And so to incriminate Nave.'

'Yes. But the attempt to involve Nave in any crime that might be committed was not at that stage designed very seriously. All that Clay was planning was a run of circumstances which would set the police hunting, for a time at least, after some private passionate crime. It amused him to think of us tumbling at length to the anagram and worrying Nave. And I think the Revenge messages may have been prompted as well by a sight of Anderson's book; that is to say he thought we might be persuaded to waste time over Malloch too. But, as Malloch himself pointed out to me, there was very little prospect of such a planted case being ultimately convincing. Clay could not reckon on Malloch being so uncovered in the matter of times and places as he was. Much less could he reckon on the amazing case built up against Nave by Giles Gott – *Leontiasis Ossium* and all the rest of it.' Appleby chuckled.

'It was a very good case,' said the Duchess with spirit. 'And according to Dr Biddle the *Leontiasis* whatever it was was perfectly sound. And if you didn't believe it yourself, Mr Appleby, you acted in a very irresponsible way.' She glanced at Appleby. 'Or Colonel Sandford did,' she said.

'The responsibility for arresting Nave,' Appleby said seriously, 'was morally mine, even if technically it was the Chief Constable's. I *was* inclined to believe the story – all but a fragment of it, as I'll explain. And anyway –' He checked himself.

'And anyway', prompted the Duchess with sudden perception, 'you thought it might loosen things up.'

Appleby looked at her with real admiration. 'It sometimes happens that way,' he said. 'A criminal is at a strain; suddenly he seems to see the last danger removed; and for a moment he goes off his guard. Which was exactly what happened. Clay's guard failed for a second and Lady Elizabeth got his middle stump.'

The Duchess did not say, '*He* nearly got her'; one must not fuss about one's chicken's skin. Instead she said, 'Poor Giles!'

'Yes; you must believe that I didn't think Sandford would call for his story in that formal fashion. At least it must have amused Clay. But to get back. We must acquit Clay of attempting – at that early stage – to get another man hanged. He was simply out to establish an atmosphere of crazy, passionate crime, and to indicate one or two suspects to keep us busy. And all this, remember, was provisional; just in case it should prove that there was a big stake to play for.

'Well, there was. We don't know how or when he got to know – though if we get at the network of spying of which he was a part we may learn yet. I suspect that before the play began he knew not only that Auldearn had this document but also something of its tenor and physical appearance. In fact, I think the original plan was a plan of *substitution*. But it was to be thoroughly violent; it was to involve murder – that was part of the fun. And by this time, I suspect, the Merkalova had become a mere lieutenant. She would do what she was told, however desperate the orders were. And this, then, was the plan –'

'One sees', the Duchess interrupted, 'how right Giles was to see the whole thing as somehow implicated with the theme of the play.'

Appleby smiled. The Duchess was evidently resolved to see justice done to the unfortunate Gott. 'Quite so. Only the relevant aspect of the play was not the theme of private revenge but the theme of statecraft. There really was a fight to the death between Hamlet and, well, the rulers of Elsinore – or Scamnum.

'But this, I say, was the plan. The document was on Auldearn's person. Very good. When Auldearn was alone on the rear stage the Merkalova was simply to shoot him from the shelter of the curtains; shoot him and make off instantly. Clay, lingering on the front stage just long enough to demonstrate that he could not himself by any trick be responsible, was to slip through to the rear stage and get the document. He reckoned to have only Bose there before him; and Bose he could send running for help. The advantage of the arrangement is obvious. It tended at once to cut out any notion of theft. For if one thought of theft one would instantly remark that Auldearn had been shot in such circumstances that the assailant could not have reckoned on time to steal anything before the entry of Clay or Bose.

'Having once got the document his plans depended entirely on what was or what was not suspected. If they didn't search Auldearn's body he could reckon that no theft was suspected; that the murder was passing at its face-value as a crazy crime by the author of the messages. In that case he would bank on getting out of the hall without a general search, or at least on getting the document to a confederate in the audience who would get out unsearched. But if they searched Auldearn's body and so gave signs of suspicion he meant, I think, to fall back on a bogus document he had prepared. He would hide that in the scroll – which he would have kicked away so that it had not been searched – and then see that the scroll was discovered. If the bogus document was accepted for the moment and anxiety thereby dispelled then again there would be a substantial chance of getting away without a general search. And, finally, he had the resource of the Merkalova's little camera. If the worst came to the worst he hoped to be able to withdraw to a dressing-room and photograph the document – not, technically, an easy task – and later get the tiny camera successfully away. He may have had some plan that gave him a substantial chance of that: I can't hit on one but I'm sure Giles could.

'Well, that – with a slight failure of plan to which I shall come – was how things stood when, just after the shooting, Clay hit on a more attractive technique. And if you think he acted fantastically you must remember that about the document *per se* he didn't care twopence. All he wanted was to be supremely clever in the eyes of Melville Clay.

'The first thing he did when this new technique came to him was to scrap provision for the old. He packed off the Merkalova's superfluous camera – packed it off through the instrumentality of Mr Crispin. That was a superb move.' Appleby paused, rather – the Duchess thought – as Lionel Dillon might have paused at the mention of 'The Burial of Orgaz'; paused in a sort of professional homage. 'It was the move of a man with the brain – well, with the sort of brain I should like to have. For it prepared the way for the *tour de force* by which he sent the Merkalova sweeping in on us in Mr Crispin's room to exclaim, "Gervase, have they found out?" and throw the camera on the bed. That scene, of course, linked Mr Crispin and the Merkalova well-nigh indissolubly together in my mind, and when I learnt that Mr Crispin could not be suspect as a spy I automatically acquitted her in that direction.' Appleby looked ruthfully at the Duchess. He liked her. 'In fact,' he said, 'I think there's some possibility of this case becoming known at the Yard as Appleby's Waterloo.'

The Duchess laughed. 'I hope so; my sympathies won't stretch further than Giles and Nave this morning. But I don't believe it. You're word-perfect already and obviously going to write an astoundingly wise report. And now, as you kept saying to everybody yesterday, please go on.'

'Clay got rid of the camera, then, and no doubt burnt the

bogus document, just as Miss – but that is irrelevant. Then he waited to put across the great performance of his career. There, sitting by herself in the front row and isolated from the audience, was the Dowager Duchess, a very old lady constantly nodding off to sleep. And beside her was Bunney's machine, purring away – so to speak – and ready to record anything murmured into it. And several people had gone to speak to the old lady; it didn't seem to count at all as communicating with the audience. So Clay waited till she had nodded asleep again after Biddle's draught, walked over the front stage, sat down solicitously beside her, made scraps of soothing conversation that the nearer people could hear – and meanwhile, bit by bit, read the whole document to Bunney's contraption. He would hold the paper, I suppose, concealed in a programme – and the whole effect to the people behind would be that of two or three minutes' courteous attention to an old lady. Presently he went away and came back with old Mr Cope – a beautiful completing of the effect. Then he simply put the document in the scroll where it would presently be found. If Bose had not found it Clay, no doubt, would have done something about it himself.

'But he had by no means got clear yet. For the Duke, despite the belated discovery of the document, still took precautions. He sent the audience away, without allowing any communication between them and the players. And then he kept the players in the hall until I arrived from London. By that time Clay had slipped the cylinder out of the machine – to do that unnoticed would not, with his peculiar abilities, be difficult – and was walking about with it. And by this time he guessed there would be a search. It is dreadfully humiliating to have to record that he thereupon got the thing away effortlessly under my nose. He simply dropped it in an empty coffee-urn which Bagot, quite automatically, would take away when bringing a full one – and which the constable at the door would, equally automatically, let through. It was all rather fantastic – too fantastic for me, certainly, as I stood there on the stage solemnly watching Bagot's exit. But remember, again, that Clay was not a common spy prosaically anxious to filch securely and make his money; he was a reckless and inspired creature playing the game of his life.

279

'And so the first act ended. There had been, from Clay's point of view, two unforeseen turns to it: the Merkalova had shot Lord Auldearn not from the shelter of the curtains but from right out on the rear stage itself; and the substance of the document was now, of all places, on a wax cylinder in a coffee-urn somewhere in the Scamnum offices. And the first of these unforeseen turns gave Miss Sandys her chance and the second gave Lady Elizabeth hers.

'The Merkalova was not quite first-class; she was not quite worthy of Clay. She was liable to muff things slightly. For instance, when she made that descent on us in Mr Crispin's room she went wrong twice. She was a little too pat, so that I had an obscure feeling that it was a put-up job. Not that that did any harm; it merely kept my thoughts centring for a little longer on the fictitious Crispin-Merkalova conspiracy. A more serious slip was a story she let fly about Miss Sandys; it was a serious slip because it tended to keep the spy idea alive. She was liable, then, to muff things slightly and one is not surprised that Clay charged her with letting Lady Elizabeth through their trap last night when actually Lady Elizabeth was not very far away.'

'I'm pleased with Elizabeth,' said the Duchess. 'It was intelligent.'

'It was genius. But the point is that the Merkalova was afraid of *missing*. And that's what Miss Sandys got to. While Giles and I were finding fine theories to account for the murderer stepping right out of cover and under the possible observation of Bose – the iron-cross, gloating-avenger, Fate-in-*Les-Présages* theory, and all the rest of it – while our minds worked like that Miss Sandys' worked like this: *Why break cover to get closer? Because you're afraid of missing*. And then she asked: *Why are you afraid of missing at that comparatively close range?* And she answered – with incomparable brilliance and disinterestedness if you consider her feminist attitude: *Because you're a woman*. And then she went further in what has been the purest detective process in the case. The revolver had been found. There would be no finger-prints on it. How does one avoid leaving finger-prints? Either by wiping the object afterwards or by wearing a glove. A glove is best, because one mightn't succeed in rubbing prints off adequately if pressed for time. The men had no gloves but the women had: they came straight to the hall to change from what had been rather a grand dinner. After the search they left mainly in their player things. Gloves would still be in the hall. So she broke into the hall with Mr Gylby, found the Merkalova's gloves, and convinced herself and myself – if nobody else – that the right-hand glove smelt ever so faintly of gunpowder – as in the circumstances it might just conceivably do. Miss Sandys had us beaten badly there and the wise report you speak of will have to say so.

'Now the other point – the cylinder in the coffee-urn. Clay knew the ways of big houses and knew that no footman up at two a.m.was going to clean out such a thing; it would be put by for the appropriate maid or boy in the morning. And he knew, roughly, where he could find it in the small hours. What he didn't know was the severe nature of Mr Rauth, who likes to lock things up. As a consequence of that he had to break into the pantry where it was and so leave traces of himself. And to avert suspicion from what he had really been after he broke open a tin of biscuits, filled his pockets with them, and later transferred them to the box in his bedroom. And that was his undoing. For Lady Elizabeth, who was familiar with the precise dispositions in these matters imposed, again, by the excellent Rauth, knew at once that he must have been the raider of the pantry. And Clay made the slip of denying it.

'Now review the position yesterday morning. Clay had the cylinder: later in the day he managed to hide it in the cow-house. The danger arising from Bose's having seen the Merkalova shoot was over, for the simple reason that he had killed Bose. What, then, had he now to do? Nothing but sustain if possible the impression that the whole affair was one of private vengeance. Did the police, indeed, any longer suspect anything else? He got his answer to that when he looked out in the morning and saw that the house was closely guarded. He knew then that we had some substantial suspicion. He may have guessed that we had intercepted a message we had in fact intercepted: the message promising delivery of the goods. If, then, we knew that there were spies his best course was to persuade us that they had been unsuccessful. And to that end he contrived another intercepted message. I had ensured that no long message could be flashed out from Scamnum in the night. But for this purpose only three or four words were necessary. And they went – a few flicks of a shaving mirror – from Piper's bedroom window to Horton Hill. And so the second message was got deliberately into police hands: the spies had been unsuccessful; the murders were quite another affair; all chance was gone. He had to send the message from Piper's room; it was the only one available to him that commanded the hill. But it was a big risk, the sort of risk he loved. For Piper, if a shade slow, has a brooding and analytical eye. And – in fact – hours afterwards Piper *saw*.

'To substantiate the particular picture of the crimes he was trying to build up he had risked dragging Bose's body about the house. And now he had only one substantial anxiety. When he had delivered one of the messages through Bunney's box he had not foreseen what part the box was later to play. And at any time now there might occur to someone the possibility of investigating the voice which Bunney held recorded. I doubt if he cared twopence for that in itself. But it involved another danger. For as soon as Bunney was given his box in order to put this idea into practice he would discover that the final cylinder recording the interrupted play was missing. At all costs that must be avoided until the cylinder with the document was got safely away. Hence the attack on Bunney. Clay boldly broached the matter at breakfast and then made sure that for twenty-four hours at least Bunney would be silent. Of course he stole the "curious message" cylinder. Doing so killed two birds with one stone; it removed any possible danger of the identification of his voice; and it gave a motive for the attack on Bunney that offered no suggestion of a connexion with the spy-theme. And there, incidentally, was the one thing I positively stuck at in Giles's theory: that Bunney had been mistaken for me. And I was just trying to work out the implications of that – that it must be a conspiratorial crime, that it might be a spy crime after all – when, well, when the final whirlwind overtook me.

'Clay made one other move to keep up the Revenge theory. He had the habit of strolling into people's rooms and yesterday evening he strolled into Nave's. Nave was in his bath. And on the table was a Shakespeare open at the play-scene. Nave, you see, had tumbled to the anagram-business before anyone else; trust a psychologist for that. He knew somebody was out to incriminate him and he wondered what more might come. And he found himself going over his Shakespeare in a fascinated sort of way, noting "ravens", "revenges", and so forth. He had just looked at this most apposite of all lines – almost fatally, he had just laid his finger on it – when Clay came in and saw it. The temptation was overwhelming; he sent the sixth message over the telephone from the Raven's own room.' Appleby paused. 'And that was a definite move to get Nave hanged. In other words, Clay was a cowardly scoundrel as well as a very, very able man.

'And now I must go and say good-bye to Giles. *Death at Scamnum Court* has not made good hunting for either of us. It has been Ladies' Day. Miss Sandys got the Merkalova. Lady Elizabeth got Clay.' Appleby rose. 'And the Duchess of Horton, in the middle of a very terrible night, remembered how to tell a story as the Duchess of Horton can.'

*

Jean was packing suitcases into the back of Elizabeth's car; Elizabeth was packing dogs into the front. And the talented author of *Death at the Zoo* and *Poison Paddock* came rather dubiously down the steps.

'Straight away, Elizabeth?'

'Straight away. They'll run for Kincrae early, I think, and I'm going ahead. By paternal decree. The affair must be blown away from the maidenly mind.'

'I wish it could be blown away. I've made a most frightful –'

'Giles, is Nave annoyed?'

'No. The unkindest cut of all is there. It's all matter of scientific interest to him. I don't believe, ideologue though he be, that he's capable of one flicker of enmity towards any living creature. And we're going for a walk together after tea to talk it all over. Think of that.' Gott's fingers strayed nervously through his hair; he looked shyly at Elizabeth. As Nave had said: painful lack of knowledge how to proceed. 'It's nice to see you with a whole skin, Elizabeth – praise heaven and Piper.'

'Oh yes,' said Elizabeth, 'Piper was all right. And I owe him an idea too.'

'An idea?'

'Yes; if he hadn't tried to make fun of you at breakfast yesterday – about Pygmalion and his statue, you remember? – I should never have thought of the Pandemian Venus.'

Elizabeth climbed into the car. Then she sighed – her mother's sigh. 'Giles, it's such a pity. That it wasn't true, I mean. It was such a good story.'

'I say, don't pile it on.'

'But it was. It *ought* to have been true. And you can tell Nave I think so when you take your walk.' Elizabeth turned to see Jean safely stowed; pressed the self-starter.

'Good-bye, Elizabeth. And I hope you'll truly blow it out of mind – our play and all that followed.'

'Perhaps we'll have the play again, Giles.' Elizabeth slipped into gear.

'You'd be Ophelia again – even if I produced it?'

'Even if you played Hamlet, Giles – mad, mad Hamlet.'

Elizabeth let in the clutch; the car glided forward. And Gott stepped back.

'Nymph, in thy orisons,' he said, 'be all my sins remembered.'

READ MORE IN PENGUIN

In every corner of the world, on every subject under the sun, Penguin represents quality and variety – the very best in publishing today.

For complete information about books available from Penguin – including Puffins, Penguin Classics and Arkana – and how to order them, write to us at the appropriate address below. Please note that for copyright reasons the selection of books varies from country to country.

In the United Kingdom: Please write to *Dept. JC, Penguin Books Ltd, FREEPOST, West Drayton, Middlesex UB7 OBR*

If you have any difficulty in obtaining a title, please send your order with the correct money, plus ten per cent for postage and packaging, to *PO Box No. 11, West Drayton, Middlesex UB7 OBR*

In the United States: Please write to *Penguin USA Inc., 375 Hudson Street, New York, NY 10014*

In Canada: Please write to *Penguin Books Canada Ltd, 10 Alcorn Avenue, Suite 300, Toronto, Ontario M4V 3B2*

In Australia: Please write to *Penguin Books Australia Ltd, 487 Maroondah Highway, Ringwood, Victoria 3134*

In New Zealand: Please write to *Penguin Books (NZ) Ltd, 182–190 Wairau Road, Private Bag, Takapuna, Auckland 9*

In India: Please write to *Penguin Books India Pvt Ltd, 706 Eros Apartments, 56 Nehru Place, New Delhi 110 019*

In the Netherlands: Please write to *Penguin Books Netherlands B.V., Keizersgracht 231 NL–1016 DV Amsterdam*

In Germany: Please write to *Penguin Books Deutschland GmbH, Friedrichstrasse 10–12, W–6000 Frankfurt/Main 1*

In Spain: Please write to *Penguin Books S. A., C. San Bernardo 117–6° E–28015 Madrid*

In Italy: Please write to *Penguin Italia s.r.l., Via Felice Casati 20, I–20124 Milano*

In France: Please write to *Penguin France S. A., 17 rue Lejeune, F–31000 Toulouse*

In Japan: Please write to *Penguin Books Japan, Ishikiribashi Building, 2–5–4, Suido, Tokyo 112*

In Greece: Please write to *Penguin Hellas Ltd, Dimocritou 3, GR–106 71 Athens*

In South Africa: Please write to *Longman Penguin Southern Africa (Pty) Ltd, Private Bag X08, Bertsham 2013*

READ MORE IN PENGUIN

A CHOICE OF NON-FICTION

The Time of My Life Denis Healey

'Denis Healey's memoirs have been rightly hailed for their intelligence, wit and charm … *The Time of My Life* should be read, certainly for pleasure, but also for profit … he bestrides the post-war world, a Colossus of a kind' – *Independent*. 'No finer autobiography has been written by a British politician this century' – *Economist*

Chasing the Monsoon Alexander Frater

'Frater's unclouded sight unfurls the magic behind the mystery tour beautifully … his spirited, eccentric, vastly diverting book will endure the ceaseless patter of travel books on India' – *Daily Mail*. 'This is travel writing at its best. Funny, informed, coherent and deeply sympathetic towards its subject' – *Independent on Sunday*

Isabelle Annette Kobak

'A European turned Arab, a Christian turned Muslim, a woman dressed as a man; a libertine who stilled profound mystical cravings by drink, hashish and innumerable Arab lovers … All the intricate threads of her rebellious life are to be found in Annette Kobak's scrupulously researched book' – Lesley Blanch in the *Daily Telegraph*

Flying Dinosaurs Michael Johnson

Hundreds of millions of years ago, when dinosaurs walked the earth, we know that there also existed great prehistoric beasts call pterosaurs that could fly or glide. Now you can make these extraordinary creatures fly again. *Flying Dinosaurs* contain almost everything you need to construct eight colourful and thrillingly lifelike flying model pterosaurs – from the pterodactylus to the dimorphodon.

The Italians Luigi Barzini

'Brilliant … whether he is talking about the family or the Mafia, about success or the significance of gesticulation, Dr Barzini is always illuminating and amusing' – *The Times*. 'He hits his nails on the head with bitter-sweet vitality … Dr Barzini marshals and orders his facts and personalities with the skill of an historian as well as a journalist' – *Observer*

READ MORE IN PENGUIN

A SELECTION OF CLASSIC CRIME

Wall of Eyes Margaret Millar

Kelsey has become bitter since the accident that left her blind. She was driving the car that night. Geraldine did die, and Kelsey will never see again. But that was two long years ago. Time enough to heal. So why would Kelsey now want to end her life with a grain of morphine? 'She is in the very top rank of crime writers' – Julian Symons

Sweet Danger Margery Allingham

'That was the beauty of Campion; one never knew where he was going to turn up next – at the Third Levée or swinging from a chandelier...' Sweet Danger is perfectly crafted, full of surprising twists and turns. What starts as a light-hearted, slightly crazy wild-goose chase becomes something much more dangerous, nasty and sinister.

Appleby's Other Story Michael Innes

The Chief Constable takes Sir John Appleby to call on a neighbouring stately home. But the owner, Maurice Tytherton, is unable to receive his visitors. He has just been killed. And Appleby, though now retired, cannot overcome his policeman's instincts...

The Franchise Affair Josephine Tey

The Franchise is the name of a large country house in which Marion Sharpe and her mother live. The Affair concerns the accusation by a fifteen-year-old schoolgirl that these two apparently respectable ladies kept her locked up in their attic for a month, beat her, and starved her.

BY THE SAME AUTHOR

'A master – he constructs a plot that twists and turns like an electric eel: it gives you shock upon shock and you cannot let go' – *The Times Literary Supplement*

An Awkward Lie

'Mr Appleby,' Sergeant Howard remarks, 'You seem to be in a rather awkward lie.'

For Bobby – Sir John Appleby's engaging but naive son – is having a hard time proving his case. He did see a well-dressed corpse with a missing finger in the sand trap off the first green. And a very attractive girl did appear on the scene. But by the time he had telephoned for the police and returned, there was no girl, and no corpse . . .

Death at the President's Lodging

Inspector John Appleby has a difficult and delicate task when he investigates the murder of the unpopular Josia Umpleby of St Anthony's College. But with the unexpected aid of three precocious undergraduates, a subtle killer is unmasked and the devious dons find that the oddest thing about the case is Appleby himself . . .

The Daffodil Affair

While Inspector Appleby's aunt assigns her favourite cab-horse. Daffodil, to Scotland Yard's missing persons file, Mrs Rideout is equally distressed at the loss of her daughter Lucy. When a London house, said to be haunted, also vanishes in mysterious circumstances, the baffled policemen begin searching for a connection.